"Kamahl! Are you okay?"

The barbarian waved Chainer off and dropped the rest of the way down to the ground, trying to evade the pollen. With his face half-buried in mulch, Kamahl coughed the pollen out and tried to suck clear forest air in.

Chainer hesitated. He didn't want to leave Kamahl in the dirt, and he didn't want to face the grendelkin without support. The huge monster took a step forward and casually snapped the top off another tree. It used the tree as a crude club, and it shambled forward, slamming into the ground and other trees with each step.

"Poison," Kamahl choked. His eyes were wet, but he had stopped coughing and was struggling back to his feet. "There aren't any poisonous plants in this part of Krosan, Chainer. We're being set up."

Experience the Magic

MAGIC: The Gathering®

CHAINER'S TORMENT

ODYSSEY CYCLE • BOOK 2

Scott McGough

Chainer's Torment
©2001 Wizards of the Coast, Inc.

Distributed in the United States by Holtzbrinck Publishing. Distributed in Canada by Fenn Ltd.

Distributed to the hobby, toy, and comic trade in the United States and Canada by regional distributors.

Distributed worldwide by Wizards of the Coast, Inc. and regional distributors.

Made in the U.S.A.

Internal art by: Brian "Chippy" Dugan, Dana Knutson, Todd Lockwood, Anson Maddocks, r.k. Post, Mark Tedin, and Anthony Waters
First Printing: January 2002
Library of Congress Catalog Card Number:

9 8 7 6 5 4 3 2 1

ISBN: 0-7869-2696-1
UK ISBN: 0-7869-2724-0
620-88544-001

U.S., CANADA,
ASIA, PACIFIC, & LATIN AMERICA
Wizards of the Coast, Inc.
P.O. Box 707
Renton, WA 98057-0707
+1-800-324-6496

EUROPEAN HEADQUARTERS
Wizards of the Coast, Belgium
P.B. 2031
2600 Berchem
Belgium
+32-70-23-32-77

Visit our web site at **www.wizards.com/magic**

Acknowledgments

Special thanks to the following dynamic individuals for their invaluable input:

Jess Lebow, my creative collaborator, who helped nail down all the details of life in Otaria before the first word of the trilogy was ever written (and then made them even better as the editor...death to the semicolon!)

Daneen McDermott, the best professional partner I've ever had the pleasure of working beside, for all her great ideas and especially for championing the concept of dementia casting in the earliest stages of the game

Rob King, for his indefatigable good cheer, endless supply of good ideas, and the opportunity of a lifetime

Vance Moore and Will McDermott, who helped us weave a world full of ideas into a full-fledged trilogy

Hiawatha Johnson, for his enthusiasm about the rough draft and his invaluable insights into the character of the First

Elena Kalikopuakeo-o-Kualoa McGough, for her patience, humor, and especially her definitive understanding of the minds and bodies of merfolk

Dana Knutson and the rest of Magic's artists, for vividly bringing our ideas to life and taking them to the next level visually

Joel, Mike, the 'Bots, and the Mads, for keeping me sane (or at least sane enough to meet my deadlines)

Dedication:

For Elena, who is inspiration, incentive,
and reward all rolled into one

PROLOGUE

Just outside the walls of Cabal City, far from the crushing waves of people and the ringing shouts in the marketplace, the young man pressed on. He called himself Chainer, and for the first time in a long, busy day he was unscheduled. He picked his way through the dwindling foot traffic, moving against the flow of people headed into the city. As he navigated around the last pedestrians in his path, he relished the rare gifts of free time and solitude.

Without a training exercise to complete, an incantation to memorize, or a schedule to keep, Chainer was determined not to be found. He was a member of the Cabal by choice, ritual, and oath, and the Cabal demanded much from its initiates. His superiors would pounce on an idle boy proclaiming, "Nothing to do? I can fix that." Chainer hated being rewarded for good work with more work. Rather than waiting for that inevitable hammer to fall, Chainer ducked down an alley when no one was looking and headed for the gates.

His pace slowed once he was clear of the city. It had been so long since he'd had any time to himself that he had all but forgotten how

1

to enjoy it. He wondered what other people did when they weren't serving their own masters. More to the point, what did they do when they weren't trying their best simply to stay alive?

As he wandered and pondered, Chainer walked through the squatters' shacks outside the city and into the salt flats toward the sparse, dying forest beyond. He ignored the sullen glares from the squatters themselves. If his membership in the Cabal didn't protect him from starving civilians, his own skills could. He was more alert for any of the dangerous wild beasts that lurked on the edges of this and every other settlement. Large predators were rare this close to the well-lit city gates and its armed guards, but the first thing the Cabal taught its members was to be careful with the Cabal's equipment, which included their own bodies.

He altered his course and scanned the path through the marshy flats. Chainer moved along by choosing which parts of the muddy path to avoid rather than which ones he wanted to take. He grew lost in the rhythm and the repetition of trekking through the flats, unaware and unconcerned about how far he had traveled. He hiked until his shadow grew long before him, until a soft, insistent whisper broke through his reverie.

It wasn't a voice, but it called directly to him. It wasn't a song, but the melody gave him chills. It wasn't an alarm, but it commanded his attention with an urgency that was soft but undeniable. He cupped a hand around his ear to help pinpoint the sound. The remains of a residential district sat to the southeast, and the sound was coming from there.

Chainer listened for a moment, then started off toward the largest house on the ruined block. Its immediate neighbors had been bombed and burned flat. The ruined mansion with the caved-in roof and exposed frame stood tall, a broken but defiant veteran of a barely remembered war.

Chainer paused at the bottom of the front porch steps. Except for the beckoning sound, the mansion was completely silent and still. Chainer expertly drew his knuckle dagger, clenched it blade-down and ready at his hip, and went carefully up the rickety porch. He doubted there was any live danger inside the mansion, but then again, he didn't want the Cabal's equipment to be damaged either.

The interior of the mansion was in worse shape than the exterior. The main floor was more hole than floor, with the basement level clearly visible from the front doorway. An ornate metal banister led up to the second floor, but the staircase itself was gone, a pile of broken wood and carpet scraps in the basement below. Chainer looked closer and saw what appeared to be bones among the wreckage of the staircase. At least three complete humans, one of whom was very small.

Chainer took one tentative step onto the threadbare floor, but before he could put his full weight down the ancient boards split and fell away. He stepped back onto the porch, which shuddered and swayed beneath him. Chainer grunted and scouted the entire first floor for a safe route down into the basement.

Finding none, he sheathed his knuckle dagger and took his weapon and tool of choice—a ten-foot length of black metal chain—from his belt. He looped the hard, polished chain around the broken base of a statue that guarded the front doorway, and with the simplest spell he knew, connected the chain to itself.

"Link," he whispered, and the spot he was staring at shimmered, then coalesced into a new link that was indistinguishable from the rest of the chain. Chainer leaned backward to cinch up the metal noose and test its strength. Then he lowered himself down into the still, musty debris.

It was incredibly dark, the kind of darkness that caused him to wonder if his eyes were still open. He listened for any other movement and waited in vain for his eyes to adjust. The sound continued to call him, growing higher and more excited as he got closer. Methodically, he made his way across the basement toward the sound, testing the stone floor before putting any weight on it.

By a pile of moth-eaten fabric and random junk, he lit one of his flare candles and immediately noticed the sphere. In a small bubble of bright light, Chainer stared in naked wonder at the treasure, hovering a clear foot off the ground, that had called to him across the salt flats.

The smooth, flawless black ball somehow seemed to radiate darkness like fire radiates light. Chainer's flare only showed it in relief, for the sphere defined itself with its own anti-light. The edges of the sphere's dark field crackled and sparked as they rippled and undulated outward.

Half-hypnotized by the black light and the triumphant crescendo of sound, Chainer had a vision of his future. The world around him dropped away, and in a flash of black light and silence he saw, felt, and knew the triumphant course his destiny would take. He would be a man of importance, of success, honored and obeyed as one of the true masters of the world. People and monsters alike would bow down before him, and at his pleasure they would live or die. He would be the Cabal's champion, its ambassador, its paragon, and he would spread its influence over the entire world.

The light from Chainer's flare began to sputter and die. He could still hear the sphere's call, still feel its power vibrating in his skull. His course was clear. *It* was the most important thing in the world and as such fit only for the most important person in the world.

"For the First," Chainer whispered. He firmly grabbed the glowing-black sphere, dropped it into his satchel, and pulled the leather drawstring tight.

The First was undisputed lord and master of the entire Cabal, patriarch and protector of its members, supreme controller of its political and magical power. He managed the Cabal and all its assets from his manor inside the city walls, and he needed to see the treasure Chainer had uncovered right away. He alone deserved it.

Chainer's eyes narrowed as he considered the trip back to Cabal City. It was one thing to walk without fear when one's pack was empty. Now that he had something worth stealing, opportunist vermin would swarm around it like maggots around a corpse. The shame and sin of losing the sphere before he had a chance to present it to the First would be unbearable.

Chainer's flare went out, and he stood for a moment in the darkness. He quickly retraced his steps across the basement and found his chain where it still hung from above. He patted the precious cargo at his hip, smiled, and began to go hand-over-hand up the chain.

Soon he would be back inside the city. He would petition for an audience with the First. And when the First laid hands on the black sphere, he would know what Chainer knew: that Chainer wanted nothing more than for his fate and his fortune to be forever tied to that of the Cabal.

PART ONE:
Cabalist

CHAPTER 1

The sun was setting by the time Chainer returned to the salt flats outside the city. He welcomed the sight of his home but did not relax.

A small armed party stood on the path between Chainer and the city gates. Chainer recognized one of the shapes as human and another as an aven bird warrior, but the other two were indistinct. All Chainer could tell from a distance was that one was tall and the other was short or crouching. The human and the aven were dressed in the brilliant white robes of the Order.

Chainer slowed his pace but did not stop. The Order were a passel of militant moral fanatics who sought to impose their rules on all the citizens of Otaria. They considered all Cabalists criminals and the Cabal itself to be a blight on society, despite the fact that it thrived all across the continent. Civilized Otarians everywhere did business with the Cabal. They willingly and repeatedly attended Cabal spectacles, borrowed Cabal money, and begged for Cabal protection. As far as Chainer was concerned, the Order only offered the possibility of a nebulous spiritual reward, and even that was contingent upon obedience to their childish concept of justice. The Cabal was far more concrete and pragmatic. It provided food, shelter, and education for anyone willing to work for it.

Chainer resumed his pace, quickly eliminating the distance between himself and the Order party. If he turned or otherwise tried to avoid them, they would surely follow. Best to confront them now.

"Greetings, traveler," the human soldier called. "On your way to the city?" Judging by the wrap of the Order members' robes and the insignias on their shoulders, Chainer made the aven as an officer and the human as a foot soldier. Beside the officer squatted an ugly, even more birdlike creature with a long neck, jagged beak, and vicious sharp talons. The other, taller figure kept its back to Chainer, but he could see that it was one of the Nantuko, a tribe of intelligent mantislike creatures from the Krosan forest. Chainer was uneasy. The bug-men rarely came this close to the Cabal's city.

"I live there," Chainer said, "and I'm on my way home."

"Have you seen the light of justice, my friend?"

Chainer was now close enough, so they could speak without shouting. "I have. I found it wanting. Let me pass."

"At ease, trooper," the aven officer said quietly. His voice was surprisingly human, but his beak clacked together at the end of each sentence. "This one is Cabal. Look at his eyes. They have that feral, vermin look about them."

"Let me pass," Chainer repeated.

The officer stepped forward. "I'm right, aren't I? You are Cabal. And according to the truce between your patriarch and our commander, we have the right to inspect any and all travelers on the road between here and the Krosan forest."

"Bosh," Chainer snarled and gestured angrily. "The First never agreed to that."

"Take it easy, son. Trooper Baankis?" The foot soldier drew his sword and stood at attention. To Chainer, the officer said, "We just need to search you to make sure you haven't smuggled anything out of the forest preserve."

Trooper Baankis stepped forward, and Chainer looked over his shoulder at the city. If he could get past them, he knew he could outrun the man and the aven, at least until he was safe inside the gates. He wasn't sure about the ugly little bird, though. Or the Nantuko.

Chainer waited until the trooper was right in front of him. When the trooper reached out to take Chainer's dagger, Chainer dropped down and kicked the man's feet out from under him with a wide sweep of his leg. He drew his dagger and fell across the trooper's neck and shoulders, the point of his blade poised over the trooper's eye. He stared defiantly at the officer.

"Get stuffed. You're not touching me."

The officer opened his beak in a cruel aven smiled. "You're hostile, even for a criminal. And now that you've attacked us, we have every right to take you down. Luckily, I think you're young enough to be successfully rehabilitated." He drew his own sword, and the bird at his feet croaked ominously.

Chainer knew that when members of the Order spoke of rehabilitation they really meant brainwashing. As he prepared to fight and run, Chainer reached down to check the satchel at his side. As soon as his fingers made contact through the tough leather, the Nantuko suddenly exploded into violent motion. The mantis rose up and shrieked a trilling, high-pitched alarm. It flailed its forelimbs wildly as it tried to strike at Chainer, and it accidentally knocked the officer into the bird.

Chainer nimbly dove over the mantis's sharp-hooked appendage and rolled onto his feet. He began to run, but the mantis sprang into the air and landed well ahead of him on the path. It was still chittering and swinging wildly.

Chainer had never fought a Nantuko before and wasn't sure where he should aim his chain. He hesitated, and in that moment noticed that the mantis wasn't trying to strike him any more. In fact, it seemed to be trying its level best to avoid touching him at all, while putting on a loud display to drive Chainer away from the city. Was the enormous bug actually afraid of him?

On a hunch, Chainer took his satchel from his waist and held it out at the mantis. The Nantuko keened and fell back, seemingly terrified of the satchel's contents. Chainer lunged forward, and the Nantuko sprang away.

Chainer didn't waste the opportunity. He sprinted away from the Order party at top speed. He heard the officer ordering trooper Baankis to pursue and the frantic trilling of the Nantuko. He risked one last glance over his shoulder and saw the bug had turned and was calling into a small, swampy, wooded area of the salt flats. From within the stunted glade, something roared in reply. Chainer felt the ground rumble beneath his running feet and heard the ear-splitting crack of live timber being splintered as something very large came forward to answer the Nantuko's call.

Chainer fixed his eyes back on the city and concentrated on running as fast as he could.

* * * * *

Roup's tavern was on a lonely side street well off the main road that led to the city center and the Cabal seat of power. Chainer thought the term "tavern" was actually too generous. Roup's was a single room with a single door and a single foul-tasting grog on the menu.

It was a welcome sight to Chainer, however. People didn't come to Roup's for the fare or the decor or the atmosphere. They came to be seen and heard at the very edge of the Cabal's web of influence. Or, as in Chainer's case, to escape from the Cabal's enemies.

"The Cabal is here," Chainer greeted Roup through gritted teeth.

"And everywhere," Roup replied.

"I need your help, big brother."

"Ask, little brother, and I shall answer."

Chainer struggled to remain patient. Roup was technically his superior, but there was a clingy desperation to his manner that made Chainer's knife hand itch. He was flabby and slow, and Chainer thought he dressed like a molting parrot dunked in bile. Roup also tried to make every conversation last as long as possible, which made Chainer and everyone else try to cut them short. It was the general opinion of Cabalists everywhere that Roup deserved to be forgotten at the edge of the city. But the Cabal was, in fact, everywhere, and Roup was the Cabal's man in this sector. He also had the only means of direct communication to the organization's headquarters in the heart of the city.

"I need to use the grapevine," Chainer said. "It's important."

Roup laughed jovially and poured himself a half-goblet of noxious green liquid. "It's always important with you young ones. 'Oh, I've lost the message I was supposed to deliver. Oh, a mean elder stole my package. Woe is me, I stubbed my toe.' Relax, little brother. You'll live longer."

Chainer patted the satchel at his side. "I have a delivery for the First. I need you to contact—"

"The First is only twelve blocks away," Roup smirked. "Did you forget the way? Go out the front door, turn left . . ." Roup trailed off, waiting for Chainer to join him in a smirk.

"I know where the manor is," Chainer said. "The problem isn't the path, it's—"

"Now that you mention it," Roup went on, "I'll bet you a silver marker that if you stood on my doorstep and shouted, the First would hear—"

"Big brother," Chainer snapped. "The Order is waiting outside."

"You led them here?"

"I had no choice. 'Here' is directly between the First and where they tried to grab me."

11

"How many are there?"

"Two. Plus—"

Roup sipped thoughtfully. "Only two? I would have thought a clever and—" he gestured with his goblet at Chainer's belt— "well armed little brother like yourself could handle a meager pair of toy soldiers." He slid the decanter of green liquid toward Chainer. "Drink?"

Chainer ignored the decanter and stared fixedly at Roup. "No thank you, big brother. And the toy soldiers are also armed. Heavily. They have one of those bug-boys with them as well, and I think something big from Krosan. They met me coming into the city and tried to arrest me. They chased me here, and they're waiting for me now, out there. I need an escort to reach the First."

Roup chuckled. "An escort, little brother? We're very important all of a sudden, aren't we? Why don't I get on the grapevine and order the First himself to come here and save you the trip?" He snorted an ugly little laugh at his own cleverness.

"All I want," Chainer said evenly, "is to deliver this package to the First. To do that, I need to get in touch with my mentor. His name is Skellum." Chainer watched Roup digest this new bit of information. Master Skellum's name carried some weight, even here.

"Well, little brother," Roup said finally, "if this package for the First is so important, why don't you just leave it with me? I can have an armed escort here by sunrise, and then I'll take it to him myself when I deliver my tally tomorrow. In the meantime, you can hide in my cellar and stay out of my way."

"It cannot wait for tomorrow," Chainer said stiffly. "And I will not surrender it to anyone but the First."

Roup raised an eyebrow, obviously slighted. "Present the package, little brother. I will decide who gives it to the First."

Reluctantly, Chainer took the satchel off his belt. Slowly, mechanically, he extended it out to arm's length and placed it in the center of the table. He kept his eyes fixed and his arm extended as Roup leaned forward.

When Roup's hand touched the drawstring, Chainer struck. He whipped his dagger out of its shoulder sheath and slammed the point deep into the table, through the sleeve of Roup's garish robe. Without pausing, he looped his chain under Roup's chin and sprang up, flipping his body over Roup's head and rolling down the tavern keeper's back like a hedgehog down a hill. Chainer's full weight pulled the chain close around Roup's throat, and as the young man came to his feet, he twisted the chain even tighter. With the same whispered spell he had used in the ruined mansion, he linked the chain to itself, creating a choking collar that didn't kill Roup outright but did make it difficult for the old windbag to breathe.

Roup struggled feebly and clawed at his throat with his free hand.

"Big brother," Chainer hissed in his ear, "I am going to show you the package now. I want us to be completely clear on one point, however—it is mine to deliver. Mine. I found it. I fought for it, and I will kill anyone who tries to keep me from giving it to the First with my own hands."

Roup gagged and choked, and the sleeve of his robe began to tear.

"Are we clear, big brother?"

Roup's head jerked up and down. He banged his chin on the table, spilling both the goblet and the decanter. Chainer touched the link that was keeping the collar tight.

"Break," he whispered, and it shimmered away into nothing. He allowed Roup enough slack to gasp and cough, but he kept the chain firmly around the tavern keeper's neck. Roup was the only one who could use the grapevine from this location, so Chainer needed him alive and conscious.

"With your free hand," Chainer said, "open the package. But don't touch what's inside. Clear?"

Roup sucked in a few more wheezing gulps of air and shot Chainer a murderous look over his shoulder. Chainer could see the dire threats of retribution forming in Roup's mind, but the chatty old bore was smart enough not to challenge Chainer's advantage. Chainer suspected that Roup had often been held hostage and was probably used to it by now. Besides, his natural greed and curiosity were piqued. Slowly, carefully, he undid the drawstring.

For several long minutes there was no sound other than Roup's ragged breathing as he stared at Chainer's sphere. Chainer himself waited patiently, resting just enough weight on Roup's back to keep him still and just enough tension on his throat to keep him obedient.

Roup's voice was a hoarse, painful whisper. "You win, little brother. What do you need?"

"Get on the grapevine," Chainer said immediately. "Contact the proving grounds and inform Skellum that his pupil Chainer is waiting for him here. Tell him it's an emergency. Tell him to come now."

Chainer released Roup's throat and spun lightly around the table. As he passed Roup's pinned sleeve, Chainer retrieved his dagger.

"And tell him to come heavy."

* * * * *

Less than an hour later, Chainer walked out of Roup's tavern. Skellum said he would meet Chainer outside, and that Chainer was to distract the Order's bully boys until he arrived.

The sun had recently set, and the night was dark, cold, and clear. Oil-burning street lamps flickered. His enemies were waiting for him in the street.

The two Order soldiers stood rigid and humorless, watching Roup's doorway. The small bird-thing squatted beside the aven officer, and it croaked unpleasantly as Chainer came out. There was no sign of the mantis or its beast. There was likewise no sign of Skellum.

"That's far enough," the officer called. "This is fair warning, boy.

If you run again, we will be forced to injure you. If you retreat back into that den of filth, we will burn it down."

Chainer glared at him, but did not speak. "Distract them," Skellum had said, but the mere sight of these fake do-gooders in their gleaming white robes galled Chainer like an abscess. He had fought many Order soldiers, both on the streets and in the Cabal's fighting pits, and he was always eager to take on another. He wondered if Skellum would consider crippling stab wounds enough of a distraction.

"I am Major Teroh," the aven said. "In the name of the Order, I hereby claim you and that satchel at your waist. If you come with us now, you will not be harmed. You'll spend a night as a guest on a warm, safe bedroll. You might even get a hot meal out of it.

"We don't want to hurt you. Quite the opposite, in fact. But whatever it is you're carrying," he paused, searching for the right words, "belongs with us. It's simply too dangerous for the likes of you."

Chainer made no effort to hide his disgust. "You don't even know what you're talking about, do you?"

"Not as such," Teroh bristled at Chainer's scorn. "But if I saw a book of spells written in a foreign language, I still wouldn't let a child read from it."

"Go find a child with a book, then," Chainer said. "I'm on Cabal business. I don't need an Order librarian wasting my time."

Major Teroh scowled. "I won't ask you again."

"Suits me. Then I won't have to ignore you again."

"Trooper Baankis," the major said loudly, and the foot soldier snapped to an even more rigid state of attention.

"Yes, Major!"

"Relieve this willful young man of his burden. If he resists . . . subdue him. No permanent damage."

"Yes, sir!" Baankis started forward, and Chainer drew his knuckle dagger. He held it expertly out in front of him in his left hand. His right hand was balled into a fist at his side, and he stood lightly on his toes with his weight evenly balanced.

"At ease, trooper." Baankis halted. The major scowled again, and shook his head in frustration. He called out to Chainer, "You're going to make this difficult, aren't you?" When Chainer didn't reply, Teroh shook his head. "Baankis, stand down."

"Sir!"

Teroh jerked the bird-thing's leash, and it spread its wings and shook itself. The major turned to Baankis and said, "Stand by to collect one bad-mannered boy and one mysterious satchel."

"Yes, sir!"

Major Teroh dropped the bird's leash and pointed at Chainer. "Subdue," he said, and the bird took flight.

Chainer watched it bearing down on him, its wingspan as wide as he was tall. It swerved so as to avoid the dagger clutched tight in his left hand. Chainer knew that with its speed and its long neck it could disarm him, knock him over, or pin him down before his blade could even touch it. Grimly, he waited.

When the bird was ten feet away, Chainer lashed out with his right hand. The length of chain he had been concealing snapped out, screaming directly toward the oncoming bird. Chainer's aim was excellent. The sharpened weight at the end of the chain smashed clean through the bird's skull, killing it instantly. Chainer caught the still-twitching corpse as it crashed into his chest and let it drop heavily to the ground.

"Callda!" Major Teroh shouted.

Chainer held onto the chain, now threaded through the ruined skull of the bird, and sneered at Teroh. "Callda, was it? Friend of yours, Major, or a distant cousin? Don't worry, it didn't die in vain." Chainer scornfully nudged the carcass. "I'll light a candle for it when I get home." He put his knuckle dagger back into the quick-release sheath on his shoulder.

"Baankis," Teroh growled and drew his sword. "Advance. If this murderous little worm survives, he is going to spend the next three years in a rehabilitation work camp."

Baankis was wide-eyed but resolute. "Yes, sir." Chainer was pleased to hear that his replies were no longer so crisp and regimental.

"Hold on, Major," Chainer said. "If you liked that, you're going to love this." Without waiting, Chainer dropped to his knees by Callda's body, clenched the end of his chain tighter, and reached out to the corpse with his mind as Master Skellum had taught him.

The bird's heart had only recently stopped beating. Robbed of any vital impetus, its blood gave in to gravity and began to pool in its torso. Its muscles drained and deflated, its body temperature dropped, and its joints started to stiffen. Chainer took hold of the energy being released by the bird's transition from life to death and channeled it up and into his chain.

"The Cabal is here," he whispered, and then he cried out as a jolting rush of energy leaped up the chain and into his own body. He felt his consciousness expand, he felt his arms and legs grow stronger and more responsive, he felt his thoughts clarify. He stood and jerked the chain free from Callda's skull. He began to twirl it around his head, letting out more and more of it as it spun. Chainer was ferocious in his joy. This was going better than he could have imagined. Perhaps he wouldn't need Skellum's help after all.

"Keep your distance, Bunkus," he said to the foot soldier, and he could hear the confidence in his voice as it echoed off the street's paving stones. Charged by the death of Callda, Chainer was flush with the arcane darkness that was the source of the Cabal's power. He felt immovable, invincible. With the barest thought, he magically added another six feet to his chain and created another sharpened weight for the end in his hand. Soon he had two lethal missiles dancing a complicated minuet around every inch of his body. The chain automatically increased or decreased in length as it flew, according to its master's will. Young as he was, Chainer was an expert with the long chain, and he even dared to mock Teroh from the safety of its whirling radius.

"Your move, Major," he called. "There's a hot meal and a safe bed waiting for me at the Cabal, too. If you let me pass, maybe we'll both sleep well tonight."

Teroh's eyes were wild, and his voice was tight in his throat. With a visible effort of will, he swallowed his fury and barked, "Reseda!"

Chainer heard a buzz and saw a blur. A sudden impact on his chest knocked him backward so hard that Roup's door rattled on its hinges. His chain snarled and tangled around him clumsily, and one of the weighted ends gashed painfully into his shin. Dazed, he looked up.

The mantis-man stood over him, chittering in its incomprehensible insect language. It jammed one of its pointed forelimbs into the solid stone beside Chainer's head and hissed at him. There was another buzz, another blur, and the mantis disappeared back into the alley behind Major Teroh.

"Reseda hates this city," Teroh said, "but he hates that thing in your satchel even more."

Chainer coughed and tasted blood. He had bitten his tongue and split his lip. His ears were still ringing, and his vision was tilted sideways. At least his ribs weren't broken, he thought. He could still breathe, albeit painfully.

"Now then, Cabalist," Teroh continued, spitting the last word out like poison. "You will surrender. Trooper Baankis and I are going to bind your hands. If you behave, we will even bind your wounds. Then you will accompany us back to our citadel where you will offer apologies and make restitution for Callda. And then, you will be rehabilitated."

Chainer grunted. "Die first. And haunt you forever."

"I don't think so." Teroh waved his hand in front of him, whispering, and the razor edges of both his and Baankis's swords began to glow brightly. "Baankis?"

"Sir!" Trooper Baankis had regained his gusto.

"Forward." The two soldiers advanced in step with their swords drawn and radiant. Chainer struggled to get to his feet but slumped back against the door of the tavern.

"My goodness," came a silky, sinuous voice. "Now this is simply unacceptable. Chainer, what *have* you been up to?"

The speaker stepped out from around the corner of the building into the light. He was a small, neat man, elegant in his manner and graceful in his movements. He was dressed in form-fitting snakeskin died midnight black, and he wore a waterproof cape with a bright red collar and black fur lining. His head was completely concealed by a bell-shaped hat made of grayish paper stretched tight between stiff wire ribs. The hat hung loosely from a hook that sprouted up from a wire rig attached to his shoulders. It had gaps between every second panel that allowed him to see, but each gap was only a few inches wide.

One of the gaps was now positioned directly in front of his face. He had clear blue eyes, an elegant beard, and a neat mustache. Beside him stood a huge black dog whose head was as big as a pony's. The dog's shoulder came up to the man's elbow, and she clearly outweighed him. Her eyes glowed dusky red in the shadow of her brow.

"My name is Skellum, and I wear a silly hat." The newcomer spoke brightly, as if introducing himself to a dinner party full of children. "Is there a problem, officer?"

CHAPTER 2

"Azza, old girl," Skellum said, and the massive dog beside him pricked up her ears. "Check on young Chainer, will you?"

Despite his pain, Chainer was thrilled. Only the Cabal elite had access to the hell-hounds, and Chainer had never seen one so close.

Major Teroh regarded the new arrivals suspiciously. Chainer watched his eyes dart from Skellum to the dog to the doorway of Roup's tavern. Chainer knew all of the Order's toy soldiers prided themselves on their ability to control every situation they encountered. Teroh was clearly weighing the odds as Azza came closer.

"Stop right there," Teroh said. Azza paused, then growled at Teroh so deeply that Chainer felt it in his spine twenty feet away.

"This boy—" Teroh began.

"Chainer," Skellum corrected him gently. "He is called Chainer."

"This boy," Teroh repeated, "is transporting contraband. When we tried to examine it, he lashed out at Trooper Baankis and ran. When we caught up to him, he killed one of my best *crusat* birds. He is coming with us."

"Oh dear," Skellum said. "That is a problem. Are you sure we can't come to some sort of arrangement?" He smiled.

"We don't make deals with the likes of you," Teroh said.

"Everyone does business with the Cabal," Skellum said cheerfully. "This is our city, after all. It's merely a question of what you want and what you're willing to give."

Teroh's voice rose. "If that dog takes one more step toward that boy, I'll give *it* the flat of my blade. Call off your dog, and leave us to our duty."

"Well now, that raises another problem. I can't 'call her off.' Azza here has been in the Cabal longer than I have, so technically she outranks me." As Skellum prattled on, Chainer stood and gathered up his tangled chain as inconspicuously as he could. Where Roup talked too much because he was lonely and pathetic, Skellum talked too much to defuse the situation and give Chainer time to recover.

"I could suggest to her that she back off, but if she doesn't want to . . . Hang on. Chainer? Are you bleeding?"

"Yes, Mentor." Then he hissed to Azza, who was closest to him, "There's a big bug in that alley. And something else, I—"

"She knows," Skellum called. "Officer . . . Sorry, I didn't catch your name."

"I am *Major* Teroh, and this conversation is over."

Skellum stroked his well-trimmed beard. "Major, officer, officer, major. What's the difference?" He looked at Chainer. "A major is an officer, isn't it?"

"This major is an ass," spat Chainer.

Teroh stiffened, and Skellum sighed.

"Anyway. Major Teroh. Was it you who damaged my pupil?"

Teroh sneered. "I had him damaged, yes. Because he resisted, just like you're resisting now. And if you don't want to be damaged, I suggest . . ." Teroh's voice trailed off.

As soon as the word "yes" passed Teroh's lips, Skellum changed. His calm demeanor grew darker, and his voice hardened. The happy gleam in his eyes became a cold, penetrating glare. Little knots of muscle formed in his cheeks, and he spoke through clenched teeth.

"The Cabal is here, Major, and everywhere. Chainer is Cabal, and more, he is under my protection. Whatever Chainer has done to you, you in turn owe us for his injury. Now we have to come to an arrangement. No one walks away from a Cabal debt. No one."

"True gods," Teroh snapped in exasperation. "Do any of you bog-wallowers live in this world? We are the Order. We are the law. And we have you outnumbered. Reseda!"

Chainer was ready for the blur this time. As the mantis sprang out of the alley toward Skellum, Chainer tried simultaneously to shout a warning and draw back his chain. He needn't have bothered.

Fast as Reseda was, Azza was even faster, and her center of gravity was far lower. Reseda's thorax crashed into Azza's driving shoulder, and even Chainer winced as he heard the insect's exoskeleton crack. Six hundred pounds of magically bred and enhanced canine reared up and slammed her powerful head into Reseda's shoulder and throat. The crippled mantis spun painfully onto the paving stones, and the hellhound clamped onto him, gripping Reseda's shoulder joint and half of his face with her massive jaws. Azza bit down to immobilize the mantis, but she did not injure Reseda further. She let out a single, explosive bark, and Reseda screamed in his eerie, alien tongue. Teroh and Baankis were wide-eyed and speechless.

"Now, Major," Skellum said coldly, "about that arrangement."

Teroh recovered first. He pointed his still-glowing sword and said, "Turn my ally loose, Skellum. Your dog is impressive, but you've just overplayed your hand."

"Have I?" He walked over to Azza and Reseda, who was hissing and chittering out a steady stream of mantis talk. Chainer didn't understand a word of it, but he guessed it was either a prayer or a curse.

"It seems to me," Skellum continued, "that we have the advantage. Granted, I'm not a military man like yourself, but still. . . ." Casually, he reached up and gave the brim of his hat a push. The yoke-and-hook rig he wore was designed to let the hat spin freely, and it did, revealing Skellum's face in brief flashes as the gaps went round and round.

A secret, electric thrill ran through Chainer as he watched Teroh's face. The major had no idea what Master Skellum was doing—or how dangerous it was.

"You're through, Major," Chainer called out. "And you don't even know it."

Azza growled at Chainer, and the next flashes of Skellum's face showed an angry glare directed at his pupil. He gave his hat another spin and refocused on the matter at hand. Baankis looked at Chainer in confusion. Teroh ignored them all. Instead, he concentrated on the words pouring out of Reseda and nodded to himself.

Reseda had been repeating the same syllable over and over, his clicking voice growing louder and more shrill with each repetition.

"What's he saying?" Skellum asked.

Teroh actually smiled, cruelly. "He's saying 'kill.'"

"Oh, it's not that bad." Skellum's voice was becoming distant, almost sleepy, and the strobe flashes of his face revealed eyes rolled back and jaw hanging slack. "A few herbs, some bed rest, maybe some time in the hot springs . . ."

"He's issuing a command, not a request. I am a military man, Mr. Skellum, and we military men know enough to keep some forces in reserve."

From deep within the alley Reseda had occupied came a rumbling, trumpeting roar. Trooper Baankis side-stepped away from the entrance, and Major Teroh waited confidently for his reserve forces to appear. Skellum gave his hat another spin.

Something huge was dragging itself down the alley. Chainer stole a glance at Skellum, who was starting to weave and list from side to side as his hat continued to whirl. Chainer nervously wound his chain around one hand, then the other. He hadn't had a real look at the mantis's associate, but he knew neither his weapons nor his skills would be enough to stop it. He was relying on Master Skellum to meet this new challenge.

The monster lurched heavily out of the alley and cracked the stones beneath it. Its skin was hairy and warty green, and it had natural armored plates across its chest and shoulders. It dragged itself forward on tree-trunk-thick arms that were taller than a person. Its huge, round head sat directly on its boulder-sized torso, which tapered off at the waist down to two spindly legs that dragged uselessly behind it. Chainer thought it looked like a cross between a tadpole in mid-metamorphosis and a whale.

"Oooh," Skellum said dreamily. "A grendelkin. I haven't seen one of those since I was a boy. Pity about its hind legs, though. Was it born stunted, or did someone cripple it?"

The grendelkin opened its mouth and roared, displaying triple rows of gnarled molars.

"Take a good look," Teroh said grimly. "You'll never see another." He waved a hand to catch the grendelkin's attention, and then pointed at Azza, Reseda, and Skellum. Reseda was still screeching, "kill, kill," over and over. Azza shook him once, roughly, and the forest dweller finally passed out.

The sudden silence seemed to drive the grendelkin over the edge. It roared again and stomped angrily toward Azza. Teroh said something to Baankis that Chainer couldn't hear, and the two soldiers moved toward Chainer once more. Chainer started his chain whirling. He hoped to slam the weighted end into one of Teroh's softer parts and then cut Baankis's hamstring with his dagger before Teroh recovered.

Even as he prepared to fight for his life, Chainer kept an eye on

Skellum. He was the only one in the street to see his mentor reach up with both hands and decisively stop the brim of his hat with a gap directly in front of his face.

Master Skellum's entire head was gone. In its place was a whirling vortex of black smoke and purple light. There was a muffled boom from deep inside the hat, and a solid nugget of smoke leaped out through the gap, trailing charnel gas and soot. The nugget expanded at soon as it was clear of Skellum's hat, exploding into a full-fledged creature straight out of a madman's nightmare.

It was still smoking and burned from its journey. It was exactly as big as the grendelkin. In fact, it looked a great deal like the grendelkin, except its lower half narrowed into a muscular serpent's tail complete with rattle. Its eyes bulged out of its skull and looked independently in all directions. It had no armor plating, but it did have a long, barbed tongue that flashed out between its jagged teeth.

"Did I mention I had seen one as a boy?" Skellum asked. His voice sounded exactly as it had when Skellum first arrived, except it seemed to be coming from inside Chainer's head. Skellum's silky tone was as calm and measured as a man lighting his pipe. "I may have gotten a few details wrong, and I've always been partial to rattler tails. . . ."

Skellum's nightmare grendelkin caught sight of its shrivel-waisted counterpart and screeched like a stooping eagle. The forest brute roared in reply. Both monsters simultaneously launched forward, coming together with a titanic crunch that partially flattened their torsos against one another. They tore at each other with their claws.

"Azza?" Skellum said, and the big dog grunted in agreement. She tossed Reseda's unconscious body at the soldiers. Baankis yelped and stepped backward while Teroh dropped his guard and threw himself in front of the flying mantis, trying to minimize Reseda's impact on the hard stone.

Chainer seized the opportunity and sent the weighted end of his chain screaming across Baankis's forehead. The deep slash began to bleed before Chainer could reel his weapon back in, and the hapless foot soldier fell to his knees, momentarily blinded.

Skellum's vortex-head boomed again, and two more smoking comets leaped out. One transformed into a scaly humanoid horror with long, dragging arms that ended in harpoonlike spikes. The other, smaller one seemed to be composed entirely of wings and legs. The harpoon-handed thing began to stalk the tangled heap that was Teroh and Reseda, and the flying thing howled like a wolf and took off into the air. It shot down the street and, still howling, disappeared around the corner.

Azza padded up to Chainer.

"Get on," Skellum called. "My other new friend has gone ahead to clear your path. I'll be along directly."

Chainer took one last look at the melee. The two grendelkin were locked in a brutal stalemate while sword and harpoon clashed, and Baankis groped along the ground for his weapon.

Azza urged him out of his reverie with a scolding bark. Chainer slung himself onto her back and took firm hold of the extra skin around her neck and shoulders.

"To the manor, please," he said, and Azza bounded off, fast as a small horse and ten times more dangerous. Chainer threw one last look over his shoulder as Azza followed the winged thing's path down the street.

Major Teroh had managed to hack off one of the harpooner's arms at the elbow, but it was still pressing its attack. The officer had planted his feet, refusing to abandon the unconscious mantis. Chainer was mildly impressed, but such bravery could well cost Teroh his life. Baankis was trying to clear his eyes with water from his canteen. Skellum's grendelkin had its tail wrapped tightly around the space where its double's throat would have been if it had a neck. They rolled over and over, crunching paving stones and flattening storefronts in their wake.

The last thing he saw before Azza turned the corner was Skellum whipping his cape around himself with a flourish, his face smiling and normal, as he backed calmly into the shadows he'd come from.

Rescued by his mentor, safe on Azza's back, and en route to the First with his package intact, Chainer allowed himself a single, short burst of joyous laughter. Then he hunkered down to make sure he stayed on long enough to enjoy the ride.

CHAPTER 3

Skellum's howling, flying thing had done its job. There was no one on the streets to observe Azza and Chainer as they galloped toward the manor. He saw several frightened faces peeking out through windows or from behind cracked doors, but no one was foolish enough to risk interfering with Azza's progress.

They raced past the initiates' dormitories, where Chainer lived after Skellum started training him. Beyond the dorms was the largest port on the continent, its docks wholly owed and operated by the Cabal. Between the docks and the dorms was the city's main arena, the bloody pits where Chainer had fought for and earned a place in the Cabal's hierarchy. Azza bounded though a sharp left turn, and there it was: the manor, where the First lived and lorded, where all the world came to bow and beg for the Cabal's favor.

Chainer had only been inside once before for his initiation, but he remembered every detail. It was a huge structure, ten stories high and two city blocks wide. The thick stone walls had been carved and set by the finest dwarf masons and further reinforced with magic and metal. It would take the destruction of the entire city and a half-mile of the bedrock below to put a dent in the First's home. The gleaming silver cathedral dome at the top was polished to a high shine, so that it reflected whatever was in the sky above it like a great convex mirror. At the very end of Manor Way, where Azza and Chainer were, the dome and the toothed drawbridge gate combined with the huge observation towers in front of it all to give the viewer an impression of a huge, grinning, metallic skull with horns.

Home at last, Chainer thought, but his good humor was already fading. Passersby this close to the manor were more used to screeching monsters than the people in Roup's neighborhood. Skellum's winged thing had only caused this foot traffic to clear a path rather than vanish behind locked doors. The sparse crowds gave Chainer and Azza plenty of space but eyed them suspiciously as they passed. Chainer touched his dagger and the satchel at his hip, mentally preparing himself for the next challenge he would face. Getting to the manor was only the first step. He would have to get inside and then convince layer upon layer of armed guards and petty bureaucrats that what he carried was for the First alone. Azza seemed to pick up on his concern, and she slowed to a trot. Chainer anxiously prodded her with his heels, but she stopped him with a menacing growl.

"Sorry," he said. "I'm a little nervous. Will you help me get inside, or are you just taking me to the gate?"

Azza craned her head around and regarded Chainer with one red smoldering eye. She coughed, unimpressed, and then sprang forward at full gallop once more. Chainer hung on, smiling slightly.

The guard on the gate was a six-foot-tall woman with three yellow eyes and vivid purple hair cropped close to her head. She was burly and broad-shouldered, with long serrated fingernails painted to match her hair. Unlike most of the guards Chainer had met in his life, she seemed neither bored nor bullying.

"Who goes?" she called. The top eye in the middle of her fore-head squinted in the dusky gloom.

"The Cabal is here," Chainer said.

"And everywhere," the guard replied. All three eyes now squinted. "Azza, old girl, is that you?"

Azza coughed again, then reared up, almost tossing Chainer off her back.

The left eye winked at Azza while the other two oriented on Chainer. "And you must be Skellum's boy."

"I am Chainer. I seek an audience with the First. I have urgent—"

The guard held up her hands. "Easy, little brother." She grinned, and Chainer saw that her teeth were serrated, like her nails, and they too matched the color of her hair.

"We've been expecting you." The guard stepped aside and waved the mounted pair in. "Proceed to the Great Hall. You will be met there and escorted to the First. Azza," she added, "don't let him wander off on his own."

Azza growled, more annoyed than angry, and the guard laughed. As the great dog padded into the manor, the guard winked at Chainer with all three of her eyes in succession.

Unlike the offices in the administration building, the interior of the manor was decidedly still and silent. The First used the manor primarily for advanced rituals and to receive important guests. All of the Cabal's actual work was conducted in the streets, in the homes and offices of syndicate executives, or in the arena. Apart from a handful of visible guards, there were very few people between the entranceway and the Great Hall. Chainer gazed around as Azza bore him on, taking in the ornate decoration, the trophy displays of wealth and prestige, and the simple, sheer power humming from the gemstone chandelier. Overwhelmed, Chainer lowered his eyes and focused on Azza's muscular neck. He was being admitted to the manor, escorted into the presence of the First, and, he reminded himself, he carried the finest treasure yet at his side.

"Eyes up, little brother." Skellum waited for them near the fireplace at the center of the Great Hall. Before Chainer could hail his mentor, Azza sat down and tossed him off with a short shrug of her shoulders. She bounded up to Skellum.

"Of course I'm fine," Skellum held his hand out, and Azza sniffed it. She quickly sniffed the air around him and then barked happily.

"No problems, I take it?" Skellum nuzzled Azza behind the ears, but he raised his voice to address Chainer as well.

"None, mentor—" Azza interrupted Chainer with a long, low, warning growl. When he quickly fell silent, she tossed her head under Skellum's hand and prodded him gently with her muzzle. She looked back at Chainer and barked once, angrily.

"I'll get to that," Skellum said. Azza barked again, and in three great thundering leaps, she was face-to-face with Chainer.

She let out another slow, deep growl. With his complete and utter attention, she stared into his eyes for a moment, coughed, and then kissed him sloppily once from chin to forehead. Chainer was only dimly aware of her bounding away, back out the front gate.

"What was that all about?"

Skellum had not moved, and he stared at Chainer meaningfully. "She likes you. She's not usually that affectionate."

"Before that. The barking. The growl."

"She's also mad at you for opening your mouth in front of that Order officer."

"She what? But—"

"As am I, little brother," Skellum said. "Or were you simply unaware of how carefully I had put things together in order to help you? Did you think it was easy to arrange for an interview with the First on short notice? So easy that you could taunt an enemy before he was defeated? Is it a simple matter to arrange safe passage through half the city while simultaneously mustering enough tooth and claw to back down an Order officer and his entourage? Did you think of these things when you opened your mouth? Did any of this cross your mind at any time, little brother?"

"No, Master."

Skellum's eyes sparkled when he smiled. He double checked to make sure Azza was gone. "Me, neither. That's how I'm able to perform such miracles, my boy. I don't know what's impossible."

Chainer laughed in relief, but caught himself. "Master, I regret taunting the toy soldier before he was beaten. I will do better."

"And better still," Skellum said, his silky voice gone cold again. "You killed that warty little bird."

"Yes, Master."

"You killed it."

"Yes."

"Killed it." Skellum's voice was fading, and Chainer waited a moment before clearing his throat.

"Yes, Master. I killed it."

Skellum shook his head. "Very bad. I'll have to explain why, but you'll have to explain first." He looked up brightly. "Ha, ha. You'll have to explain . . . first!" He shook his head, smiling.

Chainer had seen Skellum fade out before, but it was usually much later in the evening, when his thoughts were not so ordered and his control began to slip. He gently took his master's hand and pulled him a step forward, spinning his hat so that a gap was by Skellum's ear.

"Master Skellum," he said evenly, "we are meant to see the First now. You have to take me to him."

"Don't touch my hat!" Skellum flinched. "Hm? Chainer! There you are." Skellum yanked his hand free and quickly reoriented his hat so he could see out of both eyes. "Right you are. We're to see the First. You've got the . . . er. What is it you've got again?"

"A fabulous treasure."

"And you've got this fabulous treasure with you?"

"Right here."

"Keep it handy. You remember the most important rule?"

"No one may touch the First."

"Very good. And tonight, young Chainer, there is something else. The First is very interested in what you have to show him. In what you have to say, but that just means he'll be even more difficult to impress. If you had passed him at a formal dinner and said, 'Hey, look at this fabulous treasure,' it would have been an easy sell. But we've asked for a special audience, a great inconvenience to a busy man like him. We must tread lightly.

"Do not speak to the First unless he speaks to you. If he approaches you, stand perfectly still. Don't do anything that might annoy him, and for Kuberr's sake, don't flail around or duck away from him. The last man to do that was killed, reanimated, and propped up in the smoking lounge for five years, so guests could put their cigars out on his forehead. You may want to spend the next half-decade as a zombie ashtray, but I don't. For both our sakes, stand still and listen."

"All right, Skellum, all right," Chainer sputtered.

Skellum's eyes went cold again. " 'Master.' You call me 'Master.' What do you call me?"

Chainer was taller than his mentor, but Skellum had a way of peering up from the gaps in his hat with his cold, angry eyes that was ten times more threatening than sheer size.

"Master. I'm sorry, Master."

"I'm serious, Chainer. One slip and we both go down. Currently, the First thinks very highly of me, and I'd like to keep it that way."

"I understand, Master Skellum."

Skellum smiled and gave his hat a spin. He stopped it, unhooked it, and tucked it under his arm with a flourish.

"Then let's go."

* * * * *

They were admitted to the antechamber outside the First's study. They were not searched or magically bound from doing their host harm, as an outsider would have been. There were nonetheless a dozen armed humans and monsters standing ready in the First's private chambers.

The room was dark, lit only by black candles atop tall silver poles. The First stood with his arms behind his back at the far end of the room, under a massive oil painting of himself in formal robes. Four human men and four human women in matching blouses moved constantly around him, translating his commands and his movements into a complicated dance. His attendants were the only ones allowed to approach him, and even they maintained a safe distance at all times to keep from brushing against him. Two of the eight had the outline of a skull etched in bone-white on the front of their black blouses. The other six had a yellow skeletal hand. The First raised his arms high and wide, and his attendants spread out beside him, then moved forward to interact with his guests.

"Master Skellum," the First said formally. "Whose secret name is Cybariss. Welcome."

"The Cabal is here, Pater."

"And everywhere."

Chainer's life froze when the First turned and met his eyes. He had seen the First once before, but he had not seen him in such detail or in such raiment. He was dressed now in black hide, cured and tanned until it was as stiff as glass. His clothing seemed coated in a thin film of oil, especially at the elbows and shoulders. In this simple businesslike robe, head unadorned, he seemed somehow more intimidating than he did in full headdress and regalia.

"Apprentice Chainer. Whose secret name is Mazeura. Welcome." The First was old, but not wizened. His skin was gray and smooth as stone.

Chainer heard a voice from very far away mutter, "The Cabal is here, Pater," and then realized it was his own.

"And everywhere." The First's eyes were milky white, but this indicated an increased facility rather than a diminished one. It was said that the First could see through a person's soul as easily as he could through walls. The gray-white orbs darted and focused around the room.

"I understand you have something for me." From the far end of the room, the First stretched out his hand, palm up, and one of his attendants bearing the skeletal hand standard approached Chainer. "I will have it now, Mazeura."

The attendant's eyes were blank and glassy as the man waited to receive Chainer's package. Chainer hesitated only long enough to glance at Skellum. He had been determined to put the sphere directly into the First's hands, but it seemed these people were his hands. Chainer untied the drawstring on his satchel and held the sphere at arm's length, so that it hovered six inches above his hand. The sphere floated from over Chainer's hand to the hand-attendant's. Numbly, the man turned and carried the sphere to the First.

Chainer did not breathe while the First examined the sphere.

"Remarkable," he said at last. Balancing it over his right hand, the First gestured with his left. Two more of the hand-attendants came forward, bearing a sturdy black box with runes engraved in a band around its lid. The First placed the sphere inside the box, closed the lid, and muttered a few words. The lock flashed, the seam between the lid and the box disappeared, and the attendants carried the sealed cube away.

The First turned to face Chainer. "Remarkable," he repeated. He regarded the younger man, a finger tapping his upper lip. "You call yourself Chainer."

"Yes, Pater."

"Chainer. You have my thanks. Such a treasure, freely given. Do you have any idea what it is?"

"No, Pater."

The First touched his temple, and one of the skull-standard attendants stepped forward. "I think I might."

To the attendant, he said, "Make a note. I want Chainer summoned to me again when we've determined exactly what his treasure is. I want him to know as soon as we do." The attendant nodded, bowed, and stepped back.

The First glanced over at Skellum, and then stared hard at Chainer.

"I wonder, Chainer," he said, "if you would have beaten such a path to my study if you'd known exactly how powerful that sphere is. Either you are very loyal or very unobservant."

Chainer felt the back of his neck go cold. "I am your obedient child."

The First stepped behind Chainer, his attendants trailing behind him. Some of the guards shifted their positions in response to the First's movement.

"Or maybe," he continued, "you did know how powerful it was, and you knew that it was only a matter of time before it found its way to me. So you sought my favor by bringing it here directly."

Chainer felt dizzy. He caught Skellum's warning stare and choked on silence.

"Bringing it here directly," the First mused, "and en route attacking one of my children, hijacking my communications network, and killing an officer of the Order to get it here. All this for something whose value you could not precisely estimate."

The First left Chainer shaking and nauseated as he glided over to Skellum, surrounded by a silent swarm of attendants and guards.

"Master Skellum. I hope that your apprentice's sphere is very valuable indeed. It may have already cost us a great deal."

"In all fairness, Pater," Skellum's voice was as deep and as rich as molasses, "it was only an Order officer's pet he killed."

The First scowled. "A pet."

"Yes, Pater. I may have spoken imprecisely earlier. It was not the officer my apprentice killed, but his war bird."

Chainer went freshly cold as the First turned and peered at him again. The First glared at him for a moment through cloudy eyes, then snapped the fingers on each hand twice and reached forward with his right hand toward Chainer. All six hand-attendants came forward and ushered Chainer forward. He offered no resistance as they led him forward, stopping just outside the Cabal lord's reach.

The First towered over Chainer and took one step closer. His voice was calm, barely above a whisper. "You know what we do here, apprentice. You are at least familiar with how the Cabal operates."

Close up, Chainer could feel the nauseous aura that surrounded the First. Standing in his presence was like standing on the edge of a bottomless pit. There was a sick odor about the First, as well. Not a foul smell, but the sour waft of ashes from a sickroom fireplace.

"The Cabal, Apprentice." Chainer's eyes darted to Skellum, then back to the First. "Tell me now what the Cabal does."

"We survive," Chainer answered immediately. Like every Cabalist, he had gone through the Cabal's cram indoctrination program and knew the routine of call-and-response by heart.

The First took another step forward, and Chainer began to feel physically ill, and he knew it wasn't just his nerves. His throat and nostrils were becoming raw, as if he'd been breathing smoke.

"We survive," the First echoed. "We feed, we gather, we absorb." He waited, and Chainer finished the list for him.

"By the will of the First, we kill."

"By my will," said the First, "and mine alone. And my will is to kill nothing unless there's a long-term benefit. The more people there are alive, the more people there are in the arenas and gambling houses. The more patrons there are for the moneylenders and the flesh mills. We have a thousand uses for people when they're alive. We have only one or two when they're dead."

"It was an animal, Pater," Chainer said. "A bird of prey on a leash. He ordered it to attack me. I defended myself."

"By my will alone," the First repeated. "And my will in all cases having to do with the Order is no killing. I am quite comfortable with the current relationship between their governing body and ours. They claim to be the law, while we are content to be all that is outside the law. Even as they recruit and convert warm bodies, our endeavors see higher and higher profits. They suppress society's truest urges, and we release them. It is a delicate situation, one that I spent years creating. Do you understand, Apprentice?"

"Yes, Pater."

"If there is to be an escalation of hostilities, it will be according to my schedule and my agenda."

"Yes, Pater."

The First drifted back to his spot under the painting at the far end of the room. His attendants silently followed.

Chainer exhaled, drawing fresher air into his lungs. He felt stronger with each step the First took away from him.

"Skellum," the First sounded casual, almost conversational, "tells me that at least you didn't waste the death."

"No, Pater. As he taught me, I captured the bird's essence."

"Then this has not been a total loss. Chainer."

"Yes, Pater?"

"Come here."

The First spread his arms out in a wide welcome, with his attendants keeping three feet of space between themselves and his person at all times. Chainer knew Skellum would be trying his utmost to will Chainer into a state of calm, but Chainer was overwhelmed beyond panic. He stood silent and still as a stone. If the First rewarded him here and now, or killed him outright, or burned out his brain and slapped a hand-standard blouse on his back, he didn't think he'd even flinch.

The sickly odor hit Chainer again as the First brought both his arms together in front of him. In response, one of the hand-attendants stepped forward. The attendant hugged Chainer, fairly lifting him off his feet, then stepped back into the ranks. Two other hand attendants urged Chainer to his knees, tilted his head, and cupped their hands around his ear.

"I said your sphere was remarkable," the First spoke in a conspiratorial stage whisper that was clearly meant for Chainer alone. "And so I remark upon it.

"What you have done is a great service to the Cabal and a great honor to me. I offer you my hand in gratitude." One of the attendants came forward and held out his hand, palm-down. Chainer took the hand and pressed it into his forehead.

"You will be fairly rewarded for your services tonight. And more, you will be remembered." The attendant pulled his hand away, and all of the attendants around Chainer stepped back to let him rise.

"Go back to your quarters and wait. I would speak with Master Skellum about your future. He will tell you what we decide. But rest easy on the cushion of a job well done, Chainer. I see your future as one of wealth and power." The First crossed his arms behind his back, signifying that the interview was over.

A human guard tapped Chainer on the shoulder and gestured with his pike.

"The First is wise," Chainer said.

"Long live the Cabal," the First replied.

Chainer was led out, but he saw Skellum smiling. He was led all the way out of the building, past the sharp-nailed guard and out onto the street.

When his escorts turned back, Chainer walked on in a kind of daze. He touched his dagger, reassured himself that his satchel was finally empty, and broke off a three-foot length of chain with a whispered word and a shimmer of air. He began spinning the truncated chain around his fingers, one of the most basic dexterity exercises he knew.

He felt drained, but his head was still buzzing. He couldn't feel his legs, yet knew he could walk for miles. He sauntered on, spinning the chain as he strolled, faster and faster. He smoothly transferred it from hand to hand as he walked, and he realized that he was happier than he'd ever been in his life.

* * * * *

"I think he is ready, Skellum. You may begin."

"He is ready, Pater. But I would prefer to have another few months before—"

"He is ready, but needs a few more months? Speak clearly, Skellum."

"Pater. He is ready to begin his dementist training. I can have him back in the pits in six months."

The First waited silently, then said, "You are being evasive, Skellum, something I taught you. Normally, I would be proud. Right now, I want you to get to the point."

"Sorry, Pater. The point is, he would be going *back* to the pits. The ones who start out in the pits aren't usually fit for anything but guard duty or rough muscle. My method is to pick out the most promising candidates for my academy during the indoctrination cram, and most of them wind up in the pits as simple dementia casters. Chainer is capable of doing much more for the Cabal. He could be a full-fledged dementist."

"Everything you are saying is known to me, Skellum."

Skellum nodded. "We are pushing Chainer toward his strengths. I'm not questioning that. I am simply wondering if we're pushing too fast. Dementia training has snapped many a young mind beyond repair. We both have high hopes for Chainer. I don't want to lose such a valuable asset after investing so much time and effort."

The First looked mildly amused, something Skellum had not seen before. "You make it sound so clinical, Master Skellum. Hard facts, hard values. This is your favorite pupil we're talking about."

"Pater. I'm only trying to keep my personal attachment to the boy separate from my opinion of his ability."

"Why would you want to do that? Business is business, but then again, family is family."

"Yes, Pater."

"So speak, Skellum. Tell me why you want to wait."

"I want him to be a dementist, not just a pit caster. You know his history, you know his temperament as well as I do. If he masters dementia training and returns to the pits, I'm afraid he'll become unbalanced. Dangerous to himself. To others."

"You have just described most of our current crop of dementia casters and all of the truly great ones. I fail to see your concern."

"Despite what we made him recite, Pater, the Cabal is about control. We amass power, and we control it. Chainer has the potential to be extremely powerful. That power will need to be carefully monitored and molded as it grows."

"Master Skellum," the First said. "That is exactly what I am proposing you and I do for the boy."

"Yes, Pater." Skellum knew when to abandon a failing argument.

"Skellum," the First said, "listen to me carefully. I am aware of your concerns. I share them. The boy is too reactive, like all pit veterans. He assesses a threat, and he strikes. They have to be taught how to think before they act.

"But that is what you and I will teach him, my child. Imagine the perfect blend of pit fighter, dementist, and caster. To have in one man the body of an athlete, the mind of an artist, and the instincts of a trained warrior. Imagine him as a pit boss, supplying an entire games with just the monsters in his mind. Or picture the spectacle he'll put on when he enters the pits himself. And if the Order declares crusat, and the death squads come calling again, imagine how hard he will fight to defend his home and family."

"Pater?" Skellum hesitated, then blurted, "Are the death squads forming again? Has Captain Pianna violated the arrangement?"

"No. But her grip on power is not absolute. And none of us are immortal." The First smiled patiently.

"No, Pater."

"Do not worry, Skellum. Begin the next stage of Chainer's training first thing tomorrow. We will not lose him.

"And tonight," he went on, "I want you and him to join me in my private box for dinner and the main event." His face alive with showmanship, the First's voice rose with gentle anticipation. "We're having a quartet of cephalid deep-sea warriors fight to the death against four flying Nantuko bug people. The Master of the Games is going to enchant the arena—cancel gravity—to let them float around freely, so they can have a good and proper crack at each other."

"We'll be there by the opening horn, Pater."

"Outstanding." The First crossed his arms behind his back.

"The First is wise."

"Long live the Cabal."

Skellum was escorted from the chamber and went off to tell Chainer the news.

CHAPTER 4

The southern capital of Mer Emperor Aboshan's realm lay three hundred miles out from and four miles below Cabal City. Built into the luminescent coral at the bottom of an undersea canyon, Llawan City had been renamed after Aboshan's wife when she retired from public life and took up residence there.

The empress's city consisted of only one actual building, but Llawan made it the grandest city ever contained in a single structure. The coral reef provided both light and natural forms for many of its residents and guests to inhabit. Llawan's servants had magically extended the natural growth of the coral into an elegant flow of knots and bulges that crawled halfway up the canyon walls. Her coralsmiths went on to hollow out and buttress the reef into a huge, interconnected series of rooms and hallways that served simultaneously as fortress, palace,

43

and diplomatic retreat. Though any interior room could be warded and drained for use by air breathers, cephalids like Llawan lived in the submerged chambers constructed on the canyon walls. Guests from the surface stayed in the suites built specifically for them on the canyon floor.

Llawan's architects had made full use of the odd space in an effort to achieve the sheer scope and scale demanded of them. The docks on the rim of the canyon were big enough to receive both undersea ships and creatures as large as whales. The Imperial Guards' barracks outside the city were capable of housing five hundred cephalids who could be mobilized for action in mere minutes. For the Empress's more diplomatic occasions, the palace could accommodate upward of a dozen visiting dignitaries and the formal dining room had a seating capacity of over one hundred.

First daughter of a noble house, Llawan had been part of a power-sharing arrangement between Aboshan, her own father, and several other high-ranking cephalids. Aboshan got the political and military clout he needed to cement his position as emperor, Llawan's father got the post of Imperial Treasurer, and the nobles got to avoid another financially disastrous civil war. Llawan, it was whispered, got her city-in-a-palace.

Tonight, as Llawan swam around her private suite of chambers, she smiled. Gossips among her court in the south and Aboshan's in the north couldn't help but comment on her clear pattern of marriage, retirement, and relocation. The rumors describing her as a kept woman in a golden cage amused Llawan a great deal, almost as much as the ones describing her as a beaten, bitter exile. Indeed, she had started both stories to keep her name circulating around Aboshan's court, lest she be completely forgotten.

Llawan was thinking of her husband the emperor as the strangers swam off the walls of her private corridor. She only thought for a moment, however, before she spun in place and jetted back the way she'd come. It didn't really matter if Aboshan had sent the three cephalids armed with tridents and the huge, yellow shark-man who were now pursuing her. What mattered was survival.

Llawan propelled herself forward on a powerful stream of water jetted from her octopod body. Her two forelimbs stretched out to pull herself along and to steer, while her six secondary limbs trailed out behind her. Her imperial crown was both ornament and helmet, protecting her soft skull while cleaving the water before her as she swam. Over short distances, there weren't many things in the sea faster than she was. The shark-man was capable of giving her a good chase, but he seemed to be held back by the others.

The corridor was long, however, and every time Llawan stopped to draw in more water her pursuers gained on her. Two of the cephalids hurled their tridents, and Llawan froze while the spears buried themselves in the coral by her head. Before she could regain her momentum, the unleashed shark surged up and clamped down on one of her tentacles with its powerful, jagged teeth.

Llawan did not cry out. She curled her forelimb around the tridents in the coral, and as the huge creature heaved its head back Llawan and her weapons were dragged off the wall and into the center of the corridor. After a whistled command from one of the cephalids, the shark turned Llawan loose and began to swim around her in a tight circle.

"Your empress is under attack," she clicked as loudly as she could. "Assassins! Murder!" Then she drove her borrowed tridents into the shark-man's vacant, black eyes. His shriek of pain vibrated against Llawan's skin as it echoed and reechoed off the walls.

Llawan jetted toward the nearest assassin as the blinded brute flailed and roared. Her offensive charge surprised her attacker, and Llawan wrapped her forelimbs around his soft cephalid skull. She gave the assassin's head a mighty squeeze, and he went limp.

The stunned cephalid floated peacefully in Llawan's grip. The final two assassins looked at each other, then one loaded his trident into the other's crossbowlike launcher.

The shooter sighted down the center prong of the trident, targeting Llawan's head. The empress paused momentarily, listening. She could hear her bodyguards and the Imperial Guard approaching, and the water around her began to whirl and churn. She clicked at the assassins in disdain.

"Too slow, cretins," she said. The whirlpool around her solidified into a hard, transparent shell, complete with phantom eyes that blinked as the assassin's tridents bounced off their surface. Llawan's shield defenders had finally arrived. These strange creatures were pledged to put themselves between harm and their empress, and they were capable of transforming their bodies from flesh to water to a substance harder than polar ice. The assassins launched a second volley of tridents into the unyielding barrier around Llawan, and the empress turned her back on them just as a dozen lean, savage bodies exploded out of the corridor behind her. The vicious fish tore into the cephalid assassin's arm before he could pull the trigger again, and the forgotten trident fell straight to the coral floor.

Each of the empress's barracuda was three feet of tooth and muscle and killer instinct looking for a target to maul. They had been trained to tear huge, bloody scraps off of anything that she ordered them to attack or threatened her. Llawan watched impassively behind her shield defenders as her more aggressive bodyguards reduced the remaining assassins to chum and clouds of inky blood.

The survivor in her tentacle shuddered as he woke. Llawan brought him close to her face, with her harp beak a short lunge from his eyes.

"What do you want?" she said. She didn't expect an answer from a professional assassin, but if he was a zealot or a deluded patriot. . . .

She shook her captive. Behind her, she could hear the palace guard darting up the corridor. Her barracuda continued to squabble over scraps of the still-heaving shark-man.

"Answer us."

The assassin's eyes fluttered. He struggled for focus, recognized Llawan, and his face fell.

"We asked you a question." Llawan tightened her grip. "Tell us."

The assassin sneered. In a series of clicks and calls, he said, "You and Laquatus both shall fall." And then he flicked his tongue at Llawan in the undersea equivalent of a spit in the eye.

Llawan squeezed his brain again and watched his eyes roll back. As the captain of the Guard swam onto the scene, she clicked, and the transparent shell in front of her dissolved and began to reform itself into her servant's bodies. Llawan slung the unconscious assassin at the captain of the Guard like a stone.

"He probably won't say much," Llawan said, "but ask him in earnest. Just in case."

"Empress," the captain struggled to salute and control the assassin's limp body simultaneously, "are you all right?"

"We endure. But there will be a serious inquiry into this episode. Fools will be punished."

"Yes, Empress."

Llawan clicked for her barracuda, and they obediently fell in alongside her as she swam for her throne room. Her evening's rest was ruined, now that she had business that wouldn't wait until morning.

She maintained whatever power she had by staying on top of situations that involved her. Her own subjects were trying to kill her, and Ambassador Laquatus had been mentioned by name. If Laquatus was involved, Aboshan was involved. If Aboshan was involved, she could not miss an opportunity to slap him back into line like the egotistical child he was. Aboshan and Laquatus had made three attempts on her life since her retirement, all of them half-hearted affairs like this one. Some husbands send gifts to their wives. Hers sent killers. Still, she regarded the attempts more as reminders to stay alert and informed rather than actual death threats.

The empress needed more information, and she needed to know the extent of Laquatus's involvement. As one of the only merfolk on or around Otaria, Laquatus was not tied to the empire by family or tradition. Indeed, his human features reflected a decidedly human character. He was a consummate politician, a notorious opportunist, and ambitious to the point of lunacy.

Llawan needed to talk to someone with a better understanding of how he thought.

* * * * *

The Mer empire encircled the entire continent of Otaria and stretched far out into the depths of the ocean. The coastal waters around Otaria itself were called the shallows, and Director Rillu Veza lived there on the coast in an area called Breaker Bay.

Veza acted on behalf of the empire as combination negotiator, harbormaster, and customs inspector for all commerce between the Cabal's northern stronghold and the empire's southern quarter. It was not a prominent position to hold. Most of the trade between Otaria and Mer was routed through ports and storage depots further north, along shipping lanes that were better protected. In Veza's opinion, she had been confined to such a remote weigh station for not being a staunch supporter of the emperor's faction. She also believed she was in charge of Breaker Bay depot because she was qualified to run it. Her comfortable bayside cottage with access to the sea and the main road into town were proof of the emperor's partial approval. After all, he could have put her in charge of a bare piece of rock completely off the trade routes and without any other inhabitants.

Veza slept in a sunken tub filled with sea water. This morning, she was awakened by an insistent knocking at the cottage's front door. She shook drowsiness and salt water from her eyes, submerged for one last gulp of gill-filtered air, then climbed out of her tub.

Veza's hair was soft and greenish blue. After a quick wringing to squeeze out excess water, she let her unbound locks fall down to the small of her back. She grabbed a waterproof dressing gown from a hook. Though she was covered from head to toe in glistening blue scales, she respected the customs of her land-bound clients and wore unnecessary clothing whenever she might encounter them.

She was still adjusting the robe and her dripping hair when she got to the door. She opened it and found a small human boy looking nervously up at her.

"Missus Mermaid?" the boy said.

"Yes." She did not reach out to the boy. He seemed spooked enough by her huge black eyes and scaled skin. She didn't want to see him panic when confronted by her long, webbed fingers.

"There's a guy waiting for you in the water out there." He gestured vaguely to the bay behind him. "A fish guy. He says he can't come up on the land."

"Thank you," Veza said. "Did he say what he'd give you if you helped him?"

"No. He just said I should help him." Veza could see that even this scared little boy knew a raw deal when he saw it.

"Well, I think you helped him just right. How would you like to swim on my private beach today? If you come back after lunch, I'll make sure the groundskeeper lets you in."

"Thank you," the boy said glumly. Of course, Veza thought, he lives on the shore. A swim in the ocean probably isn't all that exciting for him.

Veza took a small notebook and an ornate quill pen from the hallway table. "So let's say later today, sometime after noon? I'll tell the groundskeeper to expect two of you, so you can bring a friend. Oh, and remember, the spell only lasts for an hour, so be sure not to get too far from shore."

The boy looked confused. "Spell?"

Veza smiled. "Yes, the enhancement spell. It wouldn't be much fun to swim in the ocean if you couldn't breathe and see underwater, now would it?"

The boy's face lit up. "No, ma'am."

"After lunch, then."

"Yes, ma'am."

"And bring a friend."

"Yes, ma'am." The boy ran happily off, fairly skipping back down the road into town.

Veza put the pad and quill back on the table. There was no groundskeeper, so there was no need for a note, but there was always a need to keep up the dignity of the empire. She would receive the boy and his friend herself, show them the sights only visible beneath the bay, and introduce them to some of the residents.

Now, for her other mystery guest. Veza closed the front door and backtracked into the cottage. The waters of her bay lapped gently against her living room floor, and she dropped her robe and dove in. She swam under her own floorboards and out into the sea.

The cephalid male was waiting for her a hundred yards from shore. He wore an imperial seal on his skullcap and a curved sword in his belt. His limbs twitched impatiently as he tread water waiting for Veza.

"Is that the fastest you can swim, land crawler?" he sneered, glancing at her legs. "I've been waiting forever."

"My door is always open," Veza said coolly. "And I can accommodate all callers. If you'd been braver, we could have started this discussion when you arrived."

The cephalid snarled. "It's not my bravery that's suspect, it's your loyalty. Last night our empress was attacked, and she barely escaped alive."

"Long live the empress," Veza said automatically. Llawan may live in exile, but she was still a member of the royal bloodline, and there were formalities to observe. "Our lady is well?"

The cephalid twitched uncomfortably. "She endures. I bring an inquiry from her to you."

"I'm ready to hear it."

The cephalid arranged his arms around him to float more comfortably. "You are Veza, director of this depot?"

"I am."

"Her majesty the Empress Llawan wishes to inquire if you still maintain the ability to transform between a human's legs and a fish's tail."

Now it was Veza who squirmed. "Yes," she said finally. "Tell the empress that I do." *Just as long as I have plenty of warning and a half-hour to recover,* she added privately.

"Very well." The cephalid took a small crystal gem from his courier's pouch. He turned his back on Veza, raised the globe over his head, and crushed it in his forelimb.

A high-pitched whistle blasted out of the gem, and a blue-white arc of energy radiated outward, away from the shoreline behind them. Veza watched the arc advance, growing smaller and fainter until it disappeared entirely.

The cephalid turned back to her. "The empress will contact you shortly." He handed her a small hand mirror made of tinted blue glass. "Keep this by your side until you hear our lady's voice. She has urgent issues to discuss with you." He looked Veza over once more, lingering again on her legs. "Do not keep her waiting."

In a flurry of bubbles and powerful strokes he was gone. Before she could stop herself, Veza cursed him out loud like the air breathers she spent so much time with. Underwater, the effect was minimal and she was instantly ashamed of herself for trying.

Angrily, she kicked her webbed feet and streaked back toward her cottage.

* * * * *

Three hours later, Veza sat dozing over a pile of paperwork. The seasonal winter storms had not taken the expected toll on shipping, but pirate activity was way up from last year. As much as the numbers fluctuated on the hundreds of reports she reviewed each week, the situation in Breaker Bay never really changed.

From somewhere on her desk, a fanfare of horns began playing Llawan's imperial theme.

"Director Rillu Veza, stand ready," a woman's voice sounded over the trumpets. "Your empress awaits."

Veza shoved the papers out of her lap and picked up the mirror. "Long live the empress. I am at her disposal." Veza felt a curious detached anxiety as she waited for a reply. She was the same age as Llawan and had attended the same government career training schools, but they had never moved in the same circles. When Aboshan became emperor, Veza was packed off to the shallows and Llawan retired. Veza had only heard rumors regarding her former classmate ever since.

The trumpet music finished with a flourish, and the woman's voice spoke again. "Behold, subject of Mer, your Empress Llawan."

Llawan appeared in the mirror, and Veza bowed her head. She wondered again why the empress had reached out so far to such a desolate place, and if this latest assassination attempt was tied to Breaker Bay.

"We are the Empress Llawan of Mer." The empress was obviously talking into a mirror like Veza's because only a small portion of her large face was visible. She seemed suspicious of the device and held it at limb's length.

"Empress," Veza said, "I am Rillu Veza, director of Breaker Bay depot, and your humble servant."

"We understand you are capable of walking on legs." Llawan's voice and image dissolved into static as she absently shook her mirror. The static cleared and Llawan's eye appeared in the glass, filling it from side to side. "Well?"

Veza flushed. "Yes, my empress. That is true."

"Excellent. Director Veza, you will now scan your chamber with the mirror."

"What? Forgive me, my empress, I could not hear you clearly."

"We do not repeat ourselves."

Veza hesitated then carefully held the mirror face-out, slowly pointing it at every corner of the room. When she reached the small interior fountain on the east wall, Llawan called out, "Stop." Veza's arms began to tremble from holding the awkward position.

The fountain stream froze in midair and the surface of its pool began to glow silver-white. The light was reflected in Veza's mirror and she could hear Empress Llawan in it, pronouncing the words to a spell Veza didn't recognize. A soft, insistent whine rose behind the empress's voice.

With a ripping crack, the surface of the pool became a three-dimensional disk of energy. The crest of Empress Llawan's skullcap broke the surface of the disk, and her large, round head continued to rise through the portal until it was physically in the room with Veza.

The disoriented empress's eyes darted around the room until she spotted the bay waters lapping up on Veza's living room floor. Llawan threw herself out of the portal and into the water with a splash. She rolled over once, regaining her bearing and adjusting to the temperature and purity of the bay. Veza took one last look at the glowing portal in the corner, then joined her empress under the waves.

"Greetings, loyal Veza. We must speak quickly and plainly, so listen well. You will contact the Ambassador Laquatus on our behalf. From time to time he makes use of a mirror similar to the one we gave you. We will provide you with the means to access his mirror. Something is stirring in the land to the north, Veza, and its effects are being felt down below, even in our city. News from the shores and shallows rarely filters down that far, which we would now remedy. The most recent assassination plot was conceived, planned, and launched nearby, where we would not discover it.

"Rest easy," Llawan added, "we know that you are loyal to the empire and to us. But there are others to the north who are not so reliable. You have heard of Laquatus?"

"Yes, Empress."

"You are to learn what the ambassador is doing in Cabal City. We would also know how and to whom he is doing it. There is no point in trying to keep our interest in this from him, but you must disguise your true intent. Lead him to believe that we are inspecting the emperor's newly drawn trade routes, or that we are in hiding until the threat of assassination is removed. I recommend you introduce yourself as my agent and then present yourself as a disgruntled member of my court, persecuted and ignored as a 'crawler. That will appeal to Laquatus's pride and also give him the illusion of something in you that he can exploit."

Veza swallowed heavily. "Yes, Empress."

"But you are to use every available method to discover what Laquatus is up to and how Aboshan is involved. Do you understand?"

"Yes, Empress."

"No one knows I have come to you, or what I have said. If you fail or are found out, you are the only one who will suffer."

"I understand, Empress."

"Keep us informed. We expect regular communication from you from now until we are satisfied with what you discover."

"It will be done, Empress."

"You will be rewarded for your service, Veza."

"Thank you, Empress."

"This audience is over." Llawan held out her forelimb, and Veza kissed the tip. Llawan left a small, waterproof scroll with her seal on it in Veza's hand. "Read that account of recent events before you contact Laquatus. Access to his mirror is also inside." Veza nodded and tucked the tiny scroll behind her ear. Llawan waved her tentacle carelessly over her shoulder.

"You may conduct us back to our city."

"Empress." Veza swam up and pulled herself out of the bay, standing between the empress and the fountain. The empress then shot up out of the water and landed in Veza's outstretched arms.

Llawan's weight and soft body caused her to sprawl in a manner most undignified, but Veza averted her eyes and gently placed her empress in the portal head-first. Llawan disappeared into the portal like a stone down a well, and the glowing disk snapped shut behind her.

"Do not fail us, Veza," said the empress's faint voice in the mirror. Then the mirror went dark as well and became an ordinary reflective surface.

Veza went to her personal library to review the information on the scroll and anything else she had on Ambassador Laquatus. She knew him by his formidable reputation, but she needed to know a lot more if she was going to determine his motives and report them back to Llawan. She had many duties in Breaker Bay, and now she had one that was more important than all the rest combined.

An angry knock sounded at her front door. Veza swore softly, startling her own ears. She retrieved her crumpled dressing gown from the floor and opened the door. An angry human woman stood on Veza's doorstep with the little boy who had knocked earlier clenched tight in her fist.

"Did you threaten to cast a spell on my son, you miserable sea hag?"

Veza was caught off-guard, but she was becoming sadly accustomed to this level of discourse.

"What? Of course not. He was very polite and helpful to a guest of mine, and I promised him a reward."

The woman glared at Veza suspiciously. "You threatened to make him one of you." The boy at her side looked completely miserable.

"I offered to let him swim unencumbered on my private beach."

The human sneered. "Sure you did. Well, thanks but no thanks. He won't be coming by here again, and he doesn't need your kind of reward."

"Sorry, lady," the boy muttered, and the human woman clipped him across the ear.

"Shut up," she snapped. She turned and stomped down Veza's path, dragging the boy behind her.

Veza stood in the open doorway for a full minute after they'd gone. Then, she shook her head, closed the door gently, and went back to her papers.

CHAPTER 5

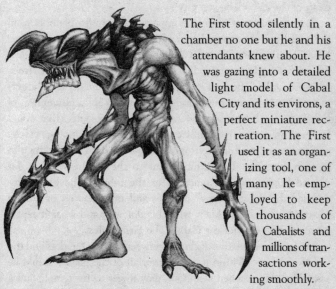

The First stood silently in a chamber no one but he and his attendants knew about. He was gazing into a detailed light model of Cabal City and its environs, a perfect miniature recreation. The First used it as an organizing tool, one of many he employed to keep thousands of Cabalists and millions of transactions working smoothly.

He focused his thoughts on the model and spoke a few words under his breath. The background buildings in the projection faded slightly, leaving a series of stark, colored dots to represent the individuals he was interested in following.

Two small, black dots waited in the proving grounds of Skellum's dementist academy, representing Chainer and Skellum himself. The

First noted with some satisfaction that the pair were still training hard, even with the progress Chainer had already made. The boy was proving to be capable of everything the First had in mind for him.

A small blue dot lurked around the shore just outside the city walls, where Ambassador Laquatus connived and plotted. The ambassador both interested and amused the First. Laquatus may have mastered the shifting tides of diplomacy, but his childish self-interest made him woefully predictable. Also, the egotistical fool seemed to actually think he could keep secrets from the First in the heart of the Cabal's biggest city.

A small cluster of white dots approached from the plains beyond the main gate. Lieutenant Kirtar of the Order coming to call, or perhaps Captain Pianna herself? Whichever of its noble heroes came, Chainer's found treasure spelled the end of the Cabal's relative truce with the Order. The First thought of himself primarily as an entertainer. While he was pragmatic enough to accept a resumption of hostilities, the host in him mourned the loss of resources that would be spent on destructive conflict rather than constructive spectacle.

Finally, and most interestingly, a single red dot was heading into his city from the Pardic mountains to the southeast. This dot glowed brightly when compared to the others. The First commanded the finest network of spies and informers on or around Otaria, bar none. He knew who this dot was, and what it represented to his plans for the Cabal. The First smiled.

He compared relative distances between the various dots and the Cabal City pits. Within a day or two, all of the players would be assembled. He touched a smooth, gray finger to his temple and a skull-attendant stepped forward out of the darkness.

"Bring me Skellum and the boy," he said.

Sometimes, the showman in him thought, the best thing to do with something everyone wants is to throw it up in the air and yell, "Catch."

* * * * *

After four months in it, Chainer grew to hate the room in Skellum's academy that was designed to recreate the pits. It wasn't anywhere near as large and there weren't hundreds of bloodthirsty spectators screaming for death and carnage, but it was as near-perfect a recreation as possible. From the black stone floor to the fixed and inextinguishable torches to the spiked wooden barriers that protected the crowds, Chainer had to hand it to Skellum: the old man had an eye for detail.

He'd had plenty of opportunity to examine those details. For endless weeks now Skellum had filled Chainer's days with breathing and meditation techniques, and extremely boring speeches about Cabal history and the dementists' role in it. After the first week Chainer had mouthed off to Skellum about the monotony of the routine. Skellum had spun his hat and left Chainer alone in the room with a two-headed harpy and a fifty-pound slug that seeped acid. Chainer hadn't complained since.

Today, Chainer perked up because Skellum was carrying an eight-inch pewter cage. The cylinder-shaped contraption was hinged in the middle and had a thick slot in the top. Chainer stared at it hungrily. It was the only new thing he had seen in weeks. Maybe Skellum would let him actually do something.

"Big day today," Skellum said. He drew a thick charcoal coin and a match out of his satchel. He struck the match against his thumb, held it under the coin until the edge glowed red, and then dropped the charcoal disk into the slot on top of the cage.

"Here," Skellum flipped the cage over to Chainer. Chainer caught it gingerly and tossed it from hand to hand until he was sure it was cool to the touch.

"Fasten it to your chain and set it on the floor," Skellum said. He spread his cape out with both arms and gracefully lowered himself into a cross-legged sitting position.

Chainer broke off five feet of chain, held the end near to the cylinder-cage, and whispered, "Link." The air shimmered, and the pewter cage became attached to his black metal chain as if it had been forged there.

"I've told you about we dementists," Skellum said. "We are the First's favorites. We work and sleep in places that would reduce lesser beings to babbling hysteria. We walk paths that would turn others' feet to ashes. We travel at will to the shores of nightmare, and not only do we return, but we return bearing captives. The Cabal serves Kuberr for a purpose, and no less than the First himself has confirmed—the dementists are part of that purpose."

Chainer shrugged. "Yes. You have told me these things."

"And I have told you about the paths we walk. How some bind their eyes and plug their ears in order to find a path. And others go without food, or water, or air until their feet find the way. And some turn to drink, or drugs, or the hypnotist's candle in order to leave this world behind and find the world within."

"So you have said, Master Skellum."

"But I haven't told you why I am the master. Why my service to the Cabal lies outside the pits. Why I am uniquely qualified to help you find your path."

"There is no need," Chainer said carefully. He watched Skellum's impassive face. "You are my master. I am your pupil. Lead, and I will follow."

Skellum smiled, gave his hat a playful spin, and caught a gap in front of his face after exactly one revolution. He reached into his satchel and took out a dusty red coin as thick as a finger.

"Put this in the censer." He showed the red disc to Chainer. "It's Dragon's Blood. Not the actual blood from a dragon's veins, mind you, but a resin we call Dragon's Blood."

"Why?"

"Mostly because it's red and stinky. Here."

Chainer caught the disc and dropped it into the slot. There was a hiss and a sizzle, and then fragrant smoke began to pour out between the bars of the pewter cage.

"Place it on a hot coal," Skellum said, "and it produces a strong scent and thick smoke. Quite a lot of thick smoke, actually."

Chainer nodded, but the choking fog from the censer stung his eyes and clogged his lungs.

"Can you still hear me, pupil?" Skellum's voice was clear, but Chainer couldn't quite pin down its direction.

"Yes, Master."

"Good. Spin the censer around on your chain. I'm about six feet away from you at ground level. Be sure not to hit me with it. When you've got a clear space around you that you can breathe in, say, 'Ready.' In the meantime, I'll tell you about Cateran."

Chainer coughed. "I understand, Master." He picked up the censer, tossed it out into space, and started it whirling around his head.

"Cateran," Skellum's voice now echoed out of the smoke from about two feet off the ground to Chainer's left, "was one of the greats. An extraordinary dementist. Before your time, before my time, maybe even before the First's time. The Cabal is here, Chainer, and some say it has always been. There are many more stories about its early days than you or I will ever hear."

Chainer had the censer spinning easily, and he was slowly creating a miniature cyclone of Dragon's Blood smoke with himself at the center.

"I'm still waiting to hear this one."

Skellum sighed. "Loathsome boy." Chainer spun the censer a few more times, then yelped as Skellum hit him on the end of his nose with a spare charcoal disc.

Skellum continued. "Cateran was a summoner. He was so good at it that he could threaten you with a monster, and make it appear between the letters in the last word he spoke."

"What was he good at? Big, scary things, or lots of little sharp things?"

"Both, and more besides. There's an old legend about him going into the pits alone on the eve of no moons and not coming out until the next one, a full month later. He must have been astounding. An inexhaustible roster of ferocity, size, variety, all at a moment's notice."

"So what happened to this dementist hero? Did he finally meet someone better than he was?"

"Of course not."

"But that's the rule. That's how it works in the pits."

"Cateran did not die in the pits." Skellum sounded hurt, almost offended. "Some say that Kuberr rewarded him, and he now sits by our god's side on a pile of gold and silver markers. Others say Kuberr rewarded Cateran with an entire world to infiltrate and colonize on behalf of the Cabal. And some among us dementists think he became too good, that he got so comfortable in his own dementia space that he simply forgot to come back."

"What do you think, Master?" Chainer took a deep breath. "I'm also ready, by the way."

"Excellent." Skellum's voice now came from the floor to Chainer's right, but he hadn't heard his mentor move. Chainer wondered if the old man had been spinning his hat as he spoke. It was possible that Skellum was speaking from inside Chainer's head again.

"I think," Skellum's voice said from directly in front of Chainer, "that Cabalists never get to lie around on big piles of money, even in paradise. And I think if you gave a dementist his own world, he would forget why you gave it to him and spend all of his time playing with it."

Chainer kept spinning the censer and scanning the smoke for Skellum. "And what if he's lost in the place that you go to find monsters?"

"That I don't know, Chainer. But together, maybe we can find out." Skellum's hand clamped over Chainer's eyes from behind and Chainer could feel whispered words hissing in his ear. "Let's go look."

Chainer heard a deafening boom, and he fell forward onto his knee. He struggled to keep the censer spinning and away from Skellum, but the old man seemed weightless as he kept his hand pressed tightly over Chainer's eyes. Angled as it was, the swinging censer should have been slamming into the stone floor by now, but it continued to spin freely.

"Keep your eyes closed. Stand up straight. Keep the censer spinning."

Chainer straightened his back and got the censer realigned. "I'm trying, damn it."

"Don't talk back. And keep your eyes shut." Skellum's hand came away from Chainer's face, and the young pupil did as he was told.

"What do you hear?" Skellum asked.

Chainer listened. "It sounds like we're outside or in a really big room. An empty one. Are we in the pits?"

"What do you smell?"

Chainer sniffed. "Dragon's Blood. And . . . dead trees? Mulch. Lamp oil. I don't know, a lot of things."

"What do you see? Keep your eyes closed."

"How can I—"

"Shut up, and tell me what you see. Now."

"We're on the salt flats," Chainer said instantly. "It's the dry season, so the ground is hard. There's been a fire recently, and all the vegetation is burned and black."

"What about the sky?"

"It's about to storm. It's midday, but there's no sun. The clouds are thick and heavy and dark. They want to rain. They're bursting with it, but they can't. All they can do is flash and rumble."

"Anyone here but us?"

Chainer focused all of his available senses on the space around him. "No one," he said.

"Keep the censer spinning. Open your eyes."

The sky was just as Chainer imagined it, but the landscape was all gray and jagged stone instead of black and ruined marsh. Skellum sat cross-legged on the ground to his left. His hat was in motion, but slowing. The spinning censer created a ten-foot ring of scented smoke with Chainer and Skellum safe in its center.

Outside the ring were a thousand slavering horrors. They crowded and jostled each other for the chance to peer directly into the protected circle. They produced an unholy chorus of snarls, growls, and shrieks as they jockeyed for position. Occasionally, one would lash out at its neighbor, and a vicious skirmish would break out, but there were too many of them to get a good melee going. Besides, they were far too busy drooling and leering at Chainer. They ignored Skellum.

"Welcome. These are my nightmares." Skellum said.

Chainer cleared his throat. An insectoid whose head was all compound eye and razor mandible was eyeing him hungrily.

"I've seen worse," he said.

"But not all at once," Skellum said. "And not all waiting here, just for you."

Chainer cleared his throat. "Okay. You've got me there." He spun the censer, and for the first time wondered how much longer he could keep it spinning.

"Master Skellum?"

"Yes, Chainer?"

"Forgive me, but . . . what in the Nine Hells is this place?"

Skellum smiled. "I just told you."

"But how did we get here?"

"I come here all the time."

"Okay. How did I get here?"

"I brought you. This is why I am *Master* Skellum. My path to this place is slow, but sure. I'm not very good in the pits without a partner, because I take too long to get going. But the creatures I produce are exceptionally stable and strong. And detailed, if I do say so myself. Look, there's my grendelkin." Skellum waved playfully at the elephantine beast prowling the perimeter of the censer's circle. "Also," his voice went serious, "I can take others with me when I come here."

"Other pupils."

"On occasion. And sometimes, people I just don't like."

Chainer was scanning the crush of monsters, picking out the ones he would most want beside him in the pits and least want to fight against.

"Will I be able to produce such creatures?"

Skellum laughed. "I expect so. But these are mine, created from my memories and my mind. Your dementia space is currently empty. Starting tomorrow, we begin to populate it."

"Now," Chainer said. "Take me there now."

Skellum scowled. "No. Tomorrow. It's dangerous enough in here, and I'm standing right next to you. If that chain stopped spinning, they'd attack us en masse without hesitation. I think I could make it out, but you'd be trapped here. Fighting forever in the darkest parts of my brain until I called you forth. And even then, you wouldn't be you. You'd be a shadow of the Chainer I knew and trained, real form without real substance. A puppet to my will."

"Then take me out of your space and into mine. If it's empty, it can't be—"

"Chainer," Skellum said sternly, "no. Trust your mentor, boy." He stood up, crouching to avoid the chain overhead, and moved behind his pupil. He covered the boy's eyes again.

"Close your eyes," he instructed, "and when I say so, start slowing the censer down and drawing it in. Ready?"

"Ready."

"Now."

The boom and the internal wrench were softer on Chainer this time. The horror's noises suddenly stopped, and Chainer felt the pressure around him change. He knew he was back in the pit facsimile inside Skellum's academy.

Skellum pulled his hand away. "Open your eyes and catch the censer." Chainer did, noting that the pewter cage was still cool to the touch, and that the smoke had tapered off to a few final wisps.

"Tomorrow," Skellum promised, and he threw his arm up and over Chainer's shoulder. Chainer took one step forward, and his legs buckled. He felt cold, dizzy, and on the verge of vomiting. He fell heavily against Skellum, who laughed as he propped his student up.

"It takes more out of you than you realize," Skellum said. "Especially at first." Skellum was physically stronger than he looked, Chainer thought, as his mentor half-dragged and half-carried him toward the door.

Before they reached it, someone knocked loudly and forcefully. "Master Skellum," a voice called. Skellum stood Chainer up and held him there with one hand while he opened the door with the other.

"Yes?"

One of the First's skull attendants was in the hallway, with the woman warrior who had admitted Chainer and Azza to the manor four months ago.

"Hello, Deidre," Skellum said to the woman. "Still on house duty, little sister?"

"Yes, Master Skellum," Deidre said. Then, over his shoulder, "Chainer."

Chainer feebly waved through half-lidded eyes and an exhausted smile.

"The First requires Master Skellum and the pupil Chainer in his chambers." The skull attendant's eyes were unfocused, and he spoke in a pathetic monotone that irritated Chainer. "Immediately."

CHAPTER 6

Ambassador Laquatus soaked himself in a hot bath. He enjoyed the steam and the bubbles, but he always kept one eye on the timer next to the tub. Ocean-dwellers like himself were built to survive in the extreme cold of deep water, but they were not normally required to cope with high temperatures. To Laquatus, the sensation of a hot spa was worth the risk of being cooked alive if he stayed in too long. He prided himself on enjoying as many of the surface's unique luxuries as he could, even when they were potentially harmful.

He smiled, and corrected himself: *especially* when they were potentially harmful. In all the depths of the ocean and all the nations of the land, he was unique. There were no boundaries for one such as he, no limits except for the ones he himself imposed.

In his legged form, Laquatus appeared remarkably human. He

was six feet tall and handsome, with two small horns at his temples which he had capped in silver. He claimed the vestigial horns were a sign of his royal blood, as were his very light skin color and smooth, almost invisible scale texture. Without his ornate robes and his horns, Laquatus could easily pass for a normal air breather.

On a whim, Laquatus switched from his legged form to his tailed one in a flurry of arcane blue light and sea spray . Now nearly nine feet long, he had to fold his lower half back over itself to fit in the spa. He gently flexed his muscles, his scales shimmering, and submerged for a difficult breath of hot water. Though he spent almost all of his time walking and talking with humans, he still needed to keep his skin moist at all times and to spend a few hours a week in his seagoing form.

The tub side timer went off. Laquatus shifted back to his legged form and signaled for his servants. Two sallow-faced humans in dreary peasant clothing stepped forward and helped him from the tub. One cooled him down with a huge, damp, purple towel, and the other draped a robe around the ambassador's shoulders.

"Be gone," Laquatus said, and the humans shuffled out.

Turg, the ambassador's bodyguard and champion, snored loudly on the floor of the next room. The huge amphibian had won four straight matches in the pits that afternoon and then gorged itself at the post-games banquet. Between the mountain of food their Cabal hosts provided and the odd body part or two from his opponents, Turg's appetite was for once completely sated. Laquatus reached out with his mind, confirming that Turg was merely asleep and not comatose, and then let the sleeping giant lie. The slightest unfamiliar sound or smell, the merest whisper of thought from Laquatus, and Turg would be as awake and as dangerous as ever. Laquatus had spent years building and strengthening the master/thrall relationship with Turg, and though the great frog still retained far too much of its own primitive drives, it was unquestionably loyal and nearly perfect in its obedience.

Laquatus heard an unfamiliar tone and a strange voice calling his name from elsewhere in the room. In a flash, Turg responded to Laquatus's confusion and rolled onto his huge webbed feet, grumbling angrily. Laquatus waved his familiar away and bid him stand ready. He then went looking for the source of the sound.

In a trunk bearing his formal attire, he found the imperial mirror Empress Llawan had given him. It played a lyrical fanfare to announce the rank and station of whoever was using it. For Llawan, it played the imperial theme. For Laquatus, it used a piece he himself had written. For this mysterious new person, it played a fairly unimpressive flute aria.

". . . for Ambassador Laquatus. This is Rillu Veza, Director of the Breaker Bay depot for Ambassador Laquatus. Are you there, Ambassador?"

"This is Laquatus," the ambassador spoke from several feet back, the mirror still hidden inside the trunk. It was a woman's voice, he noted. "And this is a private channel. Do not contact me again."

"Ambassador? I have information, and a request, from Empress Llawan."

Laquatus paused. Of course. If someone new was using Llawan's mirror, the empress must have given them instructions to do so.

"How do I know Llawan sent you?" Laquatus took off his purple robe and rooted around in his wardrobe for a finer one. Turg menacingly sniffed the trunk with the mirror in it, and Laquatus brought him to heel with a thought.

"Our lady gave me the access to your mirror, Ambassador." Veza said. "She is currently in hiding after another assassination attempt and has asked me to contact you on her behalf. Will you speak to me?"

Laquatus checked his reflection in the full-length mirror. He polished a spot of condensation off his silver horn cap, wrapped the final yard of blue silk around his waist, and tied it tight. Then he picked up the mirror.

"Assassination attempt?" he said urgently. "Is the empress all right?" In the mirror, Veza of Breaker Bay jumped at his sudden appearance.

"Yes, Ambassador. She endures. But she is very, very concerned."

She ought to be, Laquatus thought. He had spent a lot of Aboshan's money to hire the assassins, though in truth they were hired to disfigure Llawan rather than kill her. Laquatus found the empress too useful to discard just yet, but he also wanted her frightened and focused on Aboshan.

Veza was pretty, Laquatus thought, but not beautiful. She was an unknown quantity, however, and therefore interesting. Too far away to affect her thoughts, too unfamiliar to gauge her intent. Laquatus sniffed. Llawan must be desperate if she were reaching out to low-level functionaries to do her spying for her.

"Who were the assassins? Did any of them escape?" Laquatus hoped they hadn't. Survivors would want to be paid the balance of the fee.

"No. The empress's guard protected her." Veza's face clouded. "She is concerned about events on Otaria, however. Aboshan's new shipping lanes have not been well received by all. There are those in the depths and especially on the surface who feel cheated, and Llawan fears that she is being made a target for their frustration with the empire as a whole." The scenery behind Veza rolled dizzily as she sat with the mirror in hand. "I've received a number of complaints even here in Breaker Bay."

"Really." Veza was distracted and rooting for paperwork, so Laquatus was free to stare fixedly at her. "I was just discussing the shipping lanes with a syndicate of Cabal merchants. I have made great progress on behalf of the empire in the houses of both Cabal and Order. It would be a crime if my work on behalf of the empire was undone by a violent splinter group of intolerant cephalids at home."

"Of course, Ambassador. It is precisely that kind of effort that Llawan needs."

Laquatus's mind raced. She had just sat down—*from a standing position!* Veza had suddenly become far more interesting to him.

"Director," Laquatus said, "allow me to congratulate you."

"Ambassador?"

"I know how hard it is for a non-cephalid to achieve any sort of advancement in Mer. They are an old-fashioned people, not given easily to change. You must be extremely adept at your position."

Veza blinked. "Thank you, Ambassador. But I—"

"I think we should meet in person, my dear. There is much we have to discuss, for the good of the empire."

"Of course, Ambassador. When can we—"

"I am always at the empress's service." He glanced at Turg. *Growl*, he thought.

Turg let out a loud, rumbling half-roar that caused Laquatus to wince.

"Excuse me, Director, but I have an appointment scheduled, and my guest has just arrived. Please excuse this humble diplomat. By my oath, I will contact you as soon as I have arranged for our meeting."

For the first time since he picked up the mirror, Veza's expression was less than polite. She seemed to be peering at him as if seeing him clearly for the first time, sizing him up as a potential ally or opponent.

"Thank you, Ambassador.

"Thank you, Director."

"I hope I can count on you to assist me. We are both in a unique position to help the empress, the empire, and ourselves."

"Nothing would please me more. I will make some inquiries and arrange for a time and place to share my findings with you." Provided, of course, Laquatus thought, that it serves my needs, and I

71

haven't had you or the empress killed by then. "As I said before, for the good of the empire."

"Long live the empire. I will await your notice, Ambassador. I can be reached any time, day or night, on this mirror."

"Very well. I, on the other hand, will not be available. I will have to contact you. It could be a matter of hours, or a matter of days. But I will contact you."

Veza scowled. "Agreed. Until then, Ambassador, you have my thanks and those of the empress."

"Long live the empire," Laquatus said. He touched a gem on the mirror's handle, and the vision went blank. Turg belched loudly, and Laquatus muttered, "Go back to sleep," so the great frog rolled happily back onto its side.

Laquatus put the mirror back into the trunk and locked it up tight. He could sort out where to have a clandestine meeting with Veza and what kind of misinformation to feed the empress later. As intrigued as he was with the sight of another merfolk like himself, right now he needed to check in with his Cabal hosts and arrange for a meeting with the First.

Laquatus's spies in the Cabal had told him that an artifact of immense power had been recovered and brought safely into the city. Laquatus had felt the presence of the artifact himself, but he had not been able to determine what, or exactly where, it was. According to his sources in the Order, however, high-level adepts of every description were honing in on the artifact like sharks on a bleeding fish.

Laquatus felt an opportunity growing and was determined to make the most of it. Powerful, functioning artifacts were nearly impossible to come by these days, and if this one was as impressive as it seemed, then Laquatus would claim it in Aboshan's name. The emperor would use it to solidify his grip on both the seas around Otaria and the continent itself. In turn, Laquatus would also use the artifact to strengthen his hold on Aboshan. He would continue as he had for the past several years, supplanting the churlish emperor one step at a time, bit by bit, until there would be no more need for Aboshan, his exiled wife, or any of her prying, spying, low-level functionaries.

Laquatus stripped off the blue silken robe and began rooting around for something more dazzling. He would request an audience with the First, check on his hidden troops in the sea caves, and put Turg through his paces in the pits. Before he went to sleep that night, he intended to have seen the mysterious device with his own eyes.

He knew that once he had seen it and determined how to make use of it, there was nothing on land or in the seas that could stop him from acquiring it.

* * * * *

Chainer and Skellum were admitted to the First's study without fanfare. Deidre led them through the door, then began to skulk along the walls and shadows with the rest of the First's armed guards. The skull attendant returned to his post at the First's side. Master and pupil both waited for the First to hail them, but he simply stood staring at the pair calmly with his arms behind his back.

"It is called the 'Mirari,' " the First said calmly. He stepped aside and presented the treasure to them with a wave of his robed arm. The First had Chainer's sphere set floating above a polished rune-silver base, which was in turn set into a small wooden stand. The entire apparatus was enclosed in a clear glass cover that fit snugly onto the stand. Lit by torches, the Mirari seemed to be floating above a floating stand inside a floating glass bubble.

"Quite astonishing, Pater."

Chainer simply gaped. "Mirari?" he said.

"Mirari," the First confirmed. "It's an ancient word for a fantastic wish-granting artifact."

Skellum stroked his thin beard. "Simply astonishing."

"So it grants wishes?" Chainer couldn't quite pin down why that disappointed him. Perhaps because his vision had seemed so much grander than even his wildest dreams.

"It might," the First said. "Among other things. We haven't had enough time to fully determine all its uses, but simply possessing it has given me a clearer mind and more energy than I've had in years. I'm almost aglow with good ideas lately.

"Even as we speak, mages are on their way here to find out what I have. I can feel them coming like moths flitting above a spider's web. They don't even know what it is, yet they want it. It is part of this object's nature. They simply can't help but want it.

"But you," he said to Chainer. "You found it, and you brought it here. You put thoughts of the Cabal and of your First before thoughts of yourself. I must ask you to do so again."

"We are yours to command, Pater," Skellum said.

"I am speaking to Chainer." The First came within a foot of Chainer and looked down into his eyes.

Chainer fought the weakness in his legs, redoubled by the proximity of the First. "I am your obedient child," he said.

"My son." The First stepped back and gazed into the Mirari. "Tomorrow, the three-day lunar games begin. The Mirari shall be in the prize cache."

"Pater?" Skellum jumped in to prevent Chainer from doing so, but the young man simply stared calmly at the First.

"Yes, Master Skellum?"

Still covering for Chainer, Skellum said, "Your wisdom is unquestioned. But my ignorance is vast. . . . What is the advantage of offering the device up to chance before we know what it can do?"

The First stared stonily at Skellum for a long moment. Then he smiled humorlessly. "You are young, Master Skellum, and impatient. I have led the Cabal for a very long time, and served it even longer. I have seen into the hearts of men, and I have owned items of power. And I say the quest for this thing, this Mirari, will destroy many who seek its power. When their schemes are all spent and they themselves lie undone, the Cabal will be there to claim the prize once more." He crossed his arms in front, and his attendants knelt in readiness beside him. "Master Skellum, Apprentice Chainer, believe in your First. Right now there is no one on Otaria who can control the Mirari. But in time it will show us the mettle of our rivals and distinguish the smart and the strong among them from the stupid and the dead. By then, I will be ready to use it for the glory of the Cabal, and there will be no one left to interfere."

"Truly, you are wise, Pater." Skellum said. "Isn't he wise, Chainer."

"The First is wise," Chainer agreed dully.

"Outstanding. There is one more thing, before I dismiss you."

"We stand ready, Pater."

"Tomorrow, a warrior from the mountains will arrive in the pits. He is known to the Cabalists there by reputation and by first-hand observation. They say he is quite ferocious, a champion among his own violent people. He is here undoubtedly seeking the Mirari. Of all those who are coming for it, I think he may have the single best chance of winning it."

"Is he that good, Pater?" Chainer asked.

"He is easily capable of earning the right to choose his prize through combat. He is also uncharacteristically intelligent for his kind and may recognize the Mirari's value among the rest of the dross. I want you," he said to Chainer, "to guide him through the competition."

Chainer choked. "What?"

"Introduce yourself. Help him get his bearings. Offer him some tips. I would rather he be an ally than an enemy. Besides, if he wins it in the pits, he'll lose it in the pits. In this, barbarians are exactly like the hollow-eyed gambling addicts in the casino. They have to take one more risk. Eventually, the house always wins."

The First regarded Skellum for a moment, then turned back to Chainer. "I also want you to find out about him. Learn the measure of him. If he is a strong man, we would work with his strength, so that both he and the Cabal profit. If he is a coward or a fool, note exactly how, so that we can use it against him when the time comes. You are to study him, as you would study one of Master Skellum's lessons."

The First's voice dropped. "Learn from this barbarian, Chainer. They look at things differently than we do. I know you're eager to fight once more on behalf of the Cabal. Look on this assignment as a gradual reintroduction to the pits. Watch this barbarian, study him, learn from him. Whether he wins or loses, gain from him."

Chainer nodded. "I will do as you ask, Pater."

"Master Skellum," the First said. "I have a special assignment for Chainer during this weekend's games. You will suspend your lessons starting two days from now and resume them after the games are over. During that time, he will be under my instruction."

"By your will, Pater." Skellum said. Chainer thought Skellum sounded grim, almost hurt. "We will make full use of the time we have. I would like to start as soon as possible."

"Of course, of course. Chainer, report to my reception desk in two days, an hour before the first horn sounds."

"By your will, Pater." The First crossed his arms behind his back, and Chainer and Skellum bowed out.

In the hallway, Skellum was angrier than Chainer had ever seen.

"He knew this would disrupt my regimen," Skellum hissed. "I've warned him about the danger, but he insists on meddling. . . ."

"Skellum, cut it out," Chainer said nervously. "It's not so bad. I'll follow a barbarian around and see how things are these days in the pits. Maybe he'll get killed in the first bout, and my special assignment will get cut short."

"We should be so lucky," Skellum said, and grimaced. "I'm sure he's a very nice barbarian, but still. . . ." Chainer choked to keep from laughing in his mentor's face.

"You shut it," Skellum said, but his rage was mellowing. "I'll be frank with you Chainer, this dementia training I'm guiding you through can really scramble your brains. A few of my ex-students are in there," he gestured back over his shoulder, "attending the First. And they don't have skulls etched on their shirts, either. Brains non-functional."

"Well, then, I shouldn't have any trouble. The way you talk, I'm like that now."

"You haven't heard me talk yet, little brother," Skellum flicked Chainer's ear maliciously. "I wouldn't let you speak to a brain-dead flunky, much less become one. They're too good for you. Too efficient and tidy."

Chainer laughed and ducked another of Skellum's flicks.

"Ahh, to nine hells with you," Skellum said. "The First will have his way, and it will work out for the best, and you'll laugh at me all the while for being concerned. But do me one favor, my pupil."

"Anything, Master."

Skellum spun his hat and caught it with a gap in front of his face.

"Watch and learn. Do not go into the pits. Don't pick or accept a quarrel so you can go into the pits. And don't burn any Dragon's Blood without me." Chainer didn't answer right away, and Skellum glared at him. "Do you understand?"

Chainer wrinkled his nose. "Okay. But I want you to show me more before the games start."

Skellum nodded. "A lot more. More smoke, more spinning, more meditation. Starting right now."

Chainer tried to hide the secret thrill that ran up his spine. He could feel a whole horde of formidable pit fighters in his mind, just waiting for him to give them form. It would surely be worth a few days as the First's spy in order to stand at Skellum's side as a dementist in service to the Cabal. It was one more step toward the destiny that had been promised to him by the Mirari.

CHAPTER 7

Chainer watched the big barbarian, Kamahl, come through the entrance gate. He was some kind of local hero among the tribes who lived high up in the mountains. Chainer had heard the upper reaches of the Pardic mountains were thick with dwarves, but the big, bald barbarian towered over even the half-troll door guard.

The pit fighter in Chainer quickly surveyed the potential challenge. Kamahl had several ragged scars along his shoulders and chest, where the skin hadn't so much healed as it had closed and then puckered like wet leather. Chainer watched him stalk his way through the crowd, maneuvering his heavy weaponry around others' like an expert. He wasn't sure what to make of the warrior, but Chainer quickly determined to never take him lightly.

He miserably patted his hip, where his black chain should have

79

been, and his shoulder, which should have held a holstered knuckle dagger. The First had sent word early this morning via messenger. As his personal representative, Chainer was obliged to leave his fighting weapons in Skellum's care. The First did not wish to antagonize his guest, Kamahl the barbarian, and so Chainer was to leave his chain and his dagger behind as a gesture of hospitality. The note came with a long, ceremonial dagger for Chainer to wear on his hip. It was traditional, the note said.

Chainer pointed out to Skellum that in addition to being ceremonial, the dagger was also too heavy, had runes carved clean through its blade, and was entirely useless for anything but stirring gruel. The First had not offered any alternatives, however, and Chainer put on the dagger.

So here he was, representing the First and the Cabal without his weapons and without any coherent instructions. As far as he understood, he was supposed to linger around Kamahl and make sure that the big hunk of meat didn't get lost on his way to winning the Mirari and taking it away with him.

Chainer watched Kamahl a few moments as the barbarian took in one of the preliminary bouts. He was clearly not impressed, and Chainer couldn't blame him. The Master of the Games was either slipping, or he had been ordered to put on a dreary show. There was no other way such a clown act would be allowed to continue. As the First's representative, Chainer thought, I should step in here. I should steer the mighty muscle head away from the cheap seats and help him find the Master of the Games.

"My job reeks," Chainer said out loud, but he approached the barbarian, stepping up to him just as the larger man was shaking his head.

"Don't give up hope just yet, sir," Chainer tried to sound helpful, like one of the shills who roamed the casino floor.

The barbarian looked Chainer over, much as Chainer had gauged Kamahl moments ago. He didn't seem to like what he saw.

"The name is Chainer." He offered his hand. He motioned his head toward the awkward show in the nearby pit, "The pair are partners against Lieutenant Kirtar." Chainer wrinkled his nose. "A champion from the northern Order."

The barbarian brightened a little. Of course, Chainer thought. A wild warrior from the mountains would certainly share Chainer's dislike of the Order.

"Kamahl, here to win the tournament."

Chainer raised an eyebrow, but once more reminded himself that this was his mission. "You'll want to see the Master of the Games, then."

Chainer exhaled and began to relax. Perhaps this wouldn't be so terrible after all. He led Kamahl to the Master of the Games through an admittedly confusing sprawl of practice pits, betting circles, impromptu grudge matches, and gawking yokels. He played tour guide by pointing out the Mer Ambassador Laquatus, who got an excellent barbarian grunt of disapproval, and Laquatus's bodyguard Turg. Kamahl looked at the big amphibian warily, but his face betrayed none of his thoughts.

They paused to watch the end of the embarrassment that was Kirtar's match, then Chainer brought Kamahl to the Master of the Games. The master winked at Chainer and started giving Kamahl a hard time about letting the barbarian into the tournament. Kamahl didn't seem to notice he was being slighted. He was too busy staring at the Mirari.

The Master of the Games reminded Chainer of Roup: thick, stupid, and clumsy. He didn't know if the master's wink had been a signal of the assumed camaraderie between Cabalists, or if it meant the master was hassling Kamahl on the First's order, just as Chainer was accompanying him around the games. He didn't like it in either case.

Much to Chainer's delight, Kamahl didn't like the master's attitude either. In fact, he didn't like it so much that he casually tossed what appeared to be a red-hot copper coin through a nearby wall with the force of an exploding cannonball.

Chainer laughed at the master's bewildered face as the rubble smoked and the dust settled. Kamahl smiled mischievously at him.

This, Chainer said to himself, will definitely be more fun than I thought. His excitement cooled as Kamahl advanced on him.

"Look," the barbarian said, "what do you want? I appreciate your help, but I'm busy, and I don't need a sidekick."

Chainer darkened. "Then it's just as well that you don't have one. I'm here on business."

"We don't have any business. We just met."

Chainer took a breath. "My friend, I have to admit, I don't understand the point of this any more than you do. But this is Cabal City, and things happen for a reason here. I can at least explain that."

"Okay, Cabalist. Explain."

"Do you have tribal elders up in Pardic?"

"Elders? Sure."

"And do you obey them?"

Kamahl laughed harshly. "Only when it suits us, and only when they're right." He shrugged. "Sometimes not even then."

"We revere our elders here. We've all sworn oaths to obey our superior Cabalists. And the First himself, the lord and master of the entire Cabal, wishes me to learn from you. I intend to respect his wishes."

"I don't want a student."

"And I've already got a mentor. I was hoping we could teach each other something. As if we'd been randomly assigned as pit partners." Chainer locked eyes with Kamahl. "I can help you."

Kamahl crossed his arms. "Go ahead then."

"How much are you paying for your lodgings?"

"Fifteen silver a night, but I'm only here for two nights, for the games."

"You're being robbed. There are warrior's quarters right outside the arena that only charge five. I can take you there."

Kamahl considered. "All right," he said finally. "You saved me twenty silver. Now what—"

"Eighteen," Chainer corrected. "Finder's fee is two percent."

"I knew it," Kamahl growled. "There's always an angle with you Cabalists." He turned to go.

"Do you know how to bet on yourself?" Chainer said quickly. Kamahl stopped. "Do you know who to ask politely, and who to threaten? Do you understand that the Master of the Games has put you on the slow track because of your stunt with the coin back there?"

Kamahl grunted angrily. "I don't understand half of what you just said."

Chainer smiled. "Then I've made my point."

"All that stuff," Kamahl shook his head, "betting, bragging, working the pairings. It's dreck. A warrior's skill determines victory."

"In the pits," Chainer said. "But you're in the City now. The pits are the least of your worries."

Kamahl glared at Chainer, then back at the Master of the Games' station. Slowly, he said. "All right, Chainer. What is a 'slow track?' "

"Always remind yourself that this is a business. The Master of the Games is responsible for getting the most out of the contestants. Did you bribe him at all?"

"I paid a lump of gold to get in the gates."

"That goes to the gatekeepers. Did you pay the Master of the Games anything?"

Kamahl chuckled. "Just that coin."

"Then he's got to make his money off you some other way. Most likely he'll put you in as many preliminary bouts as he can, against opponents that are no real challenge. He's got to display you, keep you working in front of the crowds, just to break even on your entrance fee. He's going to work you like an animal."

"And how," Kamahl's voice was low and menacing, "do I get on the fast track?"

"You need to pay proper respect to the master. Twenty-five silver should do it. How much tender have you got?"

"Ten gold," Kamahl said immediately.

"Sshhh!" Chainer hissed. He looked around nervously. "That was a joke. Never answer that question around here."

"What? No one is going to take my money from me without a fight. No one would dare."

"Sure they would. I know pickpockets who could steal the blade off your sword while it was still in the scabbard. If I can't teach you anything else, I can at least teach you one thing. Never announce how much you're carrying in this city." Chainer worked his fingers as he calculated. "Ten gold is about fifty silver. Twenty-five to the Master, ten for your lodgings . . . You won't have much left for food and frolic."

"Food, I need. Frolic, not so much."

"Okay. The first thing we do after bribing the Master," Chainer said, "is bet. We'll get the best odds on your first fight, because you're an unknown. If we get you on the fast track, the odds get even better. Have you spoken to a fixer?"

"No."

"We'll do that next. Fixers set odds, take bets, and schedule matches. They make all the arrangements for civilians like you who want to do business with the Cabal."

"I'm not a civilian, I'm a warrior."

"In this town, you're either Cabal, Order, or a civilian. Come on. I did a little checking, and there's a match that you can help me handicap. And I can help you make some money."

Kamahl finally looked interested. "What kind of match?"

"Vampire against lavamancer. You know about lavamancers?"

"Yes."

"And I know about vampires. Between the two of us, we've got all the angles covered."

* * * * *

The stadium was divided into numerous circles, with the largest and innermost set aside for main events. It was surrounded by rows and rows of seats, and a dozen circular platforms floated silently above the arena floor, giving the important and the wealthy the best possible view. Chainer led Kamahl to the center pit and pointed out a fixer who was busily taking bets.

"He'll do. What I don't understand," Chainer said to Kamahl, "is how anyone who bets on the lavamancer thinks they're going to get their money back. The odds are good, but this is a vampire. And not just any vampire, it's a Sengir vampire." Chainer pointed to the huge, bald, manlike creature standing in the center of the pit. Its eyes were black and lifeless, and its teeth jutted out from between its lips. All of the teeth, not just the canines, were twisted and pointed like thorns, and the Sengir's filthy nails hung past its fingertips like talons. It sniffed the air like a wild dog, head darting as it oriented on each new scent, and it hissed at the crowd. Across the pit stood a dark-skinned human in tanned animal hides. His hair was loose and wild, and he carried a short sword.

Kamahl regarded the toothy brute and then continued to scan the entire arena, drinking it all in. "What's a Sengir?"

"Ancient vampire lord," Chainer said. "Possibly a myth. Some vampires prey on villages, some on cities. They say Sengir preyed on entire continents."

"And you've got an ancient vampire in the pit for the opening bout?"

"Not Sengir himself. One of his minions."

"Bet on the lavamancer," Kamahl said. "Bet it all."

"You that sure?"

"I am. Vampires burn, don't they?"

"Some do. If you can hold them still long enough to set them on fire." Chainer pointed at the vampire's opponent. "So, lavamancers. Work with lava, do they? Flames and smoke and all that?"

"Yeah. But lavamancer is a title, like champion or wizard. I say bet on him."

"It's your money." Chainer held out his hand, and Kamahl stared at it. "You're learning," Chainer laughed. He led Kamahl over to the fixer, showed him how to place a bet, and then the two settled on the rail to watch the bout.

A horn sounded, and Chainer said, "That's the prep horn. It means the match is about to start, and the fighters have fifteen seconds to prepare."

The lavamancer knelt and touched the arena floor, mouthing a silent incantation. The Sengir vampire continued to look around the arena and hiss at the audience. When the starting horn sounded, the vampire suddenly became much more focused on his opponent. Its eyes narrowed as it crouched and began stalking the lavamancer. Its pointed tongue lapped hungrily around his lips. The lavamancer stood his ground, still mouthing words that no one could hear.

The vampire suddenly charged, and the lavamancer pointed his sword and released a red-hot ball of magma and ash from its tip. The vampire caught the missile full in the chest, and for a moment its entire body was engulfed in flames and smoke.

The crowd's cheer became a collective gasp as the flaming vampire leaped into the air, soaring high over the arena floor. It swooped and dove, moving fast enough to extinguish the flames that were consuming its ragged robes.

Chainer leaned over to Kamahl and said, "Did you know they could fly?"

"No," Kamahl was impassive. "I assume they still drink blood?"

Before Chainer could answer, the blackened vampire screeched and dropped down on the lavamancer. The Sengir was so much bigger and broader than its wild-haired opponent that he seemed to swallow the lavamancer up whole. They grappled and rolled across the arena floor until the vampire pinned the lavamancer's arms and sank its sharp, twisted teeth into the man's neck.

"One less lavamancer, one more Sengir," Chainer said. "Sorry, Kamahl, but this match is all but over."

"Agreed." Kamahl said. But in the pit, it was the Sengir who shuddered and thrashed, not the human in its grip. With a roar, the vampire cast its intended victim aside and fell back, clutching at its face in agony. Flames poured from between its lips, and its lower jaw seemed to be melting.

"Earth is the body, and lava is the blood," Kamahl said. "Lavamancers believe that utterly. In mastering their craft, they embody that belief."

The lavamancer's blood, red hot and steaming, continued to jet from the wound in his neck. While the vampire flailed, the lavamancer clapped a glowing hand over his wound and seared it shut. He drove the tip of his sword into the floor, raised his arms, and completed his incantation.

A huge gout of molten rock exploded from the ground beneath his sword. The stream arced up and onto the vampire, totally covering him in thick, clinging lava. The outer layer of the covering quickly cooled and hardened, but the vampire continued to move. Step by agonizing step, it came closer to the lavamancer. The dark skinned man calmly let the Sengir approach, and when it was close enough, he struck its head from its body with a short, straight slash of his sword.

The Sengir's stone-encrusted head and carcass both fell and melted into ash. The lavamancer raised his arms in victory, and the crowd shook the walls with its cheering.

Chainer bowed to Kamahl. "I stand corrected." He stood straight and clapped the barbarian on the shoulder. "And you stand enriched. The odds were five to one against the lavamancer. You just made enough to live like a king for at least a week."

Kamahl smiled. "One less thing to worry about, that's all. I'm more concerned with winning my own matches."

"Good point, good point. When's your first bout?"

"Just before the lunch break."

"Well, then, we'd better get you where you need to be. If you're as good a fighter as you are a handicapper, you might actually make good on that boast to win the tourney."

CHAPTER 8

"Ambassador," the human servant said, "Director Veza has arrived."

Veza caught Laquatus checking his reflection in a wall mirror as she entered the room. He was dressed in splendid robes, and he was taller than he appeared in Llawan's mirror. A huge, amphibious monstrosity sat sullenly on the floor, its feral glare fixed on Veza. The rest of the huge room was taken up by a green marble swimming pool, complete with fountain.

"Ambassador Laquatus."

"Veza," he said brightly. "Long live the empire." Laquatus came across the room and warmly kissed Veza's hand. "Servants!" He clapped. "Refreshments for our guest." The dull-eyed butler shambled out of the room.

"Thank you, Ambassador." She eyed the beast on the floor and said, "May I ask . . ."

"That is Turg, my bodyguard and champion. I'm afraid a man in

89

my position cannot afford to take chances. Particularly this close to Cabal City." He leaned forward and whispered, "They're all a band of cutthroats and criminals. Without Turg by my side, I'd be afraid to leave the embassy." Turg made a grumbling noise in the back of his throat to punctuate Laquatus's comment.

"I've dealt with Cabalists myself," Veza said. "I understand your caution."

Laquatus had not released her and was staring at her intently. Veza gently pried her hand away. "Forgive my manners, Ambassador, but my time is limited. You said you had something to tell me?"

Laquatus smiled. "Of course. But first . . ." A servant bearing a bottle of sparkling wine and two ornate crystal goblets shuffled in. He poured, left the glasses and the bottle, and exited without a word.

"To the empire," Laquatus said. "And new friends." He waited patiently with his glass extended. Veza hesitated, then gently tapped her goblet against Laquatus's. Where Veza merely sipped, Laquatus drained his goblet dry.

"An excellent vintage, if I do say so myself. I received a case of it from the Cabal First himself—"

"Excuse me, Ambassador. To business?"

Laquatus laughed. "Of course. Please forgive me. And you must call me Laquatus, my dear." He abruptly shucked his robe and dove into the pool. His legs shimmered and merged in mid air. By the time he hit the water, his tail was fully formed.

"I prefer to conduct my interviews underwater," Laquatus called. "For security reasons. Would you care to join me, Director? Or would you prefer a chair?"

Veza glanced at Turg, who was now dozing. She untied her sash, folded her robe, and stepped off the edge of the pool into the water.

"Your mastery of the change is remarkable, Laquatus."

The ambassador turned his head, as if embarrassed. "Thank you.

But surely you also share the innate ability of our people?"

"I do. But it takes considerably more time and effort for me."

"Ah, that's merely a matter of practice. The nature of our magic is change, you see. To be fluid in both mind and body. Our cephalid cousins sometimes treat it as a flaw, but I see our ability to straddle land and sea as a blessing." He motioned below the surface with his eyes, then dived down. Veza followed, and the two merfolk began streaming back and forth across the pool.

"I've called you here," Laquatus said, "because I think I've got something for you. I believe that the assassins who attacked our lady were hired by the Cabal."

Veza considered. "Do you know why?"

Laquatus waved his hand dismissively. "Who knows? With animals such as these, it could be a simple matter of murder for hire."

Veza stopped. "Ambassador. I hope you didn't bring me all the way here from Breaker Bay just to tell me that you suspect the Cabal may be involved."

"Of course not, my dear." Laquatus put a comforting hand on her shoulder. "And please. Call me Laquatus." He pointed upward and surfaced. When Veza's head broke the surface of the pool, Laquatus said, "I wanted to meet you in person, and I wanted to show you something that will make it easier for us to do so again in the future."

The ambassador reached a long arm out and traced a circle on the water's surface. He was whispering under his breath, and with each new circle he inscribed, Veza tingled as if the water were conveying a mild electric shock. There was a rip and a crack, and the circle drawn by Laquatus became a disk of energy floating on the pool's surface.

"This," Laquatus said, "is a transport portal. With it, you can travel from the surface of one body of water to the surface of another. It is one of the great imperial secrets, and in the name of the empire, I share it with you." Across the room, a similar disk of energy appeared in Laquatus's fountain. With a playful grin, he rose up and dove into the disk beside him, instantly coming out of the disk in the fountain. Veza noticed that he had changed back into his legged form in mid-transfer in order to fit in the fountain's pool.

"From now on," Laquatus called, "if I need to tell you something, or if you need me, we can be together in a matter of seconds. Simply call to me from your mirror, and I will join you or bring you here."

"I'm flattered, Ambass—Laquatus. But I don't see how this is a significant improvement over the mirror itself."

Laquatus stepped back into the portal and reemerged with his tail fully formed beside Veza once more. "That's because you limit your thoughts to the task at hand. The empire rewards those who go beyond the call of duty, who take risks. You should be more fluid, Veza. Expand to fill the space around you. It is your nature."

Laquatus's penetrating eyes burrowed into hers. "I want us to be friends as well as loyal subjects. I want you to visit me as often as you can. I think we have much to offer one another, even beyond our duty to the empire."

"Of course." Veza blinked. "Have any of your contacts in the Cabal told you who hired the assassins?"

Laquatus's gaze narrowed. "No. But I will tell you as soon as they have."

"Thank you, Laquatus." Veza ducked under the glowing disk and swam to the edge of the marble. "I must get back to my duties now." She took her robe from poolside. "Can your transport get me back to Breaker Bay?"

"Certainly. In this case, that's what it's for." Laquatus waved his hands and the two disks disappeared. He quickly traced another onto the surface of the pool and turned to Veza. "The other portal should be on the surface of Breaker Bay, just outside your cottage." Veza swam back to Laquatus, and he stopped her with a raised hand.

"I hope," he said, "that you don't feel this trip was for nothing."

"Not at all. But I am unused to reporting directly to the empress, and I do not want to disappoint her."

"Impossible," Laquatus said, flashing his most winning grin.

Veza nodded. "Long live the empire."

"Until we meet again."

* * * * *

Laquatus watched Veza dive into the portal and disappear. Damn the little land crawler anyway. Her mind was tight and ordered and clear, but it was also as hard as ice. He could see it, touch it, test it, but he could neither take hold of it nor gain access to it. Like many sea creatures, Veza was immune to all but the most invasive of the ambassador's telepathic probes.

Laquatus switched back to his legged form and climbed out of the pool. He was not overly concerned. He had cracked tougher minds than Veza's in his time, and she already seemed enamored of his ability to change shape so easily. The more they interacted, the more receptive she would become. If he was careful, he could cultivate her as a political ally and as a scapegoat should anything go wrong.

For now, he thought, Veza and Llawan both could keep. He put on his robe and mentally signaled Turg. The games were about to start, and it was time for the eventual winning team to scout the competition.

CHAPTER 9

Chainer helped Kamahl find the location of the barbarian's first bout, then disappeared into the crowd. Kamahl was slowly warming to Chainer's presence, but Chainer took the first opportunity he could to break away.

He wanted to watch Kamahl fight from a clear vantage point, to see how good the mountain warrior really was. Chainer also wanted to avoid the centaur Kamahl had been given as a partner. Chainer didn't like centaurs, and he didn't trust himself to treat the man-horse as tactfully as the First required.

So he stood in the spot with the best view he knew, up against the railing in the mezzanine. When Kamahl and the centaur teamed up against a Cabal dementia caster, Chainer was honestly impressed. Kamahl was much more careful in his application of force than any barbarians Chainer had heard about. He was devastating in combat, but he was also in control. The centaur seemed competent enough, but it was Kamahl who finished off their opponent with some kind of exploding axe. It was marvelous.

Chainer gladly joined in the cheers for the victor. As he'd expected, the fixers had put long odds on the unknown warrior from the mountains, and anyone smart enough to put a bet down on Kamahl more than quadrupled their money. Chainer himself earned a tidy sum.

Until the moment Kamahl's bout started, he hadn't felt the rush of being in the pits again, hadn't recaptured the simple joy of combat. No wonder he'd felt uninvolved. The games had been lackluster, he was on an important assignment from the First, and he was unarmed except for a thrice-damned ornamental dagger. Watching Kamahl brought it all back for him. The elegant simplicity of the contest, the concrete rewards of developing one's skills, the pride of a well-fought victory, these things were missing from an apprentice's life.

Chainer picked his way through the crowd back to Kamahl's side and congratulated him personally. The centaur had trotted off to comb the nettles out of its tail or some such thing. Chainer was only glad it was gone.

* * * * *

Chainer and Kamahl were watching Turg tear apart a Krosan dragonette when the alarm sounded. The barbarian reacted a split second before the Cabalist, but both were up before the sentries blew a second warning.

"Something big is coming," Chainer said. "That's the full-on alert klaxon."

Kamahl grunted and unsheathed one of his throwing axes. "Come on, then. Let's go kill something big."

Chainer paused, trying to sort out competing priorities. The First had told him to stick with Kamahl, but the Cabal was under attack.

Chainer watched a pitiful few Cabalists standing firm against the crush of warriors and spectators trying to escape. The Master of the Games had lost all control.

"You go," Chainer said to Kamahl. "I can do more good in here." Kamahl nodded, and without a second glance charged off into the bedlam.

Chainer watched him go with a kind of jealousy. The barbarians had it good, he thought. All they needed was something to fight and their path became clear. Chainer didn't know what Kamahl was running off to confront, but then neither did Kamahl, and Chainer longed for that kind of abandon. Perhaps he should have been born in the mountains.

Chainer pulled the ceremonial dagger from his hip, tucked it into his shirt, and sprinted back toward his quarters. He would never throw away anything the First had given him, but he would be damned if he were going to wear it one second longer than he had to.

And while he could not stop the First from simply giving the Mirari away, Chainer vowed that he would stop anyone who tried to steal it from the prize cache.

* * * * *

Very few people took notice of a single, determined, unarmed young man as he dodged panicky civilians and hurdled slow-moving monsters. Two who did notice sat in a darkened room, deep inside the First's manor, staring into a scrying pool.

"He's going to get his weapons. His chain and dagger," Skellum said.

"Yes," the First answered.

"I should go to him. He's at a very dangerous stage of his training right now. A small error in judgment could cost him his life— and the Cabal a lot more."

"And yet," the First said, "if he displays sound judgment, he'll take a great leap forward. He and the Cabal would both profit."

"Very true, Pater." Skellum waited for a moment. "May I go to him?"

"Stay with me a while longer," the First said. "Let us roll the bones with your young pupil there. You can't properly evaluate a student if his mentor never stops mentoring."

"The First is wise." Skellum anxiously watched Chainer in the scrying pool. He hadn't thought of it before, but the First usually watched the games from his private box that floated high above the arena, or he didn't watch them at all. The only reason to call Skellum in to join him for a private viewing was to keep him away from Chainer.

The First also watched Chainer in the scrying pool, ignoring Skellum for the moment. Then, he said, "Everything is working out perfectly."

Skellum knew that the next few minutes would either make his pupil great or break him down into a gibbering husk. Barred from action, Skellum's mind raced through all the potential outcomes of Chainer's impromptu trial by fire. And though he swam on the shores of nightmare and kept the creatures he found there in his pocket, Skellum realized he was afraid.

* * * * *

Chainer ran toward the prize vault with renewed confidence. With his chain and his dagger, he felt fully dressed again. A tiny seed of inspiration had also led him to grab the censer and a few discs of Dragon's Blood.

He turned down the last long hallway that led to the vault and narrowed his eyes. There was already a skirmish going on outside the vault. Two Cabalist humans were grappling with a pair of reptilian pirates, dressed for the sea, and a blue-robed illusionist. Chainer recognized Deidre, the long-nailed door guard, but the other, more simian Cabalist was unknown to him.

The illusionist was bedeviling Chainer's brethren with the image of a small sea monster and a swarm of stinging faeries. Chainer guessed the illusions were as convincing as the real thing when looked at head on, but he could see straight through them. The mage must have cast the illusion so that it only affected the guards in front of her.

Big mistake, Chainer thought. Without slowing, he broke out the full length of his chain and started spinning it overhead. When he was in range, he let out a whoop. The illusionist turned just in time to catch Chainer's rounded weight square in the temple. The sea monster and the faerie faded as the illusionist swooned and fell.

"She's not dead," Chainer said to the pirates. He spoke extra loud, for the record the First would surely make of this incident.

"You soon will be," one of the pirates hissed. Neither of the raiders looked comfortable with the sudden shift in the odds. As the pirate who spoke raised his short spear, the other continued to wrestle with the simian guard.

The spear never flew. Once the pirate had raised it to his ear, Deidre's razor fingers exploded out of the center of his chest. Ice-blue blood poured from the wound, and the reptilian looked down stupidly at Deidre's hand. She yanked it back with a rough jerk, and the pirate dropped to the now-slick floor beside the illusionist.

Deidre smiled at Chainer. "That one's dead," she said, and then she turned and drove her nails into the remaining pirate's spine with a vicious thrust of her right hand. The simian Cabalist continued to wrestle with the lifeless reptile until he realized Deidre had ended his fun. He grunted in exasperation and cast the dead pirate aside.

The unconscious illusionist groaned, and Chainer looked from her to her dead companions to Deidre's brutal smile.

"You killed them," he said.

"That's what I do, little brother." Deidre flicked a drop of blue blood off her index finger.

The noises from other battles echoed down the long hallway, but Chainer was too annoyed to mind them. "I got chewed out by the First himself for killing a bird. A bird! And you butcher two pirates in the blink of an eye and stand there smiling? How fair is that?"

Deidre laughed, and Chainer hadn't realized how disturbing it was to see a tall, beautiful woman smile when she had three eyes and blue blood dripping from both hands.

"The First told us to kill anyone who tries to get through this door," she pointed at the entrance to the vault room. "And if the First says so, it's fair."

Chainer considered. "Anyone?"

"Anyone."

"Including me?"

"Including you, little brother. You're part of anyone, aren't you?"

Chainer spooled his chain around his wrist and took out the censer. "If you don't mind, big sister, I'll go back to the mouth of the corridor and make sure no one else comes down here to rush the vault."

"Please yourself," Deidre said. She rapped the simian Cabalist with her knuckles and gestured to the door. "We'll be here as ordered, just on the off chance that someone gets past you. And little brother?"

"Yes?" Chainer waited.

"You can kill 'em if you want to." Deidre laughed a raucous, unpleasant laugh that made Chainer's blood run cold. As he retreated back down the corridor and the two guards retook their positions on either side of the door, Chainer reminded himself to stay on Deidre's good side.

He lit a charcoal disc, then loaded the censer with Dragon's Blood. The thick smoke soon filled the narrow hallway, and

Chainer began to swing the censer around his head, as Skellum had shown him.

Shouts of battle and screams of pain were echoing throughout the arena, but Chainer focused on the spinning censer and the smoke. Skellum had told him that dementia summoning was all about vision. What you saw, when and how you saw it. If you could see beyond the world around you, you could leave it behind and take yourself to the new place you'd created.

Chainer stared at the pewter cage as it flew and smoked, breathing evenly. There were a dozen ways to reach dementia space, and Skellum explained them all in detail. Breathing, stance, concentration, stamina, all of these things and more could affect the end result of a dementia caster's work. Perhaps the old man thought he could give Chainer too much information, could confuse or discourage him from trying what he was about to try. Chainer grinned at the thought. He had an excellent memory, and while he didn't think he could produce a full-fledged dementia monster, he did remember enough of Skellum's lessons to defend the hallway.

Chainer heard the booted tread of an armed party heading his way, but he couldn't see them for the smoke. Deidre and the simian were too far behind to offer advice, but Chainer knew of one sure way to determine friend from foe.

"The Cabal is here," he called.

"Not for long," came the gruff reply. "Swords." Chainer heard multiple blades scraping out of multiple scabbards. "For Kirtar. For the Order." There was a bright flash, and Chainer could make out three glowing blades just beyond the miniature fog bank he had created. Behind the advancing boots, Chainer heard something heavy dragging its feet across the floor.

Chainer focused on the smoke, slowly becoming lost in its oily feel against his skin, the stifling odor, and the painful tears it brought to his eyes. He continued to breathe as Skellum had taught him, always fighting the impulse to cough. The marching feet drew closer.

Above their rhythm Chainer heard the whistling of the chain as it slashed through the air. He reached higher above his head, even going up on his tip toes to elevate the censer as high as he could.

Three members of the Order came slowly but steadily through the smoke, their gleaming swords out in front of them like torches. Chainer was gratified to see that they were crouching slightly, on guard like good toy soldiers ought to be. It gave him more clearance above their heads. He let the chain out another two feet as it spun, so that the Order were inside its radius.

"Who's there?" said the shortest of the three figures. He wore officer's robes and was the one with the gruff voice who had answered Chainer. "In the name of the Order, stand aside!" A tall, manlike figure loomed out of the smoke behind him.

"I'll stand aside," Chainer called, "but you're coming with me." He closed his eyes and remembered the feel of the place Skellum had showed him. Light-headed, he felt his balance evaporate. He might have been falling forward or backward, down or up.

He remembered what Skellum had forced him to describe before he had ever seen it. The blasted landscape, the threatening skies. Chainer saw a whole world of his own that was just waiting for him to come and claim it. Yet it was tantalizingly out of reach, and all Chainer could do was imagine it.

He felt his stomach drop and suffered an extreme wave of vertigo. He opened his eyes. The hallway, the vault, and the entire building were gone. Chainer stood in a circle of smoke on an endless black sand desert. Three soldiers and a huge limestone golem were with him. The sky above was an unbroken field of sickening mustard yellow, and a bruise-colored moon shone overhead. Opposite the moon was a hole in the sky, and from the jagged hole poured a blood-red river that was slowly creating an inland sea.

Chainer and the Order soldiers alike stared upward, disoriented and hesitant. The limestone golem shuffled forward, oblivious to the change in location. It stood well over eight feet, so

Chainer's censer was impeded. The cage clanged noisily off its cheek and bounced on the wall and floor several times before Chainer got it back under control. The world flickered around them, flashing between the vault hallway and the black desert.

Once Chainer recovered the censer's momentum, the alien landscape returned and stayed. The interruption, however, snapped the officer with the gruff voice out of his awestruck daze.

"Forward," he barked at the golem. He stepped behind the limestone man and began following it like a shield. "Fall in behind me," he said, and the other soldiers quickly lined up. Single file, the strange procession slowly made its way toward Chainer.

Chainer felt the first stirrings of panic. He had been planning on a bigger advantage from the element of surprise, but he hadn't counted on having to surprise something that wasn't alive. He wasn't sure what to do next. He couldn't simultaneously spin the chain and defend himself, something Skellum had warned him about. If he abruptly stopped spinning to lash out at the Order, would they all be trapped in the black desert? Could they ever get out? Or would they just flash back to the hallway as if nothing had happened?

Deidre sprang hissing over Chainer's shoulder before he could decide to stand or fight. She pounced on the golem, clung to its head like an insect, and began slashing and tearing at its face.

"You gonna stand there all day, little brother," she called, "or are you going to help me? Come on, they're all lined up for us."

Chainer watched the strange world around them flicker back into a normal hallway as he reeled in the censer. He quickly whispered the spell that separated the cage from the chain and replaced the censer with a rounded weight. He then gathered the chain up in both hands and whipped the weighted end into the golem's kneecap. The limestone man's leg cracked, but held together. The golem himself didn't even notice.

The soldiers started to spread out from behind the golem.

Deidre's simian partner charged into them before they could separate and clumsily bore two of them to the ground. The officer still stood, however, and he looked first at Deidre attacking the golem, then back at the tangled knot of simian and soldier. He nodded, then prepared to drive the point of his glowing sword deep into the simian's back.

Deidre wasn't faring much better. For all her effort, she was merely chipping away at the golem, doing cosmetic damage to its limestone head and throat. There were almost as many metallic shards of her fingernails as there were of the golem's face, however.

Chainer's fighting instincts were coming back to him. The dementia trap hadn't worked, but he had spent two years in the pits before Skellum pulled him out, and to survive in the pits you strategized fast and acted faster. He sent the end of his chain smashing into the officer's hand. The officer squawked and dropped his blade, which stopped glowing as soon as it hit the floor.

"Deidre," Chainer hollered, "get off him, you're not hurting him!" The simian cracked one of his opponent's arms at the elbow and then shoved the screaming man over the officer, who had bent down to retrieve his sword.

Deidre had dropped off the golem and was now trading blows with it. Rather, she was striking off tiny chips from its chest and arms and in return, it was missing her entirely. She bobbed and weaved like the veteran fighter she was, avoiding each of its slow, heavy blows.

"If I keep cracking you," she said through clenched razor teeth, "eventually you'll break." Deidre was dancing around so much that Chainer couldn't predict where she would be next, so he couldn't strike at the golem.

The simian was doing better. He had the unwounded foot soldier in a headlock on one side and the officer's sword arm in a death grip on the other. The simian hooted, amused.

Deidre turned a forward roll into a two-handed strike that landed square in the center of the limestone golem's chest. Her long nails dug in deep. For the briefest moment, she was held fast as she tried to reverse her momentum and pull herself free. In that moment, the golem brought his huge hands together in a wide, arcing clap with Deidre's broad shoulders in between. A sickening crunch followed.

"Deidre!" Chainer said. "No!" The simian echoed Chainer's howl, shoved the officer back, and angrily snapped the headlocked foot soldier's neck.

The golem let Deidre fall. The officer sprang forward and ran the simian through with his good hand before the Cabalist could get clear of the soldier he had just killed. The simian dropped, choking and grunting and clutching at its wounded chest.

The golem began to shuffle toward Chainer, and the officer fell in step beside it. His sword and the golem's hands were bloody. In the last few wisps of Dragon's Blood smoke, Chainer faced them alone.

"Surrender, filth," the officer said. He held the hand Chainer had smashed at his side, but he seemed just as comfortable with the sword in his other hand.

"You're robbing us, and we're filth?" Chainer knew he had to stop the golem first. It was too tough for his chain or his dagger. He needed something better, something more dangerous—something drastic.

"Give it up, officer," he called. He feinted at the man's face with the weighted end of the chain, flicking it back and forth to keep him at bay.

The golem was getting closer as the officer stayed back. Chainer kept up the pretense that he was focusing on the human officer and letting the limestone golem get close enough to grab him.

Two more steps to go. Chainer reached out for the Mirari, fifty feet and a thick metal door away. This close to it, he could hear its call and feel its power responding to him. It knew him. It was waiting for him.

One more step. Chainer moved slightly to his left. The golem was between himself and the officer.

"Kill him," the officer said.

Now.

Skellum had not been Chainer's first master. A Cabalist warrior named Minat lost most of his sight in the pit near Chainer's village in the salt flats. Chainer was alone, and Minat was bored. He showed Chainer the basics of pit fighting, gave him an unusual weapon to master, and amazed him with tales of the Cabal's power and influence.

He also taught Chainer the death bloom spell. "As a last resort," he had told Chainer, "to be used only when it was absolutely necessary." Minat was long dead, but Chainer remembered him well. And there had never been a more necessary occasion for the death bloom.

The golem reached out for Chainer's arm. Chainer crouched, pushed both arms out straight, and cocked his wrists back as far as they would go. With the Mirari behind him and the dark rage of Deidre's death still hot in his chest, Chainer spoke the words. He had never tried the death bloom on an artificial creature before, but it was his only hope.

A beam of black energy exploded out of Chainer's hands and slammed into the golem's chest. The cracked limestone seemed to soak up the energy, drawing it in like a sponge draws water. Chainer maintained his stance and his focus, pouring more power into the spell. The golem's innards went black, and it started to shudder.

With a roar, Chainer stepped forward and shoved the beam further into the golem's chest. The agonizing screech of ripping stone echoed down the hallway, and the golem exploded.

Driven by the unrelenting power from Chainer's hands, the shards of limestone rocketed backward, away from the vault. At least a dozen embedded themselves in the officer's body like shaftless arrows. The officer staggered and fell backward. The energy from Chainer's hands withered, and he fell to his knees, blood streaming from his nose and ears.

Chainer shook his head to clear it, wiped the blood from his nose, and stood. He could see that the simian had stopped breathing. One of the Order soldiers was dead and another unconscious with his elbow twisted completely in the wrong direction. The officer was moaning as he lay bleeding. Chainer painfully shuffled over to Deidre.

She was mortally wounded, broken beyond repair. Her arms looked like bags of shattered bone, and she coughed blood. Her legs and her face were undamaged, however, and Chainer watched sadly as all three of her eyes rolled back and forth in her head.

"Don't you dare," Deidre rasped. Dazed, numb, and mute, Chainer stepped forward.

"Don't . . . waste," Deidre managed. She choked and coughed before continuing. "Don't waste . . . us." She tried to gesture with her mangled arm and then screamed in pain.

"Don't waste us," she said again. Her eyes were wild, unfocused. She smiled one last time.

Chainer understood. "I won't, big sister."

"Don't . . ."

Chainer waited for a few silent seconds and then closed Deidre's eyes.

"The Cabal is here," he whispered, and the jolt sent him sprawling backward. Deidre had been so very much alive that converting her savage life into death almost finished Chainer off as well.

He felt better as he picked himself up. Chainer caught his reflection in a mirrored hallway decoration. His tightly rolled braids were all undone and askew. His face was a smear of blood. His eyes were two black holes that glowed with an un-light very similar to the Mirari's.

He glanced at the remaining bodies, and then walked past them to where the officer lay. He, too, was very near the end.

"For Kirtar," he said. "For the Order." Then he died.

"For the First," Chainer's voice was a bitter snarl. "For Deidre. For the Cabal."

Chainer got out the censer and started another disc of incense burning. He left the cage at the mouth of the vault hallway so that the smoke would obscure the entrance. Then he went back and finished what he had promised to Deidre.

* * * * *

Skellum and the First watched the scrying pool. Chainer's smoke did not affect the spell that powered the pool, and his Cabal masters could see him clearly.

"You have trained him well, Skellum."

"I didn't teach him that, Pater," Skellum said. "It's bad enough that he abandoned the assignment you gave him, but—"

"I have nothing but praise for your student's behavior. He showed initiative. He stood by his family and protected our property."

"But the Order . . . the tournament. We were going to give the Mirari away as a trophy. Why should he kill to protect it?"

"Because it is my will," the First said. "And you, his master, doubted his abilities. Look at him now."

Skellum was careful to keep his face neutral as he watched. Chainer was moving from body to body, standing over them, absorbing what he could of their dying energy. With each absorption, the black glow from his eyes grew stronger, and the more exaggerated and stylized his movements became.

"He continues to impress," the First said. "He does everything properly and with enthusiasm."

"He's a ghoul, Pater," Skellum said. "I know you think me overcautious, but what he's doing is exactly wrong for a dementist at his level."

"Wrong?" the First asked witheringly. Skellum bowed his head.

"Forgive me, Pater. You are wise and I see little. But I must—"

"You must be silent," the First said. He sat watching Chainer for a few seconds. The youth was casting several chains at once, creating them out of thin air with the dying energies he had just absorbed. He used them to sound the edges of the space he was in, striking sparks off the stone walls and then drawing the chains back into his body. "How like a spider he is," the First muttered, "or a snake with a dozen flickering tongues."

Skellum stood in silence. The figure of Chainer turned on some silent enemy, opened his mouth wide, and sent a barrage of chains lashing out from his fingers. He jerked the chains back and crossed his arms in satisfaction. Whomever or whatever he had been striking at had beat a hasty retreat.

The First stood, and Skellum smoothly backpedaled to get out of his way. "When your student has bled off some of that energy he's holding onto," the First said, "I want you to collect him and take him home. By this time next week, I want him ready for the pits.'"

"In his mind, Pater, he's already there." Skellum kept his head bowed, anticipating a rebuke. But the First merely gestured, and one of his hand attendants stepped forward and put a comforting arm on Skellum's shoulder.

"Your concerns have been noted. But you should be proud of what you have accomplished for the Cabal. And of what your student will yet accomplish."

"I am proud, Pater, but I am also afraid."

The First stared down at Skellum through his milky eyes. The barest hint of a smile played with the corners of his mouth.

"Then you are no different from any other father. Come. I suspect the large dragon has been subdued by now, and I've yet to hear the final result of the tournament.

"And then," he added, "we have to make sure the Mirari falls into the most deserving hands we can find."

Both men fell silent as they continued to watch Chainer's lethal dance in the scrying pool, but only the First was smiling. Skellum's eyes were far away and his face slack, as if he were staring at something enormous that only he could see.

CHAPTER 10

The empress's mirror had been silent for weeks, and Veza had quickly become desperate for anything of substance to report. Obtaining information from or about Laquatus was not a problem. He frequently called to flirt and chatter about Cabal doings. Obtaining *useful* information from or about Laquatus was another matter. Veza had exhausted her private library and her admittedly sparse network of contacts, and had even paid passing sailors and local hoodlums for any gossip or rumors about the ambassador. So far, the ambassador remained a cipher.

There were those who claimed Laquatus was a staunch supporter of the emperor, but there were an equal number who claimed he was firmly but secretly in Llawan's camp. The most prevalent opinion was that he was simply following the tide, which currently favored Aboshan. It was rumored that he had vast mental powers, and could rewrite your memories as easily as he could sign his own name. Veza heard tales of the awesome creatures he had enslaved with the power of his mind and the darkest of spells, of the pirates he had betrayed and the rivals he'd had purged. None of it was reliable or novel enough to report to Llawan.

To avoid submitting another rehash of conflicting hearsay about Laquatus, Veza had at last resorted to magic. She was not an expert in any one particular discipline, but she did have a solid command of water-to-air breathing incantations and other basic seagoing survival spells. She was extremely adept at research, however, and she soon discovered a spell that could help her. It was a knowledge immersion ritual practiced by some of the more contemplative cephalids in the empire.

It was designed to expand one's capacity to process information. Properly prepared and cast, the spell allowed scholars to read and retain a library full of scrolls in the time it took a hot bath to cool. In a sense, you gathered your data and poured it into a small body of water. Then you climbed in to soak up that data with every pore.

Veza had made all the preparations and readied herself to carry them out. If it worked, she'd have something of value to share with the empress. If not, she had lost nothing but some time.

She choked down a vial of the briny potion and grimaced. She scattered a mixture of herblike seaweed, powdered pearl, and dried fish entrails over the surface of her sleeping tub, then pronounced the words to the immersion spell. She blew on the carved driftwood effigy of Laquatus in her palm, then lowered herself into the churning, bubbling water. As her eyes sank beneath the surface, she experienced the flash and crack of lightning in her mind, and her body went rigid as steel.

She saw Laquatus in a giant Cabal arena, watching a huge frog fight. She heard the frog's bellowing roar, which nearly drowned out the continuous internal whine of the predator's natural bloodlust.

Veza trembled in the churning bath, her eyes sightless, her mouth voiceless.

She saw the frog look at Laquatus, with the merman reflected in the beast's great eye. She saw Laquatus look at the frog, with the amphibian captured in Laquatus's stern glare.

Another jolt of electricity slammed through Veza, and her paralysis broke. Still blind and mute she began to thrash, splashing even more water out of the tub. She was aware of her legs merging and melting together to form a tail, and the pain was as excruciating as ever. Her jaw locked, as it always did during these transformations, with her sharp teeth piercing her lower lip.

She heard the frog's booming vocalization from Laquatus's point of view. She heard Laquatus's voice in the frog's head, issuing constant orders and demands for obedience.

Veza found her voice and screamed just as a massive explosion of water and spray cast her completely out of the tub. Heavy, tailed, and clumsy on the wooden floor, she clawed painfully at the boards and then raised her torso with her arms. She heaved for breath and started to choke. During the shock-transformation, she had inadvertently gone into her true deep-sea form. She couldn't breathe because her lungs were empty and flattened inside her chest. With a powerful flip of her tail, she rolled herself to the edge waters that lapped at her living room and dumped herself into the bay.

Clear, cold sea water flowed over her gills, and she quickly began to regain her equilibrium. In the water, she was no longer clumsy and her increased body weight was supported by its own buoyancy. Exultant, she thrashed her tail again and shot out under the walls of her cottage, out toward the open sea.

Veza had the answer. She had seen something that would at last give Llawan direct access to Laquatus's schemes. Something to justify the imperial trust that had been placed in her.

Laquatus controlled the frog. The frog obeyed Laquatus. There was a permanent, almost palpable link between them both, mind and body. And while Laquatus's mind was too well guarded to invade, and the frog's was too primitive to understand, the link between them was neither. To a practiced psychic, reading that link would be as simple as eavesdropping on a conversation between intimates.

Laquatus's reliance on agents had just given them an opportunity to determine his loyalties once and for all. It wasn't much, Veza thought, but it was potentially the first drop in a deluge. She turned in mid-stroke, pleased at her grace underwater after so much time on land, and then she shot back toward her cottage and the empress's mirror.

* * * * *

"And you are certain this will work?"

"Yes, my empress," Veza said. She was still in her tailed form, but she had reopened her airways in order to speak. It had been difficult retrieving the mirror without switching back to her legged form, but she had managed it. Now she floated comfortably in the bay, perched on the edge of her cottage floor while she spoke into the mirror.

"And Laquatus will not know we are monitoring him?"

"Not if your psychics are careful, Empress."

Llawan paused. "Are you psychic, Director Veza?"

"No, Empress. I merely observed the existence of the link. I didn't attempt to examine it. To get the kind of information I think we can, we will need to employ an expert."

"A very subtle and gifted expert, we should think," Llawan said. "Fortunately, we have the finest mind-rider in all the empire right here in our city." She turned and clicked a few curt commands to someone behind her. Then she regarded Veza with a suspicious eye. "Are you currently tailed, Director?"

Veza flushed, giving her blue skin a purplish tone. "Yes, Empress. It was a side effect of the spell I cast."

"We understand. You will resume your land-going form at once."

"Empress?"

"We are going to test this theory of yours. We are going to give you information to pass along to Laquatus. If he sees you changed as you are, he will assume you have been to the depths and are in league with someone to betray him. He might guess Aboshan and he might guess Llawan, but if he guesses at all, he will be on guard. And we would have him as unprepared as possible when we first attempt to monitor him."

"Of course, Empress." Veza said a silent blessing for her luck. She was not sure she could change back on command, and at least now she would not have to try in front of the empress.

Llawan sat silent for a moment, thinking. Then, she said, "I will send a courier with falsified documents that prove we are in hiding. You will show them to Laquatus and offer to deliver them to him if he so wishes." She half-opened her beak in a sharp cephalid smile. "Laquatus will certainly pass the information on to Aboshan. Our imperial husband is always pleased to hear reports of our weakness, and Laquatus is always eager to please the emperor.

"If our monitors pick up our planted information in the link you describe, we will know that it is truly a window into Laquatus's mind. And you, Director Veza, will have earned our gratitude and our love."

"You honor me, Empress Llawan."

"Not yet, Director. First, we will test your flash of inspiration. This audience is over."

Llawan broke the connection, and Veza watched the mirror go dark. Then she carefully laid it down and pushed herself off the floor into the water. She felt calm and confident, but her exhilaration faded into fatigue as she floated in lazy circles around her tidal pool.

She knew she'd been ignoring her regular duties as depot director, but she also knew that however things happened, she wouldn't have to worry about them for very much longer. Either her idea would bear fruit, Llawan would reward her, and Aboshan would declare her his enemy. Or, her idea would fail, and Llawan would punish her, and she'd be stuck in Breaker Bay forever, with plenty of time to catch up on her paperwork.

In any case, she thought, she wasn't in any shape to do anything with the next few hours but take some well-earned time to herself in the gentle lapping waves of Breaker Bay.

CHAPTER 11

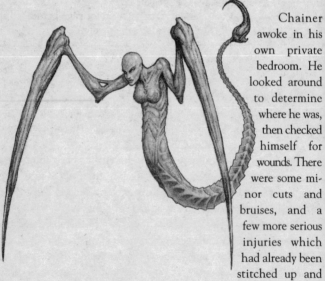

Chainer awoke in his own private bedroom. He looked around to determine where he was, then checked himself for wounds. There were some minor cuts and bruises, and a few more serious injuries which had already been stitched up and bandaged over. His scanning eyes came to rest on his chain coiled around the bedpost by his foot, and he remembered everything that had happened to him outside the vault.

Everything but how he got back to his own room, that is. He recalled Skellum leading him through the labyrinth of halls and down Manor Way to the academy, but such indistinct memories were quickly eclipsed by images of Deidre's death and the echo of the Mirari's call. Chainer lunged out of bed, but his legs failed, and he fell heavily to the floor. His muscles wouldn't flex, and he could hardly move. His head swam, and his eyes, ears, and throat were raw.

It was only then that he noticed Skellum. His mentor was sitting in a large, wooden rocker with a vague look on his face. Without so much as a flicker of an eyelid, Skellum tossed a censer across the room to Chainer.

"Catch."

Chainer slapped his hands around the pewter cage before it hit him in the chest and then winced as his arms objected.

"Skellum," he said through the pain, "they got Deidre. Did they get the Mirari?"

"Catch," Skellum said, and he tossed Chainer's knuckle dagger to him. Chainer was unable to get his fingers to work in time and had to roll out from under the dagger's point before it stuck in the floor. The abandoned censer rolled halfway back toward Skellum.

"Skellum, what in nine hells—"

"Catch." Chainer realized his mentor's hat had been spinning a split second before Skellum stopped a gap in front of his face. The vortex spat a small smoking comet toward Chainer. He yelped and reflexively snapped his hand out as if casting his chain.

To his surprise, a black chain did leap out of his empty hand. Its sharp, weighted end intercepted Skellum's casting before it could fully form. There was a small pop, an oily flash, and a foul smell.

Then Skellum was out of the chair and standing over him. Chainer had forgotten how fast the older man was. Chainer himself lie panting and helpless on the floor with his hands crossed defensively over his face.

"I give, Master, I give," he said. "What's going on? Why won't you talk to me? Where's the Mirari?"

"Kirtar of the Order has your precious Mirari," Skellum said. "A wild Krosan dragon came straight into the arena. There was a lot of noise and confusion. Kirtar and your barbarian friend stopped it, and the Master of the Games gave the Mirari to the bird-man as a reward."

Chainer absorbed this. "Kamahl let him take it? Is he all right?"

"Kamahl was buried under a half-ton of dead dragon," Skellum said. "By the time he dug himself out, Kirtar was gone, with that pretentious mer ambassador trailing behind him like a scavenger. Do fish scavenge after birds, or is it the other way around? Never mind. Your barbarian friend was half a day behind. He took off after them as soon as we told him they had the sphere."

"I wanted him to have it," Chainer said absently. "The First said he would have won it."

"And he could well have, but now we'll never know. The Mirari is gone, the First is pleased, and we have work to do." He prodded Chainer roughly with the toe of his boot. "Get up."

"Ow. Why? Don't I get to sleep in after protecting the vault? Deidre and that monkey guy were killed, you know."

"I do know, and you did get to sleep after protecting the vault. You've been asleep since I brought you here three days ago."

"Three days? It can't be."

"It is. You've slept long enough." He offered Chainer his hand, but his face was still stern and impatient.

Chainer carefully took Skellum's hand and stood unsteadily. "Master," he said, "have I done wrong?"

"Wrong?" Skellum jerked his hand away and shoved Chainer back onto his bed. The younger man clawed helplessly at the air as he fell. He had never heard Skellum raise his voice in anger before.

"You abandoned an assignment given to you by the First himself. You used the dementia exercise I expressly told you not to use. You killed three more members of the Order after the First and I both forbade you to do so, and you killed them using a spell that you never told your mentor you knew how to perform."

Chainer waited. Skellum would often browbeat him before praising him, but this was different. Chainer didn't think Skellum was going to break into a smile and laugh off these indiscretions any time soon.

"This isn't a game, Chainer. Games take place in the pits. Games have rules, they have winners and losers. People watch games for amusement. What you did, what I do—what all dementists do—it's not like anything else. You can't dabble in it. You can't polish it and put it in your weapons rack at the end of the day. Dementia space is alive. It interacts with you, it changes you. It shapes you just as surely as you shape it."

"Master—"

"Be silent. The First thinks I'm too careful with you. I don't know what you think, and I don't much care."

"Mast—"

"Be silent! I have trained scores of casters and potential dementists. The vast majority—" he tapped his temple with all five fingers brought to a point— "are gone. They only appear to be here in Cabal City with the rest of us. In reality, they only visit us occasionally. The rest of their time is spent raving, or meditating, or drooling quietly in a darkened room while they run wild in their own dementia space. Do you understand me at all, Chainer? What we do breaks minds. And the sad fact is that a broken mind won't stop you from being an excellent dementia caster. In fact, it often helps."

"But I," Skellum's voice softened slightly, "want you lucid. I want you to be a full-fledged dementist. There is far too much in this world to be enjoyed, and madness tends to water down some of life's strongest flavors. I would rather have you here, in this world, sharing a good meal and a good show while we both serve the Cabal. Not lost in the world within, constantly building monsters so you can surround yourself with them."

Skellum bent his face over Chainer's, and his voice dropped to a terse whisper. "The First also wants you lucid, for his own reasons.

You and I both serve the First, we both serve the Cabal, but that doesn't mean we can't also serve ourselves."

Chainer shut his eyes tightly, then reopened them. "I'm sorry, Master. I don't understand."

Skellum's voice grew stern again. "That is why you should listen to me and follow my instructions."

"I will, Master. I swear it." Chainer offered his hand up to Skellum. "Help me to succeed. Give me your instructions. I will not disappoint you again."

Skellum continued to stare at Chainer, sighed, and finally took his pupil's hand. "I am not disappointed, Chainer. I am annoyed by your disobedience. And I am concerned for your safety." He pulled Chainer into a sitting position, took hold of his other hand, and hauled the younger man to his feet. "Now come with me. I told you before, we have a lot of work to do."

Chainer stood, flexing his knees and ankles. The feeling was coming back into his extremities, and the pain was fading from his eyes and throat.

"I think I'm ready, Master. Where are we going?"

"To the pits. Gather your weapons."

Chainer stiffly bent and gathered up the dagger and censer. "I may be slow on the staircase, but I think I can—"

"We're not going to the pit mock-up in the basement. We are going to the pits in the arena."

"Really? What for?"

Skellum's eyes narrowed. "Because the First wishes it. And also, to prove a point."

* * * * *

Chainer stood in the empty pits, whirling the smoking censer around his head. As before, Skellum sat cross-legged on the floor in front of him with his hat also spinning.

"Remember how you got there last time," Skellum said. "Without me, I might add. You must take us there. I'm visiting your dementia space this time, not the other way around."

Chainer concentrated behind his closed eyes. The image was still there: the black sand, the endless desert, the red sea pouring from the mustard sky.

"My eyes are closed, too." Skellum sounded petulant. "Are we there yet?"

"Almost," Chainer said. He felt gravity shift beneath him, but he kept his balance. He opened his eyes. "We're here," he said.

The scene was almost exactly as Chainer remembered it. The only major difference was that the inland sea was now half-full, and the rush of red from the hole in the sky had dropped off to a steady stream. He turned proudly to Skellum, but his mentor was staring wide eyed and open mouthed at the vista.

"Kuberr's fortune," he whispered. "Chainer, is this what you saw in the hallway?"

"Yes, Master." Chainer's body was still getting used to swinging the censer, but he had already worked out the best stance to take while spinning it. He adjusted his footing and raised his chain arm higher, trying to minimize the tension on his shoulder.

"Chainer?"

"Yes, Master?" Now Chainer adjusted his grip on the chain. He would probably need to start wearing a thick leather glove again, as he had when he first started learning the weapon. Minat had told him to be careful about letting calluses get too thick or they could throw off the feel of the chain and make you lose your grip.

"Chainer!"

"Master?"

"Something's coming, and it doesn't look friendly. What should we do?"

"What? I mean . . . aren't you the expert here? Master?"

"This is your playground, not mine," Skellum's voice was gradually becoming more hollow and sing-song. "I'm just visiting."

Chainer suddenly felt very cold. He was still recovering from protecting the vault, and the smell of Dragon's Blood wasn't helping. If Skellum faded out now, they might both die here. The figure Skellum had spotted was coming steadily closer. Chainer couldn't see it clearly, but it looked big. He squinted. Between the smoke and the featureless desert, it was impossible to put the thing on any kind of scale.

"Master," he said, "what happens if I stop spinning the censer? Will we reappear in the pits, or—"

"Don't stop spinning," Skellum said. "I forbid it." His hat was also spinning, faster than Chainer had ever seen. Skellum was also twitching slightly at the shoulder, and every time he twitched, it spread across the rest of his body like a wave.

"Master? Are you all right?"

"Don't stop spinning. Not till I say."

The thing was now close enough for Chainer to see its general shape. It was humanoid but much broader and taller. It had a long, triangular head with wide jaws. It opened its mouth and roared. It was an ugly, grating sound, but Chainer welcomed it. At least now he knew how far away the thing was.

"Master, we don't have much time. Ten or twenty seconds. I don't think I can fight this thing, and I don't know how to get back to the pits if I can't stop the censer. Help me."

Skellum rose smoothly to his feet. "I thought you'd never ask." At his full height, he was well below the arc of the chain, even with the hat. He glided up alongside Chainer and held his hand in front of his pupil's mouth, just below his eyes.

"When I say," Skellum kept his eyes on the approaching monster, "stop spinning."

Chainer didn't know if it was a trick of perspective or if the thing was picking up speed as it got closer, but it seemed to be coming at them much faster than before. It charged along the ground like an ape, bent forward on all fours. It was taller than Chainer, and it had a head like a snake. Its lower jaw was distended and open wide, exposing rows and rows of short, sharp teeth. It continued to roar as it charged.

When it was ten yards away, Skellum said, "Stop spinning," and covered Chainer's eyes. Chainer brought the censer to rest in the sand. He heard the implosive sound of Skellum producing a monster and felt another shift in his gut that told him they were now somewhere else. The creature's roar had vanished.

"This is where you should have gone," Skellum said. "This is where you would have gone if you'd waited for me." He pulled his hand away, and Chainer blinked his eyes clear.

They were surrounded by mist. Chainer sniffed it to make sure it wasn't just more Dragon's Blood, but the mist was odorless and felt the same as air in his lungs. He breathed in deeply and looked around, struggling to see anything through the thick fog.

"Where you were just now," Skellum explained, "you just shouldn't have been able to get there without help. You're a gifted student, Chainer, but not that gifted."

"But I was there, Master. You saw it. And I had no help."

"Of course you did. Do you think it was a coincidence that you achieved this advanced state of dementia trance within a stone's throw of that artifact you found? The First said it was powerful. You had contact with it. Obviously you tapped into its power somehow, and that power catapulted you deeper into dementia space than you could have gone on your own."

Chainer paused. "That would make sense."

"And now, thanks to the First's meddling, the Mirari's power, and your willfulness, I have to do something I don't want to do." He looked meaningfully at Chainer, who waited for him to continue.

"Do I want you to do it?"

"Of course not," Skellum snapped. "It's unpleasant and painful, and you're going to think me heartless. But if I don't do it, you'll never make it back here."

"Never?"

"Never."

Chainer hung the censer from a loop on his vest. "Then do it."

Skellum smiled sadly at his pupil. "I already have." He whispered a few words and waved. A strong wind whipped up and carried most of the fog away with it. The bare landscape left behind was as dull and gray as an unpolished stone. In the distance several figures walked, their feet still partially obscured by wisps of fog.

Chainer watched them walk. He pointed. "Who are they?"

"They are the reason I didn't want you killing things before your training was complete. I have a confession to make, Chainer. The First only dressed you down for killing that Order war bird because I asked him to. I didn't want you to kill because every one and every thing you kill winds up here. This is the first level of dementia. The creatures here are the creatures you've seen, fought against, and bested. The memory of them remains here, in your mind. If you want to get deeper, if you want to go beyond your physical experiences, you must go through here."

Chainer brushed his dagger. "So I have to fight them." He recognized the crusat bird Callda flying over the other figures. Its silhouette was bent and ragged, and it didn't seem possible that it could fly.

"In a manner of speaking. You have to control them. They are not as they actually were, they are as you remember them to be. If you recall them as stronger than they were when you defeated them, they will be. If you believe they are still hostile to you, they will be."

"Oh." Chainer's voice was tight.

"It gets worse. You skipped this level and went right to one of the deepest reaches of your own dementia space. And when we went back there, something was waiting for us. Something that you've never actually faced but only imagined. There's no way that should have been possible, but there it is. You'll have to control that thing, too, along with these others."

Chainer nodded. The distant figures were starting to notice him.

The Callda shade set up a hideous squawking, as if trying to rally the others to an attack.

"What happens if I can't?"

"Let's not worry about that. You have to prepare—"

"What happens, Skellum?"

Skellum looked miserable. "If they don't tear you to pieces, you'll be trapped here forever, and they'll never stop hunting you. These things—" He waved— "aren't real to anyone but you Chainer, and they're not real anywhere but here. If you want to bring things out of this world, you need to be its master. You need to be the gateway they pass through, as well as the gatekeeper who lets them in or keeps them out." He gave his hat a discreet spin.

"I am ready, Master."

"That," Skellum said, "is what we are here to prove or disprove." The wind kicked up again, bringing a stream of mist with it. The mist swirled around Skellum until it enveloped him from the ground to his chin. Before it covered him completely, an implosion sounded, and he sent a smoking comet shooting toward the milling creatures. Halfway between Chainer and the inhabitants of his mind, it crashed and exploded into the shape of the snake-thing that had been charging at them under the mustard sky. It roared, angrily pounded the ground, and then turned on Chainer.

Skellum's body was fading away. His voice was distant. "Good luck, Chainer. Kuberr does not offer protection, but he does offer rewards. You must now earn yours." He looked quickly around, then added, "I'll be watching." Then he was gone.

Chainer watched the approaching monsters. There were more of them than he first realized. He tried to remember how many people and beasts he had defeated in the pits, and how many of those he had claimed for the Cabal.

They were following the aggressive lead of the snake-thing. He knew exactly where that had come from. Snakes were a constant danger in the flats, and he'd had bad dreams about them when he was a small boy, before he met Minat.

Well, he thought, he had beaten them all at least once before. Skellum said it wasn't about beating them, though, it was about controlling them. Chainer didn't even know if they could be killed again. He wondered if they remembered how he defeated them the first time, and if he could rely on the same moves twice.

In the last few moments he had, Chainer reviewed his assets. He had never been able to create fighting chains so easily and so quickly before, but he still doubted his ability to subdue the creatures one at a time or in small groups before the larger mass overwhelmed him. He wasn't even sure if his dagger or the sharpened weight would penetrate the snake-thing's hide. He would just have to find out the hard way.

The snake-thing tried to barrel straight into Chainer without slowing. Chainer sprang over it and stabbed with his dagger. He had been right, the beast's hide was too thick.

Callda the crusat bird came next. It was even uglier and more misshapen than Chainer remembered. He would have to ask Skellum about that when he got back—if he got back. Happily, Callda's skin was no tougher than it had been in the street outside Roup's, and Chainer punctured one of its wings with his chain and guided it to the ground like a failing kite.

The rest of the shambling horde would soon be upon him, and the snake thing was preparing for another attack. Think, Chainer commanded himself. How could he control a dozen-odd monsters at once? He could kill some of them with the death bloom, he could cripple some more with a dagger to the hamstrings, and he could bind a few with—

The tip of the snake-thing's claw cut the air in front of Chainer's face. It was no longer charging him headlong, but instead slashed at him with its long arms. It feinted and slashed, but Chainer stayed just out of its reach.

A half-rotted zombie bear reared up behind Chainer, roaring through its skeletal jaws. Chainer cracked his chain like a whip across its remaining eye, and when the clumsy brute lunged at Chainer, it connected with the snake-thing. Enraged, the serpent ripped the bear's paw off in its teeth and then backhanded Chainer across the chest with its claws. Chainer nimbly rolled backward, pressing his shirt into the four razor lines bleeding beneath it.

The wound was not serious, but it would force him to think and act faster before the loss of blood started to slow him down. The zombie bear and the serpent were tearing into each other, with the bear getting the worst of it. More creatures in the horde began to turn on each other, and Chainer wondered if he could let them reduce their own numbers and then conquer the survivors.

Something small and ratlike clamped onto his calf muscle with a dozen tiny needle-sharp teeth. Chainer broke its back with his dagger and kicked the wretched thing off. The snake-thing finished with the last few ghastly parts of zombie bear and immediately began stalking Chainer again. A small swarm of glowing insects spat fire at Chainer, and he shielded his eyes from a cascade of sparks. A large pool of oily slime flowed over the dull stone ground, engulfing its fellow nightmares as it also homed in on Chainer. He backpedaled, keeping the horde in front of him with his arms spread wide and his hands empty. The creatures continued to advance, focused once more as a group on the stranger in their domain.

Chainer exhaled. He thought he had the answer. It was an unfamiliar shape, and these were not ideal circumstances, but he had been making links and weights on his own for half his life. He'd been taught proficiency by an expert, then had become an expert on his own.

The snake-thing was slower, almost playful in its final approach. The other nightmares gave it a wide berth as it hissed and grinned and clawed the ground. It was trying to get him to run, to play the role of prey. Chainer smiled at it, playfully showing it his empty hands.

"Come on," he taunted. He tilted his head back, exposing his throat. "You'll never get a better chance."

The snake-thing lunged. It was lightning-fast, but Chainer's hand was faster. He cast a chain at its neck, unlike any chain he had ever created before. It was malleable in flight, solid enough only to give itself weight. When it collided with the snake-thing's throat, it folded itself completely around the beast's neck, joined itself around, and tightened. The snake-thing stumbled forward, clawing at the choking collar, and Chainer pulled it right off its feet by yanking down hard on his end of the chain. The brute went face-first into the ground and fought with the unyielding metal around its throat.

Chainer cast another collar around the fallen bird. He held neither of the new leash-chains in his hands. Instead, the ends of each hovered an inch from his open palm, following the hand's movement as if they were attached to it. With his hands thus free, Chainer was able to send collar after collar into the pack of oncoming creatures. He nimbly dodged any who came close enough to strike, and he sank sharpened weights into the bodies of those who broke or avoided the collars. He caught the shapeless mass as it flowed over another, more solid body, collaring both creatures with the same cast. As he leashed each monster, Chainer created a conduit through which he could drain its energy. He used this conduit to draw a portion of each thing's essence into himself, and the monsters invariably fell to their knees, fatigued, weakened, chastened.

Chainer floated above the heads of the now-submissive creatures, borne on a wave of their stolen energy. He no longer felt the pain of his wounds, new or old. He spread his arms wide, with dozens of chains radiating out from his hands, each connecting a monster to its new master. Chainer howled.

With a final surge of power, Chainer dispelled all of the leash-chains with the screech of metal on metal and a deafening boom. Chainer dropped to the ground and crossed his arms over his chest.

The newly released creatures growled and grumbled and eyed him angrily, but none dared attack.

"Get going," Chainer said. He brought his arm up, and when he brought it down, a ten-foot length of whip chain cracked among the creatures. "I'll call you when I need you."

The sullen, confused mass began to move away from him. Some ran headlong, terrified of being collared again. The snake-thing was the last to leave, flicking its forked tongue and clawing the ground in front of it. It hissed at Chainer, sounding almost plaintive.

"Go on," Chainer said. "But not too far. I've got plans for you later." He smiled unpleasantly, lost in childhood memories.

The creature grunted, turned, and loped off. When they were all distant and tiny, the mist returned, gently swallowing Chainer from the ground up. Chainer loaded the censer, lit it, and began to whirl it around his head in short, slow circles. He had just earned the right to continue as Skellum's apprentice. He had faced down his oldest nightmare, and for the first time in his life, he felt like he had found a place that was entirely his own.

He continued to casually spin the censer while he waited for Skellum to return and take him back to Cabal City.

PART TWO:
CASTER

CHAPTER 12

The next few months went very well for Chainer. He thought himself happy when the First praised him for delivering the Mirari and ordered Skellum to step up his training. He was even happier, however, when he had been allowed back in the pits.

After spending years in the dementist academy, Chainer was oddly comforted to be back among people who lived and died by their skills rather than their ability to lie. There was also a strange camaraderie among the contestants that Chainer never got tired of. You could be standing in a group waiting for your next bout, and when the starting horn sounded, the people around you could be your allies as easily as your enemies. Unless you had been assigned or had petitioned for a grudge match, you really had no idea who or what you'd be facing, or what the stakes were. Chainer had not seen war, but he imagined the silent, grudging respect pit fighters had for one another was like the bond that formed between soldiers during combat. Only in the pits, there were no uniforms to distinguish friend from foe, and the person who watched your back today would probably stick a rusty spike in it tomorrow.

The Cabal's house pit fighters weren't even sure if they were allowed to win. The Master of the Games plotted and paired the results every match with the fixers, on instructions from the First himself. The most important thing was to put on a good show, to make people come back either as contestants or as spectators. If the Order were out in force and a string of humiliating Cabal defeats would lure them in, then the home team was instructed to embarrass themselves. When the First specified what kind of reaction he wanted from the crowd, the Master of the Games prepared it, and the Cabal fighters produced it.

Chainer had never competed in the main pits before he met Skellum, so his matches were less structured, and he was free to fight as best he could. His youth and his skill with the chain made him something of a novelty act, however, so he was often just outside the entrance in one of the show pits. At the time, Chainer had felt like he was fighting for his life, but he later realized he was only there to impress passing foot traffic. The Cabal had taken him in, trained him, housed him, and fed him, however, so he did his oath-bound duty and put on a show for the passersby. He took that time to master his technique, and before long he had amassed enough wins to impress the pit bosses, the Master of the Games, and, eventually, Skellum.

His current return to the pits had been gradual but steady. In his first bout, an afternoon show that few spectators attended, he tore through a team of slow-moving zombie wildcats with just his chains and dagger. When the pit bosses released a maddened coal-bellied razorback at an evening exhibition two days later, Chainer kept away from it and spun his censer until he produced the snake-thing he had mastered earlier. It tore the smoking, red-hot boar into little bits and then swallowed the pieces whole. The snake-thing turned on Chainer with murder in its eyes, but Chainer quickly collared it once more and brought it to heel.

With each match he was making a name for himself. People were starting to notice his eclectic style, and more and more people filed in to watch him fight. Most dementia casters in the pits were armed only to keep their creations in line. Even the ones who knew how to fight were casters first and warriors second. Chainer could engage his opponents directly from the outset and then surprise them with an unexpected monster, or he could send something nasty at them to test their abilities and then exploit any weaknesses with his chain and dagger. Word started to spread that the young dementia caster was undefeated since returning to the pits. The quality of Chainer's competition increased, and Chainer's control and winning streak increased right along with them.

When he wasn't in the pits he was with Skellum, meditating and breathing and mastering his own dementia space. Each creature he faced in the pits left an impression on his eyes, his ears, his memory. At night, those impressions churned and bubbled in Chainer's sleeping head, and when he awoke, there were more nightmare denizens of the world with the black sand and the hole in the sky. Some nights he would retire after dinner and lie in a deathlike state until midday, and others he spent in a fitful, restless state of agitation. No matter how long he slept or how deeply, he always dreamed of monsters. The largest of his pets was still only slightly larger than human, but Skellum was pleased with his creature's durability, detail, and speed.

His mentor was also pleased that Chainer was following his instructions to the letter. Skellum worked him hard to keep him grounded in the day-to-day events in Cabal City, and he seemed satisfied with Chainer's progress. The old man had not mentioned the mental strain of dementia casting in weeks. The only objection

Skellum had to Chainer's success was that his pupil was obliged to abandon the designation "apprentice" in favor of "dementia caster."

"I didn't train a mere caster. Casters work in the mud and the blood of the pits," he huffed. "I train dementists. Dementists do important, detailed work for the First. And we know all the best people."

Chainer laughed at the old snob and tried to smear some of the dirt from the pits on his hat.

"Let me be a caster for a few more months," he said. "I like it."

Skellum blocked Chainer's grimy hand with his cape. "Don't touch me, you clod. I have a dinner engagement at the manor tonight."

"With some of the best people, no doubt."

"Indeed. And you'd do well to wipe that smirk off along with the dirt. You're invited, too."

"Is it the First?" Chainer said, suddenly interested. "Is there news of the Mirari?"

Skellum scowled. "No, then yes." When Chainer looked confused, he went on. "The Master of the Games wants a sit-down with you and me to plan for this weekend's event. Apparently, there's a couple of tough nuts coming in from the mountains, and he wants you to attend to them personally."

Chainer wrinkled his nose. "Does that mean I have to baby-sit another barbarian?" His eyes brightened. "Or has Kamahl returned? I'd like to place a few bets on him, make some extra silver." He tugged absently at his ragged clothing. "I could use a new suit."

"That's my boy," Skellum said happily. "I'll take you along to my tailor. Never forget worldly delights, my boy. They should be the reason you fight so hard."

"Master," Chainer said dramatically. "You mean that serving the Cabal isn't reward enough?"

Skellum narrowed his eyes. "You have always had a smart mouth," he said. "And no, service is not its own reward. Neither the First nor Kuberr himself have ever said otherwise. We serve the

Cabal, but the Cabal also serves you. That's how it works. That's why it works. Remember it."

Chainer nodded. "Right now, I'm feeling pretty well served. And after I clean up and join you for dinner, I'll feel even better."

"Agreed," Skellum said. "Meet me in the master's parlor in an hour. He'll meet us there."

* * * * *

Chainer sat in stunned silence as the Master of the Games prattled on. She was different from the master who had directed the games that had been interrupted by the dragon attack. No one spoke of him or his absence, and Chainer decided not to ask.

He shot an aggravated look over at Skellum. His mentor seemed calm and collected, but Chainer could tell he was not happy, either. Chainer waited for the new master to take a breath. When she did, he broke in.

"So you're saying I have to lose." He had never been asked to throw a match before. He was finding that he didn't like it.

"Not in so many words," the master said. She was a tall woman, with a tight, pinched face and her hair pulled tight against her skull. "We want the Cabal to make a good showing. But this pair has worked their way up through all the lesser pits between here and the mountains. They haven't lost yet, but we haven't been able to give them what they want."

"What do they want?" Skellum asked. He was keeping a close eye on Chainer, watching for any sign that his pupil was losing his temper.

"Oh, she's looking for her brother or something. The last she heard, he had come to fight in the pits. She and her dwarf keep beating the best we can throw at them, but so far nobody knows who she's actually looking for, or if we know where he is. He might be dead. He probably went into debt and is working it off in the side pits or in the flesh mills. Most barbarians can't resist betting on themselves to win." She smiled unpleasantly.

Chainer kept his voice neutral, but he saw Skellum note his renewed interest. "Barbarian?"

"Yes," the Master of the Games checked her roster. "Apparently, both brother and sister are from a tribe in the Pardic mountains. She's got an elderly dwarf as her partner. They seem to have worked together before, because they make an excellent team. Undefeated so far." She raised her eyebrows at Chainer. "Just like you. Think of the crowds, little brother. The Cabal's best against the toughest thing ever to come out of the hills this year."

"I think I know her brother," Chainer said.

The Master of the Games smiled. "That must be why the First gave me your names. I wasn't going to mention it unless I had to, but this directive comes from the First himself. You are to fight the pair from the mountains. The First wants them to get the information they've already earned, but we can't just hand it to them. So we're going to let you square off against them, put on a good show, and then let them walk away feeling victorious."

Chainer looked at Skellum again. He smiled. "What's in it for me?" he asked. Skellum fiddled with his hat to hide his smile of pride.

"For you, little brother? You get to do your duty for the First and the Cabal. What else did you expect?"

"He expects compensation," Skellum broke in. "His undefeated record has value. You're asking him to throw it away. It's only fair that he get something in return."

The master's eyes darted back and forth from Chainer to Skellum. "What do you want?"

Skellum started to speak, but Chainer stopped him with a raised hand. "If I'm supposed to provide information, I want that information. The Cabal has informants everywhere. I want to know what happened to Kamahl the barbarian after he left Cabal City. I want to know where the Mirari is. And," he winked at Skellum, "I want a cut of the proceeds from the match. The betting tables will be busy when we fight. I want my share."

The master's eyes gleamed. "Done," she said.

"We serve the Cabal," Skellum said.

"And the Cabal serves us," Chainer answered. "Now, then. Let's start with where my barbarian friend went. We can figure out what I'm supposed to tell his sister after that."

* * * * *

Veza never received a courier with false information for Ambassador Laquatus. Within two tension-filled weeks of presenting her idea to Empress Llawan, Veza was awakened a few hours before dawn by a ripping crack of thunder from her living room fountain. Veza had reassumed her legs the day after she last spoke to the empress. She climbed out of the tub and ran into the room.

Two cephalid imperial guards were already floating in the air beside a glowing disk of energy that used to be Veza's fountain pool. They were enveloped in liquid blue energy that kept them alive and upright as a third guard came through the portal. The two floating guards assisted him and two more like him into the water. Veza heard the crackle of portal transit, quickly bowed her head, and heard a large splash. She remained bowed until one of the floating guards touched her on the shoulder.

"Your empress awaits," he said. Veza rose, nodded to the guard, and stepped gracefully into the tide pool.

Empress Llawan floated deep, ten feet below the surface at the very limit of Veza's pool. The three tailed merfolk guards floated in formation above her, constantly scanning every possible avenue of attack. They eyed Veza as she descended, but let her pass without comment.

Veza lowered her eyes. "Empress."

"Director Veza. We require your assistance."

"I am at your service, Empress."

"We had our finest mind-rider investigate your notion of eaves-dropping on Ambassador Laquatus's link to his familiar.

"Your hypothesis proved correct, Director," Llawan continued. "Congratulations."

"Empress," Veza flushed.

"In fact, it proved even easier to interpret the signals than you projected. Our expert was able to see Laquatus's thoughts quite easily. He has but one thing on his mind lately, an extremely powerful artifact called the Mirari."

Veza nodded. "I had heard such an artifact was uncovered recently. That kind of news even reaches Breaker Bay."

"It was in the hands of the Cabal patriarch. Laquatus happened to be visiting when the artifact arrived. He has done little but connive after it ever since."

Veza started to understand. "Has the Ambassador acquired this artifact?"

"No. Currently, it is in the hands of the Order."

Veza wondered why the empress didn't seem happier about this development. "Is that acceptable, Empress?"

"Barely. The Order are honest and try to be righteous in all things. They are like jellyfish in the hands of someone like Laquatus. It can only be a matter of time before he spirits it away through violence or deceit."

Veza waited for the empress to continue. When she didn't, Veza said, "Then Laquatus will bring the artifact to Aboshan." Llawan stared at her for a moment then clicked out a sharp series of screeches to the guard above. The guard checked an instrument strapped to his wrist and nodded to the empress.

"The crystal did not glow, my empress. She is concealing nothing."

Llawan clicked again, and the guards swam off, out into the bay and well out of earshot. They maintained a clear line of sight on both Veza and the empress.

"Forgive us, Director," Llawan said, "but we had to be sure. If you had lied just now, that crystal would have flashed. I have negotiated many a favorable treaty with it by my side."

Veza simply stared uncomprehendingly.

"We can never be too careful when dealing with Laquatus. But now we must be completely frank with you. Aboshan already has the Mirari. Somehow the ambassador managed to get the Mirari away from the Order and into Aboshan's clutches without actually ever taking possession of it himself. The man's an idiot."

"So Aboshan has the artifact?"

"Yes."

"And the empress is worried that he will use it against her?"

Veza was shocked when Llawan laughed out loud. Cephalids made a high-pitched, staccato chattering when they laughed. It was too much for Veza. She burst into laughter as well.

Llawan quickly regained her composure. "If only that were our main concern! Aboshan collects artifacts, but he doesn't understand them. He wouldn't know what to do with a powerful artifact if it came with a guidebook and a tutor. If he gets his tentacles on the Mirari, he'll probably try to eat it.

"No, Director, we are concerned with what Laquatus will do once he has the Mirari. He claims to be working on behalf of the emperor, but he is a greedy and grasping child. It must truly gall him to see the prize that he so badly wanted in the hands of an oaf, and to know that he has no chance of wresting it free. If the thing is as powerful as they say—if it is as powerful as my mind-rider senses, then Laquatus will not allow Aboshan to have it for long. And when he gets it, the next obstacle between an ambassador's sash and the imperial cap is poor, exiled Llawan."

Veza's humor quickly cooled and vanished. "What will the empress do?"

Llawan extended a tentacle and gently took Veza's hand. "We will gather around us those who have served us well. Those who have served us loyally." She dropped Veza's hand and brought her other forelimb forward. On the end she wore a sharpened spike of whale's tooth. "And we will confront the oaf Aboshan. If we can push him, keep him furious and fearful of a renewed civil war, then he will cling tightly to his new toy and never allow Laquatus to take it. The harder the ambassador tries, the tighter Aboshan's grip will grow, and neither of them will be able to use it against us. Eventually, Aboshan will have Laquatus killed." She smiled a politician's smile. " It is never a good idea to be too ambitious when the emperor is feeling insecure.

"We ask you to come with us now and stand by our side in the court of the emperor. We ask you to declare yourself as our subject, and to represent our interests. You are wasted here in Breaker Bay. Worse, you are insulted by it. Come with us now, and be our subject. We have thirty executives like yourself and another dozen cephalids of noble birth. We will present ourselves to the emperor and petition him for permission to secede from his empire."

"He will certainly refuse."

"He must. But he will observe the formalities of government. He will cite the existing treaty between us. He will bluster and threaten. He will try to have us killed by assassins, and try to have us executed publicly as traitors. And all that will buy us time."

"Time, Empress? Time for what?"

"To take control of the situation. To drum up more support among the oligarchs and nobles. To turn Laquatus and Aboshan against each other and divide their strength. To take this Mirari for ourselves and rid Mer once and for all of oafs and knaves."

Veza looked up at the surface of the pool above her head. Beyond it was her cottage, her paperwork, and her depot. Beyond that, the village and all its human inhabitants, with all their human tics and prejudices. And somewhere far beyond that was Aboshan, who cared only for the commerce and not at all for the people who conducted it in his name.

"I am yours, Empress Llawan," she said. "What would you have me do?"

Llawan smiled. "Come with us now. We are taking a water portal back to our city, where the imperial transport is being prepared for the journey north. En route, we will discuss statesmanship and strategy."

Veza nodded. "There are a few items I would like to bring along."

"Personal items, Director? This is a time for leaving things behind and starting over."

Veza bowed. "Documents, Empress. Information that may prove useful to our cause." She raised her eyes and met Llawan's. "And I am Director of Breaker Bay no longer."

CHAPTER 13

Chainer caught sight of the pair from the same vantage point he had first spotted Kamahl. He recognized Kamahl's sister Jeska and the dwarf Balthor from the descriptions he had and the fact that they arrived together. Now that he saw her, he thought he could have recognized Jeska as one of Kamahl's kin without forewarning.

She was of medium height and build, but she had Kamahl's blazing red hair and brass colored skin. Where Kamahl's was cropped close to his head, Jeska wore her hair long, braided dwarf style into hundreds of finger-thick strands. Each braid was interwoven with ribbons or hide or polished stones, and she had gathered them all in the middle of her back with a heavy iron clip. Chainer recognized a weighted whip when he saw it, but he was impressed with how casually she wore a weapon that most fighters wouldn't recognize.

142

She also wore a peculiar metal gauntlet that covered her left forearm. It was etched with runes but unpolished, with two small horns at the wrist edge. It looked like a miniature slingshot, but Chainer couldn't quite credit the whole thing as a weapon. He reasoned it was either a sword baffle or some other sort of protective armor.

Finally, she carried a wooden baton that was intricately carved and ringed with metal. It was about as long as her arm, and it looked extremely solid. Her muscles lied about it, as well, effortlessly concealing how dense the baton actually was. In addition to the decorative metal rings, Chainer guessed the baton also had a metal core to give it extra punch.

Jeska carried herself and her weapons with extreme confidence. Her eyes were focused straight ahead, her jaw was set, and her pace was so stern it seemed more like a march than a hike. She didn't even glance at the dwarf by her side, though he matched her stride for stride and never fell out of her peripheral vision.

Balthor was built like all dwarves Chainer had seen, short and broad and gnarled as a stump. His long beard was split into two equal points that fell to his waist, and he wore an ornate headdress with a large red gem at the center. Instead of a fighting axe, he carried some kind of axe-staff that was neither completely weapon nor completely walking stick.

The strange duo was met at the gate by a Cabal representative and escorted into the arena. Chainer waited until the door had shut behind them before he turned from the window and made his way down to the pits.

* * * * *

Several hours later, an oily-looking fixer met Chainer on the staircase.

"You Chainey?" the fixer said.

"Chainer."

"Whatever. Come on, let's go. You're on."

The fixer's attitude annoyed Chainer. "What's the rush?"

"They are. The woman's insane, and the dwarf is really cranky. They say they're going to fight now, or they're going to start wrecking the place."

"So? Turn some stalkers and some hellhounds loose on 'em. The Master of the Games said—"

"The Master of the Games just said you should get your butt down to the main pit." He held out a sealed scroll. "See that? It's official. Now come on."

Chainer stood perfectly still. "What's your name, sunshine?"

The oily Cabalist sneered. "Louche," he said.

"Bet all you have on me, Louche. I can't lose."

"Is that so?"

"It is."

"Thanks, kid." Louche had a sarcastic tone that never wavered. Chainer couldn't tell if the fixer knew he was being misled, or if he just didn't care. He gave up trying to argue with a person who negotiated for a living and fell into step behind him.

Louche led him down the main pit floor. The stands were full, everything seemed ready to go. His opponents waited on the far side of the circle.

"Good luck, kid," Louche said, already distracted and moving on to his next assignment.

"You mean that, Louche?"

"Sure. Why not." Louche didn't even look up as he disappeared into the crowd.

Overhead, the prep horn sounded, and Chainer lit his censer. It was to be a straightforward flag match, two against one. Jeska and Balthor would attempt to take or destroy the simple black pennant that was spiked into an eight-foot-tall mound of packed dirt behind Chainer. Chainer would defend the flag. In this case, that meant he would try to stop them but would fail as convincingly as possible.

In the distance, Chainer heard his match being announced, the usual build-up of the fighters and the standard teasers about blood and danger to whip up the crowd. Chainer scanned the rows and rows of eager faces. The smoke was getting thicker around him, and he fought back a rush of dizziness. "Game on," he whispered. He had to stay focused.

The starting horn sounded, and Chainer's opponents came straight at him. They moved well, but they were terribly out of sync with each other. Balthor strode forward with his head and his staff held high, taking strides as smooth and as grand as his stature allowed. Jeska, on the other hand, was hunched low into a battle crouch, her hands free and empty at her sides. Her baton was ready at her hip, and she kept one hand near it as she stared fixedly at the flag behind Chainer.

"Let's finish this quickly." Chainer heard Balthor's impatience through the dwarf's clenched teeth.

"Just hold up your end," Jeska growled back, "and stay out of my way." They were attacking together, but they were not a team. Chainer decided to exploit that.

As they had no long-range weapons, Chainer waited until Jeska and Balthor were a stone's throw from the mound. Then his eyes rolled back in his head, he shuddered, and he threw his arms out, palm-up, at Balthor. There was a flash of black light, and for the briefest moment a purple ring of energy flickered. Through that ring came a three-foot dragonfly with a scorpion's tail. Its multiple wings buzzed with the fury of a full swarm as it shot high above the arena floor and then dove straight down at Balthor, its stinger poised for the kill. Chainer wanted to test himself against Kamahl's sister, and the dragonfly would keep the dwarf busy. The insect would bedevil and sting until the dwarf hacked at it with his axe or his fists. If he injured it, its sticky blood would spurt and foul whatever part of Balthor it touched.

As Chainer expected, Jeska completely ignored the threat that was ignoring her. As the dragonfly homed in on Balthor, she continued straight on at Chainer. Her movements became much sharper and quicker once the action began, and her approach became more like an acrobat's tumbling run. Chainer ditched the censer and drew his dagger, waiting, his stance inviting Jeska to attack.

Behind Jeska, Balthor stood straight as the dragonfly swooped down on him. The gem on the dwarf's headdress glowed, and red fire leaped from the gem to the blade of his axe-staff. Chainer could see Balthor's lips moving. His eyes were shut.

A blast of flame erupted from the head of Balthor's axe and burned the dragonfly to ash in midair. Chainer stood shocked for just a moment, and then dove forward as another blast slammed into the ground near his feet. Before he could get up off his knees, Jeska was above him and her baton was bearing down on his skull. Balthor smugly crossed his arms.

Years with the fighting chain had given Chainer extremely fast hands, and Jeska had badly underestimated his speed. He caught her baton in mid-swing, threw his weight backward, and tossed her back over his head with an assist from his boot. He held onto her hands, so she slammed painfully into the ground. Chainer released her, rolled, and came up with his hands in position. There was another black flash, and a second dragonfly buzzed out and oriented on Jeska. Chainer cursed for repeating himself. Skellum would never let that go. Chainer pushed the thought of his mentor aside, saw that Jeska had not yet regained her feet, and squared off on Balthor. He scooped his dagger up off the arena floor and dared Balthor to come forward with it.

The dwarf could not blast Chainer with Jeska so close behind, but the gem on Balthor's head was still glowing. The old devil was clearly waiting for Chainer's next casting, so he could blast it to cinders. Chainer kept his hands in front of him to keep the dwarf's attention away from the flag. Instead of giving him a target,

Chainer snapped his arm out and sent a weighted black chain singing into Balthor's headdress. The weight smashed through one of the glowing gem's supports and knocked it off center. The gem buzzed and stopped glowing. For the first time since Chainer had laid eyes on him, Balthor looked something other than haughty. He looked downright nervous, maybe even slightly embarrassed.

"You broke his special hat," Jeska called. "He's going to be *furious*." Despite the dragonfly darting all around her head, Jeska seemed savagely amused. She was keeping the insect at bay with her baton and a vicious barrage of the most obscene threats and language Chainer had heard outside of the city docks.

Chainer whistled. The dragonfly broke off and hovered in the air between them. Chainer jerked his head at Balthor, and the dragonfly buzzed hungrily toward the angry but still shame-faced dwarf.

"So you're looking for your brother," Chainer said. Jeska was not being drawn in by his stance. She had seen him sling a chain at Balthor from twenty feet away, and she didn't seem eager to let him do the same to her.

"I am. You know where he is?"

Chainer sheathed his dagger, touched his hands together, and pulled a ten-foot length of chain with a smooth, weighted end out of thin air. He held the chain out for her to see, then started it dancing around himself.

"I know where he went," Chainer said.

Jeska maintained her stance, daring Chainer with her baton as he had dared Balthor.

"I guess that means I shouldn't kill you," she said. "Tell me, and we can end this now."

Chainer began to circle around Jeska, his weapon in constant motion. "Let's come to an arrangement, you and I," he said. "I have information you want, you have information I want. If you agree to share, I'll let you walk right past me." He looked around the arena. "After we put on a good show, of course."

"I'm not making any deals with you, Cabalist," Jeska spat. "For all I know, that's what my brother did, and that's why I can't find him."

Chainer flicked the weighted end at Jeska, who easily batted it aside. "He left here free and whole. I can tell you where he went. Will you tell me where he came from?"

Jeska lunged at Chainer with her baton. He ducked under it, and slashed the iron pin out of her hair with his dagger. She looked totally shocked, then angrily shook her braids loose, spun her baton, and charged again.

Chainer snarled the end of Jeska's weapon with his and tried to jerk it out of her hands, but the polished wood slipped free. Jeska spun under the chain and tried to drive the heel of her hand into Chainer's nose. Chainer dodged and then missed Jeska's knee with the weighted end on his return stroke. They traded feints and then held their positions, facing each other.

"Look, barbarian," Chainer said. "A show of faith. Your brother is competing regularly in one of the minor pits to the north. Kamahl is alive and well."

Jeska paused. "What's he doing up north?"

Chainer relaxed but didn't lower his weapon. "Chasing after treasure."

"You mean I've been halfway across Otaria looking for him, and he's not even lost?"

"Seems that way."

"How do I know you're telling me the truth?"

"For Fiers's sake, Jeska," Balthor yelled. He was jabbing at the dragonfly with his staff, but he seemed more concerned about preserving the staff than he was about harming the insect. "Stop babbling and finish this! Did you forget the rules of this thrice-damned farce?"

Chainer saw realization crowd the anger out of Jeska's eyes. She let out an ear-splitting war cry and heaved her baton at Chainer's head. While he was distracted, Jeska stuck her gauntleted arm straight out and sighted down it like a crossbow at the black pennant. She drew a smooth red stone from her pouch and touched it to the gauntlet between the horns. She spoke one word, and the horns sparked, igniting a thin stream of fire that stretched between them like a clothesline. Jeska drew the red stone back and prepared to release it toward the flag.

"Wait," Chainer said. The gauntlet was a kind of slingshot, and if he didn't act quickly, Jeska would win the match before Chainer had gotten anything out of her. Chainer sent a collar chain slamming into Jeska's wrist and jerked her off-balance, so that she couldn't target the flag.

Pulling Jeska away from her first target was a passably sound pit strategy, but Chainer immediately realized the flaw in his execution. As close as he was to her, once he pulled her off balance the only thing Jeska could fire her slingshot at was him. Jeska barked out an incoherent warning as the red stone flew. In the eight feet of space between Chainer's eyes and the oncoming stone, the missile transformed from a shiny, glasslike bead into a glowing ball of concentrated heat. Chainer's hands proved to be faster than his brain as he jerked his arms up to protect his face.

His eyes slammed shut as a blast of heat burned his eyebrows away. He was temporarily deafened by the explosion, and the pain in his right arm was agonizing. The impact blew him back on his heels, but he didn't stagger or fall.

"Held my ground, gods damn it," he heard his own voice say. He started to sway, his eyes still squinted and unfocused. He could barely make out the old dwarf and the brass girl as they stood, side by side, staring over at him. They were curious, but they were keeping a safe distance.

Confused, Chainer looked at the flag, still untouched. He was helpless. Why weren't they finishing him off or climbing the mound?

"Do you give, Cabalist?" Chainer could see her shouting, cupping her hands around her mouth, but he could barely hear her. He recognized her tone, however, as that of someone who knows the fight is over even if nobody else does.

Chainer reached for his dagger, and a fresh wave of searing pain dropped him to his knees. His left hand seemed fine, but his right felt thick and vague and clumsy. Chainer held his arm up to get a better look at his hand.

"Or not," he said out loud. His right arm ended in a charred, smoking stump. His hand was completely gone, and his forearm now ended two inches below the elbow.

"Damn," Chainer said. He turned his dazed eyes on Balthor and Jeska. He looked back at his mangled arm. With an amiable smile, Chainer raised his arm and his stump over his head.

"I give," he said evenly. Then he collapsed face-first onto the arena floor. The last thing he heard before he passed out was the sound of the horn signaling the end of the match.

CHAPTER 14

Llawan's personal transport was a ninety-foot-long leviathan that had been specially bred, engineered, and enchanted to serve as a combination warship and yacht. Its insides were vast and hollow, with compartments that could accommodate air breathers as well as sea creatures. Its hide was thick and durable, and its head was hard and bony enough to ram through the sides of any wooden vessel. Specially trained handlers sat in the fore of the creature's skull and steered the ship based on orders from the captain and the view from a huge scrying screen.

The creature had clear crystalline chambers grafted onto its sides and back where passengers could dine, chat, and enjoy the view. These cabins could be removed or, in times of emergency, broken off to protect the empress and her armed guards inside. Though it had no offensive capabilities other than its ramming skull, the creature was fast enough to escape even the swiftest pursuers.

Veza eyed the clear wall that separated her cabin from the frigid depths of the ocean. She couldn't drown, and they weren't deep enough for the pressure to be a danger, but she was still uncomfortable. Perhaps it was because she knew that the passengers in the external compartments were considered expendable in case of attack.

The closer the craft got to Aboshan's territory, the more somber the mood became. Nobles who had ignored Veza since coming on board suddenly felt the need to chat with her, to hear what she knew, to clutch at any straws she might offer. When they found she knew even less than they did, they moved on without another word. Veza was the only legged creature on board, at Llawan's continued request.

Excuse me, honored guests. The voice was painfully loud, and echoed in Veza's head. Everyone on board seemed to have received the same amplified thought message.

The Empress Llawan requests your immediate presence in the forward viewing pod. She will make a short address there. Please hurry.

The gentle sense of forward motion eased, then stopped. The ship was no longer swimming toward Aboshan. There were murmurs and a few anguished questions, but no one knew what was in store for them. Were they turning around? Had they been met at the border by Aboshan's navy?

The tubes that connected the external cabins were only wide enough for one humanoid at a time, so Veza and the other guests waited patiently to join the single-file line to the front of the craft. Veza was one of the last ones into the forward cabin. She stepped up to the doorway, which shimmered like the surface of a pool. She cleared her lungs and walked into the flooded chamber. Magic kept the water from running out into the hallway and flooding the next compartments.

Llawan floated at the front of the chamber in complete regalia of scepter, skull-cap, and imperial robes. If everyone on board seemed anxious, it was because Llawan had commandeered all the confidence. Floating beside her was a small cephalid male with a hood pulled up over his head. His face was impassive, his eyes were closed. Llawan raised her forelimb for silence, and the room fell quiet.

"Noble guests and loyal friends," she said. "We are mere moments away from a most impressive sight. We had hoped to address you before the event began, but we fear we shall have to wait. Please remain silent. And . . . watch." Llawan swam back a stroke, and presented the forward view with a grandiose wave of her tentacle.

The guests watched in hushed awe. The ocean stretched out before them, a vast and uniform curtain illuminated only by the leviathan's lights. A full minute ticked by, and nothing happened.

Then across the vast expanse ahead of them came a deep, booming crack. Veza felt it all over her body as the water around her vibrated. Some of the more sensitive cephalids keened in pain as their delicate skin reacted to the trembling sound. A pinpoint of light flashed in the distance and grew, taking up more and more of the view as it came closer and closer. It was a frothy light, blue in color, and it boiled like a cloud of steam.

"The shock wave approaches, Empress." The hooded cephalid did not open his eyes, but he bowed his head when he spoke. The phrase "shock wave" set off a few startled cries, but Llawan's voice rang out loud and clear.

"Stay where you are," she said. "We have brought you here to witness, and we will keep you safe. Olsham," she clicked to the hooded cephalid, and he nodded. Olsham began to croon a low, haunting tune that Veza found eerily soothing.

"The Emperor Aboshan has just used the Mirari," Llawan said. "Our mind-rider Olsham has been closely monitoring the situation.

His phenomenon is almost identical to the one which occurred at Captain Pianna's headquarters mere weeks ago. Judging by the size of that—" Llawan pointed at the shock wave, which now filled the viewing window— "we would say that Aboshan's custody of the Mirari was no more successful than Pianna's."

Llawan's guests digested this among themselves. Someone from the rear chirped, "So we're safe?"

Llawan smiled. "From Aboshan? Yes. From that?" She pointed again. "Time will tell." She turned and clicked at Olsham, who bowed. The water around the empress swirled, and her shield defenders formed a rock-hard bubble with Llawan at its center.

The cephalid mystic Olsham held one final syllable in his chanted song, folded all of his limbs into a complicated symbol-gesture, and slammed his beak shut with a clack.

Just as the first edges of the shock wave started jostling the empress's craft, the hooded mystic released a flashing wave of energy that spread out in all directions. The blue-white light suffused the ship and its passengers just as the full force of the rampaging turbulence slammed through their location. Veza and the other guests stood amazed as water, debris, and the bodies of hapless creatures passed through their ghostly forms without meeting any resistance. It was if the leviathan had ceased to exist, but was looking on from the same vantage point. Even the water in the viewing chamber remained still as the storm raged around them.

Many long minutes later, when the tumult had died down and it was safe for the ship to move again, the ghostly light retracted back into Olsham. He unfolded his arms, adjusted his hood, and sank down to the chamber floor.

Llawan clicked at him. He clicked back, though his voice was low and ragged. Llawan clicked, offered him her tentacle, and he kissed it.

"Aboshan is dead," she said. A nervous cheer went up, then faded into uncertainty. Llawan smiled. "And the Mirari is gone from Mer.

We are not yet certain who has it , but we are certain of two things. Aboshan does not have it, and neither does Laquatus."

A heartier cheer went up among the members of Llawan's party. When the empress held up a half-hearted tentacle for silence, the cheer redoubled.

"The emperor is dead," someone shouted, "long live the empress!"

Veza watched the other guests take up the chant.

"Long live the empress! Long live the empress!"

Veza herself was relieved, but she didn't feel like cheering. She wondered if Llawan meant the things she'd said back in Breaker Bay about removing all the oafs and knaves. Some of each were currently onboard.

As she looked at the room full of ambitious nobles and greedy oligarchs, Veza hoped she'd have a chance to find out. She quietly edged out of the room, away from the celebration and back toward her room.

* * * * *

Chainer stood in the courtyard of Skellum's academy, carefully twirling a censer around his head with his new arm.

"Say that again," he said.

"You asked me for an update about the Mirari. I told you. It destroyed Pianna, destroyed Aboshan, and flooded half the continent."

Chainer whistled. "Which half?"

"Okay, a third," Skellum admitted. "Everything between the upper border of the Krosan and the southern edge of Cape Paradise is now underwater."

"And the Mirari?" he said, as casually as he could.

"At this precise moment in time—" Skellum made a show of looking at the sun's position in the sky— "Caster Fulla is bringing it back here to Cabal City."

Chainer kept spinning the censer, trying to get used to the pseudo-sensations his prosthetic arm was reporting to his brain. He had heard of Fulla. She was merely a caster, as Skellum would say, but one of the best. Chainer had never seen her compete, but he had spoken to a few who had fought against her. They were all glad to have survived the experience. Fulla brought out some frightful beasts, they said, but Fulla herself was scarier still.

"So the First was right," Chainer said. "All who seek the Mirari are destroyed by it." He slowed the censer and brought it to rest by his feet. It continued to pump smoke into the air around Chainer. "Except me."

"And don't think he's pleased by it," Skellum said. "The First liked dealing with Pianna. She was a rarity among Order officers. She kept her word, even when she gave it to hedonistic infidel criminals like ourselves."

"Is the Order broken?" Chainer could not keep the hopeful joy out of his voice. He nodded to Skellum, and his mentor tossed a copper coin into the air. Chainer snapped the artificial arm forward and created a lashing chain that struck the coin cleanly and bent it in double.

"Not really," Skellum said. "Bretath is still the highest-ranking officer on Otaria. Pianna's absence creates a power vacuum in this region, however, and there are a number of lesser officers looking to fill her shoes."

"Do we at least get to bury the bird-man who stole Kamahl's victory?" Chainer practiced sending short lengths of chain out of his metal palm and drawing them back in again.

"Kirtar? Yes. Dead, dead, dead. In fact, if he were still alive, which he isn't, he would have been named Pianna's replacement by acclamation."

The air around Chainer was still thick with smoke. He concentrated, shuddered, and positioned his hands for a casting. A two-headed wolf sprang out from between his hands, its tail a spitting cobra that hissed back at Skellum. Chainer nodded, waved, and the wolf evaporated in mid-growl.

"The arm seems to be working fine now." Chainer flexed it and examined his own wiggling fingers. "I've got to get used to the new feel of things, but I can do all the things I did before."

"Let's hope you can't point projectile weapons at your own body anymore," his mentor said. "That's a skill you can do without." Skellum came forward and held out his hands. "Let me see."

Chainer presented the arm, and Skellum looked it over, poking his fingernail into what would be muscles and pressure points on a flesh and blood arm. Except for the fact that it was made of metal and the fingers came to needle-sharp points, Chainer's arm was extremely lifelike. Between the steel gray of the arm itself and the polished black chrome of the brace he wore to keep it in place, it looked like he was wearing a basic warrior's gauntlet instead of a replacement limb.

Affixing the arm had been torture. The arm, which the healer kept calling a "golem limb," had to be magically infused with part of Chainer's life force before it could be grafted on. The golem arm had then been fused to the remaining bones and flesh of his stump, and despite the pain, Chainer was obliged to sit perfectly still for three hours while the graft took root.

"You can scream if you want to," the healer had said, but Chainer denied him that particular pleasure. Cabal healers were well known for their ability to get maimed or dying people back on their feet and into the pits. They were not known for their comforting bed-side manner.

Skellum released Chainer's arm and Chainer looked it over again himself. Cabal healers were also not known for their aesthetic sensibilities. Chainer had seen some hideous patch jobs in the pits. People with lobster claws instead of hands, legs fused or amputated to make room for stingers or spinnerets, heads that in no way matched the bodies they were attached to. Chainer counted himself lucky to get his new limb. It'd be just like Skellum to stick him with some dead bastard's reanimated arm. Zombie replacement limbs were far cheaper, easier to graft, and quicker to master than the metal one he was sporting. They tended to rot and stink, however, and had to be replaced at least twice a year.

Chainer grunted suspiciously. His mentor was not above childishly taunting him to put him back in his place. But Chainer had missed a lot while he was convalescing, and Skellum had so far been stingy with details. Chainer had felt something shift each time the Mirari changed hands, but his senses weren't refined enough to tell him as much as the Cabal's informants could.

"It looks good, Chainer. And try not to lose this one. Real arms are expensive enough, but the cost of replacing this one would be ruinous." He shook his head sadly. "You just don't have the silver."

Chainer saw him sneak another look at the sun, then suddenly say, "All right. Ask me what the surprise is."

Chainer had spent enough time with Skellum to become used to his mentor's rapid changes in subject. Politely, he said, "Master Skellum, what is the surprise?"

Skellum waited, listening. Then the warning bell from the guard tower that overlooked Cabal City's port started ringing, audible even at Skellum's academy six blocks away.

"The surprise is . . . Fulla and the Mirari are arriving now, right on schedule. And your barbarian friend has been in the city for the past two days, waiting for them to return." He produced a small black towel from under his cape and offered it to Chainer. "Why don't you wipe off some of that sweat you've worked up, so you can go greet them?"

Chainer snagged the towel on the end of his pointed fingers. Careful not to dig the sharp tips into his face, he wiped his brow and cheeks with the towel and dropped it lightly onto the floor.

"Thank you, Master. Are you coming to the docks?"

"No, I'm going to see the First. Once he receives Fulla and the

Mirari, he wants to see me and the Master of the Games. Once he's done with us, he wants to see you."

"How long have I got?"

Skellum shrugged. "Hard to say. Maybe an hour, maybe less."

Chainer took a step toward the door, but stopped. "Am I dismissed, Master?"

"You are dismissed."

Chainer took one last second to lash a chain into the discarded towel and haul it in to his hand. With a bow and a flourish, he offered the towel to Skellum from his artificial arm.

"Thank you again, Master," he said. "For everything."

"Go on," Skellum took the towel. "Just try not to lose any limbs between here and the docks."

* * * * *

Just as he knew where to go to get the best view of the incoming pit fighters, Chainer also knew where to go to watch ships arrive in Cabal City harbor. He sat in a second-story warehouse window as Fulla's travel fish swam up. He felt almost smug, high above the small crowd that had gathered to gawk at the amazing creature, with the best view on the pier.

The fish was whale sized, with transparent skin and organs. The only visible internal structures were its bones. A small dark-haired woman rode just inside the thing's stomach, leaning against its gullet on her elbows as she watched the fish swim into port. Her sword arm was scarred and slightly malformed, almost clublike. She wore a thick, short gladius on her hip and carried three daggers on the outside of her vest. Her skin was pale, her hair was short and unkempt, but her boots were polished and her coat well tailored. Apart from an extremely wild glint in her eyes, she carried herself at least as elegantly as Skellum did.

Behind Fulla stood Ambassador Laquatus. He looked much the

same as he did the last time Chainer saw him, only now he was not so smug or haughty. The voyage looked as if it had been a hard one for him. From the way he kept glaring at Fulla, Chainer guessed Laquatus would like nothing better than to dive straight to the bottom of the ocean with Fulla in tow and leave her there.

Fulla's fish bobbed on the water near the pier for a moment. Inside of it, Fulla stood and then backed up a few paces. She got a running start, then jumped and waved her hands simultaneously. The fish faded from view while Fulla was in midair. Her leap carried her safely onto the docks, but the unprepared ambassador was dropped unceremoniously into the sea. A ripple of laughter ran through the crowd, but it quickly died as Laquatus surfaced and angrily called for assistance.

The dock was thick with Cabalists. A handful stepped forward to haul the ambassador out of the water, but the majority hovered close to Fulla. Her reputation and her eerie, intense stare kept anyone from touching her, however, and they cleared a path as she walked toward the First's manor. Dripping, sputtering, and largely ignored, Laquatus fell in behind her.

Chainer began to scan the rest of the crowd. It was clear that no one would dare interfere with Fulla on her way to the First, and Chainer felt confident that the Mirari was safe for as long as Fulla held onto it. He was hoping to catch a glimpse of Kamahl, but there was no sign of the big barbarian anywhere on the docks. It wasn't until he looked higher than himself that he found Kamahl.

Like a mountain goat, Kamahl had scaled the outside of a building directly across the alley from Chainer and was watching the Mirari arrive from the roof. Chainer thought he looked too humorless. He seemed to have lost some of his natural joy for battle. Upon reflection, he couldn't blame Kamahl. They had both thought of nothing but the Mirari since it left Cabal City, but Kamahl had chased it halfway up the coast and back, and he still didn't have it. *I haven't moved,* Chainer thought, *and in a sense it's being deliv-*

ered back to me. He made a mental note to be sure and point that out to Kamahl as soon as the barbarian cheered up.

With a shock, Chainer realized that Kamahl had spotted him. Chainer raised a hand in greeting, but Kamahl looked startled. Then Chainer remembered his arm.

Chainer held the arm higher and flicked it, producing a high-pitched ding. "It's a long story," he shouted.

Kamahl shrugged. He rolled his hands, indicating Chainer should elaborate.

"You ever met a barbarian girl named Jeska?" Chainer yelled. "Braided hair, carries a baton?"

Kamahl nodded.

Chainer held up his metal arm. "So did I."

Kamahl laughed and pointed to the ground. "Tell me in the tavern," he shouted back.

Chainer shook his head. "I'm on duty," he said, and Kamahl shrugged again. He pointed down at the retreating figures of Fulla and Laquatus, and then resumed his humorless stance as his eyes bored into them.

He's here for the Mirari again, Chainer realized. Jeska said he couldn't stop talking about it, and Chainer had seen his share of addicts and obsessives in the pits. Kamahl's expression was somewhere between a man who's been wronged and a man who's dying of thirst. There was something he needed, wanted, and meant to have all at the same time.

Chainer felt a disquieting churn in his stomach. He'd wanted Kamahl to have the Mirari more than Lt. Kirtar. But he wanted the First to have it more than Kamahl. He flexed his golem hand and listened to the metal bend.

Chainer took one last look at his friend, then turned and headed down the stairs. The First probably had three plans for the Mirari ready and waiting to be implemented. It was entirely possible that neither he nor Kamahl would ever see the Mirari again, much less fight over it. It was more likely that he and Kamahl would fight together in the pits as Balthor and Jeska had. In fact, Chainer was sure the Master of the Games would sanction such a pairing if he requested it.

Chainer picked up his pace, his good mood restored. Besides, he thought, by now everyone knows what happened to Pianna and Aboshan. Kamahl and everyone else would eventually have to accept that no matter who won it, the Mirari belonged to the Cabal and would always come back to those who found it first.

CHAPTER 15

"Ladies, gentlemen, and other," the overhead voice boomed. "Welcome to the main event."

Chainer and Kamahl stood side by side, casually checking their weapons. Chainer loaded a charcoal disc into his censer and held it out to Kamahl. The barbarian snapped his fingers and produced a tiny, explosive blast of flame that engulfed the charcoal. Chainer let the disc drop into the censer, loaded the Dragon's Blood in after it, and waited for the smoke to begin wafting upward.

"Much obliged," he said. Kamahl grunted and nodded. He was not one for pre-match chatter.

"Tonight," the announcer continued, "they're red-hot and black-hearted. They're going for their twelfth consecutive team win, a Cabal City record. They are the Cabal's own Chainer and Kamahl from the Pardic Mountains!"

The cheers got louder with each match. Chainer waved his metal hand to acknowledge the crowd, but Kamahl ignored them. Now that he had spent some time with the big man in and outside of the pits, Chainer was getting a clear idea of the difference between barbarians and Cabalists. Kamahl only relaxed immediately after a match. Before and during, he hardly spoke a word and never so much as cracked a smile. Partnering with Kamahl had been hugely rewarding for Chainer, but it had also cured him of the notion that he should have been a barbarian. The mountain people were driven harder by their own nature than the average Cabalist was by the sternest overseer. Chainer mentally thanked Skellum for instilling a sense of discipline, but also the good sense to enjoy the time between fights.

The announcer continued to drone on. "Our champions have their work cut out for them tonight, however. The Master of the Games has sanctioned this match as a grudge match, one with no restrictions. The contest is over when all the contestants on one side either yield or are incapacitated."

"I wish they would tell us these things before we get out here," Kamahl grumbled.

"That's part of the fun," Chainer said.

"Requesting the grudge match, and representing the Order's late, lamented northern Citadel, please welcome Lieutenant Devon's crusat squad!"

Lt. Devon was another aven warrior, and though his wings were stunted, Chainer fully expected him to fly with the aid of the Order's magic. He was armed with a long pike. The rest of Devon's squad consisted of two troopers, a white-robed mage, and a huge stone beast with the head of a lion and the body of a ten-foot-tall man.

While the announcer continued with the introductions, Kamahl leaned over to Chainer and said, "What's a 'crusat?' Every toy soldier I meet these days calls himself crusat."

Chainer was pleased that Kamahl was actually speaking before a match, and that the barbarian had used Cabal slang to describe the Order. It made them seem more like a team.

"Crusat is a kind of holy war," Chainer explained. "They used to declare them every year or so, back in the days when they were trying to wipe us out once and for all. Pianna put a stop to all that, but now that she's gone, a few of their hard-liners have revived the concept."

Kamahl grimaced. "So we're fighting a death match against fanatics with a spiritual grudge against you."

Chainer nodded. "That's about the size of it." He smiled. "Should be fun, eh?"

Kamahl grumbled. "I usually like there to be more of a reward waiting for me when I fight for my life."

Chainer darkened. "As soon as the First offers the Mirari again, you'll get your chance." He nudged Kamahl. "What's that statue-looking thing?" Chainer asked.

"They're called megoliths. Animated stone, or some such thing. I've fought them before."

"Like a golem?" Chainer was eager for another crack at an Order golem.

"Sort of. They aren't carved before they're animated like golems are. They just sort of . . . come into being in the shape they have. Watch the pieces," he warned. "Sometimes you can hack off a piece, and the piece keeps fighting."

"Thanks," Chainer said. He gestured with his smoking censer. "Look, they're burning incense, too."

Kamahl looked. "Seems more like a prayer ceremony to me. I think they're blessing the bird-man."

"Think that'll make him fly?" Chainer said. He started spinning his censer around his head.

"Probably." Kamahl's voice had gone flat again, indicating that his mind was not on the conversation. The prep horn sounded. The match was ready to begin.

"You want the bird-man and the mystic or the statue and the toy soldiers?"

"I'll take the statue. I want to see if it melts or burns." Kamahl drew his massive broadsword. "Watch the mage. She's not armed, so I expect she's got some magical surprise in store for us."

"Done," Chainer said. The starting horn sounded. Devon's squad spread out, with the megolith in front and the troopers flanking it. The mage touched the lieutenant's wings, which burst into bright, glowing light. Devon yelled, "Attack!" and sprang into the air, trailing white light behind him. The mage stayed where she was, safely out of harm's way.

Or so she thought.

Chainer hardly needed the Dragon's Blood smoke at all anymore, but he liked starting the match with it because it partially hid his actions. While Devon was soaring overhead, looking for an avenue of attack, and the ground troops were marching forward, Chainer shuddered and unleashed a razor-clawed harpy with his metal arm. The filthy, screeching bird-woman dropped greasy feathers as it rose into the air, rushing to meet Devon headlong.

Chainer then dropped his real arm down by his side and let a foot-long spider fall onto the arena floor. Chainer was sure no one noticed the arachnid as it scuttled to the edge of the pit and began making a wide arc toward the white-robed mage. In the pits, he thought, there is no place to avoid the match.

Kamahl, meanwhile, had charged into the advancing wedge of Order members and started hacking. His blade bounced off the megolith with no visible effect, but Kamahl was fast enough and his strokes wide enough to keep both foot soldiers at bay while he tried to find a seam in the stone thing's hide.

Chainer's harpy was doing better than he had expected. It had latched onto Devon's pike below the blade and was using its weight to drag the lieutenant down to the ground while it struck at him with her other claws. Devon tried to pound the harpy's grip loose, but it only clenched tighter. Chainer thought he knew why the officer hadn't simply dropped the pike.

Right on schedule, Devon waved his hand and cast a spell on his weapon. The point of his pike burst into white-hot flame, which blinded the harpy and seared its flesh. It screamed and reflexively released Devon's pike. The aven warrior promptly drove the weapon clean through the harpy's body. The harpy twitched, and Devon let gravity tear the gruesome husk loose. En route to the ground, the harpy disappeared. The crowd roared.

Devon wasted no time in celebration. He raised his pike overhead, screeched out a triumphant war cry, and dived toward Kamahl. As Devon dived, the megolith caught Kamahl's blade and then lowered its shoulder into Kamahl's chest. Kamahl grunted and staggered backward, but he managed to drop one of the foot soldiers as he went with an elbow across the bridge of the nose. Kamahl was now five feet away from the megolith and the remaining trooper, with Devon bearing down on him from above.

"Any time you're ready, partner," he shouted angrily. Chainer laughed, and then there was a scream from the Order mage at the far end of the floor. Chainer's spider had leaped onto her face, and she was struggling to keep its inch-long fangs from piercing her flesh. Without the mage's assistance, Devon lost control of his forward motion. Instead of swooping down at Kamahl, Devon was now simply falling out of the sky. There was a ripple of laughter and applause from the spectators.

"Leave the bird-man to me," Chainer readied a weighted chain. He whipped a smooth, rounded weight toward the falling aven. Devon tried to block the incoming chain with his pike, but he was off balance and out of position. The weight would have slammed into the point of his elongated chin, but Devon jerked his head aside at the last moment, and the heavy ball buried itself in his temple. Even Chainer winced at the sound.

The rest of the squad hesitated as Devon crashed lifeless to the arena floor. Kamahl drew a throwing axe from his back, charged it, and let it fly. It slammed into the megolith's chest and exploded, knocking the megolith back a step and the remaining foot soldier off his feet. Kamahl weathered the blast like an oak in a summer squall.

When the smoke and debris from the blast had settled, Chainer saw that the megolith was missing a huge scoop of stone from its chest. It was otherwise unaffected, however, and it resumed its exchange of blocks and blows with Kamahl. Annoyed, the barbarian sent a stream of liquid fire shooting from the end of his sword into the megolith's face, melting and distorting it. The stone beast pressed on. Like the golem that had killed Deidre, it really didn't need its eyes to fight.

Kamahl inexplicably dropped his sword then, and Chainer saw a look of confusion cross his partner's face. Both foot soldiers were on their feet again, and Kamahl made one last effort to pick his sword up, but it wouldn't budge. He was forced to dive away from it as the foot soldiers slashed at him with their weapons.

Chainer saw that the mage had managed to neutralize the spider and was in a prayer stance once more. She must have done something to Kamahl's sword. Chainer grew angry, both at himself for going easy on the mage, and at her for taking advantage of it. He positioned both hands and sent an eighteen-foot long python shooting across the arena. It latched onto the mage's arm with its venomless fangs and quickly wrapped her head and torso in its crushing coils.

Kamahl seemed angry, too, angrier than Chainer could remember. Most things that made Kamahl angry didn't last long enough to make him really angry, but the megolith seemed to have driven him over the edge. With flames shooting from his hands, he grabbed one of the foot soldiers by the throat and lifted him off the ground. The man's flesh sizzled and popped until Kamahl threw him into his fellow trooper, tangling both men into a painful, confused heap. The crowd oohed. Then Kamahl leaped onto the megolith and wrapped his huge hands around the thing's head.

"Kamahl, get off!" Chainer shook off visions of Deidre and readied another weighted chain. Kamahl was much faster than the megolith, however. He dug his superheated fingers into the stone giant's jawline, and Chainer saw two axe-shaped bursts of red form inside the megolith's torso. Kamahl dropped off just as the megolith reached up to crush him. Kamahl dove away, rolled, and conjured a large warhammer in each hand. He charged back at the megolith, ducked under its crushing fists, and brought both hammers together with a boom.

There was a seismic shudder that cracked the stone floor, and the axes planted in the megolith's chest exploded.

This blast was different from the previous one. It was three times as strong, for one, and doubly constrained by the megolith's own body and the powerful vibrations caused by the hammers. There was a muted flash and a muffled boom, and a network of cracks raced across the whole of its body. Smoke poured from its half-melted mouth. It was standing completely still. The crowd was silent.

"Chainer," Kamahl called. He pointed at the frozen warrior. "Give that thing one last tap, will you?"

Chainer sent his weight straight into the thing's chest without hesitation. The dense crystalline creature had been transformed by the intense heat and pressure of Kamahl's magic into something far more brittle. When Chainer's weight struck it, the husk of the defeated megolith shattered into a fine, white sand that was littered with a few larger shards of broken glass.

For a moment, there was no motion or sound on the arena floor. The foot soldiers were unconscious, Devon was dead, and the megolith was dust. Even the mage was completely helpless in the python's grip. If Chainer didn't call it off, she'd soon be a meal for a nightmare.

A single pair of hands started clapping from the stands. The applause grew, louder and louder until it was a roar. The competing chants of "Chainer!" and "Kamahl!" began.

"Your winners, ladies and gentlemen. . . . Chainer and Kamahl! This marks their twelfth consecutive win!"

As the announcer prattled on, Chainer went over to his partner. Kamahl looked at him sullenly.

"That was fun," the barbarian said, "but next time, you get the megolith."

Chainer laughed and slapped Kamahl on the shoulder. "Agreed." As the crowd continued to cheer and chant, he took Kamahl's hand in his and raised them both high in the air.

* * * * *

Veza floated once more in the forward cabin of the empress's transport. She was alone, unaccompanied but for a handful of scribes and a quartet of Llawan's savage barracuda bodyguards. There were no air breathers on board, so all of the leviathan's internal and external compartments had been flooded for this fact-finding mission.

Llawan moved quickly in the wake of Aboshan's death. She and her leviathan full of Mer aristocrats descended on the ruins of the imperial palace before the sand had settled, and she quickly installed herself at the hub of a rapidly spinning wheel of circumstance.

While her servants led chants of "the emperor is dead! Long live the Empress!" in the public byways, her peers stirred up support among the rich and influential. Llawan herself addressed the population as a whole, rallying her subjects via magical broadcast and bulletins posted throughout the empire. Her message was direct: Aboshan was dead, and his policies should be interred with his bones. The widowed empress announced a lavish funeral for her husband to be held at an undetermined time in the future. On that same day she staged a rally wherein all of Aboshan's informers were chained at the neck and driven out of the capitol, and all his secret surveillance files were publicly destroyed.

While the common citizen embraced her return, Llawan was less popular among the merchants and generals. The trading sector of Mer society had never done better than they did under Aboshan. As long as the imperial transaction tax was paid in advance, Aboshan's government was extremely friendly to all forms of commerce. He controlled the trade routes to and from Mer population centers, and those who paid for the privilege were allowed to move and sell their goods unmolested. All others were usually attacked by bandits—who wore imperial uniforms—beaten, and robbed down to the clothes they wore. Aboshan had made it extremely profitable to do business with him and extremely dangerous to do otherwise. For the pragmatic capitalists of Mer, it was a comfortable situation, one that they were not eager to change.

So while Llawan held meetings and exerted influence and tested loyalties, Veza was sent to inspect the newly formed Otaria Chasm. By all estimates, an area of over a thousand square miles of land was now a half a mile below the surface, and the northern tip of Otaria had become an island. No one had done a complete survey of the new sea, but there were bound to be some human settlements, people, and animals who had been caught in the catastrophe. The law of the sea said that anything below the waves is Mer territory, however, and Llawan was eager to have this new addition to her empire explored, catalogued, and quantified. In the name of the empress, Veza was commanding the survey mission.

A cephalid officer and Olsham the mystic swam into the chamber. "M'lady Veza," Olsham said. "We are approaching the chasm. It is time."

Veza stared straight ahead. "I will return to the bridge once we've made visual contact." The officer swam out, and Veza floated alongside Olsham in silence while the mystic softly clicked and keened to himself.

The great wound Aboshan had made in the above-air continent slowly materialized out of the murky waters ahead. Veza shook her head as Olsham's prayers increased in pitch and volume. The chasm was huge, so wide that Veza couldn't even see the opposite wall from where she stood. She remembered the shock wave that had passed through Llawan's transport. Whatever caused the cave-in must have forced millions upon millions of gallons of water out of the area. As soon as the initial force was spent and the ground had finished caving, those same millions of gallons had rushed in to fill the new valley.

Olsham stopped chanting and opened his eyes. "Please excuse me, ma'am. I would like you to return to the bridge now." Veza started to object, but Olsham said, "Please. Go. I will perform the ritual alone."

Veza nodded, then darted down the connecting chamber into the belly of the ship. The captain was waiting for her on the bridge.

"We're ready to enter the chasm, ma'am. Is the spellcaster ready?"

"He's performing the ritual now. How long till we get there?"

"If we maintain our present course and speed, about half an hour."

"That should be plenty of time. When Olsham is done, this ship will be Llawan's eye, recording everything that passes around it. The crystal gemstone Olsham had installed will store it. All we have to do is cover the distance, and the empress will have a complete and detailed survey of the area."

The cephalid captain scowled. "I hope it's going to be that easy, ma'am. Any idea what we're going to find in there?"

Veza shook her head. "But," she added, "nobody does. That's why we're here."

* * * * *

Olsham completed his telemetry ritual and teleported himself back to Llawan City shortly before the leviathan entered the chasm. The ship and the crew were in top form, and they made excellent progress through the first two-thirds of the sunken zone.

Veza knew the ship was collecting and transmitting volumes and volumes of information back to the empress, but as far as she could see, the canyon contained little more than a strong current and its own stark, rugged beauty. The forward chamber commanded impressive views of sunken rock formations and a remarkably wide assortment of colorful seaweed and small fish. She would have to study the data she had gathered, but unless there was some hidden treasure, the chasm was little more than a scenic cruise.

"What in nine hells is that?"

Veza had been spending most of her time on the bridge with the captain, helping him plot the best course for the empress's purposes. The scrying screens weren't as picturesque as the forward cabin, but the screens could provide a view in any direction. Currently, they were looking forward and starboard, where a large, shadowy form was coming straight at them.

"It's a large animal, sir," one of the crew called out. "Undetermined species."

"Captain," Veza said. "Is it a natural phenomenon? Could a large predator already have staked out a territory this far in?"

The captain shrugged. "It's possible. Change course."

"It's still closing, sir. Captain, I think it's a razor ray."

The captain nodded grimly. "I think you're right."

On screen, the huge, black manta grew larger and larger. It was almost as large as the leviathan, with bony spines alongside its head that jutted forward like horns. Its tail ended in a curved barb like a scorpion's and had two red poison sacs visible at the base. Veza knew these vicious animals had first been bred hundreds of years ago, when the dominant sea powers all employed living warships.

The rays had become more specialized and horrible since then. Most leviathans had an innate primal fear of the rays, so that even they avoided being gored or envenomed, and even the larger ships often panicked and quit the field.

"Can you give me a better view of its markings?" Veza said.

"What for? Get out of my way, woman."

Veza caught the captain by the shoulder. "Captain," she said. "This is still my mission."

Grudgingly, the captain ordered a closer view of the razor ray. The monster's wings had been dyed royal blue, and its two longest horns had been capped with silver. Across its belly, it bore the Mer characters for "land" and "sea" all emblazoned over by a huge stylized letter 'L.'

"Laquatus," Veza said. Then, in a louder voice, "Empress, if you can hear me—Laquatus got here first."

* * * * *

The leviathan's handlers screamed a split second before the ship rolled violently.

"We're hit, sir," called a crewmember. "A second razor ray just stung the carapace around the head. The leviathan was not hurt."

"She's panicking!" one of the handlers cried. "Do something!"

The ship launched into escape speed before the captain even gave the order. The cephalid handlers on the creature's brain were straining to keep her from fleeing at top speed until she was too tired to swim any farther.

"Evasive action!" the captain yelled. "Go, helmsman, go!" The leviathan surged away from the second ray, which followed close behind. Farther on, the first ray remained out of the chase and out of harm's way.

"Can we outrun them?" Veza asked.

"For a short time, but we'll get tired first."

"Can we fight?"

The captain shook his head. "We can ram them, but their stingers won't miss again. They only need about five seconds of contact to kill a ship this size."

Veza looked hard at the screen, then back at the captain. "How deep are we?"

"Doesn't matter. They can go as deep as we can."

"I don't want to go deeper. I want to go up."

The captain clicked something derogatory. "This is a deep sea vessel, ma'am."

"I know captain. But it's also a fish. Is this fish agile as well as fast?"

"She can turn back on herself without missing a stroke."

"Glad to hear it. Tell me, then, does this fish . . . breach?"

Realization sparked in the captain's eye, and he smiled at Veza. "Helm," he called. "Point the nose straight up. Maximum possible speed." He swam over to the ship's handlers to make sure they understood precisely what was expected of them.

The leviathan lurched and shot up though the chasm waters toward the surface. To Veza, it felt like gravity had shifted ninety degrees.

"Give me an aft view." The screen showed the ray close behind, accelerating to keep up with the leviathan's sudden burst of speed.

"We're almost at the surface, sir."

"Forward view." The screen now showed the surface, rushing toward them like a great liquid field.

"Maintain course and speed. On my mark, I want this vessel tucked and pointed straight down, back at the water."

"Aye, sir." The leviathan broke the surface and shot high into the air. The screen showed a huge wash of spray and painfully bright sunshine. Clouds in the sky rolled around the screen.

"Everyone hang on. Mark!"

Guided by her handlers, the ship wrenched itself into a U, then snapped back into its streamlined shape with its nose pointed downward. Veza, two crewmembers, and a handler were tossed around the bridge like beans in a can. Gravity quickly overcame the ship's motion, and the leviathan dropped back toward the sea.

Below, the razor ray had stopped just below the surface, confused about its prey's disappearance. The viewscreen showed a massive shadow fall over the submerged ray just before the leviathan's bony carapace came crashing down on it—with all twenty tons of leviathan behind it.

The scrying screen went black until the captain barked, "Aft view."

Behind them, the remains of the razor ray were no longer recognizable as anything that had ever been alive. A small cheer went up.

"Back to your stations!" the captain said. Before the crew could regain control of the leviathan, however, a blue-green beam lanced out of the second ray, the one with the silver horns. The beam splayed across the length of Llawan's transport, though there was no immediate reaction.

"Resume evasive action. Helm, get us deeper into the chasm."

"Helm is not responding, sir."

The captain swore. "Handlers?"

One of the robed cephalids swam up. "The ship is entangled, sir. She is blocked on all sides and cannot move."

"Damn." He looked angrily at Veza.

"What's wrong?"

"He's tangled us in sargassum. Whatever that spell beam was, it covered us in enough seaweed to choke this vessel dead in the water."

Veza struggled to think of something, anything, that would help them. She was interrupted by Laquatus's amplified voice.

"Greetings, Mer survey vessel. This is Laquatus. Prepare to be boarded."

The captain lowered his head, then lashed out at the console before him. Veza steeled herself for a reunion with the ambassador. On the screen, a half-dozen more vessels and behemoths swam into view, each wearing the ambassador's standard.

"And if the empress is by chance on board," Laquatus said, "let me add a hearty 'welcome' from the next Emperor of Mer."

CHAPTER 16

Kamahl and Chainer stood before the First, in the public reception hall of the manor. The First was dressed formally, with full robes and headdress, and he sat on a tall throne surrounded by his hand and skull attendants. Skellum stood beaming between the First and the fighters with the Master of the Games behind him.

"Twelve wins in a row," the First said. "Quite impressive."

"Thank you, Pater." Chainer said. He nudged Kamahl.

"Right. Thanks." The barbarian was clearly uncomfortable in such a fine room. He looked longingly at the door.

"But now, I'm afraid, the winning streak must end."

"Of course, Pater."

"What?"

Skellum and Chainer glanced at Kamahl. The barbarian was genuinely confused, on the point of becoming angry.

"It's all for the best," the Master of the Games said. "We're going to put you two up against another crusat squad from the Order. They'll win, become bolder, and start sending more teams into Cabal City. People are nervous with all the changes in leadership around here. They like seeing simple fights they can understand and root for. A barbarian and a Cabalist going up against toy soldiers, over and over again. You win some, they win some. It's familiar to crowds. Comfortable."

"I agree," Kamahl said, "but I don't lose on purpose."

"We're the house team," Chainer spoke quickly to fill in the uncomfortable silence. "And the house never loses. Not in the long run."

Kamahl made a rude noise. "That's dreck. If you don't win, you lose. Period."

"Would it help," the First said calmly, "to think of this as a strategic withdrawal? You'd be letting the Order have a small victory, so that you can secure a larger one later?"

Kamahl shook his head. "I don't fight to lose. I don't think I know how."

The First steepled his fingers. "Not even if the larger victory we're waiting for includes the Mirari?"

Chainer and Kamahl both perked up at the mention of the artifact's name. The Mirari hadn't been offered as a prize since Fulla brought it back from Mer.

"You're planning another Mirari games, Pater?"

"Yes, my child. And soon."

"But we need the right kind of build-up," the Master of the Games broke in. "The Order has to feel there's a chance of them winning. If they take down our best two-man team, they'll be sure to come back."

Kamahl shook his head again. "No deal." Chainer shot Skellum an agonized look, but Skellum could only look back with sympathy.

"Forgive us, honored guest," said the Master of the Games, "but the team of Kamahl and Chainer is going to lose their next bout. It has been arranged."

"Then the team of Kamahl and Chainer will not compete." Kamahl glanced at Chainer, then spoke to the First. "You have been an excellent host, Cabal First, but I am from a different tradition. I'm here to fight. I'm here to win the Mirari with strength, speed, and skill. When you decide to offer it up, I will be ready to work for it. But until then, count me out of these games you play to increase the audience and drive up the odds."

The Master of the Games started to speak, but the First interrupted. "I am truly sorry you feel that way."

"As am I. I mean no offense, but I was raised and trained never to do less than my best."

"You are a barbarian of principles," the First said. "But if you are not going to support our agenda for the next games, I'm going to have to ask you to excuse yourself. We have Cabal business to discuss."

Kamahl nodded, glanced at Chainer, and then stomped out, his heavy boots echoing down the hall with each step.

When the footsteps had gone, Chainer said, "Forgive him, Pater."

"There is nothing to forgive. He is set in his ways, and we must find someone else to fight in his place. I only regret that we won't be able to rely on him as an ally."

"He is still our ally, Pater. He just—"

"Chainer," Skellum interrupted. "We're not here to discuss your unwilling partner."

Chainer's face fell. "No, Master."

"Master of the Games," the First said. "Can Chainer alone deliver the result we're seeking?"

"Yes, Pater."

"Master Skellum. Is your pupil ready to provide that result? And will he survive it?"

"Yes, Pater." Chainer and Skellum spoke together.

"Nothing fancy," the Master of the Games told Chainer. "Just get in there and roll over. It doesn't need to be a good fight, it just needs to be an Order victory."

"Understood," Chainer said.

"Master of the Games, you are dismissed."

"Thank you, Pater." She slipped quickly out of the room.

Chainer stood nervously before the First. Skellum fiddled with his hat beneath his arm. The First watched them both through steepled fingers.

"You have something to add, Master Skellum?"

Skellum cleared his throat. "I do, Pater. Chainer has made excellent progress as a caster. There is only one more thing I can teach him, one more lesson before he graduates from my academy."

Chainer fought off a gulp of surprise. This was news to him.

"This would be the dementist's *shikar* you've mentioned?"

Skellum began to walk back and forth, between Chainer and the First. "Yes, Pater. It is a rite of passage. A spiritual journey combined with a physical trial." He pulled himself up to his full height and spoke with as much dignity as he could muster. "It is something that separates dementists from mere casters."

"I am familiar with the ritual. Yours was a great success, if I'm not mistaken."

Skellum beamed. "Thank you, Pater."

"And you believe your student is ready for this trial."

"I do, Pater. As his mentor, I would want to accompany him. For the last time, of course. When we return from shikar, there will be nothing left for me to teach him."

"How long does it take?"

"Two days to walk to the site. Three days of trial. Two days to return."

The First considered. "Very well. As soon as Chainer discharges his obligation with the Order, you and he will take a leave of absence from the pits. You will experience shikar."

"Thank you, Pater."

"Thank you, Master," Chainer whispered. Skellum glared at him, but winked also.

181

"There is one final thing," the First said, "concerning the Mirari. Doubtless by now you are both aware that my predictions came true. The Mirari led to major upheavals in both the Order and Mer, and then it came back to us. I made one error, however. I expected the past few months to thin the field, as it were, but just the opposite is true. More and more people are following its trail, which will lead them here. This is both good and bad for the Cabal. Even as we speak, the crusat death squads are reforming in an effort to drive us out of our strongholds. Cabal City, Aphetto . . . even our minor pits in no-name villages are being targeted. They make the same old claims. We corrupt the innocent, mock the law, and generally impede the Order's righteous progress.

"The era of coexistence is over. When you return from shikar, you both will assist me in neutralizing the crusat threat."

"With pleasure, Pater."

Skellum whispered teasingly to Chainer, "A dementist at last."

"Ambassador Laquatus also continues to seek the Mirari. Today he contacted one of the crusat officers to sound him out for an alliance against us. It would be best if we could fix his attention elsewhere while we sort out the Order problem ourselves."

"We could postpone shikar, Pater."

"No, Skellum. Chainer's apprenticeship is over. It's time we made that official."

"You have something in mind, Pater?"

"I do. Since Laquatus will not stop complicating the situation until he gets a crack at the Mirari, I will announce the next games immediately. They will be held in three month's time, to coincide with the anniversary of the founding of Cabal City. The Mirari will be the grand prize, awarded to the strongest fighter in the pits. Laquatus is currently in need of a thrall. Apparently his amphibian was killed along with Aboshan. With the games scheduled, he will redouble his efforts to find a replacement thrall. This alone would not be enough to occupy a busy mind like Laquatus's, but this on top of . . . other circumstances I have yet to arrange . . . it will more than suffice.

"Chainer, I want you to meet with the ambassador to determine what sort of creature he wants. Promise him anything, but do nothing without my permission. In three days you and Skellum will begin the shikar. We will ask Laquatus to wait until you return before you create this new thrall for him."

"Laquatus will have more and better options for his thrall after Chainer experiences shikar," Skellum said.

"So much the better. Chainer. You have been a valued and trusted servant of the Cabal. Are you ready to be rewarded and carry our cause even further?"

"I am, Pater."

"Outstanding."

The First waved his hand dismissively. "The Cabal is everywhere," he said, "and so are my thoughts. You may leave me now to my meditation, my children."

The First watched Skellum and Chainer go through dry, milky eyes. Before they were even out of the room, his thoughts folded in on themselves as he dissected each infinitesimal bit of information.

Apart from Kamahl's refusal, everything was right where the First wanted it. The barbarian was absolutely devastating in combat and always made for a good show. He was also useful as an influence on Chainer. Skellum was in danger of spoiling the boy, blunting his killer instinct. Kamahl encouraged that rough, pragmatic side of Chainer, qualities he was going to need over the next three months.

The First came back to himself. Yes, the longer he considered it, the more sure he became. Skellum should stand aside and let Kamahl complete Chainer's training. With his mentor at his side, Chainer would simply become another Skellum. Teamed with Kamahl, he would return from shikar as the ancient ritual intended, as a hunter. A predator. A dangerous adversary and a valuable friend.

The First waved and a skull attendant came forward. "The mentor must set his pupil aside," he said, and the attendant copied the words onto a tablet she wore on a cord around her neck.

A knock sounded from outside the chamber. The First called, "Enter," and a hand attendant came forward bearing a silver mirror on a silk pillow. The First waved the attendant forward, and the shuffling man ascended the throne. He held the mirror up to the First's face, abjectly turning his aside.

In the mirror, a cephalid's face filled the screen. "Hail to you, Cabal Patriarch."

"You honor me, Empress Llawan. How fares the empire?"

"It fares well. Have you considered our proposal?"

"I have, Empress. I have not yet reached a decision."

"But you will continue to extend your . . . hospitality to Ambassador Laquatus?"

"As we agreed."

Llawan turned one eye to the mirror. "And the Cabal will remain neutral as we transition back into public service?"

"The Cabal has no interest in the internal affairs of the Mer empire," the First assured her. "Our relationship with all concerned parties is merely professional."

"Very well," Llawan pulled back, framing her face in the mirror. "But remember that relationships with the deep are not like those on dry land. You don't build a relationship like a house, you ride it like a wave. The wave is always changing, always moving. You must be very careful when you get off, or on."

The First smiled graciously. "Words I have already taken to heart. We have far more in common than you suspect, Empress."

"We hope so, Patriarch. We hope so." Llawan's image faded.

The First dismissed the mirror-bearing attendant, steepled his fingers under his chin, and sat in silent meditation for a time. When he next moved, it was to speak to his attendants.

"Send for the Master of the Games."

* * * * *

"Veza," Laquatus said. "This is truly a most unexpected surprise. I came to collect the empress's survey data. I didn't expect to collect her pet mermaid as well."

The captain and crew had resisted when Laquatus removed the recording crystal, but they were easily subdued by the ambassador's human mercenaries. Each had been armed and enchanted for underwater work, and Veza recognized several pirate clan tattoos among them. There was also some kind of living statue that had taken Turg's place at Laquatus's side.

"Take Director Veza to my ship," Laquatus said. "Bind the others and put them in the brig. I want this leviathan gutted and towed back to where it came in."

"Can we feed 'er to the rays, sir?"

"By all means. But save the head carapace. Hang it at the mouth of the chasm as a warning." Laquatus followed Veza as she was led out. She saw him whisper something to the purple statue, and the statue nodded, then stayed behind.

They led her to Laquatus's ray, where they untied her wrists and feet and locked her in a chamber. Before too long, Laquatus himself came to join her.

"I must apologize," he said, "but we are inches away from a full-blown civil war. I had actually hoped the information from your survey would calm some of the passions that are running so high. Alas, it seems that this chasm is another item Llawan and I must quarrel over." He stared hard at Veza. "Have you become more fluid, my dear, as I suggested?"

"If you mean, am I ready to join your side, the answer is no."

"I don't think you've thought this through, so I'll give you another chance to answer." Laquatus leaned forward to clear a floating strand of hair out of Veza's face, but she swatted his hand aside. He smiled.

"Why are you so loyal to the empress? She sent you into harm's way through sheer ignorance. She is not worthy of your loyalty. And besides, she holds no such love for you or any of our kind."

" 'Our kind,' Ambassador? What is our kind?"

"The adaptable," he said instantly. "Those of us who can respond quickly to changing circumstances. Those of us who continually define ourselves." He crouched next to her where she sat. "Let me help you, Veza. Trust in me half as much as you trust in Llawan, and I will never abandon you, as she has."

"Llawan has not abandoned me."

"Hasn't she?" Laquatus brought a blue mirror out of his robe. He held it before his face and said, "Empress Llawan?"

The empress's face soon appeared. "What do you want, pretender?"

"I have captured your spy vessel in Otaria Chasm. Your ship and its crew will be executed at dawn."

"If you damage a single scale on our leviathan," Llawan raged, "we will crucify you on the ocean's floor."

Laquatus glanced at Veza, making sure she was listening to the exchange. "What's that, Your Majesty? No concern for the crew?"

"If you have taken our crew, then they are already dead."

"Not at all, Empress." He turned the mirror to face Veza. "Your valued advisor from Breaker Bay is chatting with me now." Laquatus gave the two women the briefest glimpse of each other before turning the mirror back to his own face. "Will you barter for her life, at least?"

"We grow weary of your voice, Laquatus. If you have a point, make it."

"A trade. The leviathan and the mermaid in exchange for the chasm."

Llawan clicked angrily. "No. We are sorry to lose our leviathan and our friend Veza. But we will come for their bodies soon, Laquatus, and when we do, you will surely fall. This audience is over."

Laquatus smiled at the darkened glass and casually placed the mirror back in his robes. He closed his eyes for a moment, then turned to Veza.

"I'd say you are officially abandoned, Director. So now, the question is to you." A knock sounded, and Laquatus's featureless man came in with a heavy sack over his shoulder.

"Will you take my hand and help the Mer empire reach the very pinnacle of its power and prestige?" He took the sack from his servant. "Thank you, Burke.

"Or will you remain loyal to Llawan, who has endangered and abandoned you?" Laquatus opened the sack and pulled it away from its contents. The heads of the leviathan's bridge crew floated freely in the chamber between Laquatus and Veza. "I apologize for the rudeness of the message, but the question is pressing. Who shall you serve?"

Veza looked at the ghastly display, then Burke's expressionless face, then Laquatus's confident smile.

"If the chasm has a hidden value," she said, "I can help you secure it."

"Excellent." Laquatus extended his hands, and Veza rose to take them. "We should begin at once."

CHAPTER 17

Skellum made the short walk from the manor to the academy. He was looking forward to his dinner, but he was looking forward to the shikar with Chainer even more. He had trained dozens of young Cabalists, one at a time, and he was usually somewhat melancholy at this stage of the program. The vast majority of his students never went on shikar. Instead, they were hurled into the pits as soon as they could reliably create monsters, an arrangement that served the Cabal's needs for warm bodies in the pits far better than it served Skellum's perfectionist nature. Chainer, however, would be his crowning achievement as a Master Dementist.

The First had meddled, as he always did, but Skellum knew that

188

in this case the First's interest was well justified. He had something special in mind for Chainer from the very beginning, and though Skellum could only guess at what that might be, he was proud to have been a part of it. He was proud of his student, proud of his program, and proud of himself.

The Master of the Games was waiting outside of Skellum's office with a fixer Skellum recognized as Louche and a pair of hulking stalkers.

"The Cabal is here," Skellum called.

"Do you recognize this seal?" The Master of the Games stiffly handed Skellum a scroll with an ornate wax seal on it.

"It's from the First."

"Read it, please."

Skellum took the scroll and scanned it. It was a short statement, and it didn't take him long. He read it twice, then looked up at the Master of the Games.

"Is this a joke?"

"No joke, Master Skellum. The First has requested you to take your student's place in the pits this evening."

"But I'm not a—"

"He knew you would understand."

Skellum's ire began to rise, and the Master of the Games took a step back.

"I will see the First now," Skellum said. He looked up at the stalkers, one a saber-toothed ogre and the other a half-zombified merman with three crushing octopus tentacles on each shoulder instead of arms. The ogre, still alive and alert, took a step back from the smaller man's glare.

"Very well," said the Master of the Games, and she hurled a handful of grayish powder in Skellum's face. His hat blocked most of it, but enough got through to cover his eyes and clog his nose and throat. Skellum swooned but did not fall. With his cape wrapped around his arm, he took two staggering steps forward, as

189

elegantly as he could, and pressed his back against the wall.

Then he slid to the floor, unconscious.

* * * * *

"Forgive me, Master Skellum." The First stood alone in his private chambers, surrounded by black candles. Skellum straightened his cape and got to his feet.

"I'm afraid I really must insist," the First was saying. "You must trust in me. This will be for the best."

"But I've done nothing wrong. I've been a valued and loyal servant all my life."

The First came forward. "And you shall remain so, even after death."

Skellum looked around the darkened room. It was far too lonely and silent without all the guards and attendants.

"Pater," he said. "I don't understand."

"You don't have to, my son. I do." The First offered his hand to Skellum, and the dementist recoiled.

"Go ahead," the First urged. "None of this is real, and no harm can come to you."

"Pater, I—"

"Take my hand, Cybariss."

Skellum woodenly stepped forward and took hold of the First's cold, gray fingers. There was no pain. There was no stench. None of the things that were rumored to occur when someone touched the First happened.

"You see?" The First smiled. He pulled Skellum in close in a full, two-armed hug.

"Go now," the First whispered. "Obey me. Honor the Cabal, and serve Kuberr."

"I will, Pater."

"Outstanding."

The First released his hand, and Skellum fell back, into a soft, silent void of darkness and mist.

* * * * *

"Master Skellum."

Skellum opened his eyes. Louche, the Master of the Games, and the stalkers were looming over him.

"Are you ready to go now?"

"I am," Skellum said. He gave his hat a test spin and gracefully rose to his feet. He brushed a few imaginary bits of fluff from his cape as they led him out the front door and back toward the pits, keeping his head high, his eyes clear, and his pace measured. He was determined that no one who saw him would have the slightest idea that he was a prisoner.

* * * * *

"Ladies and gentlemen, making his triumphant return to the Cabal City pits . . . Master Skellum!"

Skellum stood alone in the pits. At least they hadn't called him "caster."

"Joining Skellum, and fresh from her recent tour of the deepest parts of the Mer empire . . . Caster Fulla!"

The crowd cheered and hooted as Fulla stalked angrily out onto the pit floor. Skellum knew her, of course. She was one of the best casters ever to take the floor, but they moved in different circles, and he had rarely interacted with her. By reputation, she was either manic from the joy of battle, or she was playful like a mischievous child. Today, she just seemed annoyed.

"Skellum?" she said.

"Fulla."

"What in nine hells is going on? I wasn't scheduled to go back in the pits until tomorrow."

"It seems we have been chosen to throw this match with the Order."

Fulla scowled. "The First is wise. But I thought you didn't do this sort of thing."

"I don't." Skellum spun his hat as the announcer introduced the competition.

". . . and their opponents, here to expose the Cabal's weakness and corruption . . . and in the process, earn a slot in the upcoming Mirari games, I present Major Teroh, Sergeant Baankis, and Justicar Gobal of the Order!"

The crowd booed, and Skellum blinked behind his spinning hat. "Did he say 'Baankis?'"

"Who cares? I just want to get this over with." She drew her sword, ran her thumb along its edge, and said, "Say, what's a justicar?"

"Tonight, the Order team will be joined by Yewma the druid and her mandrill wolf-monkeys. Place your bets, ladies and gentlemen, place your bets."

Skellum noticed that Fulla's wide eyes were such a light shade of blue that they almost seemed white. Then he realized she had asked him a question, and he glanced across the pit at the Order team. He recognized Teroh and Baankis, despite the thin beard Baankis had grown and the new insignia on his robes. The justicar stood ramrod straight on Baankis's left. He was a tall, muscular, partially armored figure whose face was hidden behind a gleaming helm and visor. Yewma was tall and wiry and carried a gnarled staff made of what appeared to be an entire sapling with the roots trimmed off. She wore the roots wound tightly around each forearm like a pair of wooden gauntlets. Yewma stood next to a large wooden box that had small, barred windows on each side. The box shook and rattled as the creatures inside jostled one another and screamed.

"I don't know what a justicar is," Skellum said, "but it looks kind of like a knight."

The prep horn sounded after the announcer's final word, and Skellum spun his hat again. He achieved a dementia trance by juxtaposing images of the world around him with the darkness provided by his hat. Then he projected his own internal landscape onto the darkness and spun the hat faster until the world within merged with the world without. When that happened, his head became an actual doorway through which he could release his monsters.

In this case, however, he had too much to keep track of in the real world. There were too many opponents for Skellum to find the footing he needed to go into dementia space, and having Fulla as a partner further distracted him. Also, he couldn't clear his head of thoughts of Chainer. I'm going to die, he realized, even though I'm rich and handsome. Even though there will be no one to protect my prize student.

The starting horn sounded. Fulla let out a yell, Yewma opened her box, and the toy soldiers drew and advanced.

The druid had unleashed eight large, baboonlike primates, each over seventy pounds and armed with a long canine snout capable of crushing stone. Colorful fur wreathed their heads and shoulders, and they screamed like lunatics turned loose in a graveyard. They were the wild predators of the deep woods, chasing down their quarry and tearing it to pieces as an organized pack. Skellum wasn't sure what Yewma had bewitched them with, but the druid was careful to leap out of their line of sight once she had opened the box.

Skellum spun his hat faster and faster. It was the only weapon he had. Fulla, meanwhile, had created a zombified rhino and a small, hissing hydra. The rhino charged directly at the Order trio, but she had to drive the hydra forward with her sword before it joined the battle.

When the rhino was twenty feet away and closing, the justicar raised his hands over his head and clapped them together. A bolt of the purest white lightning leaped from the point of contact to the rhino's body and the zombified hulk literally exploded, raining fetid flesh all over the arena. Fulla swore and charged forward herself, driving the hydra as she went.

The largest mandrill came straight at Skellum, while the others formed an attack column behind him. Two of the group broke off and circled wide around him on either side, and the main body slowed to allow them to get into position for an all-out assault. They never stopped whooping and screaming.

Skellum's view of the arena started to shudder and melt, the first signs of the trance. He opened his eyes wider, never more desperate to find that other world within and disappear inside.

* * * * *

Chainer waited outside the First's chamber until a hand attendant came to admit him. He had never been alone with the First before, and he was eager to make a good impression without Skellum to run interference for him, or Kamahl to cover for. Of course, the First was always surrounded by his attendants, but once you got used to them it was easy to overlook them as separate entities.

Inside the chamber, Chainer was disappointed to see someone other than the First and his attendants waiting. He was a tall man, slightly blue, with small silver horns. Chainer recognized him but waited for the formal introduction.

"Ambassador Laquatus of Mer," the First said, "meet Chainer, one of our best dementists-in-training."

Laquatus looked Chainer over and disdainfully held out his hand, knuckles up, for Chainer to take. "Charmed." he said.

Chainer slapped his metal hand on top of the merman's and his other hand below. He forced the ambassador's hand perpendicular to the floor and shook it vigorously, disarranging the ambassador's carefully wrapped robe.

"The pleasure's all mine, Ambassador." Laquatus quickly withdrew his hand as soon as Chainer released it. Chainer smiled pleasantly at the merman.

"We were just discussing the future of Otaria," the First said. "Grand stuff, but it has to start somewhere. Ambassador Laquatus and I are starting it here and now."

"The Mer Empire is the sea, " Laquatus said, "and Cabal City is a port city. We have always had much in common."

The First scowled slightly but went on. "But not enough in common, unfortunately. I was just describing how the crusat raids have begun again and how disruptive they are to business."

"The Mer Empire is always concerned about maintaining the flow of commerce between the land and the depths."

The First waited patiently for Laquatus to finish. "But not concerned enough," he added.

"You have to understand, Patriarch," Laquatus said, "the Empire has a long, solid relationship with the Order. They aren't like you. They don't have a single ruler who speaks for them all with a single voice. While one division prepares for crusat, the others are merely trying to rebuild. Morally and economically, I cannot turn my back on the entire Order."

Chainer choked back a snort when the Ambassador said, "morally," and he saw the shadow of a smile on the First's lips, too.

"I would never ask you to do something so drastic as to turn your back on the entire Order," the First said. "Indeed, even we don't want the Order to be wiped out entirely. Do we, Chainer?"

"No, Pater," Chainer's tone belied his words. "Not at all."

"We simply want there to be peace between our two groups. Civilized people don't kill each other because of philosophical differences. I was hoping I could convince the ambassador to join us in censuring the Order. Lodging official protests over the crusat. Demanding restitution from Bretath, if he ever returns to this region. Perhaps, Ambassador" the First said, "it isn't your relationship with the Order that needs to be solidified. It's your relationship with the Cabal."

Laquatus smiled greedily. "You have something in mind, Patriarch?"

"I do. You recently lost your champion, did you not? And while it served you well, and was formidable in combat, it was never as . . . refined as a man of your stature requires."

"Turg was an excellent jack," Laquatus said. "He is sorely missed."

"What if my young dementist here were to provide you with a new champion? As I say, he's one of our best."

"A most generous offer," Laquatus said, "but if we really want to strengthen the bond between us, might I suggest something even more valuable?" With the exception of the First's attendants, everyone in the room knew what he meant. Chainer's fists clenched.

"The Mirari has already been slated as the grand prize in the Cabal City Games, to be held three months from now. My apologies, Ambassador. It is no longer mine to offer. But please," he gestured at Chainer to step up, "accept a new familiar from us. As a gesture of good faith."

Chainer came forward. "I can make you forget the frog," he said. "Tell me what you need, and the Cabal will produce it."

Laquatus looked him over once more. "It must be powerful. Unbeatable."

"Then it will be."

"It must be obedient. Minimal intelligence, highly developed instincts."

"Then it will be."

"It must be mobile. Able to accompany me wherever I go, above ground or below the sea."

"It will be."

Laquatus looked to the First. "When?"

The First smiled. "Regrettably, Chainer is unavailable for the next week or so. But as soon as he returns, he will be at your disposal."

Chainer watched the merman building a timeline in his head. "Can't he start now?"

"Alas, no. He is still recovering from injuries suffered in the pits." Laquatus finished calculating. "A week, then. With your permission, Patriarch, I will stay on in the guest house and continue to enjoy the sights and sounds of Cabal City while I wait for the boy to heal."

"Outstanding. Now, if you will excuse us, Chainer has a report to make."

Laquatus was slow to leave, but the hand attendants gathered around him and firmly led him to the door. Chainer knew he could speak freely, for the First's attendants always escorted his guests all the way out into the street. Laquatus was just the kind to try to linger behind in order to eavesdrop. He shuddered, overcome by a fit of revulsion for the fawning politician.

Once Laquatus was gone, the First spoke to Chainer casually. Not as an intimate, but as a peer. "I'm sorry to call you away from the pits, Caster Chainer, but the ambassador needed seeing to. It was not difficult to arrange for your replacement."

"I am your obedient child, Pater." Chainer suddenly smelled Dragon's Blood. The First watched him with mild interest as the boy began sniffing the air.

"Is something wrong?"

"No, Pater. It's just that . . ." He sniffed again, absently looking behind him, above him, all around. "Something's . . . pulling me. Do you smell incense?"

"This room is scented daily."

"No, I mean . . . this room reeks of Dragon's Blood. Can't you smell it?"

"Perhaps you should take a moment to gather yourself, Caster Chainer. You're not making sense."

Chainer cried out and slammed the palms of his hands into his forehead. He smelled the smoke, he felt the black sand beneath his feet, he saw the mustard sky. . . .

"Chainer," Skellum's voice said. It was high pitched, buzzing with distortion. It cut through Chainer's head like a blade.

"Skellum?" Chainer said, as the First's hand attendant slapped him for the third time. Chainer broke the man's collarbone with his metal fist, shoved him back, and bolted for the door. Two brawny killers leaped out of the shadows and took him down before he went four steps.

"Don't harm him." The First spoke loudly but calmly. "Mazeura," he whispered, hissing the secret name and freezing Chainer in mid-struggle. "What is the meaning of this?"

"Skellum," Chainer said. He was immobile beneath the weight of the First's guards and the power of his secret name on the First's lips.

* * * * *

The lead wolf-monkey stopped five feet from Skellum and bared its teeth. Behind it, the rest of the troop chattered and pounded the ground. Skellum himself stood with his hand raised, as if in greeting. With a start, the dementist master came back to the pit and saw the wolf-monkeys closing in. The crowd booed his complete lack of motion.

Skellum stopped his hat with a gap in front. The leader was tensing for its charge. Skellum smiled amiably.

"Animal," he said. The leader snarled, then dove for Skellum's face. Before its slashing fangs could latch on, however, the vortex in Skellum's head boomed and a smoking comet erupted out of his hat and crashed into the wolf-monkey. It was a near-formless horror, all shadows and teeth, but it devoured the lead mandrill whole in a single bite. It hissed, and snapped at another wolf-monkey. Then it began to fade.

"How are you doing, Skellum?" Fulla was bedeviling Major Teroh with a pair of wolf-headed spiders and was beating Sgt. Baankis back with her gladius. She crowed happily and unleashed a zombie centaur at the justicar. Yewma cried out in horror when she saw Fulla's latest contribution, and the wolf-monkeys reoriented on the caster.

"Better now," Skellum said, the sing-song quality of his voice resonating in his own head. "I've got a lot on my mind, however." He spat out four small comets in rapid succession, each transforming in midair. While the pack of wolf-monkeys howled and gibbered toward Fulla, Skellum sent a quartet of man-sized millipedes scurrying after them.

Skellum saw that he had a moment's respite and let his mind drift away from the pits.

"Chainer?" he called. "Forgive me, my boy, but I need you to see this."

* * * * *

Chainer swooned and found himself standing in the pits. There was a match going on, a busy one with monkeys and toy soldiers and dementia castings and glowing knights. Chainer's hat spun before his eyes. He blinked. His hat?

"Skellum!" Fulla called. She was tossing out monsters left and right, but she was slowly being overwhelmed.

Chainer's vision dropped, and there were suddenly twice as many monsters fighting with Fulla. She howled again, knocking one Order soldier to his knees and ducking under another's sword.

"I know those two," Chainer said aloud, but he didn't hear his own voice.

"I'm sorry, Chainer," Skellum's voice said in his head, "but I couldn't go without saying goodbye."

"What?" Chainer's voice still carried no sound. "What do you mean? That's Bunkus and Teroh, isn't it?"

"Remember me." A vision of Skellum stood, his eyes sad and pleading. "Remember how I died." The vision put on its hat and raised a hand. "We deserve better than this, my boy."

There was a horrific screech, and Chainer turned just in time to see a glowing knight tear a hydra's headless body in half. His skin had begun to crackle beneath his shining armor, giving the impression that he was composed only of armored plates and energy. Arcs of electricity crawled over him from head to toe.

"Sergeant Baankis?" the glowing knight's voice clanged like a gong. "It is time."

The arcs of electricity on the justicar's body began to grow bigger and brighter. They increased in number and frequency, with more and more rolling over him until his body was scarcely visible at the center of an electrical storm. The air in the pit was being stirred up as if by a great wind, and Chainer felt a deep, vibrating hum in his ear. It seemed the entire building was shaking.

Disoriented, Chainer bowled Baankis over and took a few faltering steps toward the justicar. Whatever he was doing, it was affecting Chainer's balance. He couldn't see Fulla, but if she was still on the pit floor, she was caught in the same maelstrom he was. Chainer was willing to lose the match, but the longer this went on, the more he felt like the justicar wouldn't stop just because the flag was down. He couldn't concentrate enough to cast the death bloom or unleash a monster, so he snapped his metal arm out straight and tried to lash a chain across the justicar's face.

Before the chain could even form, electricity leaped in one huge arc from the justicar to Chainer's body. For Chainer, the world went white. His body was blasted halfway across the arena. . . .

. . . Chainer opened his eyes in the First's private chambers, carried by cutthroats and attended by zombies.

* * * * *

Skellum rose painfully to one knee. His hat was torn and burned and hung in tatters across his face. One eye was swollen shut, and he could feel the blood running freely from his nose. Fulla was down, halfway across the floor, and the smoking carcasses of their combined summonings were quickly fading away. The surviving wolf-monkeys turned and oriented on Skellum once more.

"We give," Skellum called, as loudly as his burned lungs permitted. The wolf-monkeys kept coming. He saw Teroh laugh and cross his arms. The major gestured and spoke to Yewma, and the druid shrugged. With a finger on either side of her mouth, she blew two short, sharp whistles.

The monkeys spread out and surrounded Skellum.

"Hello," he said. "My name is Skellum, and I wear—"

The wolf-monkey flanking Skellum's left lunged forward and hit him high on the shoulder before he could continue. Skellum felt a wet, searing slap and found himself on both knees, hat gone, face-to-naked-face with the lead primate. They stared at each other for a moment, the wolf-monkey slavering and Skellum coughing blood.

"Finish this," Teroh said. Yewma whistled again, and the wolf-monkeys piled on to Skellum with a chorus of hideous screams. The victory horn sounded over a chorus of boos, and Yewma the druid frantically blew the signal that called off her troop. It took quite a long time to get all the blood-maddened mandrills back into their cage.

PART THREE:
DEMENTIST

CHAPTER 18

Chainer and the First both agreed that the shikar should continue as scheduled. Kamahl seemed concerned when Chainer asked him to replace Skellum during the ritual hunt, but he agreed immediately and without comment. Chainer realized how much he relished the barbarian's company. He had been prepared to explain the importance of the ritual itself, how important it had been to Skellum, and how fitting it would be for Chainer's partner in the pits to become his partner on shikar. If Kamahl had been a Cabalist or a merchant, he would have bantered and negotiated and otherwise extended the discussion until he figured out a way to profit from it. The barbarian, however, simply said, "Yes."

The journey was scheduled to begin at dawn, and Chainer spent the final few hours dining with Fulla. Chainer was still too stunned to speak during his meal, and Fulla seemed ashamed of what had happened. She was not good at comforting others, but even in his state of shock, Chainer appreciated her attempts at kindness. He even asked her to accompany him on shikar, but she declined.

"Oh, Skellum," Fulla had said wistfully. She walked around Chainer as she spoke, taking long, straight strides. "Always trying to send people somewhere. 'It's a big special journey, one step at a time, watch where you put your feet.' Always trying to keep it separate." She counted her steps out loud as she walked, then went around again, trying to reduce the count.

"It's an important ritual," Chainer said defensively. "First you learn to perceive, then—"

"Where do you keep your monsters, caster?" Fulla spun on one toe in front of Chainer, drew her sword, and presented it to him, hilt-first. "Where do you go to get them?"

"I keep them in here," Chainer tapped his temple. "In my head. In the place that Skellum showed me."

"That's good." Fulla pulled her sword back and tapped the tip thoughtfully on her chin. "Look me in the eye," she said.

Chainer leaned down and put his face inches from Fulla's. He opened his eyes as wide as hers and stared into her blue-white irises.

"Don't look away," Fulla was careful to keep her head still. "But also look over my shoulder. Take your time."

Chainer sighed. Fulla's eyes were wide and bright. He could make out her half smile below them, and below that, the tapping point of her sword. If he concentrated, he could also make out the rows of beads in her hair, so similar to his own, and the space just beside her ear.

"Mine are always with me," Fulla said, and suddenly Chainer could see them. Hundreds of them, perhaps thousands, lined up behind Fulla and stretching as far back as his mind could see. Monstrous, misshapen, the shades of Fulla's monsters were always half a step behind her.

Fulla broke eye contact then, and the phantasms disappeared. "I didn't learn from Skellum," she told Chainer. "And I can't help you like he did. But I can still do what he does." They finished their meal in silence.

Chainer also spent his time ignoring Laquatus. The ambassador had sent numerous requests to Chainer, asking if he could come by and express his sympathies personally. Chainer left a pile of such requests lying unanswered by the door.

The books Skellum had which described the shikar ritual were more interesting to Chainer but harder to concentrate on. He knew that shikar would be extremely difficult without Skellum's guidance. At least the actual mechanics of it seemed simple enough, and the underlying rationale made sense. He and his partner were going to walk deep into the woods and interact with as many wild creatures as they could find. They would survive on what they could scrounge or hunt down.

The point of the exercise, as Chainer understood it, was to fill his head with fresh ideas. The more brutes he saw, the more beasts he mastered, the more he would have to draw on when he created his own creatures. Some dementists on shikar simply tried to see as many creatures as possible. Some captured the things they hunted or killed and ate them. Others were satisfied to touch their quarry or even simply to make eye contact. Each shikar was as unique as the dementist who took it, but the end objective was always the same, to align the world without to the world within and increase the dementist's ability to bridge the gap between them.

Chainer sat with an open scroll in his lap, Dragon's Blood smoking in his censer, waiting for the sky to brighten. He hadn't slept since Skellum died, and he didn't want to. All he wanted to do was leave the city behind. If Kuberr smiled on him, he might even have the good fortune to run across a pack of wolf-monkeys while he trekked through Krosan. And then, he thought, I will show Kamahl a few things about explosions and fire.

He continued to stare at the sunless sky. Absently, he created a small, buzzing mosquito with a three-pronged proboscis. With his other hand, he made a long-tongued iguana that dropped to the floor and immediately began circling under the mosquito. Chainer made a black owl with four orange eyes and a face on both sides of its skull, then a large, hissing cobra. The owl settled on the window sill and scanned the room as well as the courtyard outside. The snake coiled around Chainer's chair leg and spread its hood.

"Three," Chainer said aloud as the mosquito buzzed over his left arm, looking for a place to feed. "Two. One. Go."

The iguana's tongue snatched the mosquito out of the air. The owl suddenly swooped down and sank its claws into the iguana, and the cobra struck the owl before it could escape with its kill.

Chainer split his attention between the sky, which was at last starting to lighten, and the cobra, who was waiting patiently for the owl to stop convulsing. As the snake dislocated its jaw to enjoy a meal of bug, lizard, and bird, Chainer wiggled his metal fingers and the entire tableau disappeared.

Soon he would be in Krosan, and they all would discover just who sat at the top of the forest's food chain. And then he would return to Cabal City and teach both the Order and the Mer Empire a similar lesson.

* * * * *

It took Kamahl and Chainer two uneventful days of steady hiking to walk from the city gates to the edge of the Krosan Forest. They made their first camp about five hundred yards inside the forest's border, with another day's hike before the ritual hunt would truly begin.

"Hey, Chainer!" Kamahl called. "There's vermin over here. Are you hunting vermin?"

"What kind of vermin? Where?"

"Up there," Kamahl pointed into the trees. "It's about a foot long, with a big, fuzzy tail."

Chainer thought it over. "You mean a squirrel?"

"Yeah."

The black chain shot up into the tree above Kamahl. The dead rodent fell to the ground with a tiny thud, its back broken. Chainer nimbly pounced on his kill and scooped it up.

"In answer to your question," Chainer said, "no, I'm not hunting vermin. But squirrel aren't vermin. This one, in fact, is going to be dinner."

Kamahl scowled. "If it gnaws things and twitches its nose, it's vermin. And if you don't cook that right now it's going to stink."

Chainer put the dead squirrel in his satchel. He folded his arms and stared at Kamahl.

"What?" the barbarian said.

"You want fresh-killed meat," Chainer said, "you can kill it yourself."

Kamahl opened his mouth to swear at Chainer when the ground beneath them shook. From a hundred yards or so to their right came the sound of splintering wood.

"That sounds bigger than vermin." Chainer slapped Kamahl's shoulder. "Look alive, this is what we came here for." He started running through the woods toward the sound. Kamahl followed him.

"What do I do?" he called. Chainer was lighter and quicker through the thick brush, and Kamahl was falling behind.

"Just back me up," Chainer called. He slowed his pace. "I'll try to . . . do my thing. You make sure nothing sneaks up behind me. If I freeze up, snap me out of it. If the thing takes a bite out of me, kill it."

Kamahl nodded. They came to the edge of a clearing, and he drew his sword. Chainer was already down on one knee, peering out into the sheltered glade. A huge, elephantine creature rumbled along, seemingly lost and out of its element. When it came upon a large enough tree, it reared up and came down hard with all of its weight, snapping the tree off at the base and crushing the loose trunk into a mass of dirt and splinters.

"It's a gargadon," Chainer whispered. "A young male."

Kamahl shook his head. "It can't be a gargadon this close to the edge of the woods. They need more open space and a different kind of tree to eat."

"All I know is," Chainer said, "I'm getting a gargadon." He unhooked the censer from his vest.

"Tell me you aren't going to use that thing out here."

"Shhhh. It's important." As he spoke, he loaded and lit the censer. "Just back me up, okay? You ready?"

"Always."

Chainer stepped out into the glade. The gargadon was thirty yards upwind with its back to Chainer, so he was able to get close before it smelled his smoke.

When it turned and trumpeted, Chainer finally realized how truly big it was. A single leg was taller and wider than Chainer's whole body. It pawed the ground with one of those legs and trumpeted again, and the ground shook. It wasn't afraid of Chainer in the least, but it was going to warn him to keep clear.

This was the moment that Chainer had been dreading. He knew that he was supposed to master the creature, but it was too big for him to fight, and he knew he wasn't supposed to create any help. Kamahl might be able to blow a hole in its head with one of his axes, but that did nothing for Chainer's shikar.

He had brought his own dementia monsters to heel with a tight collar and a magical slap on the nose. How was he supposed to collar and slap something that could crush him and not notice? Chainer needed an answer soon because the gargadon was clearly not happy to share its space.

"What's wrong?" Kamahl called. "Why aren't you zapping it?

Chainer continued to spin his censer and stare directly into the gargadon's huge eyes. "Zapping it with what?"

"I don't know. It's your ritual."

"I'm getting an idea now. Just shut up and support me." The gargadon pawed the ground again and stomped gently with both front feet. Chainer was shaken almost to his knees, but he thought he might have the answer.

His dementia monsters were only alive in his mind, and Chainer's mind was his place of power. As long as he controlled his fear, he was the ultimate lord and master of his own dementia space. The gargadon had its own life outside of Chainer's, however, and it didn't know that he was its master. It needed to be shown that fact, it needed to be taught. The best way for Chainer to teach that lesson and gain the kind of control he needed was to take the gargadon out of this world and transplant it into his own.

The gargadon was preparing to charge. "Kamahl," Chainer said. "I need a big explosion, behind the gargadon. Drive it toward me."

"Say when."

Chainer felt a shudder start in the base of his spine and work all the way up to his skull. When his vision cleared, he was standing on a field of black sand under a hole in the sky, facing the exact same gargadon he was facing in Krosan. It had become so easy to take that first step, and Chainer silently cursed the fact that Skellum was not beside him to see this.

"When," he said. Kamahl let the axe fly, and the lowest-hanging branches of the tree behind the gargadon erupted into flames and thunder. The massive creature was far too heavy to spring, but it reared and charged. It bore down on Chainer, who continued to spin his censer in its widest arc yet, his eyes focused beyond the canopy overhead.

The gargadon charged into range of Chainer's censer. On its next revolution the smoking cage made contact with the gargadon's massive head, and there was a flash of black light and an implosion so strong it sucked the leaves off the trees nearby.

"Fiers's teeth!" Kamahl ran to Chainer's side. "What just happened? That thing was going to crush you like a bug, but it . . . ran into you."

Chainer kept his back to Kamahl and stared at his own smoking hands. The censer lay in the tall grass, the stalks around it smoldering. "If it ran into me, I'd be a smear." Chainer's voice sounded odd to his own ears, deeper and more hollow, as if he were speaking through a tube.

"No," Kamahl said. "I mean it ran into you, like a sword goes into a scabbard. It was bigger than you, but then you were bigger than it, and . . . Fiers's teeth."

Chainer had turned in the middle of Kamahl's sentence, and his friend immediately stopped talking. "What's wrong?" Chainer asked in his hollow voice.

"Your eyes," Kamahl said. "They're black."

"Everybody's eyes are black, you—"

Kamahl held his sword horizontally in front of Chainer's face, so Chainer could see his own eyes reflected in the flat of the blade.

"Your eyes are black, Chainer. Empty holes."

Chainer stared at his reflection while he ran a finger around his eyebrows and cheekbones. His eyes were deep, solid black, like the void of a bottomless pit. Chainer laughed, and the sound was more pleasant and musical than he had ever noticed before.

"I just swallowed a gargadon whole." Chainer tore his gaze away from the blade and looked at Kamahl. "It could take a while to digest."

Kamahl sheathed his sword. "I don't like it. Is this going to happen every time you catch something?"

Chainer held his metal hand in front of his face, concentrated, and slowly curled the hand into a fist. When he looked up again, his eyes were normal.

"Not if I learn to control it." Chainer lowered his hand and looked around the empty glen, breathing deeply and evenly. Kamahl nudged him.

"You okay?"

"I feel great." Chainer took one last deep breath, then nudged Kamahl back. "Come on. If there's gargadons here, imagine what we're going to find in the really deep woods."

"I can't," Kamahl said. "That's sort of what worries me."

* * * * *

The second day of hunting started with scorpions in their bedrolls. Chainer took his into dementia space, and Kamahl crushed his beneath a heavy boot. The further they went into the Krosan forest, the more creatures they encountered. The more creatures they encountered, the more they captured.

Chainer picked up a coal-bellied razorback near a rocky ridge, and then killed a second for its meat. Kamahl cooked his share immediately. In a marshy riverbed, Chainer took on a huge snapping turtle, a small, blue, poisonous frog, and a six-foot freshwater alligator. A deadfall yielded a sharp-clawed badger, a three-foot beetle that emitted clouds of choking spray, and a two-hundred-pound wildcat. But it was the snakes that interested Chainer most.

This section of Otaria was thick with both venom hunters and constrictors—from the small but lethal jade adder to the medium-sized razorback rattler to the enormous rock python that could swallow a man whole. Chainer's face lit up every time he saw one, and he abandoned less interesting prey the moment he spotted a forked tongue. When Kamahl asked him about it, Chainer said he admired their speed and their grace, their aim and their muscular control. He felt some kind of kinship for the sleek reptiles, and Kamahl had seen Chainer fight often enough to know that it wasn't just a flight of fancy. Like the snakes, Chainer often waited until his prey was within range, then struck so quickly that the contest was over before his victim realized it had begun.

Chainer took one of each type of snake into dementia space. The rest he killed and shared with Kamahl. Kamahl wasn't sure what his friend was doing with the half-dozen rattles he had taken from his kills, but he seemed almost reverent about preserving them in his satchel, so Kamahl left him to it. There was much he didn't understand about this trip, but at least Chainer wasn't so intensely morose anymore.

The Cabalist was sitting against a fallen tree, counting the rattles in his collection. Kamahl sniffed the air, and for the fiftieth time felt that something was going wrong.

"We're not very deep in, are we?"

"No," Chainer continued to count, transferring the rattles from his hand to a neat line he had arranged on the ground beside him.

"Don't you think it's odd that we're seeing so many creatures this far out?"

"It's odd," Chainer agreed, "but not remarkable."

"But there are tribes in the forest," Kamahl said. "Druids and Nantuko. We should have seen more of them and less of the things we've been hunting."

"Maybe they heard we were coming and fled," Chainer said. He began to put his rattles back into his satchel.

"That gargadon wasn't fleeing. It was milling around, lost, as if it had just been put there."

Chainer cinched up his satchel. "So?"

"So who put it there? And why?"

Chainer stood up. "You're never happy, are you? Either there are too many creatures or not enough. Things are either too close to the edge of the woods or too far in. Don't get all anxious on me now, Kamahl. We'll start seeing the really big stuff soon, and I'll need you at your best."

"I'm always at my best," Kamahl said. "And when you say big, do you mean bigger than a gargadon?"

"I mean bigger than a wildcat or a crocodile. Centaurs and wurms. Maybe even a pack of monkeys." The eager look in Chainer's eye did nothing to address Kamahl's concerns.

"I still say this feels wrong. It feels like a trap."

"It feels like a trap because you barbarians are constantly pouncing on each other. If I got jumped every time I went to the privy, I'd see traps everywhere, too." He threw a handful of dirt on the embers of their campfire. "Come on. We've got one more day to get to the heart of Krosan. If we don't see any leaf-eaters or dirt-farmers by then, we'll ask the First about it when we get back."

* * * * *

Later that afternoon, they heard more rumbling in the distance, as another elephantine creature stomped through the forest.

"Could be another gargadon," Chainer said. "Which we already have. Even if we were able to kill this one, we don't have time to butcher and eat it."

"So we're letting it go?"

"Hells no. Not until I see what it is." Chainer smelled something familiar, and his heart began to quicken. *Kuberr*, he thought, *smile on me now*. They jogged for a while, until they came across the thing's tracks in the loose dirt and mulch that covered the forest floor. The prints were deep, but narrow, as if the creature were walking on the balls of its feet. There were extra tracks scattered alongside the regularly spaced ones where the creature had either gone down on all fours like a bear or propelled itself forward with its arms like an ape. Chainer followed the tracks as he ran, scanning ahead to make sure of his footing and behind to make sure Kamahl was keeping up. From around a thick copse of trees in the distance, Chainer heard a terrifying but familiar roar that made the blood pound in his ears.

"It's a grendelkin," Chainer said. He stood still, staring at the copse of trees. As Kamahl came up behind him, Chainer said, "This one's for Skellum. Ready?"

Before Kamahl could answer, the rampant grendelkin burst through the trees. It was even bigger than the one Chainer had seen in the alley outside Roup's, and this one's legs were whole and healthy. With a tree in each massive paw, the grendelkin spied Chainer and Kamahl and roared a challenge. It threw one tree at them, then another, missing by a wide margin but impressing them nonetheless. It thumped its chest and then the ground.

Chainer handed the loaded censer to Kamahl, and with a snap of his fingers, the barbarian ignited it. He tossed it back to Chainer, who lashed a chain into it as it flew. He immediately began spinning it around his head, spreading Dragon's Blood smoke all around them. Kamahl readied a throwing axe.

Then a strong gust of wind blew out of the copse, carrying a wave of greenish-yellow pollen. Chainer was breathing shallow and was partially protected by the smoke from his censer, but Kamahl took in a huge lungful of the pollen and immediately doubled over in a fit of uncontrollable coughing.

"Kamahl! Are you okay?"

The barbarian waved Chainer off and dropped the rest of the way down to the ground, trying to evade the pollen. With his face half-buried in mulch, Kamahl coughed the pollen out and tried to suck clear forest air in.

Chainer hesitated. He didn't want to leave Kamahl in the dirt, and he didn't want to face the grendelkin without support. The huge monster took a step forward and casually snapped the top off another tree. It used the tree as a crude club, and it shambled forward, slamming into the ground and other trees with each step.

"Poison," Kamahl choked. His eyes were wet, but he had stopped coughing and was struggling back to his feet. "There aren't any poisonous plants in this part of Krosan, Chainer. We're being set up."

Thirty yards behind the pair, a long, legless wurm slithered onto their tracks. It opened its square reptilian head and hissed, displaying the foulest and most jagged set of dragon's teeth Chainer had ever seen. A huge, burly centaur with spotted markings and a crude wooden club trotted out from behind the grendelkin, and a crimson night tiger growled from the trees above, its brilliant red hide almost glowing under its black stripes.

"All they've done," Chainer said, "is line themselves up for us."

From above, a screaming wolf-monkey dove at Chainer. It became fouled in the censer chain, tearing it out of Chainer's grasp as the monkey itself sprang away with the chain tangled around its leg. Chainer sent a sharpened weight screaming after the retreating monkey but missed by a hair's breadth. The dementist glared at the mandrill with awful fire in his eyes.

"You're mine," he said darkly. "You are all mine." He kept his eyes locked on the monkey as he bent to retrieve the censer. A long vine whipped out of a nearby tree and wrapped itself around Chainer's wrist, and he felt an uncomfortable tingle. Moss was growing across his human hand, spreading outward from the vine. Chainer slashed his wrist loose with his dagger and scraped off the moss before it could spread any farther. The dagger took off the top layers of skin along with the moss.

"This is spellcraft." Kamahl was on his feet, standing behind Chainer. He had drawn his sword and stood with a weapon ready in each hand, his eyes darting from the copse to the wurm to the centaur to the tiger.

"Druid magic?"

Kamahl nodded. "Someone's pulling their strings." He blocked another lashing vine with the flat of his blade and chopped the offending tendril off with his axe.

"That copse of trees seems to be the center of it." Chainer flexed his bleeding hand, testing it. "Somebody's setting its pets on us. Kamahl, I want those monkeys and the grendelkin. The rest can burn, for all I care." He smiled at Kamahl and picked up his still-smoking censer. "You ready for some burning?"

Kamahl coughed the last of the pollen out of his lungs and spit. "Right now, I'd torch all of Krosan just to clear a pathway out of here." His eyes kept traveling back to the centaur. Chainer thought his friend looked disturbed, distracted by something other than the pollen or the attack vines or the platoon of wild beasts that had gathered to kill them.

"Start with the biggest one?" Kamahl asked. Chainer nodded, and the two of them charged forward dodging vines and screaming monkeys.

"Okay if I kill a few of these screaming, hairy buggers?" Kamahl shouted. A wolf-monkey had pounced on him and was resisting his efforts to throw it off.

"As many as you need to," Chainer said. He didn't even make a chain, he simply reached out and crushed the monkey's skull with his metal hand. The body shimmered and disappeared into Chainer's arm. "I've got the one I need." His eyes were black, and he touched his clenched fist to his forehead. "For Skellum."

Another monkey threw itself at Kamahl. The barbarian chopped it in half with his broadsword without breaking stride. He turned and channeled a blast of fire through his blade at the wurm. The legless dragon screeched in pain, but the blast did little more than singe its skin. It held its ground however, unwilling to risk another blast from closer range.

Chainer rolled away from the centaur's club and whipped a collar around its neck. The man-horse reared up and jerked the chain out of Chainer's hand, and the collar faded as soon as Chainer lost contact with it. Chainer sprinted past the centaur to engage the grendelkin as Kamahl was keeping the tiger and the wurm at bay with blasts of flame. The man-horse galloped after Chainer as fast as the underbrush would allow, with his club raised high overhead.

Chainer had a bigger problem with a bigger club, however. The grendelkin would not move away from the edge of the copse, and he was waving his tree trunk like a scythe in front of him. Chainer couldn't get in under the tree to attack, and the centaur was bearing down on him from behind.

Chainer jumped as high as he could over the grendelkin's next wild swing and latched himself onto the end of the tree with a collar chain. The grendelkin waved its club with Chainer trailing behind it like the tail of a kite. At the apex of the grendelkin's swing, Chainer sent a sharpened weight into the organic seam between two of the armored plates on the grendelkin's back. Chainer let go of the chain that linked him to the tree, and hauled himself onto the grendelkin.

"Eat this," he snarled at the centaur, and unleashed the death bloom directly into the back of the grendelkin's skull. The monster choked in mid-roar and froze with its hand poised to crush Chainer like a stinging fly. Except for the monkeys, who were in constant motion and never stopped screaming, every sentient thing in the area stopped and stared at the dead grendelkin, waiting to see which way it would topple.

Unfortunately for the centaur, Chainer's plan of letting the grendelkin fall forward worked perfectly. Killing the grendelkin removed Chainer and Kamahl's main adversary. Letting its body fall removed five more as the centaur, the tiger, and three of the wolf-monkeys were crushed by the three-ton carcass.

Chainer rode the grendelkin through all obstacles as it crashed to the forest floor. He spiked a short chain into the top of the creature's spine, shuddered, and the giant corpse disappeared up into Chainer's body like liquid through a sucking straw. Instead of falling, Chainer floated, surrounded by a whirling cloud of dust and black light. He felt a bomb go off in his head, and he felt a body-wide sensation similar to when the justicar fried him. Chainer screamed.

Kamahl had blinded the wurm with his broadsword and was

preparing to behead the floundering thing when Chainer cried out. He hesitated, then brought his sword down and leaped away from the thrashing coils. As Chainer continued to float and scream, Kamahl felt something angry shift inside the copse of trees. A half-dozen wolf-monkeys still howled on the battlefield, and the trees themselves were starting to move, stretching their branches down and reaching for Chainer and Kamahl. From inside the cluster of trees, a bald human figure came forward. The chanting druid held a crude pine torch in one hand and a thorny bough of red berries in the other. He was painted with bright yellow markings, and a crown of ivy spread from his head down past his shoulders.

As the first tree limb touched the nimbus around Chainer, his scream grew higher and more shrill, building to a crescendo of transcendent agony. Inside the cloud, Chainer turned his black eye sockets toward the encroaching branch. He crossed his arms over his chest, then snapped them down his sides and thrust his head back.

A half-dozen chains leaped from all parts of his body, each lashing straight into the throat of a jabbering wolf-monkey. With his body rigid and his eyes unseeing, Chainer brought all of the monkeys together in front of him with a nauseous splat. He leveled his eyes at the horrid sight he had created and smiled.

The six wolf-monkeys were mashed together like soft clay figurines. Limbs, tails, torsos, and heads were all bent and mashed together, merging into one giant gob of flesh and teeth with no discernable top, bottom, inside, or out. The ones with functioning mouths wailed piteously. Chainer's smile grew savage and cruel under his hollow eyes. Then the entire mass of monkeys burst like a balloon and disappeared in a puff of smoke.

The druid's chant grew louder, and he hurled the thorns into the air. With no animal defenders left, the trees and vines redoubled their efforts to take hold of the intruders.

"Kamahl," Chainer's echoing, musical voice called. "Do it!"

Kamahl raised his axe and charged it. He held it by his ear until steam started rising from his hand, and then he cast it high overhead, dropping it into the middle of the copse. Two seconds later, the entire copse was engulfed in bright orange flames, and the druid vanished in a cloud of flame and soot. Debris rained down all around them, and Kamahl took shelter behind the dead wurm. Chainer was less fortunate. A jagged chunk of wood slammed into him, knocking him out of the air and onto the ground.

He heard Skellum's last words again. *Remember how I died.*

"Always, Master," Chainer whispered, tears falling from the black space where his eyes had been. "I will always remember."

And then he fell unconscious to the forest floor.

* * * * *

Chainer awoke under the mustard sky. He knew he was dreaming, he could see his body from the outside as he scanned the landscape. The hole in the sky had run almost dry, only releasing an occasional drop. The red sea broke on the shore, driven by storm winds and earthquake rumbles.

Monsters milled around him in their hundreds, stretching out in all directions. They did not react to Chainer's presence but seemed to be in a state of torpor as they shuffled and bumped into one another.

There was a new addition to the landscape in Chainer's mind. The horizon was now broken by a broad, squat mountain whose peak glowed like a star. Chainer shielded his eyes against the glare and tried to focus on the peak. He must be dreaming, for the mountain was shrinking down to meet him, bowing its peak like a servant bows its head.

An indistinct figure sat on a throne at the mountain's peak, backlit by a sphere of harsh purple light. Dazzled by the mad perspective as much as the purple light, Chainer could not determine how far away the figure was, if it were humanoid, male or female. He could see the mountain, however, and he saw that it was not made of rock or mounded earth, but of currency. Huge piles of golden coins and silver markers were heaped on top of one another to create a single pyramid that stretched impossibly high into the sky. The figure leaned forward on its throne.

"Kuberr?" Chainer whispered. Was this what Skellum had wanted him to see? His mentor had sworn frequent oaths to Kuberr over the years. Did he have a vision of the wealth god as part of the shikar ritual?

Mazeura. The figure's voice was deep and sonorous, and it blasted Chainer's secret name through his head so violently that he felt blood trickling out his ears. It's a dream, he reminded himself. It's all a dream.

The mountain peak swayed to and fro, allowing the regal figure to survey the landscape and population of Chainer's mind. *Well done, dementist.*

The figure opened its arms wide, beckoning Chainer in. The mountain bowed further, and Chainer felt the ground beneath him rise up to carry him into those outstretched arms. He had pledged his life to the Cabal, and now he knew for whom he had pledged. There was power in the salt flats, power in Cabal City, power in the personage of the First. The expanding figure before him, however, was beyond power. It was that vast and nameless energy the Cabal had been created to harness, to use according to its consumptive nature. If black mana was the fuel, then the regal figure welcoming Chainer was its source.

Delirious with joy, Chainer closed his eyes and let himself be swallowed up by the dark figure that had expanded to fill the entire sky.

* * * * *

When the flaming shrapnel slowed, Kamahl rose and surveyed the battlefield. The flames were still raging in the copse of trees. The wurm and one of the wolf-monkeys lay dead at his feet, victims of his sword. The crimson night tiger and the centaur were little more than colorful smears on the grass, and Chainer was unconscious between them. There was no sign of the grendelkin or the other wolf-monkeys. It seemed he and Chainer had won, but he didn't feel much like a victor.

Kamahl sheathed his sword and crossed the field to his partner. The fight and the explosion had driven every other living thing within earshot as far away as they could get, and the forest was remarkably still. Chainer was breathing normally, but he was unrouseable. Kamahl half-carried, half-dragged him clear of the fire and tucked him safely behind a large, mossy boulder. Then he returned to the crushed corpse of the tiger.

Regret was not a common emotion for Kamahl's tribe. They spent most of their time in combat or training for it, and they tended to live short, brutal lives with little time for reflection. As he looked down on the magnificent red and black hide of the tiger, he regretted that he hadn't seen the creature hunt. It would have been beautiful in motion, a study in grace and power.

Kamahl turned, experiencing another unfamiliar rush of emotion. Kamahl had made two great friends on his first visit to Cabal City. One lay unconscious by a nearby boulder, and the other looked almost exactly like the dead centaur at his feet. Kamahl remembered Seaton clearly, his huge, apelike brow and his fierce protective streak for his home. He remembered how Seaton had become enraged when describing the poachers who raided his home, taking from the wild to stock the pits. Seaton's crusade was not Kamahl's quest, but he respected it, and he respected the centaur. Only now did Kamahl realize that he himself was one of those poachers.

Kamahl knew the shikar was only a small portion of the problem, but he was now part of it. He let himself be blinded to it because he had never had to defend his home from invaders. There was nothing in the Pardic Mountains worth taking, so invaders were completely unheard of. All the tribes Kamahl knew of, including his own, spent the greater part of their adulthood roaming Otaria looking for ways to improve their skills and their fortunes. Kamahl had spent so much time fighting in other people's homes that he'd forgotten not everyone welcomes such company. This dead centaur could have been Seaton's father, or brother, he thought. It could have been Seaton.

The fire in the copse of trees had died down, so Kamahl went in as far as he could. He found the druid's body crushed against a blackened tree. He had been a short, broad-shouldered male of about twenty. He had constructed a small stone altar in the center of the copse, which was half-disintegrated by the blast. Whatever spells or summonings he had been performing were long gone. He still held a fragment of pine wood in his charred fingers.

Kamahl's emotions had retreated. Now he felt only the clarity of the choice in front of him and the determination to see his decision through.

While Chainer slept, Kamahl built pyres for the druid, the centaur, and the tiger. He built another fire for the camp near Chainer's boulder, and then one-by-one he ignited them all with a snap of his fingers. Then he stuck his sword tip-first into the ground and waited for Chainer to wake up.

CHAPTER 19

Chainer and Kamahl hiked back toward the edge of the forest and the road to Cabal City. Chainer had slept until almost noon. The first thing he did when he awoke was to ask Kamahl to check his eyes. The barbarian reported that they appeared to be normal, and Chainer was both relieved and disappointed. The shikar felt like it was finished. He couldn't imagine anything more impressive than the vision he'd just had.

Kamahl took the news that the hunt was over as if he had been expecting it. Chainer was prepared to explain why, but the barbarian didn't ask. There was something about his manner, however, something defiant that made Chainer think his partner was planning to go back to Cabal City no matter what Chainer said. He didn't press the issue, still euphoric over his vision of Kuberr.

They saw virtually no wildlife at all as they reversed their course back through the forest. Chainer thought how vast the entire forest must be, and how many creatures it hid. He could probably go on shikar once a year, and he would still never see all of the Krosan before he died.

Kamahl was silent throughout most of the day, and Chainer was still too lost in his own thoughts to draw his friend out. They hiked through dinner and stopped to make camp only when the sun was on the verge of setting. At this pace, with the hunt concluded ahead of schedule, they were likely to get back an entire day sooner than expected.

The next morning saw them up at dawn and out of the forest by lunchtime. They stopped on the edge of the forest, ate the last of their provisions, and drank the last of their water according to the ritual. The only things they were allowed to bring back were in Chainer's head. With only a few hours of daylight left, they hiked into the deserted remains of what appeared to be a large Order camp.

Kamahl scanned the vast plain that stretched out before him. "Chainer," he said carefully, "do you see an army? Where would a thousand Order troops go all at once?"

"Crusat," Chainer's stomach went cold with hate. "They were massing for a huge raid on the Cabal City pits." He grabbed Kamahl's arm. "We've got to get back there."

Kamahl was looking down the road at the Order's stable. "The Order always brings more steeds than it needs. Can you ride, Cabalist?"

"I rode a hellhound once, I can damn sure handle whatever those toy soldiers sit on."

Kamahl grunted. "Good. Wait here, I'll go get us some transport." He paused, then added, "Provided you don't want to whip us up a pair of three-headed horses that breathe fire, or anything."

Chainer felt an unaccountable sting of insult. He smiled, however, and said, "Don't know if I'm up to a precise-creature casting right now. And in general, my monsters don't want to be ridden, and we don't want to ride them."

"Order steeds it is, then."

* * * * *

Kamahl was able to appropriate two strong chargers from the Order stables without interference. There were minimal guards on duty and plenty of animals to choose from. Two things were obvious to Kamahl. First, the Order had taken from the Krosan forest a hundred times what he and Chainer had. Second, wherever the troopers had gone, they had gone there on foot.

Both Order horses were white, of course. Kamahl muttered an angry spell and then singed a hand print into his mount's flank. Chainer tied three of his snake rattles into the other horse's mane, then they rode east all night long without stopping. They were good horses, fast and strong. As the first rays of sunlight revealed the skull-image of Cabal City's huge arena and the spires of the First's manor, the chargers were sweaty and foaming and beginning to stumble, and both men brought their horses to a slow trot.

"Do you see that, Chainer?" Kamahl asked. Chainer had excellent night vision, but he knew Kamahl's was even sharper.

"All I see is the skyline. And . . . a crowd of people at the gates. Are those arrows?"

Kamahl drew his sword. Most swords Chainer was familiar with came out of their scabbards with a crisp rasp of metal on metal. Kamahl's, however, came out with a long, protracted hiss that lingered in the air like a threat. The huge weapon looked somehow right at home in Kamahl's fist, though the sword was almost longer than its wielder.

"The Order is attacking your city," Kamahl said. "I have a problem with that. Care to join me in solving this problem?"

"Oh yes," Chainer's voice was cold. "Yes I certainly would." He shook the rattles in the mane before him. "Will they get us there?"

"They'll last at least that long." Kamahl lifted his feet to dig his heels into his mount, but Chainer took him by the shoulder and called him by name.

"What?" the barbarian growled. "The fight's started without us."

"Thank you," Chainer said. He looked back toward the woods, at the battle unfolding in the distance, and finally at Kamahl's drawn sword. "Thank you for everything."

Kamahl smiled for the first time in days. "Thank me after we clean house," he said, and spurred his charger forward, into the fray.

* * * * *

Their horses carried them as far as the main gates. There, Chainer and Kamahl dismounted. The barbarian charged forward to join the melee at the gates, where the crusat raiders were most numerous. He saluted Chainer before rushing off. Chainer himself needed to get inside, to rejoin his fellow Cabalists and determine where he could do the most good. He followed the walls of the city around to the south, where the secret tunnels were.

Cabal City was a city of over fifty thousand, but it seemed even more crowded with the entire population and over a thousand armed invaders on the streets. Chainer realized the battle at the front gate was mostly a distraction. The Order had attacked all three gates, not just the one to the east, and they were already running rampant through the city. The crusat troopers were not cutting down civilians in the street, but they were fairly trampling anything that stood between them and the Cabal strongholds at the center of the city.

Chainer had never been to war before, but he soon got the hang of it. The trick, he realized, is to treat the entire situation like a huge pit match in which you and your team were vastly outnumbered. As long as you hit what you aimed at, there was no shortage of targets. As long as you kept moving, there was no way for you to get pinned down. Also, the Order troops were focused on storming the arena, and none of them stopped to fight Chainer unless he physically blocked their progress.

After breaking a few bones and knocking a few invaders down, Chainer simply joined the headlong rush toward the arena. Cabal City's citizens were rushing there for sanctuary, or to escape via the docks, and the crusat was rushing there to burn it, or loot it, or whatever it was that righteous armies did. Chainer was headed straight for the Mirari, to defend it as he had once before. Only now, he was a full-fledged dementist instead of a pupil.

There was another crush outside of the arena as soldiers tried to get in and the door guards tried to keep them out. A few armed Cabalists grappled with sword-bearing soldiers. Chainer planted his feet, positioned his hands, and reached deep into dementia space. His hands flashed, and a carriage-sized wad of smoke and indiscriminate flesh arced high up on the arena's exterior wall, where it burst open like a balloon packed with splintered glass.

The wolf-monkeys that came out were even larger than their Krosan counterparts, and each had a small poisonous snake in place of its tongue. There were an even dozen in all, and twelve individual chains arced from the collars around their necks to Chainer's open hands. At first, the nightmare mandrills tried to attack anything that moved, but Chainer punished them with searing agony every time they snapped at a Cabalist. They quickly realized which part of the crowd was fair game, and the screams of monkeys mingled with the screams of the dismembered soldiers. Chainer even released two or three of them from their collars, and they redoubled their efforts to rip the invaders to pieces.

Chainer darted through the momentarily unblocked entrance. A hook-handed door guard touched his weapon to his forehead in acknowledgment as Chainer rushed past. Before he turned the corner, Chainer physically and mentally pulled all of his wolf-monkeys in and rechained them all to the stone doorway. Now anyone who wanted to get in would have to get past the howling troop. Anyone who made it past them would either be Cabal or be disemboweled. Chainer sprinted toward the vault hallway.

He turned a corner and came face-to-face with a trio of troopers fighting a pitched battle against a huge, black hellhound and a four-armed cyclops, the hulking result of another dementia caster's efforts. The dog had clamped on to the end of one trooper's sword, while the other two jabbed at the cyclops with their spears.

"Chainer!" Fulla cried, stepping out from behind the cyclops. One of the Order soldiers struck at her, and she angrily turned and cast a snarling red-eyed rat into the man's face. He fell back screaming.

"Fulla." Chainer cracked a chain across the sword-bearing trooper's face. As the trooper recoiled, the hellhound tore out her throat. The big dog turned and barked once at Chainer, exasperated.

"Hello, Azza," he said. Chainer, Azza, Fulla, and the cyclops all closed in on the remaining trooper.

"I give," the man said instantly. He dropped his spear and held up his hands. "In the name of—"

Fulla's ugly little sword split the trooper's skull before he could utter another word. For a moment she looked annoyed, and she held the bloody sword out to Chainer.

" 'I give.' Can you believe these maggots?" She wiped the sword on the dead man's uniform.

Azza barked, and Fulla waved the cyclops away. She stepped forward and hugged Chainer, rifling his hair like an indulgent aunt. "Azza was worried. And I've been so bored. You're not going to become one of those snotty dementists now, are you?" Then she stood and asked him brightly, "So, tell me everything. How was the forest?"

Chainer smiled. "Crowded. The shikar, however, was a spectacular success."

Azza sniffed the air and growled to let her fellow Cabalists know there was something coming.

"Well, little brother," Fulla said. "Can you show me what you learned in the forest, or do I have to clear this building of toy soldiers by myself?"

"Oh, let me show you," Chainer said. He felt his feet rise off the floor, and without seeing his reflection, he knew his eyes had gone black. Fulla's smile grew wider and crueler as Chainer drew on the power he had earned.

"This had better be good," Fulla said.

Azza whined softly, but held her ground.

Chainer crossed his arms as he floated and dropped his chin down to his chest. Fulla's cry of delight overlapped Chainer's cry of release as he snapped his arms down and his head back.

Ribbons of smoke and black light radiated out from Chainer's body in every direction. Most ran straight through the arena's stone walls without resistance, but some ricocheted back and forth inside the hallway. Chainer floated there for a few long seconds then gently settled onto the floor.

"That should do it," he said. His voice and his eyes were returning to normal. He gallantly offered his arm to Fulla.

"Do what?" Fulla took his arm but stared at him in confusion.

"I've just retaken the entire arena," Chainer said proudly. He stumbled, but Fulla caught him and propped him up against the wall. She whispered something to Azza, and the huge dog ambled over to Chainer and bent low, so that he could climb on.

"Thank you." Chainer eased himself onto Azza's strong back. "Skellum always said, 'It takes more out of you than you realize.'" The sadness and anger over his mentor's death was still there, but it didn't sting quite like it did before. Completing the shikar had gone a long way toward putting Skellum to rest. Using what he'd learned during the ritual to drive the Order out felt even better.

"To the vault, please," he said to Azza. The three walked through the suddenly silent building, but only Azza and Fulla were amazed by what they saw.

There were still small squads of troopers throughout the arena, but each and every Order soldier was covered in squirming serpents. Huge, venomous, in a wide array of unnatural shapes and sizes, the snakes covered each invader like a shroud. Those that could walk or run were being cornered and killed by the Cabal's guards. As each Order soldier fell, the body and any lingering serpents disappeared into the gloom.

Fulla made a game of counting the dead, but she had to give up when they came close to the vault and there was no one left. Outside, the battle raged on, but inside the arena, it had already been won.

"How did you do that all over the building?" Fulla asked.

Chainer was interrupted by a thud and a clatter as a live crusat trooper stumbled out of a door further up the hallway. The terrified man held his sword out in front of him with both hands, and he still couldn't keep its point off the floor. He had a sergeant's insignia on his shoulder.

"Hello, Bunkus," Chainer's voice was low but firm.

"S-stand where you are," Sgt. Baankis said feebly. His skin was pale, and his eyes were unfocused. "In the name of the Order, I—"

"I'd stop citing things in the name of the Order, if I were you." Azza growled and tried to shrug Chainer off, but he patted her neck soothingly. "No, big sister. Leave him to me."

Baankis managed to get his sword pointed in Chainer's general direction.

"In the name of the Order," the sergeant repeated, "and in the name of Major Teroh, I—"

The chain shot across the room and wrapped itself around Baankis's throat before he could utter another word. The sergeant's jaw opened and closed, but no sound came out as the chain dug deep into his windpipe.

"In the name of the Order," Chainer maintained his low, even tone, "you have broken into our home, attacked our family, and tried to steal our property. Again. I can't think of a single reason to keep listening to you. Can you?" Baankis dropped his sword with a clatter and clawed at his throat.

"Fulla?" Chainer asked. "Azza? No? Then we're all in agreement." Chainer held his position until Sgt. Baankis silently expired. As the body fell forward, it collapsed into the length of chain and disappeared up Chainer's arm. Azza growled approvingly, and Fulla rocked from one foot to the other.

"Do it again!" she cried.

Chainer didn't hear them as he stared at his hand. Before today, he had never taken a human being the way he had taken the denizens of Krosan forest. He was surprised that it didn't feel any different.

* * * * *

After Chainer stopped them at the arena, the Order troops aborted their mission and began a costly retreat. The First ordered every able-bodied Cabalist to harry the invaders until they were a mile outside the city walls, and the righteous crusat raid on Cabal City ended in disaster. The outnumbered Order troops desperately tried to break out of the city they had just successfully stormed, fighting the city guards at the gates and the Cabal's killers on their rear flank. If the First had ordered the main gates closed, the entire raiding force would have been slaughtered. As it was, almost half of their number never left Cabal City again. Of those who stayed, only a handful remained dead.

Chainer had watched the retreat from Azza's back near the steps of the arena. He knew that there were huge, gargadon-sized monstrosities hidden in the caverns below the manor, but the First was content to keep them in reserve. It seemed he wanted the Cabalists to beat back the raiders themselves, and he wanted some of the enemy to escape. Chainer reminded himself that the First had global concerns which he would never be privy to, and took faith in the First's wisdom.

Once the furor at the gate had died down and the fighting moved beyond the city walls, Chainer and Azza went looking for Kamahl.

The big barbarian might have joined the running battle, but Chainer expected to find him close by. Kamahl had been more interested in defending the city than the Cabal. Chainer made no such distinction, but he was glad that something had sparked his friend's fighting spirit after the shikar.

The dead, the wounded, and the unconscious were scattered around the main gates like leaves in autumn. Scavengers from the squatters' huts were already poking around, looking for valuables. Azza growled angrily, and the scavengers wisely withdrew.

Chainer saw a few white-robed Samites milling around as well, looking for survivors to care for. There were also two or three black-robed Cabal healers, who were known in the pits as "leeches." The two groups took pains to avoid each other and communicated only through cold stares. Azza sniffed and whined. She bounded forward, almost tossing Chainer off.

Kamahl was lying face-down in the center of a charred and smoking circle. His sword was missing, and he had taken a heavy blow to the right side of his face. His right hand clutched at a stab wound in his stomach that was filling his tunic with blood. His hands, feet, arms, and face were horribly burned.

Chainer paused only long enough to stare at the Samite healer approaching them. She was tall and willowy with a concerned air, and she offered her hand out to Chainer. "I am Nibahn. I am a Samite. I can help him, brother. I can help all who suffer." She started to kneel next to Kamahl, but Azza stopped her with a growl.

"The Cabal is here," Chainer called, and one of the black-robed healers answered. Nibahn shook her head sadly, eyes pleading, but Chainer drew his dagger and began idly cleaning his fingernails. Azza growled again, and the Samite withdrew.

The Cabal healer bowed to Chainer and Azza. He had a wide black stripe tattooed over his left eye from his hairline to his jawline and a wispy black mustache. The healer was an oily little rat-faced toad, but Chainer trusted him because he knew how to motivate him.

With a wave, Chainer whipped a collar around the healer's ankles. He yanked the healer's feet out from under him, and Azza stalked forward, so that her huge head was directly over the healer's, and her great, snorting breaths puffed into his face.

"Take this barbarian inside," Chainer said, "and keep him alive. Do nothing apart from keep him alive and comfortable until I come for him." He leaned over the healer himself, almost overbalancing, and his eyes went black. "Nothing. Do you understand?"

The healer sniveled, his eyes darting between Azza and Chainer. "I do, big brother."

Azza turned and carried Chainer away. He saw the healer rise and motion for his assistants. He clearly heard the healer say, "Gently, very gently."

CHAPTER 20

Laquatus stood in the First's private chamber at the head of a small group of Cabalists and dignitaries. They had all been summoned in the wake of the raid, ostensibly to testify about their whereabouts and report what they had seen. The Mer ambassador recognized a simple call for scapegoats, however.

He was unconcerned for himself. His contact with Major Teroh had been completely innocent, or at least, absolutely secret. Even if the First knew he had been in contact with the Order, Laquatus felt secure. There was nothing in the content of his exchanges with Teroh that was incriminating. If Teroh read a hidden meaning into the ambassador's words, Laquatus could easily feign shock and could well afford to make restitution. Besides, he was certain the First understood the political necessity of keeping in touch with one's enemies as well as one's allies, especially in these troubled times.

The captain of the city watch standing next to him was not so confident. The man had the common, earthy stink of fear all over him, and with good reason. The city's defenses were virtually non-existent during the opening minutes of the raid, and so far no one had come up with an explanation of how the Order was able to penetrate so far into the city so quickly. There were even rumors that the captain had betrayed the Cabal and given the Order free access to the heart of the city, but Laquatus knew for a fact they were false. He surreptitiously stepped further away from the captain, however, for his was the most likely head to fall.

Next to the captain stood Chainer, the young dementist who was going to provide a replacement for Turg. Chainer seemed calm, almost tranquil compared to the captain, but Laquatus was having a difficult time seeing into the boy's mind. Most of the individuals he encountered in person were as defenseless as if they had peepholes installed in their foreheads that Laquatus could peer into at any time. Chainer was more like Caster Fulla, however. Instead of a peephole, his mind was guarded by a tortured maze of mirrors. Every time Laquatus looked in, all he saw were distorted images of himself.

The boy Chainer kept glancing to his right at Louche, a sallow Cabalist who had just become the new Master of the Games. Louche's mind was more open than Chainer's and calmer than the captain's, but there was no useful information in it. It was full of facts and figures and deals and deadlines, all glued together with acrid contempt for almost all sentient being.

The First swept into the room with his attendants hovering all around him. The killers on the wall stood a little straighter as he passed them, and the entire entourage took up their positions at the far end of the room. The First's mind was even more closed to Laquatus than Chainer's.

"I will be brief," the First said. "I am conducting a basic inquiry into the recent visit we received from the crusat. Captain Fleer."

"Yes, Pater." Sweat fairly poured from Fleer's forehead.

"Explain the guards' poor performance."

"It was a well-organized attack," Fleer stammered. "They hit us on three sides simultaneously."

The First nodded to one of his hand attendants, who was busily transcribing the captain's words. "West, north, and south?"

"Yes, Pater."

"But not from the east. Not from the sea." He looked at Laquatus meaningfully, but the ambassador kept his face and his thoughts blank.

"No, Pater. There was no attack on the port or the docks."

"That you know of."

"Uh . . . no, Pater. Not that I know of."

"And yet, somehow an entire squadron of crusat fanatics was able to gain access to the arena."

"Yes, Pater."

"And storm the vault in an effort to seize the Mirari."

"Yes, Pater."

"And you have no idea how they were able to get to the arena so quickly?"

"No, Pater. We killed or wounded hundreds," he added desperately. "They took heavy casualties in their retreat."

"Because they took almost none in the attack. Be silent, Captain." The First turned his withering white gaze on Laquatus. "Ambassador," he said. "I trust you were not inconvenienced by the attack?"

"Not at all, O Patriarch. If not for the noise, I doubt I would have even known there was an attack."

"Outstanding. As you know, the comfort of our visitors is something we city dwellers pride ourselves on. We would never want to breach the sacred bond between host and guest."

"That bond is as strong as ever, my lord."

"You must understand, however, that these events will impact the plans we have already made."

"Of course, my lord." Laquatus swallowed his first taste of uncertainty. "I trust it will not impact them too . . . dramatically?"

"That remains to be seen." The First addressed Louche. "Master of the Games," he said, and Laquatus saw Chainer's mild surprise tinged with . . . disappointment? Laquatus wasn't sure, but clearly Chainer had not been aware of Louche's promotion.

"Pater."

"Your predecessor allowed the arena to be taken like some lonely mountain outpost. The pits are now in your hands. Will they be ready for the anniversary games?"

Louche's lips moved as he juggled figures in his head. "Three months from now, Pater?"

"Two months, three weeks," the First said.

Louche nodded. "No problem. The damage to the facilities was mostly cosmetic. The crowds will be down for the next few weeks because the spectators will be afraid of another raid. They'll forget, though. By the time the anniversary rolls around, everything will be back to normal."

"Outstanding. Be sure that all the shills and runners know the date. I want the arena full."

"Yes, Pater."

The First now turned his milky gaze on Chainer. He smiled warmly. "Master Chainer," he said.

"Pater." Chainer seemed completely at ease, almost disinterested.

"Once again, the Cabal owes you its thanks. It is impossible to tell how much damage the Order would have done—" he glared at Fleer— "if you hadn't arrived in time to stop them."

"I am your obedient child."

"That you are. But there should be more of a reward than my praise. Is there anything you desire? If it is within my power, it shall be yours."

"I require nothing, Pater," Chainer said. "Though my friend and partner Kamahl was gravely injured during the raid. He is not Cabal, yet he put his own body in harm's way on the Cabal's behalf."

"Then your friend and partner also has my thanks. His wounds are being seen to?"

"They are. But if it pleases you, Pater, I have chosen my reward."

"Name it."

"Give me the Mirari," Chainer said, and Laquatus fought the urge to cry out.

"Not to keep," the young dementist went on, "but to use on my friend."

"I was unaware that the Mirari had healing powers," the First said. Laquatus heard an element of suspicion in the Patriarch's voice, suspicion that Laquatus shared. How did the boy know something about the Mirari that neither Laquatus or the First knew?

"As far as I know, it doesn't. But the extent of my powers has yet to be defined. I would like to try to help my friend with the Mirari in my hands."

Laquatus could no longer contain himself. "No one yet has touched the Mirari and lived," he blurted.

Chainer smiled. "Except for me, Ambassador. And I only seek to borrow the Mirari, not to own it."

The First paused, obviously deep in thought. "It shall be done," he said. "Although I shall accompany you, to protect the Cabal's interests."

"Of course, Pater."

"I should very much like to see the Mirari in the hands of an expert," Laquatus said. "Twice now I have watched it destroy its temporary owners."

"Your presence is not necessary," Chainer said. Laquatus was preparing to argue when Chainer continued, addressing the First. "Although I would also like to employ the Mirari as an aid in fulfilling our bargain with the ambassador. I can provide him with a new familiar at any time, but with the Mirari in hand, I can exceed his expectations."

"I have no objections to the dementist's proposal," Laquatus said quickly.

The First was slower to respond. "Very well," he said. "But one use of the Mirari is a reward. The second must be paid for."

"Pater. I am always at your service."

"When shall the Mirari be employed on my behalf?" Laquatus asked.

Chainer and the First exchanged a knowing glance, then each nodded. Laquatus was beside himself that they were communicating right in front of him, and he had no idea what they were saying.

"Two days hence," the First said, and Chainer nodded again. "Now, there is one final matter that I need to address." He clapped his hands once, and the former Master of the Games was dragged, bound and kicking, into the chamber. She was gagged, but she continued to babble incoherently through the heavy cloth.

"Capau, be still." The sound of her secret name drained all the energy out of the former Master of the Games. She stood dazed and listless, her eyes glassy and fearful. The First gestured, and one of his attendants stepped forward and slashed her bonds from her wrists and ankles. The former Master of the Games stood perfectly still as if unaware of her new freedom.

Laquatus stole a glance at Louche, who had just taken over the dangerous position. For once the bitter little man was not thinking of how much others annoyed him. In fact, Laquatus didn't need to read minds to understand the sickly, haunted look on Louche's face.

"Sadget, step forward" the First intoned, and Fleer woodenly took up the space next to the bound master.

"You have failed, my children," the First said. "But in the Cabal failure is not punishable by death. Failure requires correction, not extinction. Your failures, however, have cost the Cabal too much. You will make amends for the lives and the materials wasted by your blundering." The First spread his arms wide, and for once none of his attendants jumped forward to do his bidding. In fact, Laquatus thought, even the near-mindless hand attendants were staying well clear of Fleer and the formerly bound woman.

"I forgive you, my children, for your failure." The First smiled at Laquatus, and added, "My greatest flaw is a tendency to overindulge my family. I can never stay angry at them for long." Laquatus smiled politely, but the Cabalists continued to writhe in horror before the First.

"Capau. Sadget. Accept your forgiveness, and your Pater's love. Embrace me and settle your account, so this matter can be forgotten."

Laquatus saw frenzied bolts of terror flash across Louche's mind, and even Chainer seemed apprehensive. The merman was fascinated. He had never seen anyone so much as brush the sleeve of the First's robe. He understood physical contact with their patriarch was the Cabalists' only taboo, and yet two of them were being beckoned into the First's arms by the man himself.

The errant Cabalists stepped woodenly forward, shuffling like sleepwalkers. Tears of terror were streaming down Fleer's face, and the former Master of the Games seemed almost catatonic. They came forward, however, and stood perfectly still as the First wrapped them both in his long arms.

As soon as the gray flesh of the First's hand touched the squirming Cabalists, they began to scream. The First tightened his grip and locked his hands together with Fleer and the deposed master held tight. Their skin blackened where he touched it. The patches of stricken skin spread like fire across a pool of oil, and fine tendrils of black smoke drifted from the victims into the First's waiting nostrils. The Cabal patriarch tightened his grip again and threw his head back. The two figures in his arms were now scarcely recognizable as human. Instead, they seemed to be delicate, paper-thin flowers that were drooping, dying, and rotting all in a matter of seconds. The hollow, brittle rinds of two adult Cabalists collapsed into a thousand fragments as the last of their essence was converted into ebon mist and absorbed by the First.

"Now," the First had grown larger, more robust, "all is truly forgiven." He clapped his hands together, dislodging ashen fragments from his sleeves. "Chainer," he said, "stay with me. The rest of you are dismissed with my thanks."

Laquatus followed Louche as the guards led them out and down the hallway. He would have to be especially careful now. In two days he would be in the same room with the Mirari while Chainer employed it. Everyone else who tried to use the sphere died in cataclysmic circumstances while the Mirari rolled free. If Chainer were going to destroy himself as Pianna and Aboshan had, Laquatus intended to make sure that this time he was the one who caught the bouncing ball.

* * * * *

While the others were led away, the First had his attendants hold up documents for him to read, nodding once for each when he was finished. The attendants made the First's mark on the scrolls he approved, then took them away.

"It was a terrible thing, this crusat raid," the First said.

Chainer nodded.

"Such a thing should never be allowed to happen again," the First continued.

Chainer nodded.

"There were a hundred Cabal fatalities and twice a hundred injuries. But even more than for the murder of our brethren, I want Major Teroh and the other hard-liners to pay for their arrogance. Do they think they can attack us in our own home and walk away with only a bloodied nose? They owe us restitution, and no one walks away from a Cabal debt."

"The First is wise."

"You know what I'm going to ask, don't you?" The First's eyes were calm and wide.

241

"Yes, Pater."

"And in return, you know I will grant you a second use of the Mirari."

"Yes, Pater."

"When can you leave?"

"Tonight, Pater. After I have visited Kamahl and tried my best to heal him. He was instrumental in my shikar. I cannot leave him to the leeches."

The First nodded. "What did you think of my demonstration?"

Chainer paused. "I think the ambassador either encouraged or enabled the raid. I think he still wants the Mirari. I think he intends to use it to take control of Mer, and then he will come for Otaria."

"He will try," the First agreed. "But there is value in an ally with no morals. If he will betray us to the Order, he will in turn betray the Order to us."

"The First is wise."

"Let us discuss the details of the casting you have planned for him. I may be able to . . . improve the overall result."

"As soon as I return, Pater."

"Outstanding. Now," he thrust his hands deep into the sleeves of his robe. "Let us attend to your barbarian friend."

CHAPTER 21

Thirty miles up the eastern road from Cabal City, the Samite sanctuary was filled to capacity. Nibahn the healer was on her third trip to the apothecary for clean bandages and sleeping herbs. The majority of her patients were expected to live through the night, but only if she and her staff worked round the clock. She believed utterly in the Order, but she despised the brutality of the crusat. The Samite way of universal tolerance was the only way she knew to bring about a better world.

Halfway back to the hospital, a whispered voice from the shadows hissed, "Healer." Nibahn adjusted the thick bundle of bandages and clay bottles under one arm and approached the sound.

"Hello? Are you wounded? All are welcome. All are safe. Will you come forward?" She could make out two human figures in the darkness, two men of roughly equal size. One of them took a half step forward and spoke.

"Kindness for kindness, Samite. No one walks away from a Cabal debt." Nibahn felt something round and hard strike her forehead, and she fell back in a swoon. Though conscious, she was too stunned by the blow to see or move. Someone wrapped metal bonds around her hands, and dragged her roughly by the collar into the shadows.

"You understand why you're here?" the whispering voice said to something in the shadows. The only reply was an angry, ominous buzz.

"Then go," the voice said, and Nibahn heard no more.

* * * * *

Major Teroh made a brief obeisance to the angel guarding the door and entered the hospital. The Samites were deluded fools, but their healing arts had been handed down for thousands of years and were still unmatched.

Inside, the Major scowled as he took in the rows and rows of wounded troopers, aven and human alike. Teroh cursed Laquatus for giving him the idea for the raid, but he could not blame everything on the ambassador. The merman had gotten them into the heart of the city with some sort of water teleportation spell, just as he had promised. It was a risky plan from the start, and the Cabal had offered far more resistance than Teroh had expected.

Still, he thought, as he continued to tour the hospital, it might not be a complete loss. The Cabal still held the Mirari, but now that the crusat was open and declared, other Order commanders from all around Otaria were contacting Teroh, looking to join his army. It would be well worth the loss of a few hundred troopers if a few thousand rose up in righteous fury to avenge them.

There was a scuffle at the entrance, and Teroh turned to see what was causing it. A tall, thin man dressed in what appeared to be black paper was attempting to enter the hospital, and the angel had drawn her sword to block him. The man's face was featureless, hidden under a wide-brimmed hat.

"To arms," the angel cried. "Hostile on the ward." She couldn't take flight amid such close quarters, but she spread her wings anyway to keep the man from darting past her. Teroh still did not understand the concern in her voice. The intruder looked about as substantial as a scarecrow, and he wasn't even armed.

The angel struck first, something Teroh had never seen before. Usually they waited for their opponents to strike or threaten an innocent before they attacked. From his vantage point across the room, he could see the angel and the intruder in profile. She had driven her sword straight into his torso, where it met no resistance as it plunged through. The scarecrow didn't flinch.

The angel turned her head and screamed across the room, "Run! In Serra's name, run now!" The staff of the hospital looked to Teroh, and he shrugged. Most of the wounded were dozing, and few of them were fit enough to get out of bed anyway.

"Sister," Teroh raised his voice as he addressed the angel, "what are you—" He stopped when he saw a clinging gray smoke waft out of the scarecrow's chest wound. Teroh realized the intruder wasn't dressed in paper, his skin was made of paper—or something very much like it. His chest had not been cut by the angel's sword, it had been torn like parchment.

The mist floated in midair between the two figures for a moment longer, and then it rushed at the angel. The smoke began to bubble and boil as it touched her face, her neck, her arms, and she screamed, something else Teroh had never known an angel to do.

"Swords," he called as he drew his own, and two more angels and a handful of on-duty troopers responded.

As her comrades approached, and the mist churned and boiled across her flesh, the first angel flailed wildly with her sword. It passed harmlessly through the mist, but whenever the blade touched the scarecrow, his papery skin split, and more gray mist wafted out to join the assault. The angel was in agony, but she refused to abandon her post.

A second angel lunged forward with her sword. There was a swish and a rustle, and the intruder's head dropped backward, connected to his torso only by a few papery threads. His body still stood, however, and now the gray mist poured out of his neck to attack the second angel.

"Stop cutting him," Teroh barked, but it was too late. Whatever filled the scarecrow's body was caustic and was quickly stripping the exposed skin off the two angels. Teroh grabbed a nearby Samite by the shoulder and said, "Bring bed sheets. Towels. Anything that we can wrap him in to staunch that smoke and get him out of here."

The first angel dropped where she stood, her face stripped down to the bone, and the smoke was not dissipating. In fact, it seemed to be growing, larger and thicker as it consumed the rest of its first victim. Teroh stared in horror as he realized it wasn't smoke at all. It was insects. Millions of them, each no bigger than a pinpoint, stripping the flesh from the angels' bones by the mouthful. And with each mouthful, they were growing bigger.

"Fire," Teroh yelled to a trembling trooper. "We need fire." The buzzing of the tiny swarm grew louder and more furious as the insects themselves grew larger and larger. The second angel fell, little more than a winged skeleton. The bugs on the first angel were now as big as wasps, and Teroh could see their savage mandibles working as they consumed their victims. The Samite he had ordered to fetch bed sheets came forward with them, but the healer's eyes were locked on the ever-increasing swarm that blocked the only exit.

"You," Teroh pointed at a trio of soldiers, "and you and you. That thing has to be driven outside. Charge."

"Charge, sir?"

"It's going to kill us all! Gods damn it, I gave you an order! Now charge, troopers! Defend the Order!"

Two of the three soldiers rushed at the deflating hive man and were promptly engulfed in gray mist and voracious insects. The third stood frozen while his partners died screaming. Teroh stormed over to the man and ran him through where he stood.

"Coward," he snarled.

The bugs were now as big as carrier pigeons, and they started to spread out across the hospital. New cries of pain issued out from bandaged faces and cloth partitions. The last angel on the ward leaped in and slashed one of the larger insects in two. Both halves reformed into smaller versions of the original and promptly attacked the angel's face.

The air was thick with the sounds of agony and the terrible buzzing of the hive. The insects were so numerous and so large that it became impossible to see clearly. Teroh held his sword loosely in his hand, and scanned the crush of screaming people. There were no ranks in the room anymore, however, only panicked individuals fighting for their lives.

I must escape, Teroh realized. I have to get word of this to Bretath. Though he was livid with rage at the thought of another retreat, Teroh knew his original thinking was correct. It was worth the loss of a hundred, or five hundred, or a thousand, if ten thousand more would march to replace them.

Teroh turned his sword on the cloth wall of the tent beside him and dove through the rent. He got to his feet and looked back into the hospital, but there was nothing he could do for those who remained inside. He could only take their deaths to Bretath and use them to raise more troops for the crusat.

Teroh turned and sprinted for the command tent across the compound. Without a torch, he didn't see the two spears jammed deep into the ground with a length of chain stretched neck-high between them. He felt it, however, as the chain and the spears held, cracking his larynx and slamming him flat on his back. Choking, dazed, and helpless, Teroh stared up at the starless sky. A calm, careful tread approached him. Whoever it was carried a light source on his chest, and Teroh watched a tall, slender man with braided hair and hollow eyes lean over him.

"Hello, Major." Chainer's dagger was out, and he laid the tip of it on Teroh's jugular vein. "The Cabal is here, and everywhere. Your crusat ends now. Goodbye, Major."

When he was done, Chainer wiped his dagger on the long grass and stayed on the eastern road until the commotion in the sanctuary, the command tent, and the barracks died down. Under his direction, the bugs focused their attack on the soldiers and stayed away from the ranch and stables. He knew the insects would continue to gorge until they had consumed everything in their immediate area, growing larger all the while. Then, they would turn on each other.

Chainer practiced making snakes while he waited. He was getting quite good at it.

When he activated the First's teleportation spell several hours later and returned to Cabal City, the only things left alive in Teroh's camp were an unconscious Samite healer and a stable of fine white chargers.

* * * * *

The first thing Kamahl saw when he awoke was Chainer. In the cramped, candlelit room, the Cabalist crouched over him like a smirking vulture.

"The Cabal is here," Chainer said, and Kamahl groaned.

"How long have I been out?" Kamahl's body felt heavy, drugged, and leaden.

"Just over a day. You should lie still. You've been wounded, and you aren't done healing yet."

"Wounded?" Kamahl searched his fuzzy memories. "I was fighting at the gates. We were breaking them on the walls. I remember a glowing knight, and the smell of . . . burning air. Then everything went white and jagged and hot."

"You were laid low by a justicar," Chainer said. "They generate righteous lighting, or some such nonsense. We don't know what hey are, really, but that's twice now they've surprised us. You and I are going to have to do something about that."

"I'm ready," Kamahl said angrily. He tried to rise, but only his head made it off the pillow.

"Not yet you aren't. Lie still, or you'll never heal."

Kamahl lifted his arms. They also felt heavy, and he could see thick scars running up both forearms. Or were they calluses? There was a sickly odor in the room that was making it even harder for him to concentrate.

"I've come to show you something," Chainer said. "We've been waiting for hours. You're not one of those people who jumps out of bed ready for the brand new day, are you?'"

"My arms feel wrong," Kamahl said. "My chest is too heavy. Did I breathe in some of that righteous whatever? I feel like I'm gasping."

"You were in pretty bad shape. I couldn't let those Order fools take you, and I didn't trust our own leeches to patch you up right."

Kamahl blinked. "So who healed me?"

"I did," Chainer said proudly. "I arranged to have the Mirari brought in, so I could use it to fix you. Worked like a charm, too."

"The Mirari? Where is it?"

"Safely back in its vault," the First said. He had been hidden behind Chainer, but now he came forward to Kamahl's cot. "It was beautiful to watch, however. Chainer remains one of the few people who can touch the Mirari and use it without destroying everything around him."

The barbarian turned his head and tried to breathe as shallow as he could. The Cabal Patriarch was the source of the sickening odor. Or was he? Kamahl realized his face had been burned, too, and it felt tough and callused like his arms. When the First retreated back behind Chainer, Kamahl could still smell something tainted. Unclean. With a growing sense of dread, he realized the smell was coming from him.

"Am I zombified, or just gangrenous?" he asked seriously. Chainer laughed.

"Neither. That's a side effect of my treatment. It should be temporary."

Kamahl's head was clearing fast. "Your treatment? Since when are you a healer?"

"Since never. But I am a maker. I make things, living things. And with the Mirari's help, I was able to make you whole again. Instead of an entire creature, I only created the parts I needed. The leech helped me graft them in place, but I think you'll agree it's a seamless job."

Kamahl lifted his heavy arms again. He felt more calluses on his chest, feet, and deep under the short ribs on his left side. "More light," he said, and Chainer obligingly brought the candle closer.

Kamahl's hands were covered in stiff copper snakeskin that had grown into and merged with his normal flesh. The new skin was nearly smooth, and the pattern was delicate, but Kamahl could feel the toughness of the individual scales. The edges of each scale were sharp. Kamahl ran his finger underneath one, and the finger came back bleeding. He stared at his own blood for a moment, then looked up helplessly at Chainer.

"You turned me into a snake?"

"No," Chainer chided, "of course not. I patched a few holes and touched up a few surfaces. It'll breathe and grow just like normal skin. But it's even sturdier than the stuff you lost. Anything less than a full-on sword thrust just bounces off." He smiled. "What do you think?"

"Get it off me." Kamahl spoke calmly but forcefully. "Now."

Chainer looked crushed. "But . . . I can't. It's a permanent graft."

"I didn't ask for it. I don't want it."

"You're tired," the First stepped forward again. "You need some time to adjust. It's a major change, after all, and—"

"Get the Mirari in here," Kamahl said, "and undo what you did."

The First's voice grew cold as the grave. "I'm afraid that suggestion is not a possibility. It's also remarkably ungrateful."

Kamahl shut his eyes. "Neither of you understand," he said. He lashed out and took Chainer by the shirt front, holding his new skin in front of Chainer's face with his free hand. "We barbarians don't do this kind of thing. Chop off my arm, and I must learn to fight one-handed. Put out my eyes, and I must learn to fight blind. This—" he released Chainer and shook his scaly fists at his friend— "is an abomination. It goes against everything I've ever believed." He lowered his arms. "I'm sorry, Chainer, but you've made a mistake. Thank you for your gift. I will not accept it."

"We should let Kamahl get some rest," the First said. "Sleep, barbarian. Everything will look different in the morning." He glided out of the room without another word or a second glance.

"You're really angry," Chainer said.

"Not angry, Chainer. Serious."

Chainer shook his head. "I'm sorry, Kamahl. I truly am. The First is right." Chainer followed his patriarch's path, but he backed out, so he could keep an eye on Kamahl. "You should get some sleep. We'll talk more in the morning, and I'll see about . . . I'll see what I can do."

* * * * *

Kamahl remained silent for the next several hours as his anger and frustration grew. He couldn't stand the feel of Chainer's gift. The snakeskin itched and chafed his natural skin raw wherever the two touched. He could already feel how it threw off his timing and muted the messages the rest of his body continually sent to his brain. Worst of all, it marked him as a coward and a weakling who couldn't even overcome his own injuries without spare parts from the Cabal's nightmare pantry.

He couldn't stand it—would not stand it. Kamahl let his mind drift, back in time to his training at Balthor's feet, back in space to his home on the Pardic Mountains. Pardic was not the tallest range on the continent, but it was one of the deepest. Tribal legend said that the Pardics ran right to the center of the planet, where the temperature was so hot that the elements and mana alike were combined into one glowing, red-hot ball of fire and molten rock.

Kamahl struggled to control the energy he was gathering. This would be an extremely difficult spell under ideal conditions. As it was, Kamahl would need every ounce of concentration he could muster to keep from immolating himself completely.

He stared at his hands and focused his thoughts on the sensation of the alien skin. The same sensation echoed in his side, on his legs, on his face, all the places Chainer had treated. He isolated those sensations, in effect isolating those parts of his body and those layers of skin that were no longer his own.

In Kamahl's native language, there was a word for the act of sterilizing and sealing a wound with fire. The word was "cachede," and Kamahl pronounced it now.

The huge barbarian growled and gritted his teeth as the snakeskin grafts all burst into flame simultaneously. He could not clearly recall the pain of the original injury, but he was certain that this was far worse. The horrid stench of burning flesh filled the room, and noxious smoke stung his eyes. Kamahl clenched his fists as they burned, holding them aloft so as not to ignite the bedclothes.

When the last of the scales was burned away, the fires on Kamahl's body sputtered and died. He sat in complete agony for a moment. Then he shoved himself out of the bed and clumsily began bathing his fresh wounds with water from the bedside basin.

I will live, he promised himself. I will heal. I will fight again under my own power, on my own terms.

And I will leave this place with the Mirari in my fist, or I will not leave it at all.

CHAPTER 22

Chainer moved into his lavish new quarters in the First's manor and threw himself into his new duties. The Order's crusat blossomed into a full-blown war in the wake of Chainer's visit to the camp, and the First charged Chainer with bringing the hostilities to a speedy conclusion. While the First dealt with angry communiqués from the Order's highest ranking officers, Chainer would respond to the marked increase in crusat raids around the region. The raiders were not yet numerous enough to mount another attack on Cabal City. Instead, small bands of troopers and officers were terrorizing the lesser Cabal strongholds in northern Otaria, especially those with pit facilities.

So Chainer had very little time to dwell on Kamahl's betrayal. Mere days after mutilating himself, the barbarian packed up his kit and left the leech's chambers on legs that could barely support him. Chainer realized how completely Kamahl had turned his back on Cabal hospitality. He wondered what kind of madness led a man to spit on his hosts and make enemies of his closest friends. The last thing Chainer heard about his former partner was that he was renting a room in a public house near the docks, where the rents were low and interaction between landlord and tenant was minimal.

None of that mattered in the larger scheme of things, of course. Kamahl insisted on being treated like any another contestant in the pits, and the Cabal would happily accommodate him. When he came for the Mirari he would fall to Chainer just like every other nameless challenger.

Chainer's new quarters were large and sumptuous, but he had no furniture apart from a chair and a sleeping cot scavenged from his room at Skellum's academy. He brought the cot because it reminded him of his mentor, not because he needed it. Sleep came to him in short, sudden bursts, and sometimes it never came at all.

Just as well, he mused. He had very little time to sleep, anyway. The First had sent scrolls and tomes for him to review, and the Master of the Games regularly added stacks of dates and pairings for upcoming games. Chainer himself had requested some additional reading material on his own, but all of the scrolls and heavy books and loose sheets of paper lay in a confused pile in the corner of the smallest room. Chainer had read them all and retained quite a bit of it, but he preferred to spend his time preparing for battle. He made snakes or weighted chains and aggressively hurled them at imaginary enemies as he sprinted and rolled from room to empty room.

They were all coming for the Mirari, he knew, all of them. The First had been so delighted with Chainer's use of the sphere on Kamahl that he had made Chainer its official keeper. It stayed hidden in a warded vault that would only open if Chainer and the First spoke the right charm at the exact same moment while standing side-by-side outside the door, but no one was ever permitted to touch the Mirari but Chainer, not even the First himself. Even better, when the Mirari games were staged, Chainer would represent the Cabal, and if he won the tournament, he would win the right to bear the Mirari permanently, as he now bore his dagger and censer. A victory for the Cabal meant a victory for Chainer, and vice-versa.

Chainer impulsively created two huge saber-toothed anacondas and set them on one another. He wanted to see what happened when they tried to squeeze each other to death. While the snakes wrapped around each other like a braided garrote, Chainer let his mind wander back to the sensation of holding the Mirari in his hands, of having unimaginable power literally at his fingertips.

Chainer had stood over Kamahl's sleeping body with the Mirari clenched between his palms. In his mind, he saw a bipedal snake man with copper scales standing alongside Kamahl. The two images slid together until they were two overlapping phantoms occupying the exact same space. The snake man's body faded away except for those areas that corresponded to Kamahl's wounds. Chainer felt the first giant wave from an endless ocean of power flow out of the Mirari and into his head. Something shifted deep in his brain, and when he opened his eyes the First was beaming, and Kamahl had live, healthy flesh ready for the leech's grafting spells.

Tapping into the Mirari was different than being in dementia space, different even from communing with Kuberr. The Mirari was its own power, and it didn't mingle or share with the person who held it. The sphere was more like an infinite battery in search of a will through which it could focus and release its energy.

The Mirari could change the world, Chainer knew, but it couldn't decide how on its own. Making the decision and unleashing the power had proved fatal to everyone but him, and Chainer took enormous pride in that. Not only was he the only being alive who had used it, he alone was the only one who could. It was his to employ, his to use on behalf of the Cabal. It had told him so the first time he saw it, and everything it had shown him had come true. As soon as he had annihilated the Order and won the Mirari for himself in the games, his destiny would be complete.

A soft knock and a call of "Master?" interrupted his training.

Master Chainer had earned the rank by successfully completing the shikar, and the First had formally conferred it upon him in the wake of the redoubled crusat. He dismissed the two anacondas, touched the polished marble wall to ground himself, and replied.

"The Cabal is here." He was learning to control the physical changes his powers caused. If he concentrated, he could cancel the musical reverberation of his voice. He was less successful at controlling the appearance of his eyes.

A young blonde girl came hesitantly in. She held an onyx scroll case. "The First and Ambassador Laquatus await your presence," she said. She never looked up at Chainer. He guessed his eyes were currently hollow. Had he been that timid at her age? That frightened?

"Thank you, little sister," he said. She smiled to acknowledge his kindness, but she still seemed cowed, terrified. Perhaps she had only smiled to avoid antagonizing him. Chainer felt the urge to send a rattlesnake slithering across her sandaled feet, a glowing-eyed venom-spitting nightmare that would strike but never bite, that would follow her everywhere and burrow under her pillow while she slept, rattling all the while.

He put the temptation aside. He had business with the First, and besides, he was sure the messenger would crack in less than two days. Hardly worth the effort of creating the snake in the first place.

"If you are ready, Master, I will take you to them."

"I'm ready, little sister. Lead on." Chainer saw the shadow of a thick, scaled body moving across the messenger's foot, but she didn't react to its touch. He blinked hard, and the rattler was gone.

"Are you all right, big brother?"

"I said lead on," Chainer snapped. He was suddenly irritable. Was it lack of sleep? He vowed that he would get some rest, as soon as he and the Mirari introduced Laquatus to his new familiar.

* * * * *

Chainer was taken to a small, comfortable room outside the vault that contained the Mirari. He was greeted warmly by the First and Laquatus, but the ambassador visibly fumed when he was ordered to stay behind while the Cabalists fetched the sphere. When Chainer reentered the room bearing the Mirari, Laquatus stared at it hungrily.

"Ambassador," Chainer said. "On behalf of the First and the Cabal, let me apologize for the delay. Now, as agreed, I present you with Turg's replacement." Chainer used the Mirari as he had with Kamahl, held tight between his hands with his eyes closed. He had put a great deal of thought into the casting beforehand, with constant input and refinement from the First. Every detail had been meticulously planned. Unleashing the actual creature was almost an afterthought.

Chainer saw the creature clearly in his mind. It was a medium-tall humanoid male with five fingers, no toes, and the well defined musculature of a competitive swimmer. Its body was hairless and featureless, an unbroken surface with no openings for eyes, nose, ears, or mouth. It was bruise-black in color, a dark and murky purple that was effective camouflage both in the shadows of the city and the sunless depths of the ocean. With an extremely bright light directly behind it, however, one could see that it was partially translucent with no recognizable bones or internal organs of any kind. In his mind's eye, Chainer saw a collar streak out and find the featureless man's neck. He noted with satisfaction that the figure did not struggle, or claw, or react in any way to the collar. It seemed as comfortable with it as it did without it.

Chainer gave the leash a gentle mental tug. The creature took a single step forward and disappeared. Chainer opened his eyes, and the purple figure stood in the center of the room, steaming like a lobster fresh from the pot.

"Ambassador Laquatus." Chainer presented the featureless man with a grand wave of his golem hand. "Meet your new familiar. I call him Burke." Laquatus inspected the new arrival and was clearly unimpressed.

"Quickly. Call him by name," Chainer said. Laquatus put his hands on his hips, obviously skeptical of the entire affair.

"Now. He needs to imprint on you as his master, or we'll have to start all over."

"Burke." Laquatus shot the First a long-suffering look as he spat the name out. "Attend your master."

Burke responded to the sound of his name by facing Laquatus then dropping to one knee with his head bowed and his fists on the floor.

"At least he knows his place," Laquatus said. "But what else can he do?"

Chainer had expected this reaction from Laquatus, and he smiled patiently. "Well," he said, "you specified obedient, powerful, and amphibious. Burke is all those things. You can see how quickly he responds to your voice. And he doesn't need to breathe, so both land and sea are accessible to him."

"But what does he do?" Laquatus keened. "Obedient and amphibious do me no good if there's no power to back them up. He has to be my new jack, my champion in the pits. How does he fight?"

Chainer smiled again. "Perhaps a demonstration is in order." He scanned the room. "If you'll follow me to a room with a bit more space, ambassador, I'm sure Burke will satisfy your concerns."

"If I may," the First interrupted, "I will take my leave of you now. Chainer, let us return the Mirari to the vault, so you and Laquatus can test his new jack." Laquatus sulked some more as Chainer and the First left him to become acquainted with Burke while they put their treasure away.

"Has it worked, Master Chainer? Have you created exactly what we discussed?"

"Exactly, Pater."

"Outstanding. Convince the ambassador to accept his gift and send them both on their way. Come to my chambers when you are done. I would discuss your strategy for defending the lesser pits between now and the games."

"I will be along directly, Pater." They replaced the Mirari, sealed the vault, and the First went away, trailing his attendants behind him. When Chainer returned to the conference room, Laquatus was peering into Burke's blank face.

"Can I touch him? Is he at least caustic?"

"Follow me, please. And no, Ambassador, I'm afraid not. Burke's entire body is composed of nothing more than a dense, inert gel." He led Laquatus down the hall toward one of the private pits, smaller versions of the main arena for private matches and demonstrations.

"Inert? Do you mean it does nothing?"

"I mean it interacts with nothing. A drop of his body material on your skin or in your bloodstream wouldn't harm you any more than a drop of oil. The gel is extremely durable, however. The sharpest sword or dagger might pierce his hide, but the blade will snap before it goes any deeper.

"I think you're missing the advantages of his body, Ambassador. He has no bones to break, no organs to rupture. He doesn't breathe, so he cannot be strangled. He has no eyes, so he cannot be blinded. No pores means no way for his skin to absorb irritants. No circulatory system means no way for diseases or poisons to spread inside his body. Virtually every attack he faces in the pits is going to fail, simply because his doesn't function like a normal living body. Burke's body is just a vessel for his mind, and his mind is a vessel for your commands."

"Doesn't function normally," Laquatus echoed. "It doesn't seem to function at all! All you've given me is a defensive creature, a bodyguard. And I will repeat myself. I need a jack, a fighting champion."

They came upon the closed door that led to a private pit, and Burke sprang forward to hold the door for them as they passed. "Thank you," Chainer said, and Laquatus grumbled.

"I sincerely hope, Master Chainer, that you don't expect me to be polite to this servant every time he attends me."

"No, Ambassador. The Cabal teaches us to be polite to all our guests, including their servants. And Burke is now very much yours."

"A greater treasure I have yet to receive," Laquatus said nastily. "And you haven't answered my question. How does he fight? And more to the point, how does he win?"

"Now that we're here," Chainer said, "I can answer your question. And believe me, you're going to love this."

"We shall see."

"Order him into the center of the room, please." As Laquatus repeated the order and Burke moved, Chainer continued. "He will only respond to you from now on. After a few weeks, you won't even need to talk. It'll be as if he hears your thoughts." Chainer watched Laquatus carefully, but the merman kept his expression neutral. "Won't that be an interesting sensation? To speak without moving your lips?"

"Imperial jesters have been doing that trick for a thousand years," Laquatus said. Chainer thought he saw the barest flicker of recognition, however.

"Of course. My apologies. I'm sure that the Mer learned to speak silently generations ago. Makes it easier to issue commands at the bottom of the sea."

Laquatus was staring sharply at Chainer, as if he had just realized there was a deeper meaning to Chainer's casual banter. "You mentioned a demonstration, Master. I am waiting."

"By all means. For the purposes of the demonstration, I'm going to put Burke up against a mixed group of sea creatures and land crawlers."

"An excellent idea. But that is an offensive term to some merfolk tribes."

"I meant no offense," Chainer said. "There are so many types of sea creatures in the sea that I sometimes have trouble keeping all their customs straight. It would be better for everyone if Mer could unite behind a single leader, don't you think?"

Laquatus looked intrigued, but his voice was suspicious. "I would welcome the chance to discuss the current situation in Mer with you. Later on. But right now . . . my demonstration?"

Chainer nodded, and with a wave cast four hostile monsters across the room at Burke. A twenty-foot sea serpent thrashed wildly, forcing a long-horned tiger to spring aside and stalk Burke from his left. A four-foot bat with eight spider's legs flapped and chittered madly around the ceiling, and a huge bipedal killer whale slowly moved closer to the gel man. Burke stood impassive with his feet planted firmly on the floor as the creatures all oriented on him and began their attack.

"Order him to kill them all," Chainer said. Laquatus shrugged.

"Burke," he intoned. "This is your master. Destroy your attackers."

The tiger pounced first, seven hundred pounds of snarling fangs, gleaming horns, and sharp claws. Burke stood frozen as the big cat descended on him, and then, in a motion so fast that not even Chainer could follow it, he ducked under the tiger's extended paws and sunk his arm up to the shoulder in the brute's belly. Burke wrapped his other arm around the top of the tiger's torso and slammed it head-first into the stone floor with a brutal combination of power and balance. The tiger's skull cracked, and it faded from the room.

Burke then turned his eyeless face up to the ceiling and extended his arm out toward the spider bat. The gel in his arm softened and stretched as he reached, doubling then tripling the length of the appendage until the bat was trapped in the upper corner of the room. Burke's hand dipped and weaved as the bat tried to avoid it, but he quickly caught the rabid creature by the throat. His arm snapped back to its normal size and shape in a heartbeat, leaving the bat to fall dead to the floor. Its head remained clenched in Burke's hand until both parts of the bat's body disappeared.

The whale creature was better suited to fighting on dry land than the serpent, and it reached Burke first. It grabbed the ambassador's jack like a doll in both hands and rammed him deep into its mouth. The creature ground its huge jaws together once, twice, and then threw its head back like a shark to swallow the chunks of its meal without further chewing. It turned to

Chainer and Laquatus, spread its arms, and bellowed defiantly.

"Well, that was entertaining," Laquatus said. "Perhaps we should just forget this ever happened and you can—"

"Three, two, one," Chainer said. "Go."

A bruise-black fist erupted out of the monster's sternum. The whale-thing roared and tried to tear Burke's arm off, but the gel man held on, and the creature only succeeded in ripping Burke completely out of its gullet. Burke's expressionless face showed no reaction to the layer of blood and bile that coated him. The mortally wounded whale-monstrosity fell onto its back and soon vanished.

"One more to go," Chainer said.

The sea serpent had at last found some traction and was undulating at Burke with its jaws wide. Burke regarded those jaws, and then he leaped forward. His spread-eagled body met the oncoming serpent's head, and Burke splashed across the serpent's face like an overripe piece of fruit. To Laquatus's visible amazement, the shapeless splotch of gel adjusted itself and willfully expanded across the serpent's mouth and nose until both airways were blocked. The serpent shook its head violently in an attempt to dislodge its tormentor, but the gel clung tight and would not be thrown off. The serpent's struggles grew slower, then feeble, then stopped altogether. Only when it disappeared out from under him did Burke reform himself into his humanoid shape.

"He's even better underwater," Chainer said happily. "He can smother gills as easily as lungs. The principle's exactly the same, keep air from entering the body."

Burke stood tall and silent, awaiting his next command. Laquatus woodenly began to clap, slow, measured applause that gave him time to think.

"Absolutely marvelous," Laquatus said. "Forgive me, Master. I did not fully appreciate the value of your gift."

Chainer smiled graciously. "Not at all Ambassador. There are many tasks a man in your position needs a reliable jack to perform. The Cabal is always willing to assist you."

Laquatus was still staring at Burke, his mind furiously churning.

"I'm sure," Chainer went on, "that you'll find something useful for Burke to do almost immediately."

That caught Laquatus's attention. "There are many ways I could employ such a champion. Some are more urgent than others."

"I also have urgent matters to attend to. Matters far less enjoyable than meeting with you, Ambassador. I wonder if we were to discuss these matters together, would we find a way to help each other, as we have done today?"

"I would be most interested in finding out the answer to that question, Master Chainer. I would welcome the Cabal's help and the chance to help the Cabal in return."

"Perhaps we should meet again before you head back below the sea. Tonight, for example. Over dinner?"

"I would be honored. Come to my embassy this evening, and we'll discuss the future."

"I am looking forward to it. Ambassador?"

"Yes?"

"I've heard wondrous tales of the great libraries of Mer. Is it true that they go back thousands of years?"

"Absolutely true."

"And if you had access to certain other . . . special documents . . . a man of your talents could uncover a secret that has been hidden for generations?"

"It would be my pleasure to try. More, it would be my duty. You have done me a great service here today, Master Chainer."

Chainer offered the ambassador his hand, and after a conspiratorial smile, he took it.

"The Empire and the Cabal," Chainer said. "May their interests always coincide."

PART FOUR:
MASTER

CHAPTER 23

"Master Chainer?"

Chainer started and looked for the speaker. He was in his private chambers with his hands in casting position, facing the corner of the room. Deidre stood in his doorway, all eyes and sharp edges. She appeared more nervous and timid than Chainer had ever seen her before. She seemed shorter and slighter, but she still had the eyes, the hair, the teeth and the nails.

"I thought you were dead," he said. He lowered his arms and bowed.

"Oh. Uh, the First requires your presence, Master." Deidre's face began to soften and melt, running like candle wax.

"Don't go," Chainer said urgently. His vision fogged, and in Deidre's place stood Fulla. She was smiling savagely. Slowly, she snapped her fingers in front of Chainer's face.

Chainer shook his head to clear it. Fulla had vanished. Skellum stood before him, his hat tucked under his arm, his eyes shining and confident.

Chainer's stomach froze when he saw Skellum. The fresh pain of his mentor's death told Chainer that the apparition before him was a lie. Rage churned up the pain and soon overwhelmed Chainer's grief.

"Remember me," Skellum said.

Chainer angrily waved the phantom away. He closed his eyes tight, then opened them again. The only other person in the room was the frightened little blond messenger. Hadn't she been bit by a rattler? Chainer reached for the wall, but his depth perception failed him, and he almost fell to the floor.

"Big brother?"

Chainer found himself propped up between the wall and the messenger's birdlike hands.

"Haven't slept. What day is it?" he said. He stood and dusted off an imaginary cape. The First wanted to see him about the ambassador's new jack. Or had he already seen the First about the ambassador's new jack? It was something about the ambassador's jack, but a new something.

The messenger was staring at him with an absolutely hilarious mixture of pity and fear. Chainer laughed and stood up off the wall.

"Always make that face," Chainer said. "It suits you."

"Yes, big brother." She gave him a gentle shove and guided him out the door.

He remembered now. The First wanted to ask him exactly how much control they would have over Burke now that he had bonded to the ambassador. It was a simple matter and wouldn't take more than an hour. He would lie down on his cot when he returned, force himself to rest. Not that he was tired, of course. He just wanted to stop thinking for a while. His thoughts were starting to intrude on his fun, just as the crusat intruded on his time in the pits.

He watched the back of the messenger's head as they walked, and he felt more and more clear with each echoing step they took.

* * * * *

"The ambassador has expressed his satisfaction with your efforts, Master Chainer. Another job well done."

"Thank you, Pater."

"I understand that the demonstration was quite impressive."

"It was glorious, Pater. Burke performed even better than we'd hoped."

"And he is still under your influence?"

"Yes. He is bonded to Laquatus and will obey the ambassador's every command. But his essence is Cabal. Cabal magic, Cabal methods. He is Laquatus's slave, but he is the Cabal's asset."

"And if you wanted to, you could make another?"

This caught Chainer off-guard. "I suppose I could, Pater. Yes. If I had the Mirari to power the casting, a second Burke would be as powerful and as real as the original."

"Outstanding. Let us retrieve the Mirari from the vault. I would like you to create a duplicate of the ambassador's familiar for me."

Chainer felt an idea forming, and the first tingles of anticipation before a major challenge. "Such an attendant would be more durable than your human ones."

"Precisely. And in these troubled times, I need to move about quickly. My retinue of guards and attendants is too large and unwieldy. If I could replace half of them, even a third, with a single body, it would be a great boon to my work."

"It would be my pleasure, Pater."

"Of course, you would be rewarded for this service. Is there anything you desire? If it is within my power, it shall be yours."

"I can think of nothing right now, Pater."

"Well, keep thinking. But now, let us go to the vault."

As they returned, the First peppered Chainer with questions about Burke's capabilities, and Chainer dutifully reported the answers. The First was more excited than Chainer had ever seen him, gesturing emphatically and waving his arms wide. His attendants were hard-pressed to stay close by without being accidentally brushed. Chainer carried the Mirari reverently between both hands.

Back in the First's chamber, Chainer called for space, and the First had his guards and attendants all huddle against the far corner of the room. The First waited eagerly opposite his servants, and Chainer stood between them. He held the edge of his left hand against his stomach with the Mirari floating above his palm. He held his metal hand palm-down over the Mirari, and closed his eyes. He held this position and concentrated for a long time, until some of the braver guards began to grumble and jostle the people around them. The time was now, he told himself. This was what he had been preparing for. It was time to truly impress the First.

"Pater."

"Yes, my child?"

"There are two things preventing me from doing what you have asked."

The First frowned. "What are these things? Can they be removed?"

Chainer's eyes snapped open, the void in his sockets endless and impenetrable. "I thought you'd never ask. The first impediment is that it's far too crowded in here." He unfolded his left arm and left the Mirari hanging below his right. A yellow glow shot out of the sphere, up Chainer's arm, and traveled across his body to his out-stretched left hand. A massive bolt of black light exploded out of Chainer's hand and slammed into the throng of guards and attendants in the corner. The room shook as the death bolt impacted, and some of the servants screamed before the entire group fell dead where they stood.

"Chainer! What are you doing?"

"The second impediment," Chainer said evenly, "is that you sent Skellum into the pits to die."

"Mazeura," the First was regaining his composure, "attend me." Chainer felt the dominating power of his secret name take hold, and his muscles froze where they were.

"I am the Cabal First," he snarled, "and I do not explain my actions. Look at what we have gained, what you have gained, from the death of a single man. Skellum's time had passed, and he knew it. I think you know it, too. These are dangerous times, my child, and not everyone is going to survive. You are the future of dementia, you are the future of Cabal. That future needs to be fast, focused, versatile, brutal. We need you more than we needed Skellum."

"Do not say 'we,' Pater. You do not speak for me in this."

"I speak for the Cabal in all things. And you are Cabal. The oath you took is not some clubhouse initiation ritual, it is a powerful magical bond. You don't just quit the Cabal because your best friend is gone. You are mine, body and soul, for as long as I want you."

"I've been thinking about my oath lately. In Mer they say an oath is nothing more than a contract, and all contracts have loopholes."

The First crossed his arms behind his back. "There are no loopholes in your sacred oath, Mazeura."

"My name is Chainer," he said. "And of course there are. You only have power over me because I gave it to you when I accepted my secret name."

"You accepted much more than that."

"True. But if I could discover your secret name, Pater, wouldn't the roles be reversed? Wouldn't you be as docile before me as I am before you now?"

"No one has known my secret name for a hundred years." Chainer heard the initial strains of uncertainty in the First's voice, and he breathed it in like delicious incense.

"I'm sorry, but that's no longer true . . . Calchexas." Chainer jutted both palms forward, leaving the Mirari to float freely at his chest. An even larger bolt of energy burst from Chainer's hands and totally engulfed the First. His panicked white eyes were the last thing Chainer saw before the First vanished behind a cloud of black light.

Chainer continued to pour energy into the spell, keeping the First's body surrounded by the roiling field. The First had lived a very long time, he reasoned, and would take a lot of effort to kill. He hadn't dropped yet, and Chainer had never seen anyone withstand the death bloom for so long. In fact, the First was still standing upright as Chainer continued to hurl killing magic at him.

"Die," Chainer whispered. With the Mirari he could keep this up for a week. He increased his efforts, and the First was physically driven back into the stone wall. He still stood, however, straight and tall, against an attack that would have overwhelmed an army.

After a full minute of pressing the First against the wall, Chainer broke off. The First's body had been crushed into the stone behind him, and his fine robes were in tatters. He was panting and shaking, but he was very much alive."

"You cannot kill me Mazeura. There is no way you can kill me."

Chainer blasted him again, a brief slap. "Chainer. My name is Chainer."

"You can never kill me, Chainer. I am not merely called the First, I am the first. The first to worship Kuberr. The first to receive his gifts. The first Cabalist. I have lived for centuries. I have fed on bloodlust, greed, and brutality since Otaria was wild and the Mer empire was just another school of intelligent fish. I have been Kuberr's servant since the very beginning, and nothing you do, not even with the Mirari, can prevent me from serving him."

Chainer ran his tongue over his teeth, perturbed. He expected the First to tell outrageous lies and convenient half-truths to save his own life, but here the old viper actually seemed to be telling the truth. At least, he was telling the truth about the death bloom, because it was having almost no effect on him at all.

"So you're immortal?"

"In a sense."

"Then I really can't kill you."

"No. You can't."

Chainer sent a sharpened weight flying toward the First's face. It buried itself in the patriarch's forehead, and Chainer watched the

First's corruption crawl back along the links toward Chainer's hand. Chainer dropped his end before the toxic patina could reach him, and the First actually fell to his knees, clutching feebly at his wound.

"I can try, however." Chainer returned his hands and the Mirari to their position in front of his stomach. The First slumped to one side, groaned, and then got back to his feet.

"We need to settle our account, Chainer. This city . . . the Cabal itself may not survive an all-out conflict between us. I suggest we come to an understanding." With as much poise as he could manage, the First pulled the sharpened weight out of his head and let it clatter to the floor.

"Very well. You ordered Skellum's death. In return I demand yours."

"Your price is too high and can never be paid. I have a counter offer."

"Name it."

"Cabal City is yours," he said, "if you give me safe passage. The manor, the arena, the pits, even the Mirari."

"And where will you go? Do you really expect me to believe that you'll just disappear?"

"I will go south. Our . . . my stronghold in Aphetto City. The Parliament of Knives is weak and ineffectual. I have been ignoring them of late, and they could use a firm, guiding hand."

"And in five years you will come back at the head of an army of mages to retake Cabal City by force."

The First laughed. "That would be wasteful and unnecessary. In fifty years . . . less, given your recklessness . . . you will be gone, and I shall return unopposed. The Cabal is here, and everywhere. I will take it with me, and it will be here when I come back for it."

"You think so."

"I know so."

Chainer grunted. "I accept your terms. Here are mine." Chainer raised his arms over his head. The Mirari stayed between his hands.

"You will use the city-wide grapevine to announce that you are leaving the City under my control. The Cabal still runs things, but now I will run the Cabal."

"No one will follow you, Chainer."

"Everyone will follow me. I am the Cabal's response to the Order crusat, as you always intended. The entire city knows and fears me. And I intend to keep everything running smoothly. The anniversary games will happen as planned. People will come from all over Otaria to claim the prize. And I will destroy them all in one fell swoop."

"I agree to your terms," the First seemed sullen, angry, and Chainer wondered how long it had been since he had been at a disadvantage during negotiations.

"I'm not finished yet. My personal representatives will be sent ahead to Aphetto to prepare it for you. To clear the road before you and to keep an eye on you once you arrive."

"Spies, dementist? That hardly seems like a warrior's style."

"Not spies. Cabalists. They do not report to me, but they are loyal to Kuberr. You may lead them, if you can. But they will be harder to dominate than the Cabalists you're used to."

"What do you mean, 'will be?' " The First sounded as if he already knew and dreaded the answer.

"I mean they *will* be. Observe." Chainer put his hands out in the casting position with the Mirari between them. His eyes went black, and he shuddered. From between his hands, a long tendril of smoke curled outward, growing thicker at the front end. There was an implosion and a flash, and Chainer's new Cabalist stood ready before him.

The creature was a huge, ten-foot serpent as long and heavy as an alligator. It sat on a coil of its own body, propped up by two small hornlike claws where the coil rose off the floor. It had thin, flexible arms that collapsed against its body for quick strikes or rapid motion. Its head was big enough to swallow a cannonball without dislocating its jaw. It appeared to be a rattlesnake man, complete with a warning shaker on its tail and venom dripping from its fangs.

"I've been thinking about snakes recently," Chainer said, "and I've decided I like them better than people. A snake only strikes to hunt or defend itself. It specializes in graceful motion and deadly accuracy. Nature designed them to be elegant killers. I, in turn, have designed them to be perfect Cabalists."

There was another shudder and another flash, and a second snake-person appeared. This one was longer and broader, rippling with muscle. It had no rattle, and its fangs were dry.

"The constrictor caste is especially good at stealth killings. Once it embraces you, you can't even scream. You should get along famously with these, Pater. You have so much in common."

Another shudder, another flash. "And the king snake. Bigger brain, stronger arms, and deadlier venom. They will be the ones who give you the most trouble as you try to take over."

"What are you talking about, Chainer? How many of these things have you made?"

Chainer grinned. "All of them." The final flash blew the First against the wall, and even drove Chainer back a step. The entire building shook. When the First had recovered, there was no one else in the room. No snakes, no attendants, only Chainer and the First.

"My serpent Cabal is now on its way to Aphetto. Scores of them, hundreds. They will hunt and kill and feed and fight on the way. Those that are successful will become real—indistinguishable from things that were born instead of conjured. They will breed and spread throughout Otaria. Who is running Aphetto City for you now?"

"The Parliament of Knives," the First said warily.

"Within a week of their arrival, my snakes will have overthrown the Parliament. If I were you, I'd get down there quickly, before everyone who knows you is killed or driven out."

The First nodded, angry but resigned to his defeat. He was

staring at the Mirari as he spoke to Chainer. "Well done, my child. I can't help taking pride in—"

"Shut up," Chainer said. "The only thing I want to hear out of you is your announcement to the city. And then, Calchexas, you will leave. If I ever see you again, I will make it my life's work to cut you to pieces, burn the remains, and scatter the ashes. I may not be able to kill you, but I can make you wish I had." Chainer closed his eyes, the Mirari glowed, and the First was once again bathed in black light. This light did not harm him, however. It merely cascaded around him.

"Speak clearly, Pater. All of your children are listening, and you won't get a second chance."

The First folded his arms into his sleeves. After one final glare at Chainer, he began to speak. "Attention, my children. This is the First. . . ."

Chainer tuned him out as his mind sizzled and sparked from one topic to the next. First, he would honor his agreement with Laquatus, who had been instrumental in pinning down the First's secret name. Then, Chainer would crush all who came for the Mirari, including the Order and Burke and Kamahl, if they were foolish enough to compete.

And then, he would devote the rest of his life to punishing the First. If he couldn't kill the patriarch, then he would take the one thing from him that mattered most, the Cabal itself. With Chainer's snakes in Aphetto and the Mirari in his hand, it was only a matter of time before all of Otaria danced to Chainer's tune. In fact, he noted with a laugh, the music for the dance had already started in his head.

CHAPTER 24

From inside the Otaria Chasm, Veza watched the conflict between Llawan and Laquatus escalate toward civil war. Since the water portals only worked from surface to surface, the two sides were forced to grind out a victory the old fashioned way, face-to-face on the battlefield.

Llawan's first move was to send an armed force large enough to blockade the gorge, but not to storm it. Laquatus mocked her for not coming in person, and concentrated all of his mercenaries and undersea monsters at Llawan's end of the chasm. There were frequent skirmishes as the imperials tried to press in and the mercenaries labored to keep them out. The two forces continued to grow stronger and stronger as the days wore on.

Veza had never witnessed a full-scale military engagement before, though she had heard vivid stories from her grandfather describing Aboshan's predecessor's rise to power. Where her grandfather described noble duels and magnificent noble beasts, Veza saw ambush and sniper attacks alongside the hideous spectacles of razor rays tearing into leviathans.

Massive orcan warriors surged out of the chasm to engage the empress's troops, and though each was driven back, each took its toll on the imperial guard with their massive fists and powerful jaws. Laquatus's mercenaries were unwilling to fight hand-to-hand. They preferred to pounce from the shadows in overwhelming numbers, or to not leave the safety of the chasm.

The ship-to-ship combat was even worse—giant, graceful, deep-sea creatures roaring and tearing at each other like wild dogs. Llawan's troops took heavy losses to the razor rays until they began using a school of electric eels that cooked the giant fish in mid-battle. Huge, paddle-footed beasts with long necks grabbed guards like fruit from a tree and were in turn choked by sargassum blasts or poisoned by lances coated in lethal puffer-fish extract.

When she wasn't watching the endless stream of carnage and patrol ships, Veza spent her time sifting through the survey data she'd collected. She couldn't reconcile what she'd seen in the chasm with what she reviewed. The data indicated gemstone deposits, precious ores and metals, and a freshwater underground river that could easily be tapped for drinking water. Laquatus was delighted, and the more value she discovered, the more troops he brought in to hold it.

Veza also had duties assigned to her by Laquatus. With the ambassador's armed guards by her side, Veza inspected the canyon walls for stability. Under their careful watch, she enchanted a series of blue crystals and affixed them to the walls along the entire length of the chasm. They crystals could relay magical impulses to one another. Veza used them to transmit data up and down the length of the flood zone. She also knew Laquatus intended to use the crystal arrays as a weapon. If he were forced to quit the chasm, he would send a signal to the crystals that would bring the walls crashing down around whoever was inside. He smiled when he told Veza of his plans, but he made it clear he did not fully trust her yet. He made sure that she was not allowed to alter the spell that powered the stones, so they could only transmit magical impulses, and only within the chasm. If anyone but Laquatus tried to use them in any other way, they would shatter.

Finally, Llawan herself arrived at the head of another flotilla of ships and leviathans. Laquatus had sent Burke to collect Veza and politely forced her to sit and watch the show.

Beyond the front, safe from the fighting, sat Llawan's private yacht, a smaller, slower version of her transport leviathan. Laquatus made sure the empress was indeed on board, and that Veza had an excellent view before he rolled out his surprise. The long, familiar shape of Llawan's transport leviathan streaked out of the chasm and plowed through her forces on a direct line of attack for the empress. Laquatus had not in fact slaughtered the empress's transport vessel, he had commandeered it and sent it into battle against her. Veza almost wept when the empress's troops were forced to strike the leviathan down with spell blasts and giant ballista bolts.

Hours after the destruction of her transport, Llawan unleashed a squadron of heavily armed cephalids. Just as they came into range of the mercenaries' weapons, the squadron vanished from sight. The invisible squadron did a lot of damage to their unsuspecting foes before the enchantment wore off, and they were only captured and killed when they tried to storm Laquatus's command ship.

After the initial exchange of hostility, the front stabilized just outside the chasm and each side settled in for a long siege. Not in the strictest sense of the word, Veza knew, because either side could abandon the battle any time they pleased by simply turning around and swimming away. Veza had been close enough to both Laquatus and Llawan to know that neither of them were going to do that. The entire empire was watching this conflict, and whoever came out of it victorious would have enough political and popular support to claim the imperial throne.

Meanwhile, Veza continued to watch and research, Laquatus stayed safe in his canyon, and Llawan stayed safe in her luxury vessel while their troops tore each other to bits at the mouth of the canyon.

* * * * *

Kamahl strapped on his broadsword and took a few tentative steps across his tiny room. He was nowhere near full recovery, but he could walk. If he could walk, he could fight.

Kamahl was sensitive to the Mirari, and he could feel the powerful forces gathering around it. He was uncertain but unafraid. Unknown challenges were a barbarian's stock in trade, after all, and the promise of a good contest was more than enough incentive for Kamahl to meet this one.

Kamahl left the public house and joined the crowds of people heading for the Cabal City pits.

* * * * *

Cabal City's anniversary games drew more spectators and more combatants than any event ever before. Everyone in and around the city either wanted to take a shot at the Mirari or wanted to watch others do so. From his vantage point high above the arena floor, Chainer watched the crowds and the fighters buzz and vibrate like a huge hive of wasps.

Chainer looked around at the former First's private box. It was a luxurious, round, floating platform with all the amenities visiting dignitaries expected. The First often watched important games from here, or rather, watched the crowd watching the games. Among the First's finery, with the Mirari safely hidden in his chambers, Chainer understood what Skellum meant when he spoke of the good things in life.

Chainer leaned over the side of the platform with a dizzy grin on his face. All of the contestants had been assembled in the main pit below, and it was literally full of hundreds of humans and monsters crammed together under Chainer's box. Down there, they were waiting. Up here, he simply was, and would be until he decided to start the action.

"Ladies, gentlemen, and others!" The announcer's voice was much louder up here than it was at ground level. "Welcome to the Mirari Games." A small cheer went up through the crowd.

"Today we have something truly unique in store for you. The largest collection of fighters in the world has gathered for the right to claim the Mirari, the sphere of wonder. There will be only one winner. There—"

A bolt of lightning shot up from the floor into the magical apparatus that amplified the announcer's voice, and his introduction sputtered and choked. Intrigued, Chainer peered more closely at the tall figure standing alone at the center of the only clear space on the arena floor.

"Murderer," the figure cried, his voice echoing like a gong. "Destroyer of the innocent. The Order is here for retribution."

"I know, justicar," Chainer said softly. "I've been counting on it."

Justicar Gobal's hood and robe had been burned off by his initial blast, and he stood sparkling and crackling in his polished armor. Beside him, three more robed figures cast off their outer garments to reveal terrible, white-winged angels armed with flaming swords. All around the arena, other fighters began to unsheathe their weapons. Others who were wiser, or perhaps more cowardly, quickly tried to exit the arena.

"Your attack on our hospital killed more than healers and wounded soldiers. It killed the angels. In their place, Angels of

Retribution have arisen. Your end comes now, Cabalist." The justicar pointed his hand at Chainer, and the angels took wing. The justicar sent another bolt of lighting up toward Chainer's platform. The platform was thoroughly warded against all types of attack, however, and the justicar's bolt faded into nothingness before it ever touched Chainer.

"Oh, no," Chainer said dramatically. "Angels and justicars! The Order has come for me! Whatever shall I do?" He focused on the Mirari back in his chamber, concentrated, and every door in the huge arena slammed shut and melted into the wall around it. His eyes were long gone, and his voice boomed out louder than the announcer's. "Come one, come all. The Mirari awaits. Who is strong enough to take it from me?"

* * * * *

Veza was poring over a scroll when Burke entered her chamber. The gel man wore a small, circular hand mirror around his neck, and from it came Laquatus's voice.

"Please follow my jack," Laquatus said. "There is something I want you to see."

Burke kept pace as Veza swam through the ship. She noticed that his hands and feet became flatter and wider when he swam, and he stayed by her side easily no matter how fast she went. She stole as many glances at his expressionless face as she dared, searching in vain for some flicker of recognition, or at least independence. Burke was as inscrutable as a mask.

Laquatus had taken to filling his command ship with air, both for his mercenaries and in case anyone tried to teleport in. A cephalid assassin would find himself floundering on the floor as soon as he arrived, and they would drown without so much as touching Laquatus. Veza and Burke stepped into the chamber, and Laquatus greeted Veza with a warm, loud call.

"Hello, Director. I'm about to contact the former empress to discuss terms of her surrender."

Veza's eyes darted to the viewscreen, which showed the exact same standoff she had seen for the past week. Laquatus nodded, Burke gently nudged her forward, and Veza took the seat Laquatus offered her.

"Get Llawan on the scrying screen," Laquatus said. He took out his own hand mirror, and Veza watched him whisper into it. She could see a thin man with braided black hair, but she did not recognize him and could not hear his voice. Finally, Laquatus said, "Done. A pleasure doing business with you, as always. And may I add, congratulations on your recent ascension." He paused while the other man spoke. "After today, you will be able to offer me similar sentiments." The mirror went dark, and he put it away with a smug little smile.

"We have the empress, my lord."

"Excellent. Put her on, and have the troops in the chasm stand by."

Llawan appeared in the screen, with the mystic Olsham—his eyes closed—and another cephalid officer at her side. "What do you want, Laquatus?"

"Greetings, Empress. I hope you are well. Isn't it a fine day?"

Veza's dread was like physical pain. She didn't know what Laquatus was up to, but she guessed he had been preparing for it since before he captured the survey vessel. She continued to stare at Olsham, willing the mystic to hear her silent message of warning.

"Speak, irritant. You waste our time."

"This is something in the nature of an official call, I'm afraid. I'm here to offer terms."

"Then you will abandon this farce and submit yourself to imperial justice?"

"Actually, Empress, I was going to offer you one last chance to surrender. You have already lost here. If you leave now, and cede the chasm to me, I will spare you the embarrassment of losing each and every one of your loyal guards. I may even spare your life."

Llawan chittered. "You are a fool, Laquatus. We mock you and spurn your offer."

"Are you sure?" Laquatus's obvious joy twisted Veza's stomach, but Llawan was unimpressed. She began to turn away from the screen.

"Inform the troops," Laquatus said loudly. "Launch an all-out attack on the empress's forces. Begin immediately."

Llawan paused and shook her head. "Your ego has finally grown past the point of your good sense," she said. "But the imperial guard will be happy to accommodate your lunacy."

The occupants of both vessels heard the sounds of renewed combat. Llawan stared grimly at Laquatus, who stared, smiling at Llawan. Veza fought the urge to cry out to Olsham. Whatever was about to happen, the empress's ship would be better off if it were intangible, as her transport had been during the catastrophe that created the chasm.

Olsham opened his eyes. Veza was the only one on board who had seen the empress's shield defenders in action, and so she was the only one who saw their almost transparent bodies stream up and encircle the empress. They did not harden into their defensive formation, but they stood by, ready to do so.

"Forgive me, Empress," said the yacht's cephalid captain. "But I think you should see this."

Llawan turned, and Laquatus's bridge had a clear and unobstructed view of Llawan's, complete with the image that appeared on its scrying viewscreen.

Both bridges stared silently at the images they saw. On Llawan's screen, a steady stream of dark, serpentine figures was pouring out of the chasm and surging forward to attack Llawan's troops. There were thousands of them, a multitude. Along with the ambassador's mercenaries and monsters, they slammed into the empress's line like a crashing wave, and slowly drove it back.

When the empress spoke, it was to her crew, her voice thick with anger.

"What are we looking at?"

"I don't know, Empress. Those creatures seem to be coming from just outside the chasm rather than inside it."

Llawan turned back to Laquatus. "They attack our loyal guards. What are they? What do they want?"

Veza stared as the skirmish grew steadily bigger. Her memory had been jogged by the sight. She remembered a Cabal barge that docked in Breaker Bay some years ago. The Cabalists had set up a makeshift arena and staged a fighting demonstration. A wild-eyed woman with green eyes and a bald head challenged all comers, and she had beaten every one. Not her, Veza corrected herself. The monsters she created.

"They are dementia creatures." Veza's voice was hushed, muted by fear.

Laquatus beamed. "Yes," confirmed the ambassador, "and they are here to kill you, Llawan."

CHAPTER 25

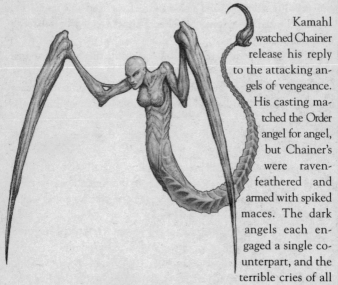

Kamahl watched Chainer release his reply to the attacking angels of vengeance. His casting matched the Order angel for angel, but Chainer's were raven-feathered and armed with spiked maces. The dark angels each engaged a single counterpart, and the terrible cries of all six warriors could be heard throughout the arena.

While the angels continued to battle high above the arena floor, old grudges erupted all around Kamahl and desperate fighters lashed out at each other in an effort to escape. The Mirari Games were quickly turning into a bloody melee, and the crowd loved it. Kamahl wondered how long they would cheer before they realized they, too, were in danger. Neither Chainer nor the Order seemed to care about protecting innocent bystanders.

The crowd around them cleared, and Kamahl got what he'd been waiting for, a line of sight on the justicar.

He sent a small fireball blasting past the armored visor, and called, "Hey, sparky!"

The justicar turned.

"That's more warning than you gave me," Kamahl said. "And more than you deserve. This is twice now you've attacked the Cabal at home. I think it will be the last."

"Stand aside, barbarian," the justicar said. "The Order will settle with you later."

"For you, there is no later." Kamahl hauled his huge sword out and charged.

The justicar sent a jag of lightning at Kamahl, but the barbarian easily drew it into his sword. "You think I don't know lightning? We pick our teeth with lightning up in Pardic." The justicar hurled another bolt which Kamahl also countered, then had to draw his own sword to defend himself.

Kamahl's brass-colored blade rang against Gobal's silver one. The justicar tried to charge up for a larger bolt, but Kamahl was so close that he bled the armored figure's energy off before he could use it, storing it in the blade of his sword.

"You fight like an officer," Kamahl jeered. He butted his head into the justicar's visor, denting it. "Welcome to the pits."

Enraged, Gobal put a crackling hand on Kamahl and shoved him backward. Kamahl staggered but was able to block the justicar's sword stroke as it came down toward his head.

"Is that it, shiny man? Are you really only dangerous when nobody knows your power?"

Another Order soldier threw his spear at Kamahl. The barbarian caught the shaft in midair and burned it to ashes with a glare, but the distraction allowed Gobal enough time and space to raise his arms above his head. Hot, white light from all around the arena streamed into his hands, forming a swelling, crackling ball of energy.

"You're done, justicar." Kamahl launched his broadsword with all his might, skewering Gobal through the chest. The energy stored in Kamahl's sword joined that in the justicar's body, and Gobal screamed. The circuit of energy fed on itself, and light began sparking out from all the seams of the justicar's armor. Kamahl conjured a small throwing axe, knocked Gobal's visor back with a wide round kick, and jammed the axe deep into his enemy's armor.

Kamahl dove to the ground and covered his head just as Gobal exploded. The combination of lightning, fire, and fury was so intense that the sharp metal bits of the justicar's armor melted even before the force of the blast scattered them across the arena. All around him, Kamahl saw warriors and monsters alike cut down by the hail of molten silver.

Without the armor, Gobal was unable to control the electricity that gave him his power. He became a much smaller, broken figure draped in rivulets of melted metal, a figure that grew ever smaller as jags of lightning leaped off his body and dissipated.

Kamahl picked up his sword and stood ready as the justicar collapsed into a ball of flaming debris. Except for a charred pair of footprints and a few droplets of steaming metal, there was no evidence he had ever existed.

"Bravo, barbarian!" Kamahl looked up and saw Chainer politely clapping. Kamahl touched the tip of his sword to his forehead, a gesture of recognition.

Then he pointed at Chainer and drew the tip across his throat, beckoning the dementist down with a wave of his hand.

* * * * *

Chainer laughed with delight at the shows both above and below his platform. On his level, the battle of angel versus angel prevented any other flying things from soaring too high. On the ground, Kamahl had just revenged himself on the justicar, and all of the other contestants were either killing each other to get at the Mirari, or killing each other to escape from the pit. He had planned it carefully, but he hadn't planned it anywhere near as well as it was happening.

One of the Order angels broke free of its nightmare twin and tried once more to reach Chainer's platform. He waited until it was almost on top of him and then threw one of his anaconda people into her face. The snake wrapped its twelve-foot-long body around the angel's wings and torso and sank its venomless fangs into her sword arm. The angel cursed the snake, and both creatures fell out of sight.

"What are you staring at?" Chainer yelled at the dark angel who no longer had an opponent. "Fight!" The angel bared her sharp teeth and hissed, but she complied. She slammed her mace into the unprotected shoulder of one of the Order angels then followed the wounded creature to the floor as she fell, striking as often as time and gravity permitted.

Chainer was starting to see why the First treated everyone like children. There wasn't a single Cabalist left who could think and act for himself. He took one last look at the carnage on the floor and suddenly became bored. Why was he offering the Mirari when he already had the Mirari? No one but he could use it. It was a cruel waste of time to even offer the illusion of obtaining it.

Chainer flipped the control switch that would bring the platform down. It was time to end this charade, clear the building, and start from scratch. New Cabal City would be twice as grand as the original, and there would be no Order to interfere with the Cabal's business.

As the platform descended, Chainer hoped that Laquatus was putting his borrowed dementia monsters to good use. Once he had settled with the Order, Chainer vowed that the Mer empire would become nothing more than a subsidiary of the Cabal. He may have sworn an oath with Laquatus, but it was Laquatus who taught him that oaths could be broken.

* * * * *

Llawan's bridge was in chaos. Cephalid sailors and imperial guardsmen swarmed around the ship while her advisors counseled her to escape while she still could. She cleared the room of all but the command crew and Olsham, then she turned to the captain.

"Take us into the battlefield."

"But Empress—" the captain stammered.

"Do as we command. We will not allow our most loyal subjects to be killed by phantoms." She turned back down to the mirror clasped in her forelimb. "Silence! You have broken our bargain, Cabalist. We have a personal guarantee from the First!" she screeched. "There was to be no interference!"

"The First has gone south to Aphetto," said a young man with black braids and a void in his eyes. "Who are you again?"

"We are the Empress Llawan, rightful heir to the throne of Mer."

"Never heard of you. Sorry."

"We demand to speak to your patriarch."

The young man paused. He seemed amused. "Who's we?"

If the braided man had been in the room, the look on Llawan's face alone would have struck him dead with fear. "What is your name, Cabalist?"

"My name is Chainer, and if you don't leave me alone I'm going to change my mind. And then you'll be sorry." The connection broke, and the mirror went dark.

Llawan lowered the mirror. "The man is mad." She turned to Olsham. "Have you any ideas, mystic? Can this endeavor end well for Llawan?"

Olsham closed his eyes and bent his limbs into a complex sigil. "There is always a chance, Empress. But in this case, chance is not enough."

* * * * *

Laquatus sipped at a fine white wine as he watched the destruction of Llawan's hopes for the throne. With Chainer's monsters, his forces outnumbered Llawan's four-to-one, and he had major sea serpents and an orcan behemoth still in reserve.

Burke stood at Laquatus's side, silent and subservient. Laquatus was sorry to miss Chainer's Mirari Games, but he knew the treasure would keep. Someday soon, he would sit in the First's luxury box, watch Burke tear the competition limb from limb, and finally lay claim to the prize. Laquatus smiled. That is, he would do these things if the foolish boy Chainer hadn't destroyed himself and all of Cabal City by now. Laquatus truly hoped that Chainer was still alive, so he could watch his own creation steal the Cabal's greatest treasure for the glory of Mer.

"Ambassador." One of his mercenary chiefs stood in the doorway to Laquatus's chamber.

"Emperor," Laquatus corrected him. He sipped his wine.

"We are forcing Llawan's guard away from the mouth of the chasm. We should have room to bring out the behemoth shortly."

"Excellent. Keep me informed."

"There is one other thing, Amb . . . Emperor."

"Yes?"

"Llawan's command ship has left the edge of the battle."

Laquatus rose and struggled to keep his voice calm. "She is abandoning the field?" He had expected more of a fight before she accepted defeat.

"No, Emperor. She is joining the battle."

"That cannot be. She would never . . ." Laquatus stopped as the chief pointed to the scrying screen. It clearly showed a host of Cabal serpents battling a host of Llawan's cephalids. It also showed Llawan's yacht and the obvious positive impact it had on her troops' morale.

"Why, that reckless, soft-skulled witch," he said, amused. This was even better than he had dreamed. Defeating Llawan's army would earn him the throne, but killing Llawan in the process would ensure that his reign lasted for the rest of his naturally long life.

"Take us farther into the chasm," he said. "Oh, and Veza? I heard you trying to contact that psychic octopus. I'm very disappointed." He turned to one of his mercenaries. "Kill her." The mercenary drew his knife and advanced on Veza.

She had been waiting for this, fully aware that Laquatus would have detected her pleas to Olsham. Veza was not a warrior, but she trusted her own speed and strength when compared to that of a surface dweller. The man's knife flashed, and Veza stunned him with a sharp blow across the face. Blood flowed, but the mercenary did not fall.

Laquatus and the rest of the bridge crew laughed. "You're fired," Laquatus called to the bleeding mercenary, and the man growled in anger. He drew his sword.

Veza didn't wait for Laquatus to order more mercenaries into the fight. She ran from the room and hit the flooded corridor in a running dive. The laughter stopped, and Veza heard more bodies break the surface of the corridor as the mercenaries pursued. She pressed on, confident that no human being, no matter how well enhanced, could swim faster than a mermaid.

She had been in and out of the ship numerous times, and she knew she could make it at least as far as the edge of the chasm. Better to die randomly in the battle as a subject of the empire than as a coward on a traitor's command vessel.

Veza found the exit hatch and opened it wide. The last thing she heard before plunging into the frigid waters of the chasm was Laquatus's amplified voice, echoing throughout the ship.

"Burke?" he said. "Retrieve the prisoner."

CHAPTER 26

Chainer made his way back to his chambers. He did not go unchallenged, but he might as well have. A small band of Nantuko pounced on him as he came off of the platform, but they were quickly collared and absorbed. Chainer broke a few bones with weighted chains as he went, but for the most part the fighters gave him a wide berth, and the spectators ran at the sight of him.

One of the First's toys was buzzing as he opened the door. It was a handheld mirror with a talking octopus in its glass. Chainer made a half-hearted stab to figure out what she wanted, then shattered the mirror over his knee. He had more important things to occupy his time.

The Mirari was where he left it, under the pyramid of paper in the corner of the smallest room. No one dared enter his chamber after he had deposed the First, and he doubted anyone would have believed him audacious enough to hide it there anyway. He took the glowing black sphere in his hands, and once again marveled at the depth of the power it contained. He should have used it to find a way to kill the First. Cabal City was nothing to him now, and worse, it was an obstacle. He would have to tear it all down before he could build it back up again properly.

Chainer drew the power into him and began to shape it. What he had in mind was complicated and would happen on a scale undreamed of even by the most fervid dementist. He reached out into Cabal City and beyond to Aphetto. His mind flew out past Krosan, across all of Otaria, and beyond into the depths of Mer. He could see and feel every dementia caster there was, each of them linked by their power and their oath to the Cabal. He felt a few dead spots in his continental sweep, a few individuals who could not be contacted. Fulla, for example, and a handful of casters in Aphetto. Perhaps the truly disconnected were beyond even the Mirari's reach.

No matter, he thought. He had more than enough. The Cabal taught them the ways of power, and they in turn used that power to benefit the Cabal. But the Cabal was dead now, just waiting to be buried. It was time for a new covenant, one that Chainer would enforce.

All across the land, he felt casters stop, freeze, and remain rigid. Skellum had always said that a master needs pupils, and in one stroke Chainer had more than any master who had ever lived. With the Mirari, he could enter each of their minds and commandeer them. He could occupy all the dementia space there was and turn it toward his goals. He could assemble the largest and most diverse army of dementia monsters that had ever been.

"Like this!" he cried, and he was suddenly back in his own dementia space even as he remained in his chambers. Both locations superimposed on top of each other, fusing and separating over and over. It was as empty there as it had been when he first arrived, and Chainer suddenly felt very small and lonely. He had been expecting a multitude, and he was unnerved by the complete lack of company. Where had they all gone?

He heard a fresh scream nearby, and he appeared back in his chambers. They were all around him. Sprawled across his floor and spilling out in to the hall, visible in the courtyard outside his window and throughout the streets of Cabal City, a million monsters or more howled and hunted and rampaged and roared. Twisted nightmare versions of people, animals, birds, snakes—fantastic beasts of the forest and terrifying monsters from the depths all lashed out at themselves and the world around them. Chainer had opened the floodgates of his mind, and the Mirari was keeping them open.

Chainer laughed and sat on the pile of paper with the Mirari in his lap as the entire city wailed in horror.

"The Cabal is here," he cackled, "and nowhere else."

* * * * *

Kamahl had never seen such chaos. It became difficult to tell who was real and who was a summoning, and impossible to tell which side they were on. Harpy fought angel, zombie fought trooper, and all manner of things that never had names fought beasts from the forest that had never been seen. Kamahl did not consider himself a brilliant man, but he knew how to learn from experience. An out-of-control catastrophe spelled Mirari, and a flood of monsters spelled Chainer. Kamahl concentrated. He could feel the sphere's presence. His former partner had finally fallen victim to the Mirari's curse.

It was not hard to locate the Mirari, and Kamahl made his way through the killing floor as fast as his wounds permitted. There were plenty of victims to go around, and Kamahl encouraged a few of the monsters to find easier pickings with the tip of his sword. Before long, he was at the end of the long hallway that led to Chainer and the Mirari.

"Chainer," he bellowed. A hissing snake man attacked him, and Kamahl burned its throat out where it stood.

"Is that my old friend and partner?" Chainer's voice called back.

"Come on out, 'old friend.' Let's finish this."

The flood of sprawling monsters pouring out of the chamber door momentarily increased just before Chainer came through it. The creatures fled past Kamahl without looking at him. They were far more interested in getting away from their master.

Chainer's braided hair splayed out around his head like a crown. His eyes were black again, but the void had spilled out of his sockets and was obscuring the top half of his face. His feet floated six inches above the ground, and he held the Mirari in his metal hand. He was smiling.

"Kamahl."

"Chainer."

"Have you come to apologize, or to kill me and take the Mirari?"

"Neither. I've come to stop you."

"Stop me? From what?"

"From destroying yourself. From destroying this city." He shrugged. "From destroying everything."

Chainer's smile faded. "Still looking out for me, big brother? I have a bad history with authority figures, you know. They always die or betray me."

"I'm not your brother, Chainer. I'm your friend. Listen to me. You've got to put the Mirari down. You're going to get us all killed."

"We have to get killed," Chainer flared. "Have to destroy before I can rebuild."

"If you don't put it down, I'm going to put you down."

Chainer smiled again. "Aaah, threats. You don't really think you have a chance, do you?"

"Enough talk." Kamahl drew his sword. "Now we fight."

"You don't look healthy enough to fight."

"I'm healthy enough to fight you. Not your monster pawns, not the Mirari. You.

"I don't need pawns," Chainer said darkly. He gestured at Kamahl's weapon. "Don't you know that no one with a sword can get the best of someone with a chain? That's why I carry this thing."

"Then let's go. You're right, Chainer, I'm not healed. But this isn't the pits. There isn't a scheduled conclusion to this fight. Care to test your skill?"

Chainer's eyes twinkled. "Are you proposing that we come to some sort of arrangement?"

"No arrangement. No tricks. Just a plain challenge. I say I can take you using nothing but my sword. Can you take me with just a length of chain?"

"And my dagger. I used to use that, too."

"And your dagger. Come on, Chainer, it's you and me. We both fought for the Mirari. Now we can fight fair, and may the best man win."

"Done," Chainer said. He tossed the Mirari through the open door into the next room and squared off against his former partner.

Kamahl breathed a sigh of relief. At least the building wouldn't go up in a black cloud of debris and body parts while they were fighting. Now all he had to do was overcome the pain of his wounds and the fatigue in his body to defeat his insane ex-partner who could kill with a gesture and created both weapons and monsters out of thin air.

After he had done that, Kamahl promised himself he would look into some other kind of work.

* * * * *

Veza swam for all she was worth, but Burke caught her just outside the chasm. He never seemed to get tired, and Veza simply could not keep up the pace. From the mirror around his bodyguard's neck, Laquatus watched as Veza was recaptured.

"Now you are mine," Laquatus said, "along with the empire."

Veza struggled in Burke's grip, but she was staring at the war being waged around her. In the distance, something new was happening on the battlefield. Veza allowed herself a small smile.

"Nothing is yours yet, Laquatus."

"Emperor," a mercenary's voice said, "are you seeing this?"

"Seeing what?"

"Look at the battle. Look! By the depths, what's going on?"

Veza looked. Inexplicably, the hundreds and hundreds of serpent warriors who had been grappling with Llawan's soldiers were vanishing in mid-blow. His mercenaries found themselves face-to-face with trained imperial guards, and the guards adjusted much more quickly than their new opponents. Within seconds of the final serpent's disappearance, a hundred of Laquatus's mercenaries fell dead, and the rest fell back in disarray.

"Perhaps you only rented those warriors from the Cabal," Veza called into the mirror. "I'll bet it's not too late to get your deposit back."

"Get my troops back inside the chasm. Burke, kill that wench and bring her body back here."

Veza didn't wait for Burke to comply. Instead, she clamped on to the gel man's thumb with her short, sharp teeth. With a wrench that nearly dislocated her jaw, she tore the digit off and spat it back in its owner's face. Minus his thumb, Burke could not maintain his grip on Veza's wrist, and she was able to kick her way free and dart out into the open ocean.

Burke was close behind, however. Apparently he took any order Laquatus gave him to heart. He elongated his feet to give him more drive, and with each stroke he stretched his arms a little closer to Veza.

When his finger brushed Veza's foot, she panicked and dove for the sea bed. Burke changed course even quicker than she did and actually gained on her before she could hide among the seaweed and silt. She needed to go faster. She needed her tail. It was impossible, though. She couldn't change while moving, and the transformation was extremely painful. Burke would be on her before the process had even begun.

Just as his hand closed around her leg, the empress's ship swam into view. Burke snapped Veza's ankle, and she sank painfully to the sand. She cradled her injured leg and wondered why he wasn't finishing her off. She looked up, and saw the reason.

Burke was beset by the empress's barracuda. All twelve of the spindly killer fish circled around him, breaking their teeth on his body and occasionally ripping small chunks off. The pieces of Burke's body immediately floated back and rejoined the main mass. The barracuda were ill-equipped to deal with something that didn't panic, bleed, or feel pain.

Burke, on the other hand, was killing the barracuda with both hands. They were strong and they were fierce, but they were not faster than Burke, and they had bones he could break. Five of the fish already floated dead in the water around him. In a matter of seconds he would be through them and ready to finish Veza.

Veza concentrated. Laquatus was wrong, magic wasn't about being mentally, physically, and morally flexible. It was about understanding the world and your place in it. Veza felt the powerful tides flowing out of the chasm, felt the palpable force of the civil war around her, felt the bond between the barracuda and Llawan. I am a servant of Mer, Veza reminded herself. I am of the sea.

"Change," she commanded, and her legs merged seamlessly and painlessly into a powerful fish's tail. Burke was just finishing off the last of the barracuda when he noticed Veza's metamorphosis. He elongated his arm across the gap between them to clutch at her throat, but she shot off like an arrow through the air. She laughed, exhilarated as she screamed toward the empress's vessel, until she felt Burke's hand close round her lower extremities once more.

The gel man's arm had continued to stretch after her as she swam, and now he had her snared in a long, tough line of his own bodily substance. He didn't have much power at this distance, but he was able to hold her fast. She now outweighed Burke, so he couldn't draw her toward him, but he was quickly pulling himself closer to her by retracting his arm and letting her weight carry him forward. Veza thrashed and clawed at Burke's unyielding hand.

Suddenly, the featureless killer stopped. Through the water, Veza could make out Laquatus's voice from the mirror around his servant's neck. Burke stood still, nodded, then released Veza's tail. He struck out, back toward the chasm.

Laquatus must have summoned him home. There was a cloud of bubbles and a whirling sensation, and Veza found herself and the remaining barracuda on the bridge of the Llawan's vessel.

"Greetings, Veza. We are so glad to see you alive. Is all as you described it to Olsham?"

"It is, Empress."

"Then, my mystic, if you would begin?"

The cephalid mystic nodded and once more formed a complicated symbol with his multiple arms. Llawan joined him, and between the two of them they wound up looking like a strange new alphabet.

Veza looked to the screen. All of Laquatus's mercenaries had retreated back into the chasm and were fending off Llawan's troops.

Veza tapped the captain on the shoulder and said, "Pull those guards away from there." He looked dubious, but he decided not to question her authority. Several seconds later, the imperial troops backed off.

"All clear, Empress." Veza anxiously counted the seconds. Once more, Veza spotted the flow of the shield defenders' transparent bodies as they positioned themselves in front of the chasm. "The shield is in position."

Llawan clicked, and her shield defenders formed their barrier, larger and thinner than they had ever created before. It sparkled like a sheet of ice, and Veza could even see a ghostly reflection of the empress's troops in it. Olsham reached out and traced a huge circle in the water before him, and the huge convex shield tilted slightly, sparking at its edges and reflecting the light back upon itself.

At last, a huge silver-white plane of energy flickered across the transparent shield. The energy flowed past the empress's servants and continued out to cover the mouth of the chasm. It was almost a mile across, wide enough to overlap the chasm opening by several hundred feet on both sides. It stretched from the ocean floor to the water's surface, and Veza knew it would stretch across the entire chasm, the magical impulses relayed by the crystals she herself had installed, to enclose the entire flood zone in a huge tunnel of mystical energy. A cheer went up among the bridge crew.

Olsham and Llawan opened their eyes. Olsham smiled and said, "Behold, Empress. The largest water portal ever created. Or rather, the largest portal barrier ever created. Nothing outside the chasm can get in, and—"

"Nothing inside can get out. As always, Olsham, you exceed our expectations." Llawan turned and noticed Veza's wound. "All hail the noble sacrifice made by our comrades, warriors and defenders both. And captain, get a medic to the bridge," she snapped. "Our valued sister is injured. Are you blind?"

"Sorry, my empress."

Llawan floated down and gathered Veza up in her forelimbs. "Is the damage permanent?"

"No, Empress. I think it's a simple fracture." She flexed her tail and winced. "A very painful one, but a simple one."

"Veza," Llawan said softly. "Are you sure that Laquatus and all his troops were inside the chasm when the portal was created?"

"Yes, Empress."

Llawan smiled. "Then we have won." She handed Veza to the medic, then began floating back toward the view screen.

"Empress," Veza called. "You planted the survey data that proved the chasm was valuable, didn't you?"

Llawan smiled. "Olsham altered the recording device before he teleported off the ship."

"So you used me."

"Not at all. We employed you. We assigned you a task, and you performed it. It is the right of the empress to demand service from her subjects."

"Service, Empress, or sacrifice? Your leviathan, its crew, your soldiers and shield defenders. Even me."

Llawan scowled. "What is your point, Veza? Laquatus would have sunk the entire empire into economic warfare and decadence. This is why civil wars are fought. To preserve that which is worth preserving, at any cost."

Veza nodded, then floated quietly as the medic examined her tail. "Forgive me, Empress. My wound has made me light-headed."

"Of course. When you are healed," Llawan said, "you will join us in the palace as our Imperial Counsel. We have risked much together, and we do not refer exclusively to our personage. You and all of our loyal subjects either made us empress, or welcomed us as empress. Now that we have earned that title fairly in combat, we will not forget those who made it possible. We expect a steady flow of consistently good advice from you, Counsel."

"Yes, Empress." Veza felt herself being taken away, and though she didn't know exactly where she was going, for the first time in months that wasn't something she had to worry about.

* * * * *

Chainer sent three separate chains screaming at Kamahl's sword. The first two locked and held onto the blade, while the third snared

Kamahl's wrist. Chainer hauled with all his might, but he could not pull the sword loose or Kamahl down.

Annoyed, he sent another chain coiling around Kamahl's foot. With a brutal tug, he finally hauled Kamahl off his feet. Kamahl dropped his sword as he fell, and took hold of the chains himself. When he hit the ground, he yanked hard to pull Chainer toward him, but the chains vanished before Kamahl could bring his superior strength and weight into play.

A rounded weight broke Kamahl's jaw before he could get up. "Guess you'll have to learn how to fight without teeth now too, won't you barbarian?" Chainer's voice was high-pitched and grating. Kamahl sneered and spit blood at Chainer. He reached for his sword, but Chainer struck it and sent it skittering across the floor.

"I'm getting bored now." Chainer sank a sharpened weight into Kamahl's thigh, and another into his shoulder. "I can stand here, twenty feet away, and whittle you down to nothing. I told you. The sword is useless against the chain."

Kamahl stood firm, his breath ragged and blood streaming from his wounds. "You should just kill me now, then. There's no audience to be disappointed by a short bout."

Chainer wagged a finger at his partner. "Now, now. We both know you're not that weak." He slashed another chain at Kamahl, but the barbarian ducked under it. "Not yet, anyway."

Kamahl conjured an axe and hurled it down the corridor at Chainer. Reflexively, Chainer threw out his hand and released a large, gelatinous mass which absorbed and muffled the explosion.

"I thought you said no magic."

Kamahl shrugged. "I was just trying to clear us some space."

"Now you've done it," Chainer said. "You've made me angry." He jutted both arms out in the casting position, but instead of the death bloom or a nightmare casting, ten sharp chains exploded out of his hands, streaming and curling in twisted spirals as they flew toward Kamahl. The hallway was not wide enough for him to dodge them all. Six of them found their way into his body, linking his sword arm and both legs to Chainer. Kamahl stiffened but did not fall. He couldn't move, but he would not go down.

"The best man wins. That's what you said, isn't it?" Chainer walked casually toward the immobilized barbarian. He waved his hand, and the Mirari appeared in it. "I think I'll do something really special for you, Kamahl. You rejected my gifts once. If I remake you from the bones out as one of my snakes, however, you won't have any choice but to accept it." Chainer stood less than an arm's length from Kamahl. He reached out his metal arm and daintily flicked Kamahl in the chest. The nudge sent Kamahl teetering backward, and he began to topple like a great tree. Before he fell, however, Kamahl reached out and grabbed on to Chainer's metal arm.

"Let go of me, you lump of rock." Chainer jerked his arm back, but Kamahl didn't let go. He clamped onto the artificial limb with the other hand and steadied himself on his feet.

"I'm sorry, Chainer," he said, and channeled a withering blast of heat from his own body into Chainer's arm.

The metal limb instantly became red-hot, and Chainer screamed. He dropped the Mirari and drew his dagger, stabbing it into Kamahl's forearm, once, twice, a half dozen times. Kamahl grimly held on through it all, pumping more heat and more energy through his hands.

Chainer's arm melted into slag with a wet, angry hiss. He fell backward and lashed his foot out at Kamahl, finally knocking the barbarian onto his back.

"That was a gift from Skellum," Chainer hissed. "Can't you barbarians lay off my thrice-damned arm?" He kicked Kamahl in the ribs as he stepped over his prone body to retrieve the Mirari. He took the sphere in his remaining hand, closed his eyes, and concentrated. The smoking end of his stump started to swell, and a new arm began to unfold like an inflating balloon. It wasn't Chainer's arm, or any human's. It was a thin, segmented claw like an insect's, and Chainer looked at it in confusion.

"That's not right," he said. The insect claw vanished, and in its place a large, black rattlesnake sprouted. Chainer scowled at it until it withered. Another attempt produced a mewling, eyeless monstrosity that wailed like a baby until Chainer shook it away.

"Chainer, what's happening?"

"I don't know," he said. What was happening? How could the Mirari keep failing?

Unless he had overtaxed it. Of course. He had been communing with the sphere for days, actively using it for the past half hour, and then had simply cast it aside. Of course it was malfunctioning, he wasn't using it properly. He ought to have pulled himself out of the sphere's bottomless well of power before he tried to do something else. Also, it was probably mad at him for abandoning it.

"Chainer, wait."

"Shush." Chainer absently flicked his arm toward the helpless barbarian, and a torrent of misshapen snakes and monsters swamped Kamahl where he lie.

Chainer tried one final time to make himself an arm, but it came out as a lifeless and callused roll of flesh. Nearby, Kamahl was grappling with the tangle of horrors and losing. Chainer shook his head. That wouldn't do. He had promised Kamahl a fair fight.

In fact, the entire building was getting too noisy and crowded. Chainer needed peace and quiet to kill his friend, and he held the Mirari up to help him get it.

"Chainer," Kamahl gurgled from the bottom of the pile. "Don't."

"Hold on," Chainer said. "I'm almost done." With the sphere in his hand, he once again felt all of the minds he had broken into and pillaged, all of them still frozen and empty. Instead of reaching into those minds, this time Chainer reached out into the world. The other dementists were merely relay stations for his dementia space now, and there was no reason to give back what he had rightfully stolen. He wanted to finish Kamahl man to man, however, and for that he needed quiet.

Chainer used the Mirari to locate each and every one of the monsters he had unleashed since the games began. He was surprised how many of them were left. In fact, there were very few people left alive in the arena around him, and the monsters there had turned on each other. All the more reason to call them home, he thought. The battle's nearly over, and we've already won.

All around Otaria, the flow of power reversed as a million nightmares began to flow back into the fragmented brain that created them.

"This kind of hurts," Chainer said. "Is it supposed to hurt?"

*   *   *   *   *

Buried by hostile monsters, Kamahl was helpless to stop Chainer. He watched the Cabalist as the Mirari sent blasts of light out in all directions, and then a thousand smaller beams began flowing back into Chainer's body.

"This kind of hurts," Chainer said. "Is it supposed to hurt?"

"Drop it, Chainer!" Kamahl tried to yell more, but something with hooves instead of fists punched him in the mouth.

The swarm of monsters stopped tearing at him as the lights beaming into Chainer began to grow larger, faster, and more frequent. Kamahl was still unable to move, but at least he wasn't being damaged any further.

Chainer was screaming now. They were no longer merely beams of light slamming into him, but elongated streamers of flesh, eyes, fangs, stingers, and claws. Not just energy, but mass was pouring into him, and his physical form was not prepared to deal with it. In a final burst of triumphant, agonizing sound, the air around Chainer's body imploded and a flash of purple light blew outward, knocking stones loose from the wall and almost reburying Kamahl in rubble.

Many silent minutes passed. Then Kamahl broke the silence by shoving one of the larger stones off of his chest and letting it crash loudly to the floor. The barbarian painfully got to his feet and limped down the hall to where Chainer writhed.

At first Kamahl thought his friend was coated in some kind of undulating ooze, but as he looked closer, he saw the truth. It wasn't something on Chainer's body that squirmed, it *was* Chainer's body. Though he still had the same build and the same shape, Chainer's arms, legs, chest, head, even his hair was now a turbulent mass of wriggling monsters. Tiny eyes looked up at Kamahl, and miniature fangs formed, struck, then melted again. Sometimes a head or a hand would rise above the surface of his skin, and snakes swam all through the unstable flesh like sharks in a feeding frenzy. His nose and mouth were only shapes, and those shapes were crammed full of tongues and scales and fingers and talons. Even his missing arm had been replaced with the cancer of living monsters.

Worst of all were his eyes. Chainer's brilliant blue eyes had returned, and they bore mute and tragic testimony to the agony he suffered.

The Mirari had rolled free and sat unobtrusively on the floor. It seemed smaller and drab, its eerie black glow extinguished. Kamahl marveled that he and so many others had fought and bled for something that appeared to be nothing more than a spent cannonball, or a discarded child's toy. He knelt down next to Chainer.

The hideous parody of his friend's body reacted to his closeness, and Chainer clumsily flopped a boneless arm toward Kamahl's hand. Kamahl took it, and he fought the urge to release the hideous squirming thing and start hacking it with his sword. Chainer pulled on Kamahl's arm, and the barbarian leaned forward to put his ear next to the place that had been Chainer's mouth.

"Mu. Ra. Ree."

Kamahl had no idea how the sound was created, but he understood. He shook his head. "You don't need it. It'll only make things worse."

Chainer shook his head, his eyes pleading. He tried to point at it with his free arm.

"Yours. Take. You. Take it."

"I'm not so sure I want it anymore."

Chainer's horrid grip grew tighter. "Must," he gurgled. "Not. Safe."

"All right, Chainer. I'll take it, and I'll keep it safe." A hundred battles had taught him not to argue with a dying man.

Chainer's grip relaxed. "Sorry," he said. "So sorry."

Kamahl held his friend's hand until the squirming stopped and his ragged breath stopped completely. He stood, remembering the simple courtesy he had paid to dead enemies and allies alike. In this case, it was the least he could do to free Chainer's spirit from the hideous form it had been shackled to.

With a wave, Kamahl burned Chainer's twisted body to cinders. When he was alone, he caught site of the Mirari once more, so unassuming in repose. He had told Chainer the truth. He wasn't sure if he really wanted it anymore. But he also had made a promise to his friend, and he thought he understood why Chainer had insisted and why he had agreed.

After a few moment's hesitation, Kamahl bent and picked up the Mirari. For a brief moment, he saw a huge, smoking battlefield littered with corpses and an ocean of multicolored flames. And then he was alone, surrounded by the memory of monsters and the death of his friend.

EPILOGUE

Laquatus and his mercenaries had explored the length and depth of the chasm, and the news was the same: There was no simple way out. All the water in the chasm was surrounded by Veza's barrier, one giant, permanent portal that only led to itself. Anyone who touched the barrier from within or without instantly appeared on the exact opposite side of the chasm, on the same side of the barrier that they started on. Those inside couldn't step out. Those outside couldn't step in.

The trap for Laquatus also served as a source of income for Llawan. While Laquatus and his forces were trapped inside, Llawan's functionaries had already fixed a price for merchants to use the portal's external surface as rapid transit for shipping from one side of Otaria to the other. He was not only trapped, he was isolated from any and all Mer commerce.

Disrupting the barrier from the inside was costly and difficult. Since the field was powered by the newly formed tides in the chasm, penetrating the field required enough magical power to baffle the elemental force of the tides themselves. For the time being, Laquatus couldn't do it alone for long, and he could only open a hole big enough for a few people at a time.

Still, he had the resources and the time he needed to breach the barrier. He still had his contacts inside the Order, and a good working relationship with the First, should the Cabal patriarch ever return. And the Mirari was still out there, in the hands of one ignorant savage or another.

Laquatus accepted defeat as he did victory. Each was merely a shorter step in his lifelong campaign for greatness. He had been bested and embarrassed in Mer, and it was his own fault. His mistake was to go after the Mer imperial throne and the Mirari at the same time. In the future, he would focus all his attention on obtaining the sphere and then use it to carve out a kingdom for himself.

Llawan may have temporarily exiled him from the deep, but that simply meant that he must turn his sights inland. There were a million land crawlers to conquer, a dozen factions to play against one another, and a priceless source of power to be obtained.

First, the sphere. Then Otaria. Then, the empire. After that? Laquatus laughed in his spacious prison.

If his ambition was as bottomless as the seas, why shouldn't his power extend as far?

* * * * *

Kamahl stepped out of the Cabal City arena and squinted in the bright, setting sun. He was preoccupied by thoughts of the Mirari, the way it reacted so swiftly to its handler's thoughts. Therein lay the real danger of it. Chainer's thoughts had been dark and troubled, and Kamahl's own were violent. He wondered what would happen the next time Jeska gave him lip. Would she spontaneously burst in to flames because Kamahl thought about it?

The street was full of surviving spectators and pit fighters. The crowd was murmuring, and all eyes were on the Mirari.

". . . killed the entire Cabal . . ."

". . . the only survivor . . ."

"I challenge you, barbarian."

Kamahl looked up at the Order officer who had stepped forward. She was a tall and immaculate aven, almost blinding in her white robes. She drew a long sword and a short dagger.

"For the Mirari," she continued. "I will fight you for the Mirari."

"When you've killed her," said a burly Cabalist, "I will fight you for the Mirari."

"Then me."

"I will fight, too."

One of Kamahl's own people, a barbarian from Pardic, stepped forward. "Forgive me, cousin. But I will fight you for the Mirari. It is our way."

Kamahl stared out at the growing number of challengers. His sword felt heavy, and he had never felt so tired. His burns still ached, and for the first time in his short, brutal life, Kamahl wanted to rest rather than fight. The other barbarian was right, however. It was their way to compete for the things they wanted, to constantly improve their skills and their situation through combat.

Reluctantly, Kamahl drew his sword and almost dropped it from his clumsy, aching hands. He looked at the long line of challengers, growing longer all the time, and the crush of others who edged closer, unwilling to wait for their turn. Warriors and monsters and dementia beasts all jostled for the right to kill him and collect the spoils.

Kamahl snorted a bitter laugh. Improve through combat? If he survived the next few hours, according to the ways of his people, he would be very much improved.

* * * * *

Fulla and Azza made their way through the plains due south of Cabal City without incident. Azza sometimes forced Fulla to get on her back as she was now, but the caster preferred to have her own feet on the ground.

Azza's spirit seemed muted. She was still in mourning for Skellum. Fulla was also sad that she would not see Chainer or Skellum again, but Fulla was easily distracted when she was not in the pits. While she remembered that she was sad, she did not always remember why.

For days before the First's surprise announcement that he was leaving, Fulla had strange dreams. They were of a jovial figure who sat on top of a huge pile of money. The figure's voice hurt Fulla's head, and he kept insisting that she should get out of Cabal City and head south. Fulla eventually agreed just to get the figure to leave her alone, and Azza had refused to let her make the dangerous trip by herself. They were hardly outside the city walls when the commotion at the arena began, but they were too far away to make it back in time for the fun.

As they came over a rise in the road, they saw a tall man standing before them in the distance. Many bodies were strewn around his feet, as if his party had all fallen asleep at the same time. When the tall man turned toward them, both Fulla and Azza straightened up.

"The Cabal is here," Fulla called.

"And everywhere," replied the First. Closer to the scene, Fulla could see that the bodies of four or five snake-men lay dead and blackened around the First's feet, along with a handful of humans in Cabal clothing. He smiled as his children approached, ignoring the corpses around him.

"It seems we are all going to Aphetto," the First said.

"Yes, Pater." Azza carried Fulla past the First, slowing her pace but not stopping.

"I would offer you Azza's back, Pater," Fulla said, "but that wouldn't be good for either of you."

"No, my child. You two go on ahead. I have already sent for an escort from Aphetto, which should be here shortly." He dipped his head toward the dead at his feet. "The first three escorts were waylaid on the road as soon as they picked me up. Then their waylayers fell ill. Such a waste."

Azza and Fulla were now completely past the First, and the caster had to turn to continue the conversation. "We shall see you in Aphetto then, Pater."

"Indeed. I have much to ask you about the final Mirari Games."

"The First is wise."

"Long live the Cabal."

Fulla and Azza rode on over the next rise, and the First disappeared behind them. Azza began to trot, but Fulla tugged on her neck.

"We're in no rush, sweet Azza," Fulla said. The hellhound dropped back to a slower pace, and they rode on.

A world begins anew...

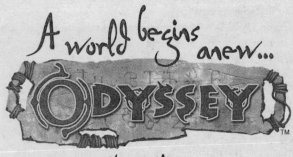

Vance Moore

**A hundred years has passed since the invasion.
Dominaria is still in ruins.**

**Only the strongest manage to survive in this
brutal post-apocalyptic world. Experience the glory and
agony of champion pit fighters as they enter the arena
to do combat for treasure.**

In September 2001,
begin a journey into the depths of this reborn
and frighteningly hostile world.

Legends Cycle Clayton Emery

Book I: Johan

Hazezon Tamar, merchant-mayor of the city of Bryce, had plenty of problems before he encountered Jaeger, a mysterious stranger that is half-man and half-tiger. Now Hazezon is caught up in a race against time to decipher the mysterious prophecy of None, One, and Two, while considering the significance of Jaeger's appearance. Only by understanding these elements can he save his people from the tyranny and enslavement of the evil wizard Johan, ruler of the dying city of Tirras.

April 2001

Book II: Jedit

Jedit Ojanen, the son of the legendary cat man Jaeger, sets out on a journey to find his father. Like his father, he collapses in the desert and is left for dead until he is rescued. But rescued by whom? And why? Only the prophecy of None, One, and Two holds the answers.

December 2001

Tales from the world of Magic

Dragons of Magic
ED. J. ROBERT KING

From the time of the Primevals to the darkest hours of the Phyrexian Invasion, dragons have filled Dominaria. Few of their stories have been told—until now. Learn the secrets of the most powerful dragons in the multiverse!

August 2001

The Myths of Magic
ED. JESS LEBOW

Stories and legends, folktales and tall tales. These are the myths of Dominaria, stories captured on the cards of the original trading card game. Stories from J. Robert King, Francis Lebaron, and others.

The Colors of Magic
ED. JESS LEBOW

Argoth is decimated. Tidal waves have turned canyons into rivers. Earthquakes have leveled the cities. Dominaria is in ruins. Now the struggle is to survive. Tales from such authors as Jeff Grubb, J. Robert King, Paul Thompson, and Francis Lebaron.

Rath and Storm
ED. PETER ARCHER

The flying ship Weatherlight enters the dark, sinister plane of Rath to rescue its kidnapped captain. But, as the stories in this anthology show, more is at stake than Sisay's freedom.